I0658872

THE RISE

BOOK 2 IN THE LAZARUS STRAIN CHRONICLES

SEAN DEVILLE

SEVERED PRESS
HOBART TASMANIA

THE RISE: BOOK 2 IN THE LAZARUS STRAIN CHRONICLES

Copyright © 2019 Sean Deville
Copyright © 2019 by Severed Press

WWW.SEVEREDPRESS.COM

All rights reserved. No part of this book may be
reproduced or transmitted in any form or by any
electronic or mechanical means, including
photocopying, recording or by any information and
retrieval system, without the written permission of
the publisher and author, except where permitted by law.
This novel is a work of fiction. Names,
characters, places and incidents are the product of
the author's imagination, or are used fictitiously.
Any resemblance to actual events, locales or persons,
living or dead, is purely coincidental.

ISBN: 978-1-925840-73-5

All rights reserved.

"My Zombie apocalypse plan is simple but effective; I fully intend to die in the very first wave."

Graham Parker

From:

Field Marshall McKenzie,
Chief of the Defence Staff

ATTENTION!

By order of her Majesty Elizabeth II, Queen of Great Britain and the Commonwealth, I
am hereby authorised to implement a nationwide curfew effective immediately.

No person shall be allowed travel between the hours of 8PM and 8AM.

Stay in your homes unless instructed by the Military or Civilian Authorities.
Food distribution centres will be set up. Stay tuned to terrestrial television and radio
networks for more information on their locations.
Acts of disobedience to the authority of the temporary military government will result in
summary detention.

Do not congregate in groups.
Do not attempt to deal with the undead yourself.
Do not break Curfew
Do not break imposed quarantine

Failure to follow commands WILL be met with lethal force

If you suspect an infected individual in your household, phone 999, or email
report@pandemicresponse.gov

THE RISE

21.08.19
Hounslow, UK

The streets were empty of the living. Soon they would be owned by the dead.

Cowering behind curtains and locked doors, humanity watched as the resurrected rapidly began to take control of the world. In the distance there could be heard the almost futile sounds of gunfire, but here, in this place, mankind could only stand helpless as the undead made their way through the urban landscape, killing everyone and everything in their path.

Helpless and afraid, the people of the London borough of Hounslow waited expectantly for the police and the army to come to their aid, to save them from this living nightmare. *Surely they would come* they said to reassure themselves…*surely it was only a matter of time.* It was a pointless hope, however, the uniformed bodies walking amongst the ever-growing battalions of the undead a testament to that.

Humanity was already losing the war… and really, it hadn't even started yet.

Then there were the other sounds that filled the hapless humans with growing dread. The chorus of doors and windows being breached, interspersed by the tortured screams of the abandoned. Glass shattering. Wood splintering. Unseen by the terrified, teeth gouged flesh whilst limbs were torn. The dead were coming, and all anyone could do was wait for fate to deliver her final judgement. Some were initially lucky, the rolling horde passing their houses by. But most weren't so fortunate, the attacked homes breached easily. The virus worked quickly at expanding the ranks of the damned.

Many were killed outright in the frenzied onslaught, dying from shock and blood loss. For those who suffered less serious damage, the zombies simply seemed to move on. The victims weren't spared of course, the virus that now infested them rapidly corrupting the flesh around fresh wounds, spreading via the bloodstream throughout the rest of their bodies. Within minutes, those injured could feel the changes starting inside them, the burning that spread out from their injuries an irritation that would become an agony.

Dullness began to gather in their minds as their humanity was methodically stripped from them.

The majority of those infected chose to sit, clutching the bleeding limbs, realising the inevitability of what now awaited them. They would watch in horror as their attackers withdrew so as to go in search of fresh flesh, knowing that the endless hunt for the living was to be their own ultimate fate. It wasn't long before the desire to breathe became a chore, hope draining from them with every passing second. As the fever took them and the virus went to work on their brains, the will to resist and fight was destroyed. In their hundreds, the newly contaminated accepted their fate almost willingly.

They died…and then they came back.

Some tried to flee from the undead, only to be run down by fiends whose speed defied logic. Some tried to fight, but how could a relatively disarmed population hope to battle such an enemy when the professionals were now retreating on all fronts? The only way you could "kill" a zombie was to destroy the base of the brain, and nobody had, as yet, shared that information with a population that thought getting a nasty comment on social media was a hardship. Soft, succulent and weak, the people of Britain were ripe for the coming slaughter.

Alive, they had mainly lived mediocre lives. As one of the undead, they became legion.

It was as if the virus knew what it had to do to defeat humanity. Whatever the truth, Lazarus seemed intent on wiping the human race from the very face of the Earth.

21.08.19
Manchester, UK

David Campbell didn't know who he was more annoyed at: himself, or the MI13 team that had left him trussed up naked and zip tied to a cold metal chair. His hands ached painfully, a gift from the sadistic Brodie who had, before leaving the premises, popped into Campbell's room only to tighten the restraints way past what was required.

"That should keep you out of trouble," Brodie had said mischievously. "Interesting shade of purple your hands are going mate. Hope your rescue team gets here before your appendages drop off."

"Go fuck yourself," Campbell had spat back at him. Probably not wise considering the predicament he was in, but defiance was all he had left. He hated Brodie, and he didn't try to hide that fact.

"Careful now," Brodie warned, "or do you want me to get Natasha in here to tie off your balls. She'd do it too, tie them real tight. You know that's how they castrate sheep?"

"I don't think you heard me, so I'll say it a little louder. Get fucked." Brodie had laughed at that and had playfully slapped him about the head a few times. Campbell had no choice but to let him inflict the humiliation.

"Good times," the MI13 man had said before making to leave the room.

"You should kill me," Campbell had warned. "When I get out of this I'm going to make it my life's mission to hunt down all of you."

"Yeah?" Brodie had responded. "Good luck with that. You'll be lucky your own side don't just shoot you and leave you in a ditch."

That had seemed hours ago. How many hours, Campbell had no idea, the ache in his hands and feet turning from an annoyance to a mind churning pounding. Even though the ends of his limbs felt numb, they pulsed with an unrivalled intensity. It wasn't the worst pain he'd ever experienced, but his life would have been infinitely better if he had been spared the experience.

Noises of hope came to him. Downstairs he heard the back door being breached as the retrieval team came for him. His superiors had persuaded the hierarchy of MI13 to let him live, to which Nick and his team had reluctantly been forced to agree to. There was no real excitement at the prospect of being released. As Brodie had wisely stated, the men coming to rescue him could just as easily be here to put a bullet through his skull, punishment for his failure to extract the asset. Campbell had failed in his mission, and his superiors did not take kindly to such failure. Especially when Campbell had warned said superiors that the plan to kidnap Jessica was, to put it into technical terms, *fucking idiotic*. Those at the top of America's intelligence community did not cope with embarrassment well.

Perhaps his one saving grace was the fact that the organisation he worked for, the US Defence Intelligence Agency, was in the public eye to a degree and had to account for the majority of their actions to the US Congress. But that did not change the fact that Campbell's failure was an embarrassment for himself and everyone associated with the ill-fated operation. So if not a bullet, perhaps he would simply be shipped to a black site in some third world hell hole and be left to rot.

It was safe to say his future did not look particularly bright.

"Clear," he heard someone shout downstairs. His countrymen were clearing the house now, mindful of what had happened to the last American team to be caught on UK soil. Even Campbell was surprised when the rest of his men had been executed so clinically. How did MI13 think he was going to let them get away with that? And even though it was Brodie who had pulled the trigger, the bulk of Campbell's ire was aimed solely at Lieutenant Colonel Nick Carter, the man in charge. There needed to be a reckoning there. Campbell wouldn't be happy until he choked the life out of the bastard with his own hands.

"Clear," another voice said, closer now. Creaking stairs, careful, measured feet coming up to his level. A door smashed open on an upper room.

"Clear."

The door to his room was closed causing a horrifying thought to suddenly come to him. Had the MI13 men booby-trapped it? Was this some ruse to just mess with his head only for his life to be ended by hidden explosive devices? Campbell felt his body tense, but he didn't cry out. He had to trust that the men coming for him knew what they were doing.

The door to his prison flew open, smashing into the dresser at the side of the room. The world didn't erupt into flames. Two men in black combat gear stared at him, their faces hidden behind balaclavas and protective goggles. One of them raised his machine gun ominously.

"Found him," the other man shouted, pushing past his partner slightly. Campbell couldn't tell, but he suspected the rescuer's eyes were scanning for booby traps.

"Any threats I should know about?" an American voice asked Campbell.

"None that I'm aware of." The second man nodded and stepped into the room. A knife appeared and the plastic ties holding Campbell down began to be released. Campbell knew what was coming, and the agony increased in his extremities as the blood rushed back to them. Most men would have instantly keeled over from the pain, but Campbell did his best to ignore it, although waves of nausea rocked through him. His second hand came free, and the fire intensified there as well. Blackness almost took him, but one of his rescuers must have predicted that. Smelling salts were thrust under his nose and consciousness rushed back into him, his body jerking as the Vagus nerve was stimulated.

His body screamed with the torture, but that was good. Pain hopefully meant there wasn't lasting damage. Pain he could deal with. Losing his hands or his feet would decrease his operational effectiveness and thus end his covert career. He'd been worried, the fingers of both hands having felt frozen for a considerable time.

Campbell tried to stand, but a gloved hand held him in place in the chair. In his condition, he wasn't going anywhere without help.

"Don't move please." Polite but authoritative, not treating Campbell as an equal. He was merely an object that had needed acquiring.

So that was how it was. He hadn't earnt an execution, at least not here, but he wasn't seen as a colleague in his rescuer's eyes. At best he was an irritant, at worst a prime fuck up. A third man appeared and threw a blanket dismissively at Campbell. Tentatively, his hands still pretty useless, he wrapped the material around his bare shoulders. He ignored his own nakedness, it held no shame for him.

"Clear," another voice shouted in the last room of the house. The agent standing next to Campbell spoke into his microphone.

"Riker to control. We have the asset, over." Riker? Campbell didn't know the name. He also didn't hear the response. "Wilko. Extracting asset now, over and out." Men pushed their way into the room, and two men forcefully grabbed him under the arms. With the fact his feet were still a beautiful shade of purple, they knew they would need to help him walk, but they were none too gentle about it. Campbell didn't complain because that would just lower him even more in the eyes of these men.

"Am I going to make it out of this alive?" Campbell enquired. There was no pleading in his voice. It was said in the manner one would ask a stranger for the time.

"Above my pay grade," the man called Riker answered. "All I know is I'm to take you in for debriefing." Riker gave the order for his team to leave, and they dragged Campbell with them, the feet a cruelty of pins, needles and recirculating blood. Out of the room now, they hauled him down the stairs, Campbell helping as best he could, trying his best not to slow the team down.

Three more men joined them at the base of the stairs, more outside making eight men in total. So likely Seals or Delta force. Wow, his superiors had pulled out all the stops, Campbell joked to himself. Free of the building, he was finding it easier to walk, and the men made their way with him over to two Land Rovers.

The morning was dark, the road outside the house devoid of streetlights, the sun still not fully up. On the distant horizon, a building was on fire, perhaps evidence of the way the city had tried to consume itself in the riots.

"God I hate this country," Campbell advised as he was bundled onto a back seat. Two men climbed in either side of him, which indicated he was nowhere near out of the woods with this crap. Neither of them spoke to him.

"ETA, twenty minutes to extraction," Riker said to his men. Sitting in the front seat of Campbell's transport, the soldier turned to the DIA operative.

"We are moving you to the nearest airfield where we will transport you to RAF Alconbury. There you will be debriefed and it will be decided what is to be done with you."

"Sounds peachy. I have information for my superiors…"

"It can wait," Riker said. "Shit's hitting the fan. I honestly don't think anyone will want to listen to be honest."

"Why, what have I missed?" Campbell had concern in his voice now.

"Oh nothing much," Riker said reassuringly, "Just little things like the President trying to eat his Chief of Staff. You know, inconsequential stuff like that."

Christ, thought Campbell, it was worse than he thought.

21.08.19
Hounslow, UK

For the last ten years, Carl had driven a London tube train deep below the surface of the teeming metropolis. The job wasn't particularly satisfying, but the pay was reasonable as were the hours and he was thankful that he made enough to live in the city of his birth. Many of his co-workers had objected to the twenty-four-hour tube service that now ran a limited service, but not Carl. He loved working at night. Isolated in his cabin, he was safe from whatever life threw at him and he watched the world go by, content to grow a little older with every day that passed. There was nothing wrong with living a humdrum life.

Or so he thought.

It was perhaps ironic then that on that fateful September morning he had been working a normal day shift, and it had been mid-rush hour when he was informed that his train was to be held at Hounslow Central Station. The morning rush had been in full flow, the platform and the train packed with those wanting to get to jobs that were utterly despised. Carl had quickly realised that the persistent red traffic light would back up the entire Piccadilly line, and would thus likely have a knock on effect to other lines.

Mandatory morning chaos to add to the depression of the average Londoner's existence.

The commuters would become angry, some verbally so, the bubbling resentment that their lives were less than their hopes and dreams rising to the surface. Any oral ejection would be muted though, mumbled in words most would be unable to hear. Even in their ire, Londoners would often do everything they could to prevent drawing attention to themselves. Occasionally, an emotional dam broke with voices raised, but such complaints never mattered to Carl. Any fury thrown his way was always unseen and unheard.

That morning, before the truth of everything was revealed to him, he had sat in his cabin and had waited for the light holding him to turn green. He had even done his duty and told his passengers that there was a delay of indeterminate length. At that specific moment, there had been no cause for alarm.

Carl couldn't tell people information he hadn't been given himself. And as the minutes had ticked by, Carl himself became agitated. They could have at least told him what the delay was being caused by. Signal failure? Jumper on the line? Power outages? He never did learn officially what the problem was...but that was okay because he got to see it first hand with his own eyes.

"Sorry folks, I'm still being held at a red light."

He wondered how many people in the carriages behind him had sworn when he told them that over the communication tannoy. The thing with Londoners was, they generally bottled everything up, the cult of non-communication whilst present on public transport almost a part of the culture. Still, he'd seen some things in his time. Nothing to match what he was to witness that morning.

At the end of the platform were TV monitors that allowed the drivers to observe what was happening on the platforms. The day prior he had seen a man trying to barge his way onto the train using a pushchair as a kind of battering ram. The fact there had been a child in the chair didn't seem to matter. The week before that, he'd been a spectator to two men fighting. Not particularly unusual for humans to engage in that activity, but perhaps not a common occurrence at eight thirty on a Saturday morning. At that hour, one couldn't even blame alcoholic indulgence for such unrestrained violence.

Carl was well aware the ties holding civilisation together were frayed and weakened, but he never expected the world to end the way it did.

As he had waited out the red light, his attention kept being drawn to the platform, which was full of people. The doors to the train were open and passengers were constantly stepping off the train to go and seek alternate means of transportation, only for their places to be taken by someone who still had hope in the London underground network. The majority waited, well aware that delays were common and unpredictable. It was a familiar dilemma...wait it out, or try and get a bus in the knowledge that the trains could start moving the minute you left the station.

"Carl," the call came in from the control room, "sorry mate, all trains have been suspended." Bloody hell, Carl had said to himself.

"Why, what's happened?" he asked. The not knowing was always the worst of it.

"I'm…I'm not allowed to tell you at this time," came the sheepish response. *Not allowed to tell me?* He let those words sink in. What the fuck did that even mean?

Time to tell the passengers the good news. Before he had been able to do so, however, a scuffle broke out on the packed platform. The presence of the train meant that there was little risk of anyone ending up on the tracks, but the violence still needed to be dealt with. Not by Carl, there was no way he was leaving his cabin. But until the people were out of his train, he couldn't get it back to its endpoint and relieve the pressure that had been steadily building in his bowels. That curry the night before had perhaps been a mistake.

"Control," Carl radioed in giving his train's registration, "we have a fight on Hounslow Station platform. Can you get Transport Police down here pronto?" Nobody gave him any kind of response, and he sent the message again. Again, no response. Looking down at his radio handset, he almost threw it to the cabin floor in disgust. With admirable restraint he carefully placed it back into its cradle.

If they weren't talking to him, perhaps there was a reason. Terrorists?

The fight seemed to spread even as he tried to speak to control, the crowd of people surging away from the epicentre of the violence. What he could see was limited, but it looked like two men were lashing out at those around them. Then things really descended into chaos because it wasn't every day you saw a child's arm get ripped out of its socket.

Thirty minutes passed by as the world had the sanity ripped from it. The chaos had spread rapidly throughout the whole station and through his train. Even with the train cabin's soundproofing, Carl had heard the harrowing screams. Carl had sat there helpless as the zombification of the station's commuters had occurred. He had even tried to close the train doors to protect those inside, but the doors were obstructed by humanity and by the relentless dead.

In terror and fascination, he had watched through his cabin door peephole into the tube compartment directly behind his cabin. At the height of it, people could be seen trying to fight off a tall man who was almost manic in his attack. Some people tried to flee, hampered by the sheer volume of those around them. Others had punched the man, with little apparent effect. The scenes he saw through that spying device would forever haunt him… for the rest of his soon to be shortened life.

Things seemed calmer now, Carl remained in the cabin, waiting. The platform and his train were strewn with bodies, some lying on top of each other in parts. Many of those caught up in the violence had long since wandered off, either nursing their injuries or through death and resurrecting. When the dead rose, they easily seem to traverse the steps off the platform and into the body of the station. It hadn't taken Carl long for him to figure what this was all about. Hollywood had taught him much. Nobody from the control room bothered to relay any further information to him, not that he cared because things just continued to get worse.

With the power to the train now cut, the only way he was getting anywhere was on foot, a prospect that did not appeal to him in the slightest. To be abandoned like this was such utter betrayal.

Carl looked again through his peephole. The carriage behind was relatively empty now, perhaps only two dozen bodies left. As he watched, one of them twitched, pulling itself up off the floor like a drunk who had no sense of its awkwardness. Not the first time Carl had observed the phenomena, but still he watched with horrified absorption. It took the zombie two attempts to get to its feet.

Carl wiped tears from his eyes as he witnessed the dead face turn towards him. Several of them had done this, and the zombie staggered towards his cabin door, the black eyes quickly becoming large enough for Carl to see. Carl moved back from the door, a hand hitting the other side uselessly. How did they know he was in here? There was no way it could get through to him, but likewise, there was no way Carl could get out that way. Even if the whole train and platform cleared, the station and the road outside would likely be teeming with the things. And then there was the blood and the body parts he would have to step through.

The creature hit the door again, but then Carl sensed the thing backing away. Carl didn't step back to the spy view, he had seen enough. Instead he waited for the zombie to leave the train, and Carl sighed with relief when the TV monitors at the end of the platform showed exactly that. It stepped over a floored form who tried to use its brother to climb up into the world. All it did was drag its fellow zombie down.

His bowels churned again, an insistence that couldn't really be denied for much longer. Pressure was building, and there was only one way to ease the suffering that was coming.

Carl decided he'd had enough of this. He couldn't wait around here any longer with his bowels threatening to explode. At the very least, he had to relieve himself. The driver's cabin on this particular train had a door that allowed him to access the track whilst avoiding the platform, and he opened that door now, the stench from the dead hitting him. Carl had expected to hear moaning, but the only sounds he heard were the movement of the departed. Why were they so silent?

As carefully as he could, he climbed down from his cabin and stepped to the side, well away from the live rail just in case there was still juice running through it. A more athletic man might have been able to hang his arse out of the cabin door, but Carl was in his late forties and to attempt that would just end up with him flat on his back lying in his own shit.

Feet firmly planted on the tunnel floor, he got his britches down just in time and the relief was almost orgasmic. Mistakenly, he moaned with the release which caused the zombies on the platform to stir, drawn towards the only sound of humanity. Within seconds a set of arms was reaching for him through the small gap his train made with the platform's protective barrier. That sight alone seemed to spur his bowels on to greater feats of explosiveness, and this time he was washed with a wave of pain and nausea. So not only was he caught in the zombie apocalypse, but there was a strong chance he also had a full-on case of food poisoning to deal with. The only positive in all of this was the fact that he had managed to avoid shitting himself.

Another arm shoved its way through the gap, and he could see them massing, pressing to get at him. Could zombies climb? Whilst they wouldn't be able to get through the barrier, if they put some effort into it, the average human could get over. Carl felt his third and likely final expulsion building, sweat now building on his skin. The horrors occurring in his intestines were competing with the horrors occurring in the world around him.

When your adrenaline is heightened, you often spot things you would otherwise have missed. That was the case with the movement to Carl's right, the small creature balancing along the live rail. Rats, of all things to come along now. Carl hated the little bastards, always had. Driving the train gave him a certain amount of satisfaction in that he knew in his working career he would get to kill at least some of them. It was their teeth that did it for him, the very thought of what they could do sent him cold.

Another rat came into sight, and Carl's fear notched up another level. Rats were not brave creatures and generally tried to avoid humans wherever possible, but these two were less than two metres away. They seemed to sit there staring at him as if Carl was some rare curiosity. One of them edged closer, just as fresh fluid poured from Carl's raw and stinging anus.

He had to get back into his cabin, but his expulsions just wouldn't seem to quit.

"Come on," Carl begged as the cramps inside him subsided. One final push and what he hoped was the last of it came. With nothing to wipe himself with, he was halfway to getting his trousers up back around his waist when the first rat pounced. It landed on Carl's leg, the tiny claws digging into the fabric, and Carl tried to hit it off with the back of his hand. All that did was to give the rat another target, and its teeth dug into the side of his wrist.

The pain was like fire, and it shot all the way through his arm. Carl waved his hand in the air to try and dislodge the attacking beast, but it would not let go. His trousers fell back around his ankles hampering his ability to retreat. Ample opportunity for the second rat to attack. Jumping from the rail, it scurried towards Carl, initially disappearing in the bundled clothing on the floor. Then it re-emerged, clambering up his inner thigh, only to take a chunk out of the flesh there. Carl roared in panic, ripping the rat away with his free hand and hurling it down the tunnel.

Swinging his compromised hand again, he smashed it against the side of the train, the rat hardly noticing. Finally, it came away, but not because it released Carl of its own benevolent volition. His flesh had simply worked loose and the rat fell to the floor complete with a tasty morsel to tell all its friends about. It disappeared from his sight, and he dragged his trousers up from the ground again. By some miracle, Carl had been able to keep his feet through all of this.

As he fastened the button, there was a tugging on the back of his leg, a rat scaling him yet again. Carl had yet to tuck himself in, and the rat slipped under the cloth of his shirt so as to attack his back. Unable to reach the rat, Carl's mind broke, and he went into full-on frenzy. Roaring, he propelled himself back against the train in a hope of crushing the vermin. As he slammed his overweight body against the hard metal, he felt something give in the creature, and it dropped out from under his shirt. Moisture spread across his back, trickling down into the crack of his arse. It took everything within him to keep the vomit from rampaging up his throat.

"You fucking little bastard," Carl bellowed and stomped down on the remnants of his defiler. And all the time, the puppet arms were uselessly reaching for him, dead eyes witness to everything that had occurred.

Carl, turning to get back into the cabin, saw two rats sat on the doorstep. Time seemed to pause as he felt rather than saw the onrushing masses coming towards him. Turning his head, Carl looked down the tunnel as far as the station platform lights would allow. Hundreds. There were hundreds of rats heading for him, their eyes sparkling in the blackness. Rats naturally have black eyes, so it didn't occur to him, not until he was uselessly fighting off their onslaught, that the rats were also carriers of the zombie virus.

Carl never managed to get back into his cabin, and it took him nearly ten minutes to die. When he eventually stopped his struggling, only then did the undead rats decide to leave him alone. Another zombie for the world sat up off the tracks and dragged itself to shaky feet. With no way to get back onto the platform, Carl(Z) wandered off down the tunnel, tripping over several times. It would eventually find a train blocking the next platform and never would get to taste the delights it craved.

21.08.19
Manchester, UK

It had taken everything within him to let the little bastards live. When he had rescued Susan from the clutches of the rioting yobs, Brian had felt the all too familiar red mist begin to descend over his mind. And whilst he had delivered grievous injuries upon some of them, he had resisted the temptation to end their sorry ass lives. Twenty years ago he wouldn't have been so forgiving, but experience had taught him such actions would have unacceptable consequences. Killing people was fine, it just had to be done in a controlled and planned fashion so that the bodies could never be found. Spontaneity was what got you into trouble with the law, something he really wanted to avoid from now on. Brian would rather die than spend one more day at Her Majesty's pleasure.

All of the gang members would have required hospital treatment, but Brian had left enough of them still able to walk so they could help their less fortunate friends out of Susan's violated home. Even so, the yobs had been lucky. Despite his understanding of the need for restraint, if he had arrived any later (forcing him to do his White Knight rescue whilst they were actually engaged in rape) things likely would have been a little different. Instead of pistol whipping the boys, he would have surely shot out knee caps and removed genitalia. That would have resulted in one or more deaths, and there would have been no way for him to come back from that. If he had killed one, he would have had to finish the lot off. Even with his gangland connections, you couldn't cover up the murder of multiple people in the middle of Manchester. In the unlikely event he could arrange to get rid of the bodies on such short notice, there were still too many people who had seen him brandishing a gun out in the street. People who knew and feared him likely wouldn't grass, but frightened people still had lips that flapped when put under pressure by Her Majesty's Constabulary. Someone would have eventually talked, and then he would have ended up straight back in the cells. That would have been the end of him.

Brian knew he would get away with sending a few scumbags to the hospital at the height of the worst riots the country had ever seen. Mindless murder was out of the question though. That was all before he learnt that perhaps the police would no longer care, what with it being the end of the world and all.

So, through restraint and luck, he had done just enough to teach the youngsters an important lesson, the Lion laying down some knowledge on their naïve and pliable minds. Brian gave instruction on what the rules were, what rules they had broken, and an explanation as to why the punishment was required for their transgressions. Okay, the two he had initially encountered in Susan's kitchen were pretty worse for wear, but that was because one of them had thrown a perfectly decent bottle of vodka at him. Restraint only went so far.

For the boys upstairs, a few slaps and a few broken fingers with the threat of future violence was what had been required. Then there was the reinforced assurance that a recurrence of their activities would result in severe penalties.

"If I encounter any of you again," Brian had told them, "I'm going to start collecting balls." They also needed to understand that talking to the rozzers was not in their long-term best interests. Snitches had a tendency to end up face down in the canal along with their loved ones.

"Talk to the police, and you will wish you had never been born. Some of you undoubtedly know me, so trust me when I say your lives won't be worth living."

Was fear and his threats enough though? Brian had actually spent much of the morning wondering if he shouldn't just have the shits dealt with. It wouldn't take much to find out who they were. They were a loose end and although unlikely, there was still a risk they could go to the police and complain about their harsh treatment. He preferred the old days when the cops used to turn a blind eye to this sort of thing.

He gave Susan the vengeance she was owed and left a modicum of the youth's dignity intact. Brian had learnt the importance of that from his time in prison. He hurt them, but in a way they could use as a rite of passage. Humiliation and degradation were the last things you wanted to inflict on a human being you intended to leave alive and free to roam. Brian put them in their place and then sent them packing to nurse their injuries. One broken arm. A crushed hand, a dozen dislocated and snapped fingers. Three concussions and a smattering of smashed noses. Nothing they wouldn't recover from. Some of these lads had little if nothing to live for in their future, and as hardened as Brian was, he didn't want some little scrote trying to revenge shank him as he locked up his own gym one night. He thus made sure that whilst he damaged their bodies, he did not catastrophically damage their egos.

With the new day well under way, he had a new problem. Despite what the lads had tried to do, Susan had initially seemed relieved by his ability to limit the beatings he unleashed. Part of her wanted vengeance, but she also realised they were basically children, with brains that were still developing and still establishing a concept of morality. Plus, it was her home, and for Brian to have left a mound of corpses lying around the once marital bed would have definitely been going too far. He had defended her honour when there was no one else around to do so and saved her from the worst they were threatening. Brian sensed that was enough for her.

However, even with the kids vanquished and their like no longer a threat to her, Susan had been hesitant to offer him any kind of thanks. She had made the call begging him for help, and when the help was offered, it was like she resented him for it. Now he was in the annoying predicament where he felt strangely obliged to look after her in his own home. Her house was a shattered wreck, and she wasn't hurt badly enough to warrant a hospital visit. Her living room window needed boarding up and the front room cleaning out, which was something he planned to arrange for some time today all being well. The carpet in the bedroom probably needed burning as well.

This all meant that Susan was now in his spare bedroom, sleeping off the trauma of the previous night even though the afternoon was almost upon them. Brian did not need this kind of commitment in his life right now. He could really do without playing nursemaid to someone who, over their last few meetings, had made it clear she no longer wanted anything to do with him. Where once he had felt some sort of affection for her, now she was a burden that he carried stoically. The sooner she was gone, the sooner he would be happy, and yet his own sense of honour prevented him from abandoning her in her time of need.

Why hadn't he just put her up in a hotel? That was a question he kept asking himself, and he hadn't yet found an answer that made any sense. *Fuck my life.*

If his brother had still been alive to defend her honour, things would have likely gone very differently. Brian's brother, in his heart, had been a pussy and a coward, so likely he would have suffered a beat down at the least, and Susan would have likely have had to worry for the rest of her life about the possible diseases the little runts had passed onto her. Brian's unique abilities were often frowned upon by society, but there was no denying that occasionally a man like him was needed.

Brian knew Susan had distanced herself from him because of his resemblance to the man she had loved. The only child they had raised together had been murdered by a nonce that really should have chosen his victims with much more care. Not a wise move to rape and kill the niece of a man like Brian. Brian had let the paedophile bastard live, but his body and mind were now irreparably damaged due to what Brian had done to him. The nonce wasn't of any use to anybody anymore. The guy even needed help just to go to the bathroom.

It felt weird having Susan in his home, and with the faint sound of snoring still coming from the guest room that rarely saw guests, Brian sat on the sofa of his penthouse flat and watched the news channel with growing alarm. He had expected to be watching stuff about the riots, but they were hardly mentioned. The Prime Minister was dead, and there was talk about martial law. Troops were apparently fighting running battles on the outskirts of Heathrow, and the news anchors looked genuinely scared. In the bottom right-hand corner of the screen, an insert ran a drone flight image over the streets of Bangkok. Thousands of people could be seen running amok there.

Only they weren't people.

Brian was just about to flick to the next news channel when his phone rang. He looked at the number and knew he had no choice but to answer. He muted the TV so that he could give his employer his full attention.

"Mr Clay?"

"Brian, I need you here ASAP."

"Is there a problem Mr Clay?" Clay, the boss of the criminal enterprise Brian worked for, sounded agitated.

"Yes, and it's only going to get worse. I'm sure you are aware that I have powerful friends that protect my interests?"

"Yes Mr Clay." Such matters would never be discussed in detail over an unencrypted phone line.

"My friends have informed me that the shit is hitting the proverbial pan. I'm calling all my lieutenants in. I need you here at my home." This obviously wasn't a request, and one didn't survive long if you failed to follow one of Clay's orders. He looked after you and paid well, but only so long as you maintained your usefulness and did what he said. The criminal underworld did not issue P45's.

"Yes Mr Clay, I can be there in about thirty minutes. I have a problem though." Brian almost winced as he said it.

"I don't like to hear about problems Brian, especially now."

"I know Mr Clay, and I'm sorry for that. It's just that I had to rescue my dead brother's wife from some home invaders last night. Little shits tried to rape her. She's not in a good way and it will worry me to leave her alone." Perhaps worry was the wrong word, but he still felt he had some form of obligation to her.

"Is this Susan we are talking about?" Clay's voice seemed to sparkle as he said the words.

"Yes Mr Clay." Clay and Susan had met several times. Clay was known for his 'charity' work and often held exclusive parties that some of the rich and famous wanted to be seen at, allowing themselves to be blinded by Clay's ruse as a legitimate businessman. Clay always invited the family members of those who worked for him, and before the suicide of her husband, Susan had attended several times. She always seemed to protest her attendance, but secretly, Brian knew she enjoyed the thrill of being around footballers, actors and even the occasional politician. Whenever Clay had greeted Susan, he had always spent too long looking at the wrong parts of her.

"Hmm. Tell you what you can do, bring her with you. I have plenty of rooms, she can stay here for now, until things settle. I'm sure we can find a job for her." *What things?* thought Brian.

"I'm not sure she will like that," Brian insisted, although he felt relief that Clay was making the offer. He had to be careful though, he could feel the eggshells cracking under the weight of this precarious conversation. If the offer was made, and Susan said no, that might not go down well. Brian was not so naïve as to think this was some sort of altruistic offer being made by Clay. He always wanted something in return whenever he helped someone. Always.

"Then persuade her, I wouldn't be asking you to come here if it wasn't important. And having a woman as attractive as Susan in the house will be a welcome distraction. I'll expect the two of you here within the hour. Oh, and Brian, don't bother bringing anything with you. You might be here a while, but I have everything covered." With that the call ended.

"Shit," Brian said to the living room. He hadn't heard Susan entering the room behind him.

"Who was that Brian?" Brian turned to see her dressed in an old dressing gown he had left for her. Her face was free of makeup, and her hair pulled back. She looked surprisingly good considering what she had been through. There was a nice bruise developing on her left cheek though.

"My boss."

"You mean that gangland maniac Clay?"

"You shouldn't talk about him like that," Brian insisted. He was still surprised by the urgency he had heard in Clay's voice. No, not urgency, fear. That was a first for Clay.

"What did he want?"

"He needs me. Something is going down, something important enough that his contacts on the police force warned him." He was about to say something else when Susan suddenly clasped her hand over her face.

"Oh my God," surprise ripping through her.

"What?"

"The fucking Prime Minister is dead!" Susan was reading the news off the teletype running along the bottom of the TV set.

"Oh that. I suspect that has a lot to do with why Clay wants me."

"But that doesn't make any sense."

"Clay sounded worried, which doesn't happen very often. I have no choice but to go round there." Brian hesitated. He was three times the size of Susan, and yet he felt nervous about informing her she would need to come with him. "There is one thing though."

"What?"

"Mr Clay has requested the pleasure of your company at his house. He says with what is going down, it would be safer for you." That wasn't technically true of course, but it was better than Brian saying there was a strong chance his boss was possibly going to try and get all romantic with her. "And I'm not happy about leaving you here on your own." Brian didn't elaborate on that last part. Susan's eyes kept flicking between Brian and the TV screen.

"Christ, the Health Minister is dead as well." Another message from the television. Brian turned to the TV and used the remote to turn the volume back up.

"We are getting reports that the Queen will be making a declaration to temporarily dissolve Parliament," the news anchor said. "Everyone is being advised to stay in their homes…" Brian flipped the channel. The news on the alternate channel was pretty much the same. Except it then went into reporting about supermarket riots in some UK cities. Things were falling apart, the images of violence on the screen reinforcing the urgency in Clay's demands.

"This doesn't sound good Brian," Susan insisted. She sounded scared, vulnerable.

"That's why I don't want you to be alone. Sounds like being at Clay's, even if it's only temporarily, would be the best thing for you. The place is a fortress. Susan, are you OK with this?"

"Will I be safe there?"

"Of course you will. You've been to his house, you've seen the walls around it." There would be armed men too, lots of them. Susan looked at him with a pensive look. She didn't want to be beholden to Brian, but right now only an idiot would deny that she needed his protection. This no longer seemed like a world safe for civilians, women in particular. Staying here was only a short-term option at best, and she couldn't go back to her own house. She had experienced how easily its defences had been breached. Where else was there to go but with Brian?

"Can I at least shower first?" came the response.

That was easier than I figured, thought Brian.

21.08.19
Flight, West Coast of Hawaii

"Air traffic control, Echo Foxtrot 421 again requesting an emergency landing. Please advise." The captain of the flight out of Singapore looked at his co-pilot who shared his desperation. They had followed protocol, radioing ahead with the outbreak of violence that had occurred on their flight. Only things had become much worse. For the last thirty minutes, someone had been relentlessly attacking the cabin door. Whoever it was couldn't get in, but still they persisted, the camera that made the attacker visible almost useless now as its field of vision was obscured by splattered blood. The Captain wasn't sure, but he thought it very likely the loud monotonous sound was the person using his head as a hammer.

Jane, the senior flight attendant, had contacted them over the internal flight intercom several hours before to inform them that the passenger in seat 22J had fallen ill. Minutes later, her frightened voice had come back over the coms to tell the Captain that the passenger had turned violent, that he was biting people. She had warned the Captain not to come out of the cabin, because something was very wrong with the man, that he was being restrained by fellow passengers and that at least a dozen of them were now injured. The heavy turbulence that hit then didn't help matters, and the Captain had radioed ahead to inform the authorities of the situation. At that point, they were four hours out of Hawaii.

They had managed to get the passenger shackled down to his seat, his immense fatty bulk making it difficult, his strength surprising for someone who had clearly never stepped foot in a gym. In the middle of the Pacific Ocean, their only option was to fly on and land at the nearest available airport. Two hours from Hawaii, and some of the other passengers had begun to fall sick, the news of what had happened at the CDC finally being widely disseminated to federal authorities, including the aviation authority. The Captain was asked questions about the nature of the illness, something he hadn't really been able to answer.

"You might have to do a quarantine landing," he was told.

Again the Captain had wanted to come out of the cabin, but Jane had persuaded him not to. What if it was something contagious? They needed both pilots to get the plane down on the ground, and there was nothing the Captain could do out here anyway. She'd started to implement emergency isolation procedures, moving those who were injured towards the back of what was thankfully a lightly occupied flight. Some passengers protested, but she was blessed to have an Air Marshal on board whose armed presence silenced most of the dissent. The Air Marshal, who had helped restrain the passenger in 22J, hid the fact that his left hand had a nasty bite mark. He felt fine, he'd kept telling himself, even though he clearly wasn't, the nausea and the fever slowly building inside him.

Things were different now, and not for the better. The two air force jets flying either side of his plane had come out of nowhere and worried the Captain. There was no risk that the flight would be hijacked, so why were they there? Yes, there were violent passengers on board, and he had lost contact with the flight attendants. But he still had control of the plane.

"Flight EF421, be advised you are to land at Kalaeloa Airport," the air traffic controller responded, reading out the airport's coordinates. The Captain felt relief wash through him. "Be advised, you are ordered not to deviate from this flight path. Follow all commands given to you by your fighter escort." As if to accentuate the order, the air force jet out the Captain's left window moved in closer. And still, the forehead pounded on the cabin door.

Jane shook as the sickness owned her soul. She was almost mad with the sound of fists beating on the flimsy toilet door that she had locked herself in. Likely the only thing keeping the crazed teeth at bay were her feet planted firmly on the inside of the collapsible door. Whatever madness had taken hold of the passengers, it had erupted quicker than she could have imagined.

She had managed to escape being bitten by 22J, but many hadn't, and those injured by 22J had eventually started to turn. Turn, what did that even mean? She had been standing over one of the first of them to die, the elderly woman's spasms a replica of how the original victim to the virus had reacted. And all the while, the passenger in 22J had thrashed and writhed in an attempt to escape his bondage. Several times, she had seen the Air Marshal nervously fondling his sidearm. That was when he wasn't busy mopping his sweating brow. Any minute, she had kept expecting the armed officer to start shooting.

Jane didn't understand what was happening here. She just knew that she was terrified. It was the deep black eyes that scared her the most.

The second person to die and resurrect had been the one who bit Jane. This one the Marshal did shoot, but not before several more passengers had received nasty and vicious bites. The shot didn't stop the freshly born zombie however and half a clip later, the thing was still on the rampage, Jane amazed a bullet hadn't gone astray and punctured the pressurised cabin.

One man was so grievously wounded by the old woman's insane attack that he bled out in his seat, the attempts to stem the arterial bleed from his neck an exercise in utter futility. It was then that Jane began to understand what was happening on the plane, even though it went against everything she believed could be possible. When science fiction suddenly became reality any rules you thought applied quickly stopped making sense.

Jane had looked at the deep chunk of missing flesh at the base of her left thumb and had panicked. All professionalism left her, and she backed away, two more passengers starting to buck and gyrate in their seats. Just as Jane retreated into the toilet stall, she saw the Marshal get overpowered, the whole cabin erupting into chaos as the zombies began to rise up from their deaths. Nobody on the plane really stood a chance.

Now it felt like the very minions of hell were trying to reach her. As crazy as the revelation was to her, she knew what this was. Zombies. How could it be anything else? The violence of their attacks, the blackness of their eyes, the strength with which they were able to resist the attempts of multiple grown adults to hold them down. It was the only explanation that made sense to her. And even through the fear and the sound of the toilet door being attacked, confusion descended upon her terrified mind.

She suddenly found she couldn't spell the word zombie. The letters just sort of floated there, not joining together in any logical order. They just didn't seem to fit, and she shook her head, grogginess coming over her. Susan started to lose the ability to understand what some words even meant, the very surroundings an enigma to her. If it wasn't for the relentless attack on her meagre defences, she might even have forgotten the predicament she was in.

Then it struck her, a wave of humanity sweeping back, Jane's old self cutting through the fog that threatened to strip her of who she was. Looking at her hand, Jane gave out an almost silent whimper. *No, not that. Please, anything but that!*

As the tears truly began to well up in her eyes, Jane suddenly felt a great hunger build within her. So bad was it that she was actually in enough pain to almost double her over. That would have been catastrophic because she would have had to drop her legs and they were the only thing keeping the creatures from pushing their way into where she sat.

Jane's mouth suddenly filled with saliva, and it poured from her mouth causing her to have an explosive coughing fit. The cough seemed to catch in her throat, the air no longer able to move. Jane battled for breath, her lungs just refusing to inhale. In her last moments, her finger nails clawing at her neck, Jane went mad. That was how Jane died, asphyxiating on her own spit

Flight EF421 never did make it to land, shot down by one of the jets when it became evident that most of the passengers on board weren't human anymore. The loss of the airline wouldn't even make the news.

21.08.19
London, UK

Colin Macready watched the news with growing alarm. Not because of the horrors he witnessed, but because of the opportunity that was being stolen from him. How could he bring devastation to the city when it was already ripping itself apart? At this rate, the chance to make his mark, to make his statement, would be lost in the unravelling carnage. It wasn't fair, it just wasn't fucking fair.

The BBC was no longer trying to pull the wool over everybody's eyes. With the Prime Minister and most of the Cabinet dead, the military had taken charge. All social media had been shut off, and the terrestrial TV channels that were still on air played a combination of news channels, archaic comedies and curfew instructions.

Where possible, stock up on food
Stay in your homes
Lock your doors and windows
Fill all containers with water
Avoid large crowds
Do not break curfew

The list of seemingly contradictory advice played sporadically at the bottom of the TV screen. Colin wouldn't be doing any of that. He had a bomb vest and he was determined to use it for maximum effect. His sick mind was determined to go ahead with his plans for mass destruction…even though at present he didn't even have a target.

A pain filled scream rose from the street outside, and Colin carefully peaked down from behind the curtain, his curiosity irresistible. Three stories above the developing madness, Colin watched in fascination as a middle-aged woman was chased down the centre of the road by two lumbering, bloodstained creatures. This was the first time Colin had seen THEM first hand, finally believing what the news had been telling him all along. Zombies! Well, wasn't that just a kick in the teeth?

There were other people around, obviously desperate shoppers intent on emptying the shelves of the numerous establishments that were still foolishly selling their wares. Colin didn't understand the insanity of that. This was clearly the end of days. If he had owned a shop full of provisions, he would have locked that shit up tight. Why sell your future survival for a piece of paper with a picture of the Queen's head on it? If this truly was the zombie apocalypse, did people actually think the economy was going to survive this?

But if those shops did shutter up, how long before the mob came to force their way in? The breakdown in society and law and order was a single spark away. The riots over the last few days had shown how fragile civilisation had been. Was there any way a semblance of order could be maintained?

An inevitable wave of panic rippled through the people down below. Nobody came to help the woman, and as she was felled by the first of the zombies, the inhabitants of the street scattered like frightened mice. Doors locked and people scrambled into cars in an attempt to drive off. Nobody went near the woman and her attackers.

Colin watched almost mesmerised as the two zombies started to devour her, one ripping the flesh off her bare arm with its teeth. The satisfied zombie reared back its head, thrashing from side to side as it chewed on the meat, its partner in the assault ripping the clothes from the woman's chest to expose the breasts. The woman tried to hold it off with her free arm, but the second zombie just grabbed the limb as if it was an offering, taking the fingers as easily as if it was biting into a hot dog. The woman's agony could be heard by everyone, and yet nobody seemed to care.

Despite the destruction to his plans that this turn of events represented, Colin suddenly found himself approving of what was going on. Yes, let the masses be consumed by whatever this was. Let the sheep fight for their lives in the coming apocalypse, dying in their billions to free the land of the scourge of man. No more pollution, no more deforestation. And the only species going extinct now would be the one that most threatened the planet. It was absolutely perfect.

Both zombies were now intent on dining on an arm each, and Colin felt himself urging them on. For some reason, he wanted to see the woman die, wanted to see her lifeless form rise up from the asphalt so as to join the hunt of humanity. He was almost about to stick his head out of the window to shout encouragement to them, when the first zombie's head was thrust back, the momentum taking the rest of the body with it. The sound of the shot arrived a fraction of a second later, making Colin jump. Now he did open and lean out of the window, just as another bullet took the second zombie in the left shoulder. More bullets hit it.

Up the street, several soldiers could be seen. One of them was kneeling, and he fired again, this time ending the other zombie with an accurate brainstem shot. Colin's fingers gripped the window frame in frustration, the fingertips beginning to hurt with the pressure he was exerting. The bastards were spoiling all his fun. He didn't want to see this. Colin didn't want to see humanity winning for Christ's sake. Right then and there, Colin became more determined than ever to inflict as much carnage as possible.

Still alive but bleeding badly, the woman tried to push herself up off the floor, her hands a mess of pain. Despite her injuries, she managed to struggle valiantly to her knees. Sobbing loudly now, her heart must have filled with thanks for the men who had saved her. Colin didn't know how, but he knew what was coming, sensed it as if it was in the air. From this distance, he couldn't tell the rank of the soldier that walked up to the woman, but he reckoned it was an officer. You had to be a cold-hearted upper-class twat to be able to shoot a defenceless woman in the face like that. That's what his abusive father would have said if he'd still been alive. With his sidearm, the soldier put more rounds into the heads of the woman and the undead, before holstering the pistol he had used. Some would claim it was murder, but let's not kid ourselves. It was an act of mercy when you looked at the big picture.

The few civilians who had been unable to escape the scene watched with mesmerised fascination as the soldiers moved off down the street. Nobody berated the armed men. Perhaps everyone understood that this was the only way now to deal with the threat.

"Stay in your homes. Obey all instructions from military and police personnel. This area is now under Military Quarantine. Arrangements are being made to relocate you to a secure location. Anyone found on the streets will be subject to immediate detention and risks summary execution." The voice now booming out was a recorded message being played from an armoured personnel carrier that was trundling down the centre of the street towards where the soldiers had engaged the enemy. It came on regardless of the cars in the road, many of them being forced to pull over to let it pass. They were no match for the tracked vehicle, and several of them had the paint and wing mirrors scraped from their sides. There would be no insurance claim to cover that kind of damage.

It would seem the rules had changed.

Colin now knew what his purpose was, the idea dropping into his head out of nowhere as monumental ideas often did. The great purge had begun, the removal of humanity from the planet. But it would go a lot more efficiently if there weren't men with guns running around killing the agents of the undoing. It would also go a lot faster if there were more zombies on the loose to help with the unravelling of it all. Perhaps Colin's final mission was to help with all that.

21.08.19
Preston, UK

The door to Jessica's room was no longer locked. Blood tests had confirmed that she was no longer infected and thus not a threat to anyone. She still represented an opportunity though. By some freak of nature, she was immune to the deadliest virus humanity had ever known. So even more than an opportunity, she represented hope. That was probably why the Americans had tried to grab her from the hospital. That was why she had been locked up and treated like a lab rat for the last couple of days. Even the bite wound that had been inflicted seemed to be healing faster than she expected. She told herself to stop peeking under the sterile dressing, but she kept doing it anyway. The flesh there gave the impression it was knitting together quicker than was possible. Jessica wondered if she was imagining it.

It was the man called Nick who had come and unlocked her door. He said there was no need for her to be a prisoner, not now. Jessica was grateful that someone had finally acknowledged that she had indeed been held against her will. All Nick had asked from her was that she not try and run off, because that wasn't going to be allowed to happen. She could go outside and get some air, but she wouldn't be allowed to leave the base. Partly for her protection and also because of how valuable she clearly was to the scientists who would be fighting this thing. Her blood might be the key to everything. Nick just didn't want her locked up anymore. She wasn't deserving of that, and never had been.

People like her might even be the saviour of the human race so a bit of respect might even be in order.

Jessica had assured him she wasn't going anywhere. Her own brother Peter had died and then returned from the dead, only to then try and kill those around him. To make things infinitely worse, Pete had then attacked her, even whilst she begged him not to. There wasn't any denying that the safest place for her to be, right now, was around men with guns, men who felt she was an asset that needed protecting. Having witnessed the undead first hand, she didn't want to be alone in a city that might very well soon be teeming with them. She could still remember visibly the image of the dead police officer as he had walked past her hospital bed during the initial outbreak. The way the blackened eyes had watched over her still sent chills down her spine.

Nick had even given her a satellite phone and told her she could ring and talk to whoever she liked. No restriction, not now, at least not until the mobile network went down. Even when that happened, Jessica should still be alright. Her phone would work regardless, and living out in the middle of nowhere, Tom too relied on satellite communication due to the isolation of where he lived. To think twenty-four hours ago they had been watching her like a hawk watches its cowering prey. Had things really gone to shit that quickly? Could her blood really hold the secret to ending all this? She hoped it did, they had certainly taken enough of it. What she wouldn't do to go back to her own life though.

Little chance of that.

"You could be the key to stopping all this," Colonel Smith had said several times. Jessica had no love for the Colonel. He was a cold fish and she detected something dark within him. He had never been anything but polite to her, but she sensed more to his personality than what was being shown to the world. Maybe it was female intuition that told her not to trust him. Maybe it was her experience as a criminal defence lawyer. Whatever it was, she knew the Colonel did not have her best interests at heart, and most likely cared only for himself. Where the hell was he anyway? Jessica hadn't seen Smith since yesterday. Perhaps that was something she shouldn't really be complaining about.

Jessica had spent an hour on the phone with her mother, as well as speaking with her one remaining brother, Tom. They were both safe, holding up in Tom's remote farmhouse. She had only been there a few times and even with satnav, it had been difficult to find. It was also easy to defend. To think Jessica had playfully mocked Tom and his end of the world prophecies. Well, she wasn't laughing now. If only she could just get in a car and go there now, to be with the family she loved. They reciprocated her affections, despite the way she had been stupidly neglecting them due to the dreams her career hypnotised her with.

What use was a law degree when the undead marched across the Earth?

Now was the time of fighting men, men like Nick. She liked Nick. Jessica knew he was a dangerous and damaged man, and he always looked at her with that piercing stare that seemed to rip the secrets out of her inner core. She couldn't even fathom the things he must have seen in his life. Rarely did he ever smile, life obviously too serious for any kind of frivolity with someone like her. Still, there was something there, a humanity that she could trust, a resilience and formidable competence. He was driven by duty and a personal sense of honour that was rare in this day and age, especially amongst the people she normally associated with. Jessica recognised he would do what needed doing, even if it meant committing unthinkable atrocities. He was the kind of man you wanted to be around when the shit truly hit the fan, just so you could forget about who he was and what he did when normality returned. Nick was also most definitely the kind of man you didn't want as an enemy.

Even though she felt safe for the first time in days, she struggled to deal with what had happened. Working as a defence lawyer for some of the most vicious criminals in the city hadn't prepared her for the brutality she had witnessed and personally experienced since she had driven her dying brother to the hospital. Jessica realised now that she had been totally naïve about the nature of society, living a masquerade provided her by the powers that be.

She had thought that law and order always prevailed, especially if you had the money to pay for it. It had never occurred to her that there were men and women employed by the state who had no hesitation to act with extreme violence if the order came that a bullet in the head could solve a pressing problem. They had no concern for the rules of Judges and laws. Nick and his team were clearly such people. The defining moment had come when the man called Brodie had helped rescue her from the American assault team. Dazed and confused, she had still watched almost mesmerised as Brodie had mercilessly killed all but one of her surrendered kidnappers.

Was that what Britain was?

Were these the people who protected her whilst she slept through her illusion of reality TV and expensive electronic devices?

She didn't condemn anyone, rather she accepted the wisdom that had deemed such men and women to be a necessity. If not for them, there was no telling where she would be now. There was a reality that she had never been exposed to until this moment, a world of violence and covert activity that she had only ever been subjected to through the occasional fiction novel and TV programme. Today it was real, and she was glad she was around people like that. She didn't care if they had no respect for the law or for human rights. Jessica realised she was fortunate that she was surrounded by people who were willing to kill anyone and anything so as to keep her safe.

She would shortly find out just how fortunate she was.

21.08.19
Hounslow, UK

It had once been nicknamed Sid. Now it had no name, no identity except for the craving that grew ever stronger, the yearning that forged it on despite the injuries already inflicted on its dead and slowly decaying flesh. The clothes that indicated it had once been a female police constable were now ripped and stained, soiled by its inability to eat the flesh it tried to consume. Gore dripped from its mouth, the tongue there half destroyed in its frenzy to bite and chew the meat it had detached from the neck of its last victim. What was left of its brain told it that it had to eat, but there was no consciousness left to tell it why.

It was not alone. Sid(Z) was buffeted by the crowd of undead it wandered amongst. The group walked clumsily down the centre of the road, ever vigilant for the sounds and smells that told them their prey was around. Frequently, groups of two or three would break off to attack a random door, or to force their way through a front window, their sudden bursts of speed shocking to those who bore witness. The bulk, however, moved on, a surging wave that brought destruction with it. Their numbers grew with every hour, time their ultimate friend in the coming battle for supremacy over the planet.

The virus now attacked humanity on two relentless fronts. Through the air man breathed, and through the teeth of those it converted.

Sid(Z) was rare in that it was still relatively intact, the bullet laceration to its scalp an irrelevant wound. The missing fingers were of no consequence. Most of those of its kind sported more grievous injuries. Some lacked limbs. One had lost an entire shoulder to a shotgun blast, the arm hanging there precariously, in danger of finally detaching at any moment. It seemed to swing with a rhythm of its own making, totally useless now to the body that carried it.

Further behind them, a zombie crawled across the ground, one of its legs crushed and useless. There was no discrimination amongst the armies of the dead, although occasionally one of its kind would step on it.

Sid(Z) and her ilk were the lucky ones, having survived the battle that had not gone well for the humans. And all the while the virus worked its way through the population, spreading the coming undead across the capital of a once great nation. For the first time since 911, no commercial planes filled the skies over the area that housed the UK's biggest airport.

Sid(Z) sensed something, and it turned as one with its brethren towards the building to their left, drawn by the sound that it couldn't name. Ripples of what might have once been called anticipation spread through its decaying nervous system, the sound of the baby crying sweet music to its dead ears. Barely audible at this distance to human senses, it was like a clanging dinner gong in its zombified being. Weeks from now a scientist would discover how the undead were able to hear enhanced sound, despite the death that had occurred in their brains. But that knowledge wouldn't do the human race any good. By then there was barely anyone left to tell.

Ten went with Sid(Z), working in unison, enticed by the noise. Within seconds it was at the door, the frail PVC only able to withstand the assault for mere minutes. Sid(Z) felt a panel in the door give way, and it forced its head in, the aroma of frightened flesh caressing it as Sid(Z) writhed its head and one shoulder into the gap, squirming as best it could to get through.

The barrier rattled in its frame, the pressure of the massed undead against it too much. Finally, the door relented, and Sid(Z) was almost taken with it, coming loose at the last second as the door was ripped from its hinges by fingers that were flayed and broken in the process. The dead poured in, Sid(Z) with them after pulling itself free, more joining as the portal was breached. With undiluted focus, the zombies went in search of the meal that was calling to them. As luck would have it, Sid(Z) was the first to hit the staircase, and it ascended out of some primal instinct, it's brothers and sisters following behind it, speed abandoned due to the awkwardness that the steps presented. The dead could climb, they just had to take their sweet time about it.

"Go away," a voice screamed. Sid(Z) didn't understand the words but sensed a younger version of its prey at the top of the stairs. Sightless, it staggered upwards, unaffected by the object that struck its forehead. Two-thirds of the way up now, and Sid(Z) lost its footing, still relatively uncoordinated from its rebirth. It fell onto its chest, its fingers reaching for some type of purchase. Those following did not help. Instead, they clambered over its prone body, a boot landing hard on one of Sid(Z)'s ankles. The bone there broke, the sound cutting through the persistent terror of the building's inhabitants. It crawled upwards, grabbing what leverage it could, reaching the upper floor landing behind several of its kind. They all went right, following after the teenager who had tried to fight off the undead with her feeble missiles.

Despite the fractured ankle, Sid(Z) had regained its footing. Limping, not through pain, but purely from the deficiency in its own body, Sid(Z) ignored the teenager. There was something else here, something tantalising. The thing that had enticed it here in the first place. Defenceless and ripe, the baby cried again.

The door offered no real resistance, and Sid(Z) left the thin wooden barrier shattered and obsolete. It stood in the door frame, knowing where the wriggling form was, somehow knowing that it alone had the best meat that the prey had to offer. There would be no respite for this meal. Such a young child would be useless in the coming battle, and the viral laden saliva almost gushed from Sid(Z)'s mouth in a contagious torrent.

Something pushed against its back, but Sid(Z) did not yield from its position, seeming to savour what was coming. This food, this banquet, belonged to it. Stepping forward, Sid(Z) bent down and plucked the baby from its crib, the wriggling form helplessly held in a grip that was strong enough to shatter the young pliable bone. And that was exactly what the hands did, the baby wailing a final time as the teeth began their mutilation.

***

Charlie Section had managed to get back to the Hounslow Civic Centre, only to find mayhem at what was supposed to be the Army's command centre in this military action. The defences were intact, but there were numerous bodies strewn about the streets and the car park surrounding the Army's only remaining defensive position in this region. Not all those bodies belonged to the undead, more corpses than he could ever accept were seen to be wearing army fatigues. Several of the deceased soldiers sported obvious gunshot wounds to their heads.

Corporal Whittaker was stunned to discover his was the only section to make it back alive from the reconnaissance patrol.

"Alpha, Bravo and Delta sections were all overwhelmed," said a stressed Sergeant who looked like he'd fought in a thousand wars. This was not a battle for the unblooded. Only veterans had a chance of defeating this enemy and even then...

"They came at us out of nowhere," Whittaker advised, the sound of helicopters overhead a reassurance to him. If it hadn't been for the Apache attack helicopter that had covered their retreat, Whittaker had no doubt that his section would have been slaughtered too.

"Save it for the Major," the Sergeant said almost unsympathetically. "He wants your report and he wants it now."

"Yes Sarge," the Corporal said. Before he could fulfil the Major's wishes, however, the Sergeant grabbed his arm. It was a rare gesture of respect.

"Good work out there Chris." Whittaker nodded. This particular Sergeant was renowned for being a hard ass. Praise from him meant it was truly warranted, and a part of Whittaker was saved by the gesture.

"The men did what they were trained to do. I want to put them all in for a commendation."

"Again, tell the Major," the Sergeant sighed, "although I doubt commendations will amount to much soon." Whittaker watched as the Sergeant walked off, an air of defeat seeming to descend over both of them. Briefly, the Sergeant stopped as a sneezing fit took him. *If a man like that can be beaten by this...* thought Whittaker. He'd seen things he had hoped to never witness, the enemy like no other he had ever encountered or even imagined.

Were things really as bad as the Sergeant made out?

Major Pickering was in one of the offices of the civic centre, with three other harassed looking officers. The two military police soldiers guarding the entrance let Whittaker through without a word. Neither MP showed any kind of emotion, nor did they meet the Corporal's eye. How long would that kind of discipline last in the face of all this, the corporal suddenly thought?

Whittaker stepped into the office and snapped to attention. The room was dimly lit by three high windows and a fluorescent light. The officers were stood around a central table with a map on it. All but the Major initially ignored him.

"At ease soldier. Corporal, what happened out there?" Major Pickering demanded. The tone wasn't accusatory, but it relayed the urgency of the situation.

"Sir. Approximately two hundred of the enemy came at us out of the tube station, then from the surrounding streets. We weren't warned to expect such vast numbers."

"None of us were which is why we are in the shit we are in. What was your impression of them?"

"Sir?" Whittaker didn't understand what the Major wanted.

"Tell me about my enemy," the Major insisted. "What am I up against?" The Major had witnessed them first hand when they had attacked this fortified position, but there had only been a few dozen then. The heaviest mass of zombies had yet to descend upon his position. It was the troops he had sent out on patrol who had borne the brunt of it, as well as the men guarding the road chokepoints. And that strategic miscalculation would be forever on him. Major Pickering had already lost too many men. He would shortly lose many more.

"They are difficult to kill. Faster than I can run for the most part, and they seem to work together. They tried to outflank my position and if that Apache hadn't been there..."

"Corporal, having engaged them, do you think we can win this?" Whittaker looked at the Major and saw what he never hoped to see in the eyes of a commanding officer. Fear. This wasn't good, and his eyes wandered across the faces of the other officers. The same emotion resided there.

"Permission to speak plainly sir?"

"Granted."

"The intel we were given was for shit. We were expecting a few scattered..." Whittaker paused. "Sir, are we officially calling these things zombies?" The Major looked at his other officers, then back at his Corporal.

"I think zombie is as good a name as anything."

"Well sir, we were expecting to encounter small groupings. None of the men really believed what they had been told in the briefing, it just seemed so ridiculous. But they believe it now. I don't think this is something we can win!"

"Why don't you think we can beat this, Corporal?" asked one of the captains present.

"Because we don't understand what's happening. And there's something else…"

"Well, spit it out man," the Major said curtly.

"Whilst the bulk of the zombies came after us, groups of them broke off to attack the houses and buildings all around. We left hundreds of civilians defenceless back there. If you ask me, these things were actively working to increase their numbers." The sound of a helicopter flying low overhead briefly drowned out any conversation, specifically the expletive that escaped Major Pickering's mouth. When the noise passed, Whittaker was about to speak again, to tell the Major about the way the zombies moved, their raw power and feral nature. But a shot came from outside.

"Incoming," the roaring voice of the Sergeant could be heard through one of the room's open windows. "Here they come again."

21.08.19
Manchester, UK

This was a level of wealth Susan had only ever dreamt of. Clay's house was a multi-bedroom mansion on the outskirts of Manchester's city centre. Surrounded by walls and thick reinforced iron gates, it was a stronghold that should be able to defend against the undead, even though it had been built to withstand the might of man.

Brian had driven, their conversation stilted and forced, the roads they travelled on barren of commuters. When the car had pulled up outside the main gates, two men in surgical masks had kept him waiting so they could spray the car down with bleach, the smell penetrating through the car's ventilation. That job done, the gates opened, gates that were specifically designed to survive forced entry. Twenty metres of gravel drive led to an ornate front porch, where more guards stood ready. These men were conspicuously armed with submachine guns. Despite the masks, Brian recognised them as people who were painfully loyal to Clay, more loyal perhaps than Brian himself was.

As someone who helped to screen the men Clay chose for his organisation, Brian knew that none of the men he had seen so far had anything in the way of family to speak of. Each was a military veteran who Clay had rescued from the poverty of their life outside the army. Some of them Clay had even paid for intense counselling to help beat the PTSD that had put them on the streets.

Clay looked after his own, but only to reduce the future chances of betrayal. That was how Clay created loyalty, by paying well, and by salvaging those the state had chosen to betray. Many of them might even lay down their lives for Clay, the man who was ultimately seen as their saviour. Brian stepped out of his vehicle.

"Mr Metcalfe," one of the guards said respectfully, "I need you and the lady to follow my directions please. Mr Clay's orders." As Susan also stepped out of the car, Brian looked to where the guard was pointing. A large sand coloured marquee style tent had been erected on the front lawn, something Brian had clocked as he had driven up. As if on cue, a woman in surgical scrubs, mask and gown stepped out of the tent and beckoned to the guard.

"What the hell is this?" Brian demanded. He recognised the woman. Her name was Florence, a doctor that Clay had on speed dial for when those he employed were "damaged" in the course of their employ. Florence was an accomplished surgeon from a very well to do family. She was also a functioning addict that had been unfortunate enough to be arrested trying to purchase the heroin she needed to feed her habit. Florence had chosen the wrong time to go out and see her dealer.

Her misfortune had been tempered, in a sense, by the fact that the undercover officer who arrested her was in Clay's back pocket. The story went that the officer, hoping to increase the money he received in his monthly brown envelope, had experienced a sudden wave of genius about how Florence could be used after she had so foolishly tried to appeal for leniency due to her being a doctor. With Clay's blessing, he had made her a deal. It was either work for Clay or get arrested and lose her livelihood. The General Medical Council was not a fan of heroin smoking doctors.

The story was an elaboration. Florence had no idea that she had been set up for exactly this from the very start. Clay had been looking for someone of just her skill for several years and had been tipped off by someone working at the local hospital who was also in his employ. A rumour that turned out to be true. Although he objected to the use of drugs, Clay had sweetened the pot by being a safe source for her addiction. He also paid her a significant sum which was spirited away in an account in the Cayman Islands. Really, there was no way she could refuse

"The doc can explain everything," the guard said. Florence beckoned to Brian and he sauntered over, Susan close behind, not wanting to be alone around rough looking men with guns.

"I don't want to be here," Susan suddenly whined.

"And where will you go?" Brian asked her. Susan was about to protest further, but she really didn't have an answer to that. Where would she go? Brian turned his attention to Florence.

"What's all this Florence?" Brian asked. He didn't like the doctor, found her to be a tad snobbish as if she was somehow better than those around her. More than once Brian had needed to remind her that she was here because of her own frailty. If she hadn't been sucking that shit up into her lungs, Clay wouldn't have had any hold over her.

"What has Clay told you about what's happening?" Her upper-class accent was out of place for the people she served. Nobody was ever openly critical of her, Clay laying down the law that she was here to save lives and keep people out of going to prison. You couldn't turn up on the official medical radar with knife and gunshot wounds without the police getting involved, not these days. Clay had thus demanded that, as long as Florence did what he demanded, the foot soldiers were all to treat her with respect. He even had a miniature medical facility set up that she could use should the need arise. Not here mind, Clay liked to keep such things off site.

"Nothing really. And its Mister Clay to you."

"I want to leave, I want to leave now," Susan persisted. She grabbed Brian's arm lightly, then thought better of it.

"You know where the way out is. But if you go you are going alone." Brian didn't for one second think he was being too harsh.

"Trust me my dear," the doctor said turning to her, "this is the safest place for you. I'm sure Brian will protect you from these scary men." Brian scowled at the mocking doctor.

"They don't scare me," Susan lied.

"Well, they should. They scare me."

"Florence?" Brian insisted.

"Mr Clay," Florence said emphasising the title, "received word from one of his confidential sources this morning. There is a virus, loose in the country. It's very deadly and very contagious, which is why Mr Clay has everyone he trusts now behind his spiked top walls." Susan seemed to cringe at the word virus.

The Clay estate covered about three acres and comprised of several buildings. There was the main house and a guest cottage. The old stables had been converted into accommodation, housing many of those who guarded Clay day and night. The select few would be invited into the main house. The walls were indeed topped with evil looking spikes, and there were no trees on the external that could offer any means of scaling the wall which was significantly higher than the usual six feet seen around most British properties. Even if someone could get over, the ground a metre inside the perimeter was lined with further spikes to penetrate any boot that should be foolish to land upon them.

"Is that why you are all dressed up?" Brian quizzed.

"Yes. And now I need you to follow me into the tent. We have certain procedures that now need to be followed."

"Procedures," Susan sounded alarmed.

"We need to ensure that you aren't infected. And if you still want to leave I'm sure that can be arranged. Not sure being on the other side of that wall would be wise over the following days, however."

"No, I'm good," Susan said, defeated, her eyes drifting between the doctor and a man she knew she shouldn't really resent. And yet she did, even though he just seemed to keep saving her. Perhaps that was why. Perhaps the knowledge that she owed him more than she could ever repay was the thing eating her up inside.

There was something else, something that she didn't even realise herself except in the fevered imaginations of her sleeping mind. Brian had dealt with the maniac who had killed her beloved daughter, but not once had he come to Susan and ask how SHE wanted the man punished. Brian had reaped out his own form of vengeance, but Susan would have taken so much more from the man.

Brian had denied her that.

21.08.19
Birmingham, UK

People had once called her Helga. Now they would just call her what she had become, a monster. The body that defied everything that medical science understood to be true, walked, even though all the organs within it had shut down. Skin swelling slightly under the soiled clothing, the normal decomposition of the corpse was not occurring.

Routinely in death, there would be a four-stage process to the body's breakdown, but that would make the vessel useless to the virus due to the eventual liquefaction of the muscles and the joints. Although Lazarus was not a conscious entity, it was still designed to propagate itself. This meant preventing, as much as possible, the degradation of the vehicles it moved about in. Bodies, such as the one that had once been known by the name Helga.

Helga had once been the name of an attractive woman, despite the ravages of her hard life. Now it was a sexless being intent on only one thing...the consumption of warm human protein. And in that hunt to consume, it would spread the virus to every living thing it touched.

The night before, Helga(Z) had been born and had attacked a bunch of rioters who failed to see the truth behind the threat she represented. It had come out of the altercation damaged but intact, some of those Helga(Z) had bitten with it now. Its right arm hung uselessly, the bone there shattered. The feet and legs still worked, and it walked down the centre of the deserted street, the scent of humanity occasionally hitting it. Deserted except for others of its kind, the surrounding city breathing with an anxious anticipation. The ones Helga(Z) had created and converted flocked around it, the group moving with an eerie fluidity. When together, they seemed to almost move as one unit, the fall of their feet almost synchronised.

Two dozen zombies shared the street with Helga(Z) and it sensed more were coming, converging together. The army was building, the great battalions of the dead rising up from where their human precursors had died. All day Helga(Z) had been relentless in its destruction of humanity, nearly dozens of hapless people suffering the ravages of its teeth. At some point during the day it had lost a finger on its good hand, but there was no memory or thought process within the skull to register that this was a problem. Bit by bit the body degraded, but still it walked on. Even now, it chewed on the tough flesh it had ripped away several minutes ago, the ability to force the food any further down its gullet long since passed. It would carry on chewing until a fresh food source came to hand, the hunger within it never satiated.

Being home to an international airport, Birmingham was one of the worst cities affected by the virus in the early days. At that moment in time, there were just over three hundred zombies either walking the streets or trapped in buildings, clawing to get out. One hospital had even been stormed by armed troops to rid it of the scourge of the undead that had sprung up there. An easy number to deal with perhaps, but not when one realised there were over twenty thousand people infected, some unknowingly. As the minutes ticked by, each one of them got that little bit closer to joining the risen, time bombs waiting to bring forth the end of the world.

As a group, Helga(Z) and its followers turned the corner, only to be faced by the futile resistance of mankind. About twenty soldiers had blockaded the road, a strategic choke point where they could wait for the undead to come to them as well as control the flow of people throughout the city. The soldiers looked on horrified as the undead turned together and ran with a speed that would give many of the young soldier's nightmares. Even the hardened veterans would find difficulty dealing with the things they would see that day...not that many of them would live long enough to suffer psychologically though.

Helga(Z) didn't feel the bullets as they ploughed into it, merely sensing that its progress was being hampered. It tried to put on an extra burst of speed, but a bullet blew out its left knee sending it sprawling to the moist asphalt, the light drizzle having started about an hour ago. Helga(Z) proceeded to crawl, its brothers and sisters falling all around. A bullet struck the side of its skull, taking off a large chunk of scalp, the missile actually ricocheting off.

One of its fellow zombies fell on top of it, but still Helga(Z) pulled itself along the ground as best it could. Using one arm and one leg, it tried its best to get at the dangerous humans, the desire for the taste of them greater than the risk their guns represented. Chips of the road's surface were propelled into its face, the bits getting into its still chewing mouth. It crunched down on the small stone-like masses, breaking several teeth in the process, the red liquefying flesh in its mouth dribbling down a grazed and bloodied chin. Then a well-aimed shot hit it in the centre of its forehead, wiping out the viral part of the brain that allowed the virus to work its magic. Helga(Z) returned to join the truly dead.

The soldiers celebrated the slaughter of a dozen zombies, not fully understanding the scope of the battle ahead of them. Already the virus was working through their ranks, their officer showing early signs of infection. They could battle on against an onslaught of these limited numbers, but every hour the enemy grew stronger whilst the defenders of human civilisation grew steadily weaker. Some were already saying the battle was already lost.

How right they were.

21.08.19
Manchester, UK

Within the confines of the tent and out of the prying eyes of Clay's minions, Florence told Brian and Susan that they needed to strip out of the clothes they had come with so that they could take a chemical shower.

"What, naked?" Susan objected.

"Darling, I'm a surgeon. There's nothing you have that I haven't seen before."

"It's not you I'm worried about," Susan persisted.

"For fucks sake," Brian sighed, "it's going to be bloody difficult to walk about with my eyes closed. Besides, I have seen you naked before remember."

"Hmff," Susan said moodily, "how could I forget."

"Easily solved," Florence reassured. "Mr Metcalf can go first." Florence turned to Brian. "Once you've been through the chemical shower, you may find it stings the skin a bit. You will find goggles to stop the stuff getting into your eyes and I highly advise you wear them. There's a second spray of water after that to wash whatever chemical residue is left on you." Brian started to remove his clothes, the ground hard underfoot suggesting that the grass had been boarded over.

"You won't need those clothes once you are done. A fresh set is waiting for you."

"Where the hell did Mr Clay get his hands on a bloody decontamination tent?" Brian asked.

"Mr Clay doesn't tell me these things," Florence informed him. As it happened, Clay had realised years ago that weapons alone weren't sufficient to enhance his financial interests. The Middle East and North Africa were in dire need of medical assistance, which carried much less risk to his organisation. Clay had taken shipment of a whole field hospital he was in the middle of selling to the Syrians. The tent was designed for use in a combat zone, to deal with the effects of biological and chemical weapons. It hadn't taken much to get parts of it shipped from the Liverpool warehouse and assembled on his front lawn.

When Florence had turned up, she had understood almost instantly what her role was to be. She had read the various internal NHS memos that were being passed around by hospital management and had no guilt at all about phoning in sick. She certainly wasn't the only person. If this was the zombie apocalypse, the last place Florence wanted to be was in a hospital. If the zombies didn't get you, then the virus would.

Florence Cameron was not on speaking terms with her parents or siblings. Although Clay kept her safe from the claws of the medical regulator and the police, her behaviour out of work had become erratic, the odd hours demanded by Clay taking a toll on her family and social life. Florence's sister, supposedly worried about her sibling's wellbeing, had turned up unannounced one evening to ask Florence what the hell was going on. When Florence didn't answer the doorbell, the sister had let herself in with a key Florence had probably forgotten she had given the meddling woman. The sister found Florence spaced out in the kitchen, the evidence of illegal drug use laid out on the expensive marble-topped counter.

The sister had taken great delight in telling her parents of her unfortunate discovery. Mindful of the damage this could cause to the family name, the parents had almost instantly disowned their once favourite daughter. They had also cut her out of the will, leaving more of a share for Florence's borderline sociopathic sibling. Also, there was no man in her life because regular drug use kind of got in the way of that sort of thing. So now she was here, where she designed and implemented an infection control system to keep Mr Clay safe. By doing so, Florence realised it gave her a sanctuary to ride out the worst of what was coming. Those NHS memos had become increasingly desperate in the scenario they were painting.

She was glad to see Susan here. In her late forties, Florence was too thin and bony to be considered attractive. But she was well versed in the realities of human nature. Men like Clay needed women, and Florence was more than happy that there was a much more viable candidate for the role now present.

Brian removed his shirt, the scars evident there from fifty years of street fights and altercations that he had mainly prevailed in. Three knife wounds, a bullet hole from a young punk who now no longer had any fingers. There was a burn mark about the size of the palm of his hand across his back, the result of someone trying to throw sugar laced boiling water at him in prison. Even being at the top of the prison hierarchy didn't protect you from the insane wankers who could suddenly take a grudge. Although now scarred, the burn hadn't been deemed bad enough for a skin graft which Brian was thankful for. Florence said nothing, she had seen it all before, having patched him up on two previous occasions. Florence caught Susan staring at him though. She clearly had a lot to learn about what Brian's life actually involved.

"Turn around then!" he admonished Susan. This was not the body she remembered from years ago, the damage inflicted surprising to her, the muscles bigger and more refined. She didn't protest, and Brian removed the rest of his clothing as she turned away from him. Naked, he stepped through the slightly opaque hanging plastic door curtain that led to the showers.

The goggles were hanging where he could easily access them, and he pulled them over his face before stepping onto the shower tray. A pungent yellow liquid descended upon him, and he gagged at the smell of it. He had no choice but to breathe through his nose because he really didn't want any of this shit in his eyes. Fortunately, the shower was of short duration, less than twenty seconds, and it was only a further second before water replaced the chemical concoction that felt like it was burning into his skin. Brian wondered if everything was automatic, or was Florence outside activating it. Probably not the latter, because he suspected that, if Florence was in charge, the first shower might well have lasted a lot longer.

He knew, right there and then, that Susan was going to do nothing but bitch about this to him for at least the rest of the day.

"I hope you are well stocked up on alcohol Clay," Brian said to himself as the lukewarm water brought relief to him, "because I'm going to need a crate load."

21.08.19
Houston, USA

Houston was a city of nearly two and a half million people, many of them asleep when the first zombies rose up from wherever they had died. Those not working nights would awaken to the knowledge that their President was dead, shot by the Secret Service who felt they had no choice when they witnessed the commander of the free world on a murderous rampage. As the rest of the city's residents woke up, Houston would quickly realise the truth about the threat that lurked within its midst.

Deputy Clarisse Reece of the Houston Sherriff's department had sat speechless in the pre-shift briefing as her Assistant Chief had boldly informed her and the rest of the roster that zombies were real. The room was at maximum capacity, what with all leave being cancelled and every able man and woman being dragged in to deal with the new threat. There were no no-shows, the true nature of the emergency being kept from them until everyone was present. Right after the word zombie had been used for the first time, the officer sat next to Reese had suddenly sneezed, the tissue he had been frantically trying to drag from his pocket becoming useless. It would be several hours before Reese realised how mind-numbingly terrifying a simple sneeze was soon to be.

There had been reports that the state Governor was going to call out the National Guard and the Texas State Guard, that all leave was cancelled indefinitely, and that martial law might even be implemented. If that happened, then the military would deal with the growing numbers of the undead whilst the police and the sheriff's department kept order on the streets. The Governor and the city mayor both wanted the city flooded with armed uniformed personnel before the activation of the Federal emergency broadcast system. If panic started, and likely it would, that shit had to be kept off the streets.

Panic was a greater enemy than the undead at this stage in the game.

"We also expect the governor to order the unofficial state militias to be deputised." There had been a murmur of disapproval at that news. Some of those militia types could be nothing but trouble, the majority of them having no love for the structure and workings of the US Federal Government. They saw it as their god given right to meet up every weekend and practice being soldier, all because some piece of paper written hundreds of years ago said it was what they should do. The US Constitution was all well and good, but when the shit hit the fan, Reece was of the opinion that, as a former President had once reportedly said, it was just a goddamn piece of paper. Perhaps not the most popular view for a Texan to hold, so she kept such opinions to herself.

"You have got to be shitting me?" Reece had said. She'd instantly regretted the act of disrespect, but the information had been too unbelievable. The last time she had been forced to deal with a militia group, it had ended in an armed standoff that had very nearly turned into a firefight. And all because some idiot city bureaucrat had insisted the flagpole flying the militia's favourite flag (a rattlesnake with the words "don't step on me") did not meet city code. The pencil-necked twat probably got a promotion for that act of lunacy.

"Are we going to have a problem here Deputy?" the Assistant Chief had admonished.

"No sir. But half those guys are more likely to shoot us than the…zombies?" She had struggled with the word, still finding belief in what she had been told difficult. "You can't…"

"I can and I will because the decision doesn't rest with me." The Assistant Chief had stared her down, Reese finally breaking eye contact. Her boss had turned and looked at the person stood behind him, a short man in an ill-fitting suit, who was, it turned out, from the local branch of the Center of Disease Control.

The stranger had fidgeted nervously before accepting the Assistant Chief's invitation to step up to the lectern so that he could tell everyone in the room exactly what was going on. Reece remembered the man, recalled thinking that public speaking wasn't something the guest did very often, if ever. Somehow

33

that had made the situation more real. *They just sent a nervous nelly to tell us all it's the end of the world.*

"I'm Doctor Cooke," the CDC man had said. Cooke looked like he hadn't slept this millennium, the dark bags that lived under his eyes at risk of becoming a permanent feature. "A few days ago a senior member of the Atlanta CDC died in his office. The report I have been given states that the body came back from the dead and began..." Cooke had paused, dabbing at his lips with a pristine white handkerchief before continuing. "He began to attack people in the building, killing several."

"OK, someone tell me this is a joke," someone had shouted from the back of the room.

"Shut the fuck up deputy," the Assistant Chief had roared. That shut the room down instantly, quiet descending like a shroud. Reece could hardly remember ever hearing of the Assistant Chief raising his voice. And as for swearing, he was renowned for never letting a vulgarity pass his lips. Shit had definitely got real at that moment. "Please continue doctor".

"We think this is the same virus that has devastated Bangkok. It's already spreading through the population here and in other US cities. Those who contract the virus die, only to reanimate." The deputy next to Reese had sneezed again, this time catching the aerosol. Reese remembered giving the man a nervous glance.

"Reanimate?" Reece asked, genuinely confused.

"They come back," the doctor explained, "from the dead."

"So you really are talking about zombies?" Reece was known as being a troublemaker, but she was also good at what she did so her occasional insubordination was tolerated. It was true to say that her inability to tolerate fools had hampered her career progression, but someone like her had been needed in the room then. Many of those present had wanted to ask that question but hadn't dared for fear of being judged by those they worked with. Reese had never cared about peer pressure, even in high school.

"Yes exactly. Zombies. I know it sounds impossible, but really it's the only word to describe what we are faced with." The confirmation of the word had caused another concerned murmur to spread through the room. The fact that the Assistant Chief remained stony-faced solidified the truth of what everyone was being told.

"Fuck," someone had said behind Reese.

"We will be issuing respirators and protective clothing," the doctor had continued, his hesitancy evaporating when he had seen that most of the people in the room hadn't rejected his message. "The CDC are working on a field test for the virus because at present it is spreading through the population like flu." Reese had put her hand up then rather than just shout out as she often did. She had figured the guy talking to them was now one of the most important people in America. "Yes, deputy?"

"Does that mean some of us could be infected? I mean Simmons here is sneezing up a storm." The Deputy next to her had flipped Reece the bird.

"Fuck you Reece, I've got allergies." Voices had started to be raised, and Reece had noticed how several of her fellow deputies had moved their chairs away from Simmons slightly.

"Please," the CDC man had begged to the room, calming down the raucous before it could get established. "In answer to your question, yes some of you may be carrying the virus. Which is why before you go out on shift you will all be volunteering for blood tests."

"Volunteering!" another dissenting voice had muttered.

That had been an hour ago. Now she was out on patrol, hunting for the undead, her partner Rodriguez sat silently next to her. He hadn't said anything since getting in the car, his face a ploughed field of concern. Reece noticed that he was definitely on edge, so it was probably better that she was driving. The respirator she wore was stifling, even with the car's air conditioning. In the heat of the day, she knew it would make it difficult to breathe.

"Talk to me, Rodriguez. What's going on with you." Normally her partner of two years was an outgoing, jovial character, but today it was as if he was attending a funeral. Rodriguez looked at her, much of his face hidden by the breathing apparatus.

"I'm scared Reece, and I don't know how to handle it."

"Bullshit, nothing scares you!" Wasn't that the truth. The number of commendations for valour her partner had received put the rest of them to shame.

"Well this does. I've got kids Clarisse. How am I going to protect them from this?" he slammed his hand on the dashboard of the car. "In fact, what the fuck am I even doing here?"

"To serve and protect, Rodriguez."

"Yeah?" Rodriguez almost laughed. "And who is going to protect my family with me out on the streets? I need to be with them. And yet I'm scared to even go home. What if I pick this shit up out here on the job? What if I bring it back to them?" Reece could tell he was conflicted, and strongly suspected that he was raising this with her in the hope that she could somehow change his mind. He wanted to do his duty, but he also wanted to be the protective father for the most important things in his life.

"The best place for you, right now, is here with me. If we lose control of these streets, then that's game over." In reality, as frightening as the idea of zombies was, she hadn't as yet seen anything to prove to her they even existed. So her bigger fear was in the risk of a breakdown in law and order. If chaos got hold of the city, then there would be no containing the virus. There was already no telling how far it had spread.

"I need to be with them," Rodriguez insisted. "Maybe get out of the city. My father in law has a cabin on Lake Conroe." He turned in his seat to face her. "Seriously, we all need to get out of here."

"You really want to spend the last of your days with that arsehole?" It was an attempt at humour and it almost broke through. Rodriguez had never clicked with his wife's father, and he complained about him loudly and frequently to Reece.

"Better than here," Rodriguez insisted.

"All units, all units. Reports of shooting at the corner of Washington Avenue and Sandman Street. Please respond." The voice was loud over the car's radio, and Reece was glad of the interruption.

"We good?" Reece asked her partner.

"Shit," he said, picking up the radio's handset. "Unit 43 to dispatch, that's right near us. We are responding." The handset clanged off one of the filters, the respirator making it difficult to talk to the dispatcher.

"Copy that unit 43."

Reese switched on the lights and the siren and watched as the traffic began to drift out of their way. Within hours there would be little if no traffic on these roads, but right now they were close to being jammed.

They weren't the first deputies to arrive. The street was sealed off, one officer directing traffic, another questioning a large man who was stood defiantly with his arms crossed. There was a naked body lying in the middle of the road, the dark tarmac hiding any blood that might be escaping from it.

Reece parked the patrol car up, and they both got out to face the malevolent heat. Walking up to the questioning deputy, Reece noted the empty holster on the civilian's hip and the lack of handcuffs on his wrists. Texas was an open carry state. The fact that the man wasn't in restraints told her everything she needed to know.

"Craig," Reece said as she stepped next to her fellow deputy. Rodriguez walked over to the body that was lying on its back in the middle of the road. He couldn't fail to notice the severed and gnawed child's arm that lay next to the man's corpse. There were numerous gunshot wounds penetrating the torso and a single hole that had shattered the lower jaw.

"Tell me this isn't what I think it is?"

"Well if I was to do that it would likely be a lie Reece," Craig said. "Mr Johnson was walking to his store when he witnessed our deceased walk out of that building."

"Damn straight," Johnson said. "Guy was eating a fucking arm, can you believe that shit?"

"Mr Johnson told him to stop, but the deceased ran at him, causing Mr Johnson to pull his sidearm. Multiple witnesses state it was a lawful shooting, the arm being wielded like a weapon." Rodriguez stepped over, his face was pale.

"How many bullets did you fire?" Rodriguez demanded.

"All of them," Johnson said warily. "Bastard wouldn't go down, probably on PCP or something. Who the hell does that to a kid?" A kid's arm? Jesus, how bad was this going to get? More sirens could be heard in the distance, and as they quickly got closer, Reece expected them to pull into the street. Instead, they shot right past the intersection. Four cars in total.

"What the hell is going on folks?" Johnson asked. Reece had to remind herself that there would still be people out of the loop regarding the news that zombies now walked the Earth. That was going to change in a matter of seconds. As if in unison, everyone's mobile phones went off. Just to add to the fun and games, the city's emergency sirens also began to wail their ominous music.

It looked like the government had finally decided to tell the people of this fair state the shocking truth. Reece read the text message, which really hit everything home.

This is a Presidential alert
It is not a test
This is an emergency action notification
Be aware there is a nationwide threat of biological contagion
Keep tuned to terrestrial and radio channels for more information

"Does that have something to do with what I just shot?" Johnson quizzed, his face seeming to light up with the reality of it. Holding his phone, his eyes were almost bugging out. Reece looked at the officers around her.

"Most likely, yes. Sir, you need to get home." Reece was now the senior officer on the scene, and she indicated for Craig to give the civilian back his sidearm.

"Are we at the end of days?" Johnson persisted, carefully holstering his sidearm.

"I think claiming that may be a bit premature," Reece answered. But was it? She wasn't a religious person, she left that sort of thing to Rodriguez who was even now fondling the cross around his neck. You had to wonder though.

21.08.19
Huntingdon, UK

They had left Campbell in a room with access to an en-suite bathroom. It wasn't luxury, but it was a damn sight better than what he had been rescued from. At least now he didn't have to piss and shit all over himself. He had even been granted the luxury of a shower, but he suspected that wasn't for his own wellbeing. When he was rescued, he must have stunk.

The room was an office and had a plush leather sofa as well as a TV set. He sat now watching CNN, his body no longer naked due to him being provided with military issue clothing. The remnants of an adequate meal lay on a small wooden table next to the sofa, the medic who had examined him on his arrival determining that he needed no immediate medical intervention. Hands and feet still ached, but there was no sign of permanent damage from his forced restraint. You had to take your wins when you could claim them and he didn't have much else to be thankful for at the moment.

The door to the room was locked from the outside and there were no windows for him to look out of. There was also no way for him to communicate with the outside world, the room's desk having been stripped of a telephone, the PC also absent. All he could do was continue to wait and hope that the next person through the door to his temporary cell had good news for him. Everybody had declined to take any kind of statement and every time he had tried to tell someone what he knew, it quickly dawned on him that they either didn't have a clue what he was talking about or had no interest whatsoever.

On his arrival at RAF Alconbury, it was clear that the US Airforce stationed there were packing up to leave. Would he eventually be on one of those flights? Man, he hoped so.

CNN was not reassuring him. He now understood why his superiors had wanted Jessica taken. There were multiple events across multiple cities in multiple countries. Campbell cared only about one country, the USA, home to his birth town of Houston. Would he ever get back there? He had family but he hadn't really seen them in forever. The covert world had become his true family, so it was better and safer that he distance himself from former friends and relatives wherever possible.

The door to his room suddenly unlocked and opened, a woman stepping through. She was dressed in a smart dark blue suit, her thin, athletic frame making her look of average build. Campbell didn't know her, but he knew what she was. This was the woman who was going to decide his ultimate fate, the answers to her questions either satisfying her or reinforcing the need to have him killed. Campbell stood up. He was lacking in many things, but he was a gentleman at heart.

"Please sit down, agent," she said almost tersely. His display of chivalry had obviously not had the desired effect. She had short hair rather than having it pulled back, which hinted she had field training. It wasn't good to give a potential enemy something to grab in close quarter fighting. Although she wore glasses, they could easily be swapped out for contact lenses. What Campbell noticed more than anything though was the way she carried herself. Total confidence, no hesitation, no hint of self-doubt. She looked like she could fight. Unlikely she would be a match for Campbell, but she would be able to hurt him for sure if they went head to head.

"Okay," Campbell said. "I assume you are here to decide what to do with me."

"That would be correct, agent." She grabbed a lone standing chair from beside the desk and dragged it over to the couch. When she sat down, Campbell found he was seated lower than her. Was that done on purpose?

"I don't mind if you call me David," Campbell said hoping to build some sort of rapport. It didn't work.

"Unfortunately, I do," she responded. There was a coldness in her voice that Campbell didn't like. She was being deliberately distant from him, aloof, probably to help protect herself from any decisions she might need to make. It would be important to her to avoid forming any kind of empathy. "You may call me Ms Winters. I am to be your debriefing officer. DIA flew me in from Washington especially, so I'm jet lagged and pissed off to be on this moss covered rock the Limey's call a fucking country. Let's get this over with shall we? I'd like to get home before the world rips itself apart." She sat with her legs crossed and a legal pad rested in her lap, a pen ready to bear witness to his testimony.

"Certainly."

"Tell me why you failed in your mission." No messing around. Right to the point.

"There was an external factor I didn't account for," Campbell told her, taking complete ownership of the failure. He had been thinking over the best way to answer this question ever since he got here, so he'd had several hours to formulate the best way to respond. In the end, his mind told him the best way was to just tell the total truth. "The assassin I had been sent to help try and find ambushed my team outside the hospital when we were extracting Jessica Dunn. We had no reason to believe he was in the vicinity. He was armed with grenades and an automatic weapon. He fired at us from a concealed and protected position, taking out our extraction vehicle. In having to counter this threat, he delayed our exfil enough that it allowed two agents of MI13 to open up a second front on us."

"How is it only you survived?"

"Even with those odds facing us, we still would have got away. But with the outbreak at Wythenshawe Hospital, SAS were in the vicinity. MI13 called in one of their Blue Thunder teams. By then we were already low on ammunition with two men definitely dead, and one bleeding out from a leg wound. Also, despite being Tasered, Jessica Dunn showed surprising resilience and made a run for it. I regret now that I didn't put her in restraints, but it wouldn't have made any difference. We soon became surrounded and overpowered by superior numbers. The survivors of my team were rounded up by the SAS and lined up against a wall. The MI13 agent Carl Brodie killed each of my remaining team in cold blood. I have no explanation why that happened." Campbell watched the woman's expression, a slightly raised eyebrow giving emotion away.

"MI13 executed your men?" She seemed surprised at that.

"Yes. I never got a reason why. It's not something I expected the British to do."

"What information did you give MI13 during your interrogation?"

"They didn't interrogate me," he said truthfully.

"You expect me to believe that?" Winters said sternly.

"Use scopolamine if you don't. The British found it very effective when they tortured Azrael." She looked at him with a confused expression. "Sorry, that was the name of the assassin I was hunting."

"It's unusual for the British to be so cold-blooded," Winters said.

"What do you know about MI13?"

"That's classified," Winters said. Campbell read that as an admission that she knew very little. The organisation was a ghost in the covert world.

"From what I've seen, MI13 agents are obviously a rare breed. They have little or no oversight and are well trained and well-funded. They are basically a law unto themselves. But none of this is important."

"I don't think you are in any position to make that kind of judgement," Winters said, her body language indicating that the interview was coming to an end. Campbell decided to stall that decision.

"What level of clearance do you have?" Campbell asked. "I need to know if you are cleared to hear what I have to tell you."

"Higher than yours. You know that because otherwise I wouldn't be here."
True, they wouldn't let some desk jockey make a decision on whether to
rendition or retire a senior field agent like Campbell. It was important for her to
say it though because he had no doubt this conversation was being recorded.
The notes she occasionally made on the legal pad were just part of the dance
being played here.

"Good. Because I know who created the virus." He looked at Winters. She
definitely wasn't leaving now.

"What?"

"I thought that would tweak your interest."

"You need to tell me what you know," Winters demanded.

"And I will. For the record, I've been trying to tell someone since I arrived.
Now I just need assurances that I won't be left in a hole in the ground after I give
you what I know."

"You don't get to make demands. Whatever you know we will get from
you."

"Yes, you will." Campbell sighed to show his disappointment. "But how
long will that take if you use force? A day? Two? Or I can tell you everything I
know now, freely. I just need your word I will be treated fairly."

"I think we have treated you more than fairly, considering."

"Your word," Campbell insisted. This was the only card he had to play.

"My word doesn't mean shit."

"It does to you," Campbell observed. If he was reading her right, Winters'
honesty to herself was part of who she was. She seemed to soften just a tad.

"Okay, I give you my word that anything you tell us will be taken into
consideration in any defence you might need. Good enough?"

"Good enough," Campbell nodded. "When I was taken, I was able to witness
much of the MI13 interrogation of Azrael. Azrael is an assumed name. Before
that, he was called Kevin Jury. A lawyer of all things. He was a sleeper agent of
the old Russian Illegals programme."

"The Russians? What has this got to do with the virus?"

"I'm getting to that. Azrael was activated by someone who calls herself
Mother. It shouldn't be too hard to figure out who this Mother is. I'm sure the
CIA have someone inside the Kremlin who can dust off the old files. There
wouldn't have been that many women running Illegals in Western Europe."

"I can get onto Langley about that."

"Mother used her network to create an organisation, the goal of which was to
eliminate the problem of overpopulation." Campbell watched Winters' eyes. He
could see the reality dawning on her. She had stopped any pretence of writing
on the pad now. "That organisation activated Azrael, and used him to eliminate
some of the best scientists the west had."

"MI13 got all this from Azrael?"

"No. Nick Carter, the head of the team I was seconded to, managed to
acquire Mother's telephone number. MI13 were unable to trace it, but the two of
them had a little chat."

"Can you remember the number?"

"No, I never got to see it." Winters wasn't happy about that.

"Why was this organisation killing scientists?"

"Because the plan was to release weaponised flu across the planet. They wanted to limit the ability of medical science to fight off the disease. Turns out they created another virus as well."

"The Lazarus strain?"

"You got it. I was in the room during their conversation. It appears Carter didn't care what I overheard. And there's no reason any of it could have been faked. The virus escaped from a secret laboratory north of Bangkok several days ago. I guess from there it spread across the globe."

"Anything else?"

"Yes as it happens. It is clear to me that Azrael was warned that MI13 were coming for him. MI13 have a mole in their ranks."

21.08.19
London, UK

Parliament was on fire, but the building had already been mostly abandoned. With the now deceased (and resurrected) Minister of Health having brought the virus back with him from his trip to Bangkok, the contagion had spread through the hallowed halls of government like…well, like the most contagious disease known to man or beast. Much of those who ran the great machine of government were either falling sick with the effects of the virus, or were already dead and intent on destroying the very soul of the human race.

The troops outside were thus guarding a decaying and useless relic, so when the fire started, the response from them was virtually non-existent. It was almost poetic, the home of British democracy burning, just as the rights of the country's citizens had been burnt on the altar of political correctness by the dying politicians who once dwelled within those very same hallowed chambers. By the time fire engines arrived, the soldiers were fighting running battles with a horde that had seemingly appeared out of nowhere. Although not great in number, the zombies were enough of a distraction to stop any attempts at containing the blaze. The building was thus allowed to burn, the fire crews unable to leave the surprising safety of their fire engines.

One by one another phenomena began to happen. The men and women on the front line began to melt away. Either through concern for loved ones or understandable fear, many of those with the vital job of defending the country against this unbelievable horror began to abandon their posts.

As the evening drew on, the roads around Parliament and much of Westminster fell to the zombie menace, the overwhelmed soldiers retreating by helicopter and by river. By that time the streets had become impassable with people trying to flee the city, the infected lurking within their ranks, spreading the virus further. This was of course the streets that the average man knew about. Beneath the restless city, the subterranean secret heart of government also fell. Those entrusted to protect the elite of government succumbed to the virus just as easily as with those they had promised to defend.

One such man was Nigel Peterson. His life's ambition as a police officer had been to enter the ranks of the Metropolitan Police's Elite Protection Command. Specifically, he had wanted to be part of the Parliamentary and Diplomatic Protection Division, and had reached his goal sixteen months previous. It was a proud day for his mother and father and meant more money and safer working conditions. Better to guard the rich and the powerful with a gun strapped across your chest than be fighting gangs on the crime-ridden estates of London. With the exception of the occasional crazed terrorist, the most dangerous people Peterson encountered in the days of his early career were lost tourists who seemed to have an insane fascination with getting a glimpse of the Queen.

Peterson had gone even further along the career path, obtaining his sergeant's stripes, working his way up the political ladder that existed for those who knew how to climb. With that, his primary role became that of guarding the people who used the subterranean complex known as PINDAR, the UK government's crisis management and communication centre. It was supposed to be the safest government facility in London, but in the end, it was just as deadly and as vulnerable as everywhere else.

His ambitions had failed him. Now he was running for his life, chased it seemed by the very hounds of hell.

He ran as fast as he could along the connecting underground tunnel, his lungs burning, his legs feeling weak as if he had run a thousand marathons. Nobody had been in the right place to stop the breakout and the spread of the undead in the underground realm. The zombie menace had arrived in the form of a meaningless, humdrum bureaucrat who died in his office deep in the facility. That pen pusher of vague usefulness was the first of the undead to circumvent the protection that the vault-like doors to the underground fortress sheltered. It first killed its former secretary, and then three unarmed junior personnel who came running at the sound of the secretary's screams. One zombie quickly became five, which became ten, and only then was the alarm raised. All the while, the virus was floating in the air, expelled from breath, surfing on the droplets of moisture that were sucked up and moved around by the facility's air conditioning. The air from outside was filtered and sterilised, but nobody thought to do that with the air within the bunker itself.

By the time armed resistance was thrown at the zombie uprising, it was already too late. The depleted numbers of armed officers present were unable to stop the infection quickly taking control of the whole facility. Despite their excellent marksmanship, their ammunition soon became depleted in the maze of offices and corridors, their foe hardy and resilient. If only PINDAR had been guarded to the same extent as the MI13 Central facility, with autonomous drones that were designed to deal with any unwanted intruder. Alas, it was not, so it became the undead against an outnumbered and demoralised police protection detail. The end result was Nigel running out of ammunition and running for his very existence.

That was why he was now running for his life. He could hear them behind him, their feet pounding on the tiled floor. Nigel could tell they were gaining on him and he somehow expected them to be screeching in their pursuit. Not a sound escaped their lips, the lungs no longer able to push air out through the vocal cords. Their silence was perhaps the most unnerving aspect about them.

Turning a corner, he saw the security door that was his only chance of salvation. If he could get through that, then he knew it would be strong enough to hold the demons off. He risked a glance behind him, noticed that the zombies hadn't navigated the corner well, and had collided with one another, two falling to the ground. They were fast, but they lacked the nuances of coordination it seemed. The rest stumbled over their necrotic kin, but not before giving Nigel an increase in his lead and a chance at life.

He knew then that he was going to make it.

If there had been more officers on duty, they likely could have contained this, at least until the virus had managed to work its way through everyone present. But so many had phoned in sick, all victims of the illness that was now running rampant through this part of London. Instead, Nigel had watched his friends and colleagues be killed by remorseless fiends who he found ridiculously difficult to kill. Round after round he'd fired into them, only for them to weather the onslaught. Occasionally some would stay down, but most kept on coming, even when limbs were destroyed. He'd even tried headshots, which seemed to have a greater success rate. But that wasn't guaranteed, most of the brain useless to the virus that resided there. It would later transpire that the most efficient way of killing the undead was to destroy the base of the brain right where it met the top of the neck. That was home to the reptilian part of the organ, the bit that controlled instincts, the part where the virus lived and thrived. Everything else was just useless jelly.

Such an injury was a surprisingly difficult shot to make. Heavy calibre and armour piercing rounds were not standard issue for a police protection detail. Their standard issue hollow point ammunition, whilst specifically designed not to over penetrate and thus minimise the risk of friendly fire, lacked effectiveness against the dead.

Nigel reached the door and wafted the ID badge that dangled from his lanyard so that the door could be opened. He was through and shutting the door before the zombies chasing him could stop him. Nigel's heart leapt with relief as the barrier clicked into place, sealing the threat away behind its unbreakable steel. Seconds later a zombie impacted the other side, smashing its face and hands into the reinforced glass window that the door contained. In fascination and morbid curiosity, Nigel watched the zombie obliterate its own visage in its attempted frenzy of destruction. The ferocity of what the zombie was capable of was incredible, and it quickly became impossible to see anything through the glass. Nigel didn't think that was such a bad thing.

Adrenaline still pumping, Nigel removed the glove off his left hand, noticed the marks there. A zombie had tried to bite him, but the leather of the glove had not been penetrated. *Thank God*, he thought, *thank fucking Christ and all his little wizards*. Bruised was better than bitten any day of the week. Bruised was paradise by comparison. A dull thud came from the door as the zombie head-butted it again, but Nigel ignored the sound.

He wanted to discard the blood-stained gloves, but he also didn't want to lose the protection they offered. That protection was now irrelevant because Nigel hadn't noticed the spots of blood that had splattered across his face, a result of the firefight that had occurred minutes before. Up till now, he had been one of the minority to have escaped contamination by the virus, something that was no longer the case. The infected blood had already started the process of infiltration, the virus worming its way through his skin and into his pumping bloodstream. If he had known he was now on a rollercoaster to zombie-ville, and if he'd possessed any more bullets for his sidearm, Nigel would have likely shot himself. Instead, he made his escape from PINDAR intact and through stealth and cunning, he managed to make it home where his loved ones waited in mortified horror.

Later, as he clung to his two young daughters, he had no comprehension that he had brought the virus home with him and that he had just condemned his family to the fate that would befall so many.

21.08.19
Hounslow, UK

Whittaker was barely breathing heavily, despite running up several flights of stairs to get to the roof. He took up position along the rear of the building, which was bordered by an open playing field, home to countless games of football over the years. Whittaker found himself wondering if a ball would be kicked across that grass ever again.

Kneeling behind a wall topped with sandbags, he surveyed the situation. The earplugs he had in were the only thing protecting his hearing, the loud roar of the machine guns deafening. To his right on the ground below, a Warrior armoured vehicle was laying down 7.62mm rounds into a medium sized grouping of the undead that were running in parallel to the defensive line. Despite the heavy ordnance, the majority of the zombies seemed to just ignore the hail of gunfire, trees and buildings offering them a degree of cover. They had yet to emerge out onto the open field. Many fell, some for good. Others almost seemed to dance as they ran through the deadly metal rain. Whittaker noted they didn't seem to be charging the defensive position, not yet at least.

From what Whittaker could see, the visible undead numbered in the dozens, not the hundreds as he had previously witnessed in his retreat from them outside the tube station. There were likely more that he couldn't see, surrounding this human stronghold which was all that could be mustered in such a short time.

"They are breaking through the houses to the north," a manic voice shouted over a radio handset nearby.

"They have broken through Kingsley Road," another voice shouted, crackling static breaking up the reception. It was difficult to hear, especially with the roof mounted L111A1 fifty calibre machine gun to his left laying down devastating fire. The only problem with the fifty calibre was its tendency to use up its ammunition quickly and its slower rate of fire compared to the L7A2's which had smaller 7.62mm rounds. Very effective as they were against infantry, the L7A2 just wasn't as good against the necrotic horde. Shooting a man in the chest usually stopped them in their tracks. The same injury on a zombie just sometimes seemed to spur them on.

He should have been with his men, but with the chaos, Whittaker had no idea where they presently were. Whittaker could also see that their defensive position was weak, the area surrounding them a mass of residential properties that offered ample opportunity for the undead to hide in. *"The Undead"*, he still found it unbelievable that he was saying those words.

The Corporal watched for several seconds and soon realised that they clearly didn't have enough men to defend this position if the recently deceased decided to come at them in significant numbers. It had been over seventy minutes since he had first engaged the undead, and now the enemy's numbers would likely have swelled to frightening levels. What also confused him was how they could be so fast. Ignoring the fact that the dead shouldn't even be able to move, how the hell could they move with such ridiculous speed?

Looking around, Whittaker recognised his sector's sharpshooter, Tod, further along the roof and Whittaker went over to him. It was reassuring to see a familiar face. For his part, Tod barely registered the presence of his Corporal, the shit eating grin on the private's face reinforcing what Whittaker had always known. Tod was one of those men who enjoyed the killing a little too much. Often a liability in war, but perhaps exactly what was needed now. His sniper shots seemed to be doing the maximum amount of damage to the enemy for the bullets he expended, each round finding its mark, some even having a permanent result. A significant number of those he hit failed to get back up again when they fell.

"Make your shots count lads," a Lieutenant shouted, stalking along the roof's defensive line. "Make them keep their heads down." *Keep their heads down*? thought Whittaker. Is this guy for real?

Whittaker had to remember there were men down on the ground as well. They would be the first for the undead wave to hit should it come. As it was, it felt like these things were just playing with them. The scene out of the film *Zulu* came to mind, where the Zulu warriors sacrificed their men to test the defences of the British encampment. Was that what was going on here? Did these things think as well as attack? Tod chuckled to himself as he scored another 'kill'.

"Corp, why aren't they attacking?" Tod asked Whittaker. The Corporal could only just hear him over the raucous firefight. The .50 calibre was suddenly swung towards the houses to the north, eating into the brickwork of the lower floors there. And then its belt ran dry, silencing it until it was reloaded. How much ammunition did they actually have? How long could they sustain this?

A quarter of a million people lived in Hounslow. Those were numbers the whole British Army couldn't match.

21.08.19
Preston, UK

Nick sat on the bunk he had been reluctantly given by the base commander who didn't seem to appreciate non-military personnel having the run of the place. It didn't matter that Nick was still officially a Lieutenant Colonel in the British Army. Nick Carter was a different kind of soldier, and the base commander knew it. Nick could understand the commander's point of view and had issued reassurances that he had no intention of getting in anybody's way. That didn't alter the fact that Nick had been given ultimate authority to be here and had been put in charge of organising the protection for Jessica.

Fulwood barracks was the home of the Duke of Lancaster's Regiment, and the barracks had lived under a shroud with the pending government spending cuts that now seemed totally ludicrous and short-sighted. It was really the only military facility of any size left in the North West of England, and it was where Jessica had been brought. Partly because of the number of soldiers that would be able to protect her, but also for the mothballed medical facilities that were on hand. With no comparable military installations closer to Manchester, it was far from ideal location wise, at least forty minutes' drive from the North Manchester General Hospital where Dr Patel was doing his research, but helicopters were supposed to ease that pressure. Much of the frontline troops stationed here had been deployed to keep order in Manchester leaving just enough men to guard the base and to watch over the growing numbers of infected soldiers that were quarantined away.

The rest of his team were asleep, their provided quarters a barely adequate room near the building they had housed Jessica. Natasha had shown no sign of hesitation when it came to sharing cramped quarters with three other men. They all respected each other and were already bonding in the way effective teams often did. When you operated in the clandestine field you either detested the people you worked with or you became friends and allies for life. And not the, "going out for a pint on a Friday night" level of friendship. This was more the "willingly giving your life to save the other" kind of comradeship. If a live grenade had been chucked through the window at that moment, Nick would have gladly thrown his own body on it to save the lives of the men and woman under his command. From what he could tell of them, he was reasonably sure that Jeff, Natasha and Carl would all have done similar if the unfortunate opportunity presented.

Nobody wore their protective gear in here, there was no point being burdened like that. They had been together during this from the start. If one of them carried the virus, then it was clear that they all did. If that was the reality, then nothing really mattered anymore. Unless the scientists could pull a fucking rabbit out of a hat, Nick knew exactly the action he would take if he discovered he was infected by the virus everyone was now calling Lazarus.

Lazarus? Who comes up with shit like that?

There was a rap on the window, the signal Nick had earlier agreed with Captain Haggard. Morse code, dot, dot, dash, dot, dot, dash. V for victory...or perhaps V for virus. Nick rose wearily and pulled the curtain back. 'Mad Dog' stood there, the evening light almost gone, his tired face showing the first signs of stubble. There was still enough illumination to see that he was alone, his gas mask removed so that he could smoke the cancer stick that dangled from his lips.

The window was open a touch to allow them to speak, but the inside was sealed with clear plastic and duct tape so the odour of the cigarette didn't penetrate. The sudden desire for a fag hit Nick expectantly, as it often did in times of crisis and uncertainty. Even now, ten years after he had stopped smoking, his brain still hadn't unwired itself. He pushed the desire back down under its rock.

An open window seemed a simple way to keep the lines of communication open. The entrance to this building had a decontamination station to wash off any chance of Lazarus being walked in on the protective suits everyone now wore outside (on the instruction of Colonel Smith who had implemented strict cross infection protocols for the whole base). Easier to just chat through a window than go through all that hassle. They could use phone and handheld radios of course, but sometimes you wanted to see the face of the person you were talking to. Besides, you also wanted to say things without electronic eavesdroppers or third parties listening in.

"You still here then?" Nick asked light-heartedly.

"Whatever is left of the powers that be seem to feel me and my lads should hang around. Seems your girlfriend has got everyone in a tizzy." Haggard was referring to Jessica.

"Any word when you will be moving her?" There was a plan in place to transfer Jessica to Porton Down, but it had yet to be finalised. Seems Colonel Smith was putting the brakes on that so he could finish whatever mad scientist concoction he was cooking up, his infection and impending death perhaps clouding his judgement somewhat. Then there was the fact that all those involved in the transfer had to be isolated and tested to ensure they weren't carrying the virus. The military's primary biological research lab wouldn't be much use if it was riddled with the sick and the dying. As a result, the SAS were all hunkered down away from the main military population of the base. Fortunately, it was hoped that some of the blood tests could eventually be done in the base's own medical facility which would save on having to ferry blood to and from the hospital that housed Doctor Patel's research team. Testing hundreds of men every day wasn't quick work mind, even with the means to do it on site.

"No. All I know is I'm to hang around and act as her escort when the order finally comes. I assume you will be tagging along?"

"Might as well," said Nick. "Doesn't look like there's anything else for me to do at the moment." They certainly wouldn't be going back to Central, the London command and control bunker of MI13. With the death and resurrection of Sir Arthur Gant, the subterranean complex had been deemed off limits until it could be thoroughly sterilised. It was on lockdown, and even Nick's ultimate boss, Sir Osmond, wasn't allowed out until the results of the urgent blood tests that had been done on all the building's occupants were received. Nobody had envisaged the virus breaking into the heart of MI13's sacred citadel which was perhaps an unforgivable oversight considering all the other eventualities they had foreseen. It also wasn't reassuring that the battle against the undead on the streets of London wasn't going exactly to plan. Exactly to plan? It was a total cluster fuck. Whole sections of the city had already been abandoned to the undead.

"How many men have you lost?" Nick asked. When news of the virus and its effects became known, the squaddies had started deserting. Many of them had family and had chosen to help defend the people they loved rather than prop up a collapsing government. There had been talk of bringing military families onto the bases, but with the risk that so many of them could be viral carriers, that had been abandoned. When Colonel Smith had realised he had been infected, it hit home how easy the virus could infiltrate the military's ranks. There was only so much capacity for the blood testing that needed to be done to prove people were clean of the virus. The more pressure the testing facilities were put under, the more likely a mistake was going to be made.

"Only one as it happens and fortunately he didn't desert. Instead, he asked for permission to leave. He's got a newborn kid, so I let him go. Many of my lads don't have any family to speak of, so we are lucky in that respect. As for the army here, looks like they've lost about a quarter which is a significant number."

"The single life. Best way to be for men like us." Nick had rejected the conventional path of the western male at a very early age. He knew from his teenage years that he had no interest in marriage or kids or a nine to five office job. School irritated him more than it educated, learning shit by rote that would be useless in the outside world. Going straight into the army from school had only solidified that philosophy, and it had been the natural path for him. He enjoyed a good shag just like the next bloke, it was all the baggage that came with such frolics under the sheets that Nick could seriously do without. There had been one woman who had nearly broken through his armour, but that relationship had never flourished. Nick just hadn't let it.

The life path he had chosen had been tough and Nick soon became a hardened man. Men like him told themselves they purposefully didn't get bogged down in the complexities and distractions of relationships. Whilst he was well aware that there was every chance that he could find a woman who could penetrate through his concrete exterior, he simply had no interest in searching for such. Sex fine, but he wasn't going to settle down and devote his life to anything other than the country he loved. This conviction had only grown stronger over the years as experience had played its heavy toll on his body and mind. This was certainly not a world to bring children into. And hadn't recent events just vindicated that?

"I reckon my ex-wife would agree with you," Haggard stated. There was meant to be humour in the comment, but it didn't seem to work. "What about your deadly assassin?"

"What, Azrael? Smith has something all *mad scientist* in mind for him apparently. I can't say I approve, but I'm not going to stop what needs to be done. Smith is the expert. If he thinks sacrificing Azrael for the greater good is a price worth paying, he won't hear a word of objection from me. And you have to appreciate the justice in it all." Nick had written Haggard into everything about Operation Pharmacy, so the SAS Captain knew about Azrael's slaughterous rampage through the ranks of Europe's (and perhaps the world's) scientific elite. Wouldn't it just be ironic if experimentation on Azrael led to the discovery of a cure for the whole of mankind? Haggard took a last drag from his cigarette and stubbed it out on the grass at his feet. There were already four butt stubs there, an indication of how many of these chats the two men had engaged in. At this rate, there might be a small mound of cancer castoffs before they got Jessica out of this place.

Waiting around was merely part of the job they had both signed up to do.

21.08.19
London, UK

Colin had waited for the relative dark of night. The streets were still brightly illuminated by street lights, but from his observations during the hours before his planned expedition, he saw very few people brave the insanity that now ruled the city he persevered in. That's all his life had been for several years now, grinding survival, and part of him was glad that the tolerations of his existence were coming to their end.

He found himself revelling in what everyone else feared.

The execution of the woman by the soldier before the eyes of everyone had solidified the dangers the world now represented to a population that no longer knew what to be more afraid of. The only ones he had seen brave enough to defy the military order were a gang of youths. Just children really, living off adrenaline and masculine stupidity. About an hour ago, they had appeared out of a side alley and had foolishly tried to force entry into an off-licence across the road. Whilst two kept watch, four of them had haphazardly assaulted the thick roller shutters that were the establishment's benign guardian. Five minutes into their noisy attack and the barrier had proved to be more than a match for them. The little shits should have learnt to drive, then they could have at least rammed the place with one of the many cars scattered around. Colin reckoned they were already drunk or high and they would have carried on with their futile mission if not for the helicopter that had come into view. Threatening to fly low over their position, the gang had vanished into the night, scattering in all directions.

Colin easily realised that the dregs of humanity would be as big an issue as the zombies themselves, at least in the early stages. This wouldn't be the time of heroes.

Colin predicted the yobs would be back. Their type always persevered when it was something as important as alcohol. Likely they figured they had been denied their fun. If not for the actions of the soldier, the road below would probably be burning now, swept up in a rage of destructive carnage as the pressure valve in the oppressed and the opportunistic popped. The scum that passed for humanity cared only for their own self-indulgence, and with the lowest forms of human life merely waiting for their ideal moment, opportunities for lawlessness often manifested in a depraved desire to utterly destroy the property and lives of those around them.

Colin knew he was better than that. Even though he was also intent on destruction, at least he had an overriding purpose. He would be doing it for the greater benefit of the planet, not for some cheap thrills. His death would have meaning.

Now fully kitted out as best he could, Colin looked at himself in the full-length mirror that he somehow had found space for in his miniscule flat. He looked ridiculous, but this wasn't supposed to be a fashion contest. He wore a waterproof poncho over a thick leather coat. Two pairs of jeans would hopefully offer some sort of protection should the undead find and attack him, the poncho extending to well below the knees. The thickness of the joint material made walking awkward but he could live with it. The pink marigold gloves were the crowning feature on his outfit, as were the respirator unit and goggles he wore. The latter had been needed when he was mixing the household chemicals up to make the explosive he was now hoping to thoroughly weaponise. With the chord of the poncho pulled tight, most of his face was protected.

In his left hand, he carried a bucket full of nails and ball bearings. He hadn't yet gotten round to adding this added bonus to the pouches lining his crudely constructed explosive garment, and he was glad of that. What he was about to do was to make his suicide even more devastating. The freezer bags in his pocket were the secret ingredient. They would be used to carry the deadly projectiles into the vest without contaminating the fabric of it too much.

The bucket also contained a large carving knife. It would be left on the street when he was finished with it. No amount of washing up liquid or bleach would salvage it for the mediocre purpose of cutting up food, not after he was finished with it tonight.

There was nobody in the corridor when he left his flat, and he made sure to close the door behind him, the keys safely placed where he could get at them in a hurry. The marigolds would be difficult to negotiate, but that was why he wore nitriles underneath so the bulkier gloves could be ditched once he had done most of the dirty work. And it would definitely be dirty. Colin had no illusion about what he was about to do and had deliberately not eaten since the thought had popped into his diseased brain. It was almost a certainty that he was going to throw up at least once during this. He was willing to pay that price.

He didn't see anyone as he traversed the corridor and the staircase, and apart from the dulled sound of a neighbour's TV set, he didn't hear anyone either. So he made it down to the ground floor unhindered and most likely unobserved, which was exactly how he preferred things. He didn't like interacting with people at the best of times. When he went out there, he knew there would be the twitching of blinds and curtains, so he accepted that as an inevitability. They would have no idea what he was really up to, just that he was a sick son of a bitch who clearly needed to be avoided. With what he had planned, he had to admit that they would be right in that assumption about him.

Colin was no longer a person any reasonable person should have anything to do with, not if they knew what was good for them. His own psychosis had gone too far for him to be salvaged now. And to his credit, Colin actually realised this. He wasn't in denial about the sickness that had grown inside him, in fact, he actively embraced it.

This was the quietest he had ever known London, a shroud of gloom and silence encasing the once vibrant city. Keeping the main street door propped open with a discarded telephone directory, Colin tentatively walked out into the still night air. If he ran into trouble, Colin wanted to be able to get back into the illusionary safety of his apartment building without having to mess about with keys in locks. He'd seen enough horror films to know that keys could be dropped at the most inopportune moments, usually when some knife toothed demon was about to pounce on your back. He was many things, but a fool wasn't one of them. At least, that's what he told himself.

Truth was, Colin Macready was a sad, weaselly little man who had allowed himself to become a victim to life. His overriding emotions for as long as he could remember were anger and resentment. Anger at those who ridiculed and pitied him. Resentment towards a society that stopped him getting the rewards he felt he deserved. People like him always blamed the external rather than pointing the accusatory finger at the true reason for their failures. That finger should first and foremost always be pointed at themselves.

With all the layers on, he didn't feel the coolness of the evening. In fact there was a nice sweat building on him now. Part of that was also caused by the nervous tension that gripped him, his penchant for danger almost non-existent. Fortunately, everything out here was as he had hoped and expected. The three corpses were still lying where they had been left, and he wasn't alarmed to see black shapes moving over one of them. Rats, brought out of hiding by the rich pickings the decaying flesh represented.

Millions of them lived on and below the streets of the nation's capital, and if anything, he would have expected more rats given the plentiful bounty that was being offered to them. He wasn't really concerned by their presence, but he was somewhat shocked to see a black raven suddenly land on the shattered skull of the woman. The bird sat there as if it owned the place, its attention partially on Colin as he carefully approached. Occasionally it would peck at the flesh below it.

The raven's nerve finally failed it and it took off back into the air. Colin wasn't sure, but he thought the bird had an eye firmly lodged in its beak. Had the fucking thing been scavenging as well? Well of course it had, ravens were carrion creatures. Colin had learnt that at school many moons ago, and he had no idea why that snippet of knowledge suddenly leapt into his cranium.

Could the virus be passed onto the other creatures of the planet? That was a worrying thought. The whole point of wiping out the footprint of man was to save the other species that were dying under homo sapiens' relentless onslaught. Would the Earth be able to self-correct and heal itself in the millennia to come? What if the building army of the undead turned on and wiped out what was left of the already depleted mammalian species that were struggling to survive mankind's onslaught?

Colin didn't want to think about that.

The rats showed no hint of bravado, scuttling away as soon as Colin could threaten them, the infected meat they ate still yet to take its devastating effect on their physiology. The road around him was still clear of everything but the creatures of the dark and dirty places, but Colin didn't dawdle. Placing the bucket next to the nearest body, he clutched the large carving knife. Despite his determination, he faltered. Could he really do this? Could he open up the cadaver of a human being and stick his hands deep into the abdominal cavity. That was what he reckoned he needed to do to be successful in this.

With the body he chose lying on its back, Colin lifted up the soiled and still moist t-shirt to expose the blackened, tendril marked skin. There was a sheen of moisture present, almost like thin jelly and Colin pressed down with his gloved hand against the corpse's belly. Soft and pliant, the best place to get what he needed. He would have preferred the brain matter, but even with the skull injury, getting inside the body cavity would have been difficult. Plus, damaged bone was sharp, and he really didn't want to come away with an injury that would likely result in a death sentence that might kill him before he was ready. The scientist he had been listening to on Radio 4 had hypothesised that mere exposure to the bodily fluid of the undead could prove fatal. He reckoned that was where the idea came from for his miniature doomsday device.

Somewhere down the street, something metallic fell over with a loud clashing sound.

Colin shot to his feet and did a full three-sixty, the goggles he wore already steaming up. He adjusted his respirator whilst it was still safe to do so, his breath hot. It was difficult to breathe with the apparatus on, but there was no way he was removing it. From what he could see, he was still the only living soul around, but his nerve almost failed him. Should he even be out here, this was not the sort of thing a coward like him should even be attempting? Dressed like a complete idiot, he had dragged himself out of the sanctuary of his flat to risk this fool's errand. Colin nearly turned and ran. Instead, he went back down to his knees and plunged the knife straight down. It might well have been the bravest thing he had ever done.

He'd pushed with such force, that the tip of the knife hit the road surface underneath. Black matter welled up from the knife wound, the respirator sparing him from the ungodly smell that must have been leaking out of the wound. The knife moved sideways, cutting through the abdominal muscles easily, its razor sharp edge finding no resistance. Bubbles erupted from where the knife led, the bacteria already putrefying the organs and the meat. The gas found its freedom to escape. The zombies were disgusting enough now. What were they going to be like in a week? In a month? Would they even still be able to move?

A window smashed unseen on a side street. There was something wrong with that sound, not seeming to fit with the present situation. The road was supposed to be deserted, who would be out breaking windows when civilisation was at its end?

Colin started to panic. Abandoning the knife, he forced his hands into the hole he had made, the texture slick and disgusting. Even with him being double gloved, the feeling sickened him. His fingers closed down on what were probably intestines, and he pulled what he could free, incredulous that he was actually doing this. The thick tubing came surprisingly easily, allowing him to get better access into the body. Bile began to rise in his throat, and then he realised the basic error he had committed. If he threw up, it would make the respirator useless, and he couldn't take the respirator off without first removing the now gore-stained gloves.

He swallowed hard and did what he could to control his breathing. *Hold on for just a few seconds*, he demanded of his body.

"Come on, you can do this," he insisted of himself, not really believing a word of it. Giving quick glances up and down the street again, his hands once again descended into the abdominal cavity, and he scooped the dead viscera and blood into the bucket. There were things in there that he didn't recognise, plump and pliable. Once, twice, a third time, Colin managed to get handfuls of Christ only knew what out of the zombie's now useless body, sometimes using the knife to cut it free. How many people were watching him do this? The thought struck him as almost amusing. Colin Macready, mediocre office worker and defiler of death's own sculptures.

"That's enough," he said perhaps louder than he should have. That has to be enough. The knife now abandoned, he carefully stripped off the outer gloves, holding his hands away from his body. They fell to the floor together, his hands still protected by thin nitrile. That was when he heard the sound of people running.

Up the road, a single figure came towards him. She was a good sixty metres away, so Colin easily had time to grip the handle of his bucket and retreat back to his flat. He'd made sure to only fill the bucket enough to cover the shrapnel that resided in it, so there was no danger of any escaping over the sides.

"No, wait," a harassed and frightened voice pleaded. But Colin didn't wait, in fact, he did the exact opposite, speeding up as fast as his outfit would allow. Inside the lobby of his apartment building now, Colin turned to close the door just in time to witness what the woman was running from. She was making directly for him, drawing the small detachment of undead with her, so Colin did the only thing that made any sense to him. He shut and locked the door. What the hell did she think she was doing going out there alone?

Seconds later she was pounding on it, demanding entry. The profanity she called him was shocking to a mind that rarely used such words.

"Open the door you utter bastard", were the last words he heard her utter. The mystery woman slammed her fists on the door a final time, only to suddenly abandon her attempt at entry, taking off again at a pace that was unlikely to save her.

Colin retreated away from the door. It was strong enough, designed to resist forced entry, but still, Colin didn't trust that it could withstand a persistent attack by the undead. Any second he expected their hands to start pounding, but they never did. They had obviously not detected his presence out on the street and through the small frosted window by the side of the door, he saw their shapes pass by at a frightening speed. Could they all move that fast?

A sigh of relief escaped him, and carefully he took his contaminated bucket up the steps, mindful of any drips that were falling from underneath. His last scoop of guts had only half gone into the receptacle. But he had what he needed now. Not only would his suicide vest be lined with viscously sharp nails and pulverising bearings, those metal implements of death and disfigurement would also bring the virus to whoever they inflicted themselves upon. Now all he needed to do was find himself an unsuspecting crowd.

On his corridor now, his apartment at the end, Colin left the bucket by the side of the door so he wouldn't have to endure the stench that was undoubtedly coming from it. Looking at his repository of death for one final moment, he withdrew his key and let himself back into his apartment. Colin was sure nobody would disturb his morbid collection.

He didn't see the mayhem that was occurring outside. If at that moment Colin had looked out of his living room window, he would have been witness to dozens of the undead rampaging down the street. It would seem he had just had a very lucky escape.

21.08.19
Manchester, UK

Stuart had wanted to phone his father, but in the end he didn't bother. They hadn't spoken for over two years, ever since his dad had lost the battle with his own prejudice. If his mother was still alive, it might have been different. But Stuart's father had seemed to take it as a personal insult that his son was a homosexual. It was as if it somehow threatened his own masculinity. Stuart didn't see why he had to put up with that.

He had intended to call though. Stuart had held the phone with his thumb over the dial button for almost ten minutes, nervousness preventing him moving the digit bare millimetres. The shot from outside his apartment had made him jump, and any resolve for reconciliation had dissipated in that moment.

Stuart had been horrified by what he saw out of the window. Three armed police were crouching behind a parked police car, the blue lights blazing hypnotically. He was confused by what was going on, only for there to be the sound of another shot. Stuart instantly saw the motion, a man behind a tree shooting at the police who were choosing, at this time, not to return fire.

What the fuck was this, 1920's Chicago?

It was after eleven in the evening, way past the military imposed Curfew that had been placed across the city of Manchester. Somebody had clearly been caught out after hours and had chosen the path of death by cop. Because really, this was the only way it could end. Already back up units would likely be on their way. If the lone idiot with the gun didn't give up, and soon, he would be going home in a box.

One of the police officers lifted his head up above the car's bonnet, only for another shot to come his way. The officer didn't duck back down, the distance was clearly too much for the silly twat shooting at him to have any real chance of effective aim. There were too many guns on the streets of Manchester these days, but fortunately, nobody knew how to use the bloody things. It wasn't like some countries where you could nip down the shooting range and pop off a few shots as practice.

A second officer appeared from where he was hidden and aimed his machine gun, leaning his elbows on the boot of the police car. Stuart opened the window and only three floors up, he could just about hear what was going on. The rest of the city was quiet, hundreds of thousands of people having retreated to their homes.

"Armed police, drop the gun now or it's over. I won't ask again."

"Screw you pig," the man said, fear evident in the words. If there was bravado there it was brought on by pure desperation. He barely looked like he was an adult. Just a frightened youth full of piss and vinegar most likely. The boy came out from behind the tree and let off two more shots. Then there was a third, and the kid wasn't shooting anymore because the organ pumping the blood around his body suddenly had a catastrophic hole through it. When the gun fell from his hands, two of the officers made a tactical advance towards him, the third obviously radioing everything in. Stuart closed the window, he didn't want to see anything else. But he did, he saw the worst of it. The officer who shot the man got up close enough to accurately put a second bullet through the now dead man's head. Was that what it had now come to?

Stuart naturally couldn't sleep with all that was going on. He was still haunted by the mistake he had likely made. Jessica had phoned him and told him to go to her brother's place because it was safe, secure and out of the way from all this madness. Only Stuart hadn't listened because he'd had important shit to do. Well, it wasn't important now, and Stuart was likely trapped in a city where people were openly killing each other.

He reckoned he could still be accepted there if he went, but how did he get out of the city? Public transport had been suspended, and all the main roads in and out of the city would be blocked off. The military didn't want people moving around because that risked spreading the infection. So they had simply shut everything down, the TV saying that only essential personnel were allowed to travel. There was no way Stuart's job classed him as essential personnel. He was a lawyer, not an engineer or a paramedic. Maybe his dear departed mother was right after all, maybe he should have become a doctor. They could get rid of all the lawyers, and the lights would still stay on and the water would carry on flowing from the taps.

Stuart realised he was going to have to wait it out. He'd managed to get some canned food on the way home and had enough in the house to last him about two weeks. Surely everything would be back to normal by then. There was no way he would allow himself to envisage anything but a happy outcome here. I mean, okay, the TV now seemed to be telling the truth about what was occurring, but it wasn't like there were legions of zombies crashing through the streets outside. Stuart was more than confident that the police and the military would get things back under control. And if what he had witnessed outside was widespread, there was likely going to be a bob or two to make out of the impending lawsuits. There were undoubtedly massive infringements of people's human rights going on throughout the city and the country. So there was definitely an opportunity for himself and his firm once all the insanity ended. Some would consider it strange that he was still thinking about money when zombies were walking the Earth, but it was just who he was. It would end though, right? This couldn't go on for much longer, humanity always won out.

The sneeze took him by surprise, the droplets forming into an infectious cloud that spread out through the apartment. With no other lungs to breathe them in, they slowly drifted down onto the furniture around him. Invisible death with nobody to infest.

21.08.19
Hounslow, UK

Night was fully on them now. The civic centre's surroundings were illuminated by piercing spotlights, but virtually every building around their position was internally dark, the inhabitants likely long since dead. The relentless undead moved around the perimeter, and Whittaker thought he understood why now. It occurred to him that the undead had some sort of animal cunning and that their present actions were merely to taunt the soldiers. He had no idea if he was correct in his assumption. After all, he was just a Corporal. He'd barely managed to leave school with four GCSE's, so he didn't consider himself to be particularly smart.

Smart people rarely did.

Ammunition stocks had been dangerously depleted throughout the day, and whilst the last supply run from their barracks had arrived successfully, the one before that had never turned up. The last they heard of it was a garbled radio communication that the convoy was being attacked. There had been nothing heard since, twenty men most likely lost to the horde rampaging through the streets of Hounslow. That was all assuming it had been the undead that had been the attackers.

The Major was now relying on helicopters to keep the supplies flowing, determining that the roads were becoming impassable to anything except a fully armoured column. At the moment, only the occasional sniper shot could be heard across the night's sky, the Major now ordering the heavier stuff to hold fire until an assault actually came. Unbeknownst to the bulk of the men, Major Pickering was already deciding that he had to get his men out of this shit-fest. He just had to try and figure out how. The Major silently cursed the senior officer who sent him and his men on this fool's errand.

"Do you think this is the end, Corp?" Tod asked. He sat with a satisfied air about him, the rifle resting across his lap. Whittaker wouldn't be surprised if Tod suddenly started stroking it. He'd heard a rumour from some of the other lads that his section's sharpshooter sometimes talked to the rifle. If he did, he certainly wouldn't be the first soldier to do so.

"The end of what?" Whittaker was surprised by the question if he was honest. Tod may have been a bit of a nutcase, but he always had an optimistic slant to his personality.

"The end of everything. I mean, fucking zombies right."

"It's not looking good, I'll give you that."

"At least we get to go out doing what we love." Tod sucked on the cigarette he held between his lips, savouring the hit of the nicotine. Nobody as of yet had told them to don NBC protective gear.

So far by his count, Tod had killed seventeen zombies today. Whittaker figured he might have embellished that figure somewhat, and if this continued, he also reckoned it wasn't long before Tod started to keep some sort of visual tally. If the stock of his gun had been made of wood, that probably would have already happened.

"Sometimes I think you enjoy the job a little too much." Whittaker said it playfully, but he meant what he said.

"I won't lie," Tod said, "I do like killing these things. When I was told I could put on a uniform and kill for Queen and Country, I jumped at the chance."

"Well looks like you are going to get plenty of practice tonight." Whittaker had met a few men like Tod during his stint in the army. He wasn't shocked by them, it was only natural for such characters to find their way into the armed forces. What surprised him more was that people like Tod seemed to be a bit of a rarity. The majority of the men and women he met could go through their whole careers without firing a single shot against an enemy.

Until today that was. Today changed everything. Every man here would be doing their part.

Whittaker was distracted by the sound of a helicopter in the distance. He wondered if it was the same one that had saved him and his men earlier in the day. He'd tried to find out who the pilot was with a view to one day maybe thanking him, but nobody seemed to know the information. There was the distant sound of something laying down machine gun fire, and he wondered how long those flying angels of death would be up there.

Down the line, five men distant, someone had a coughing fit.

Behind him, the Sergeant from earlier walked past with the Lieutenant in tow. The officer had a computer tablet, which he was obviously monitoring the video feed from a drone that had been sent up earlier.

"They are massing on the other side of those buildings," the Lieutenant could be heard to say. "We have a Yank airstrike incoming any minute. Should take out the majority of them." The RAF didn't have the ordnance needed for this sort of attack. As a NATO ally and with jets stationed in the UK, the Americans had agreed to do limited strikes on selected targets before they bugged out of the country entirely.

"Let's hope those flyboys know friend from foe," the Sergeant replied. Whittaker had yet to catch his name, but he felt reassured by the Sergeant's presence. Sensing something, Whittaker joined the two men in looking up at the skies, even though the night was overcast, the moon fully hidden from sight. They weren't looking, but listening. He heard it, the distant roar of fighter jets, what every soldier wanted to hear when their position was in danger of being overrun. Their technology might just be the edge they needed to beat this thing.

Who am I trying to kid? thought Whittaker. The scratchiness of his throat was really starting to irritate him.

They came in low and quickly, their engines a fanfare to their arrival. Some of the men around him cheered. As the cacophony rose, Whittaker just managed to hear the Lieutenant shout "My God, they are scattering," and then the planes seemed to be overhead, the aviation lights briefly the only visible indication of their existence. A second later a line of fire erupted above the buildings bordering one side of the recreational ground, the flames billowing into the night's sky. It didn't take long for the smell of the burning to reach Whittaker and it seemed to stick to the back of his nose, the chemical fire bringing with it the stench of burnt flesh, exacerbating the soreness there.

The Corporal found himself coughing for the first time that day. He didn't know the Americans even still used such incendiary ordnance.

On the opposite side to the military stronghold, another line of fire engulfed a whole street. The visible buildings began to burn, a wave of warmth washing over the defenders. Whittaker had read about the firestorms in German and Japanese cities of World War Two and knew there was no threat of that here. This was precision bombing, almost surgical, creating a barrier whilst hopefully destroying as much of the undead as possible. A secondary explosion went off some ways in the distance.

With the politicians out of the way, the military seemed to have no hesitation in sacrificing the British public for the greater good. Any civilians that had survived the undead were scorched to death now. Whittaker just hoped fire could kill these things. They were horrific enough, the last thing he wanted was to face burnt zombies running across the battlefield.

Two more strikes hit streets further out, the plan obviously to create a buffer zone of burning death. How long would that hold the zombie armies off, Whittaker wondered? How many would it kill?

"Corporal," the Sergeant shouted at him, Whittaker jumping to his feet.

"Yes Sarge?" Whittaker stood at attention, the Lieutenant completely ignoring him.

"You told the Major you thought the undead used strategy, is that correct?"

"Yes Sergeant. They tried to outflank us." That was when the Lieutenant looked at him. The officer seemed nervous, but then he was young and inexperienced. This was likely his first time in battle, so it was wise that he was listening to the veteran Sergeant.

"Where is the rest of your Section, Corporal?" the Lieutenant asked him.

"Not sure sir."

"Go and find them mate," the Sergeant said softly. "Better to be together with lads you know when the attack comes." Whittaker nodded. Giving the officer a salute, he went off in search of his men, leaving Tod to savour his next kill.

21.08.19
Manchester, UK

The clothes fit him surprisingly well. Brian had always felt that his body was difficult to shop for due to his height and relative bulk, but this was military gear. It was designed to fit men of his size. The black fatigues gave him a menacing appearance, which was only hardened by the black gloves and the respirator he wore. He absently scratched at the small plaster that covered the needle mark in the crook of his arm. Florence had taken blood from both he and Susan, and whilst Susan had squealed when the needle penetrated her, Brian hadn't felt a thing.

Everyone had to have the blood tests so they could be checked for the virus. Brian didn't ask how Clay could get those blood tests done. Somebody at some hospital somewhere was obviously being paid a lot of money to provide that service. Brian knew that the time when money would be seen as irrelevant hadn't arrived yet. People would likely cling to the hope of it for a few more days yet, and it gave Clay the edge he needed.

He sat and listened to Clay, the three other men present with him of similar rank in the organisation to Brian. They were all dressed as he was, and they all kept at least two arms distance away from each other. Clay wasn't taking any chances here.

"Is there anyone here who doesn't want to stay?" Clay asked. The gang boss had just spent the last twenty minutes outlining the information he had been given by his contacts inside MI6 and the British military. Selling guns across the world was a lot easier when you had the unofficial blessing of the powers that be.

Some of those present had sat mouths agape under their masks as Clay told them about the zombie outbreak at Wythenshawe Hospital. Nobody asked how Clay had acquired this knowledge, they all knew his wealth and his business empire created information tendrils that reached further than any of them could imagine. Nobody indicated they wanted to leave.

"Good," Clay said. Clay was sat in a plush armchair, a cigar planted between his teeth. The smoke rose lazily in the air, dissipating as the air-conditioned room he was in sucked the particles of burnt plant matter away. Nobody else smoked. Nobody else was allowed to, and it wasn't feasible with the respirators they wore. In Clay's mansion, you only smoked what Clay said you could, and sometimes he would even offer you one of his own. Unlikely that would be happening anytime soon. There was a high probability that Clay would suddenly get very stingy with his stash. Cigars were likely something that was going to be in very short supply soon.

It didn't matter that Clay was in a different room from them, these were still the rules to follow. For now, with the ever-present risk of infection, Clay was locked away in his master bedroom. The fifty-inch TV set that had been set up in one of the mansion's living rooms was how he was now video linking with his most trusted commanders.

"The plan now is to fortify this position. I want it locked down, nobody in or out without my express permission." Clay took another pull on the cigar, the smoke lingering in his mouth before he blew it out. "Some of you will be going out first thing tomorrow morning. There are several warehouses I want you to hit, but the military presence is too strong for us to try that tonight. Tonight I want you to get some sleep whilst we wait on your blood test to be returned."

"And if any of us are infected?" the man to Brian's direct right asked.

"Then you will be isolated until such time as we need to deal with you. Any other questions?" The room indicated that there weren't. "Then that will be all for now. Brian could you stay behind please." The other three men gave Brian a glance that he couldn't determine due to the paraphernalia on their faces. It could have been curiosity, pity or jealousy. Either way, Brian could do without it. He watched as the three men left, the last one closing the door behind him.

"Take that shit off your face Brian," Clay insisted. Brian hesitated for a moment, and then stripped off the mask.

"What can I do for you, Mr Clay?"

"Of all my men, you are one that I trust more than most. You have proven to me countless times that you are loyal. And yet I always wondered why you never made a power play for your own organisation."

"It was never something I was interested in. I'm a follower rather than a leader." That was the truth. Brian didn't feel he had the temperament or the desire to lead. He was more than happy to grow rich serving someone else's agenda. Rich, that was a laugh now.

"Well, that's good to hear. Would be a mistake for someone to try and overstep their station in life. I trust you noticed Gary's absence from the room." The man Clay was referring to was perhaps as close to a second in command as Clay's organisation had. It was said that Clay declined to trust anyone implicitly, which was probably why he had lasted so long. But Gary was perhaps one of the few men who got his ear the most.

"I did Mr Clay."

"He was absent because he thought he could instigate a coup against me. Very foolish if you ask me, I have eyes everywhere. Be good to get his blood tests back so I can deal with him personally. As I am sure you can imagine, these events are turning out to be very stressful to me."

"I'm sure they are Mr Clay." The man called Gary would not be enjoying the several days Clay would draw his torture out. Clay wasn't forgiving at the best of times, but betrayal was the one thing he dealt with in person when possible. Over the years the crime boss had become quite accomplished at making men severely regret the error of their ways. And some women too, Clay was not one to discriminate. Clay did have an appetite when it came to the ladies.

"But that's not why I held you back Brian. You may not have heard about it, but there was a shootout at the North Manchester Hospital yesterday."

"No I didn't hear about that," Brian stated. With everything that was happening, it was unlikely it would even have been reported in the news, even if there wasn't a restrictive D notice placed on it.

"Turns out the army might have a patient immune to this terrible disease stashed away. I don't know where, but I know they might be on the way to creating a cure to all this."

"That's good news, Mr Clay." Why was Clay telling him this?

"It's even better news if we can get our hands on that cure, don't you think Brian?"

"I'm not sure how we can do that, Mr Clay. Not if the military are protecting her."

"Never the optimist are you Brian?" Clay's eyes seemed to grow as he spoke, the cunning that had kept him alive so long seeming almost to live there.

"No, Mr Clay." Always best not to argue, thought Brian.

"I hear you are acquainted with the patient as well." Brian didn't respond, the confusion on his face answer enough. "Turns out her name is Jessica Dunn, the lawyer who ran your defence. I'm not sure if we can pull it off just yet, but there's a small chance you might shortly be re-acquainted with her. Wouldn't that be nice Brian? Wouldn't that be just ever so peachy?"

"Yes, Mr Clay." What the fuck was Clay planning now?

21.09.18
Houston, USA

Reece stood leaning against her police cruiser, the midday sun scorching the world around her. She had changed her gloves, the stifling heat making the replacement set difficult to put on, the sweat sticking to the insides like glue. As she had predicted, the respirators made it difficult to breathe, but rather that than catch the disease everyone was now talking about. The man they had just arrested shouted abuse at her from the back of the car. It wasn't anything Reece hadn't heard a hundred times before. Being a woman only added to the litany of insults that could be hurled at her, especially from the macho types who couldn't seem to believe that a woman could slap handcuffs on them so easily. Reece enjoyed taking those scumbags down, she couldn't deny it.

What made today more worrying was that everyone they arrested might be someone who could pass the virus on. Just being spat on could be a death sentence. Thus they had been ordered not to engage in any physical takedowns now. Anyone who refused their lawful orders was to be either tasered or shot if the situation warranted it. Only when the suspect was lying face down on the ground with their arms spread were law enforcement to approach. An anti-spit hood would then be placed on right after the cuffs were slammed on the wrists. Even worse would be to end up in a scuffle and get bitten. Reece had been bitten twice in her career so far, and she was determined that today wouldn't see a third occurrence.

The Presidential alert, unsurprisingly, had not produced the desired effect causing the city to explode initially. Fortunately, the National Guard had not failed in their duty, and their presence on the streets had shut that shit down hard and fast. Even with the increased law enforcement presence in the city, continuing reports of mayhem were all over the police bands. Even worse, three deputies from her department were dead, killed in an ambush by people who hadn't believed that Lazarus was real, that somehow this was a power play by the Federal Government. An armed populace was only a benefit if everyone was working on the same side of the hymn sheet. Desperation and fear were making people act like idiots. And then there were the people who were just basic utter twats. Sometimes after a long day at it, Reece wondered if there were any decent folks actually worth protecting.

Despite his doubts, Rodriguez was still with her. His earlier indecision about staying on the job had apparently dissipated, although Reece reckoned that when the blood test results came back, she wouldn't see him for dust. The man wasn't a coward, he just loved his family to the degree that he would risk everything for them. She strongly suspected he would be phoning in sick tomorrow...or not phoning in at all and just not turning up.

Reece didn't personally have that kind of handicap, so she would keep coming into the job until this thing was fixed or someone told her not to bother anymore.

"Dispatch says not to bring him back to 1200," Rodriguez said exiting the front of the car, leaving the driver's door open. 1200 was the unofficial name given to the Sherriff's headquarters where she was based. "Apparently we now have to take everyone to the FEMA processing centres that are being set up around the city. There they will be put into the system and transported to holding at the Astrodome."

"The Astrodome? How many people are we supposed to arrest?" Two national guards walked past them, and Rodriguez went quiet until they were safely out of earshot. Reece noted the look of distrust in his eyes.

"I don't like this Clarisse." Most of the time she preferred to be called by her surname. Clarisse sounded too soft for her, but she made allowances with Rodriguez. He was her partner after all. He wasn't quite like a brother to her, but she still gave him a degree of slack.

"I hear you," Reece agreed. "But we have a job to do."

"But I'm hearing things," Rodriguez said, his eyes flitting around the car park they were stood in, the Stetson he wore shielding his sight from the sun. They had been called to a small department store that the guy in the back seat had attempted to rob. Unfortunately for him, the store had Korean owners who had shown no hesitation in defending their store. Two would be robbers were dead, the third being detained for the Sherriff's Department to collect. "Word is, it's not just criminals that are being sent to the Astrodome. The army are rounding people up."

"Have you been listening to conspiracy radio again?"

"No, you need to listen to me. My cousin is a nurse, she texted me whilst I was onto dispatch. They are emptying the hospitals of anyone they deem to be infected. She said the Guard are piling them onto buses. Nobody is being given a choice."

"Well doesn't that make sense?" Reece reassured him. She was about to say something more, when there was an uproar from the back seat of the cruiser.

"Hey, haven't you forgotten about someone?" the prisoner shouted. Reece ignored him. At least he wasn't throwing up like some they had arrested the past few days.

"If the hospitals are getting overloaded, then surely shipping them to a larger medical facility is the wise thing to do."

"I guess," Rodriguez said. He didn't sound convinced.

"Let's get this guy dropped off and then we can have a break."

The first problem they encountered was the processing centre wasn't ready for them. Some harassed looking FEMA personnel said they weren't yet set up to take prisoners in as the army weren't here yet to man the holding facilities.

"You will have to take him direct to the Astrodome."

Reece wasn't surprised. Houston was a big city, coordinating something like this must have been a logistical nightmare. Rodriguez seemed to like the idea of going to the Astrodome, and Reece hoped it would put her partner's mind at rest. For a sheriff's deputy, he did spend a bit too much of his time feeding his inherent distrust of the Federal Government. He wasn't the only one in her department either. Many of her fellow deputies did not have a favourable opinion of Washington DC and all its myriad tentacle-like organisations.

Even to this day, Rodriguez still believed that 911 was an inside job. Reece humoured him, but she never let any of his crazy theories infect her thoughts.

Fortunately, he was wise enough to keep most of his strange notions to himself, occasionally sharing something of pressing interest only with her, never with the rank and file. She would humour him, and then offer a counter-argument to the one he was wrapped up in. Sometimes she was able to defuse his fevered imagination. She could see the conspiracy juice flowing through him now, and she hoped getting a first-hand view of what was being done at the Astrodome would dilute the toxic mix bubbling in his mind.

Unfortunately, their arrival at the Astrodome did not dispel the creeping paranoia that was most likely forming in her partner's overheated head.

The first thing that struck Reece was how quickly all this must have been put together, which meant that somewhere there had been a plan made ready. She knew FEMA prepared for likely disasters, but she had no insider knowledge of the workings of the bloated and inefficient Federal Emergency Management Agency. When they arrived, what they saw was the result of a plan put together several years ago to combat a virulent pandemic, something the then state governor had actively encouraged. The Astrodome had been selected as the central holding area for infected individuals. It was hoped that placing everyone in the same facility would help to better distribute resources and allow for more effective disposal of the inevitable casualties.

Kirby Drive had been blocked off by a checkpoint just where it cut under the freeway. As they drove up, both deputies were unnerved to see heavy calibre machineguns being pointed at them from sandbag emplacements, a Bradley fighting vehicle adding to the strength of the National Guard defensive post that spread across the road. Two rising arm barriers were there to allow the flow of traffic in and out. Although the Astrodome's car parks already had fences all around them, army engineers could be seen putting up higher and more formidable structures topped with razor wire. To keep people in, or to keep people out?

"What the fuck?" Rodriguez said under his breath.

As they slowed for the turning, an army corporal in full containment gear motioned for them to stop so that he could approach them on the driver's side. Rodriguez wound the window down, the dry hot air rushing in to overwhelm the car's inadequate air conditioning.

"Can I help you deputies?" the Corporal asked. There was a terseness to his voice detected even from under the respirator. *The guy must be roasting his butt off in this heat*, thought Reece.

"Prisoner for processing," Rodriguez said, pointing in the back.

"Man, I ain't no prisoner. I'm innocent man," the prisoner shouted. Reece told him to shut up. The guy was still obviously high on whatever had given him the courage to watch his two buddies die.

"You need to take him to the processing centre on Hiram Clarke Road," the Corporal said.

"Did that, they aren't set up yet. They told us to bring him directly to you," Reece said, leaning across to speak to the Corporal. As they spoke a large grey bus pulled up behind them and beeped its horn. Who the fuck had the guts to sound their horn at a Sheriff's Department cruiser?

"All units, all units, shooting on the corner of Creekbend and Cliffwood Drive. All units respond, possible hostage situation." The call was loud over the car's radio.

"Let us drop this creep off, so we can do our jobs," Rodriguez pleaded. The Corporal hesitated a moment, the bus honking its horn again. Reece looked into her side mirror and saw a second bus come up behind the first. It was the same grey colour. The Corporal stepped back from the car and said something into the radio mike that was linked to his breathing apparatus. Neither deputy could hear what was said. After a moment, the Corporal stepped back to their car.

"Ok, follow the blue channel. Do not deviate into any other direction," the soldier ordered. "When you have dropped him off, leave by this gate only. Everything else is blocked off to civilian traffic."

"Blue Channel, got you," Rodriguez agreed. The Corporal gave a hand signal and the road barrier was raised to allow the car entry. Behind them, the two buses didn't have to undergo any kind of questioning, they just followed the deputies straight through the barrier. With the traffic passed, the Corporal disappeared under the shade of an awning that had been set up to get some relief from the oven he was working in.

To her right, Reece saw that the Astrodome car park was being filled with huge tents, military personnel and people in hazmat gear braving the Texas sun. The blue channel was marked out by spray paint along the centre of the road and led to one of the many car parks servicing the Astrodome. There were other colours marked out, obviously for different classifications of people, guiding a path that even an idiot could follow. They drove slowly, a red line veering off to a turn off to their right. The buses stopped following and followed the red line, Reece wondering what classification of person were being carried on board.

Shortly their own channel filtered off and they pulled the car past a smaller car park, another checkpoint waiting for them. This one was only manned by two soldiers and a single Humvee and their car wasn't stopped. Instead, they were directed towards a large white tent-like structure. Rodriguez stopped the car in front, a large sign saying *Criminal Processing* indicating they were in the correct place. The tented structure must have covered a space the size of an NFL football field and was being borrowed for its new purpose.

It was cool inside the tent, the bulk of the interior not visible due to partitions that had been set up. An army sergeant sat behind a metal desk in the same gear the Corporal had been wearing, and he watched the two deputies bring their prisoner in. Reece was surprised to find the air cool, the tent obviously air-conditioned. Before them, metal barriers were set up to create channels that led to six processing desks. Only the Sergeant was presently manning the desks at the moment, but three MP's were stood off to the side. This area of the structure could accommodate two hundred people easily. There was no queue to hold Reece up. The fun was obviously yet to begin.

"We were told to drop this off," Rodriguez said as she approached the desk. The Sergeant studied them for several seconds, perhaps contemplating whether to make an issue of their breach of whatever the new rules were. He handed Reece a clipboard with paperwork on it. Rodriguez was given a netted bag.

"I'll need your names and badge numbers. If you know your prisoner's name, put that down as well with the incident that caused him to be arrested." Reece looked at the form, noticed the barcoded stickers at the bottom of the sheet. There were two other pieces of paper underneath. "Prisoner's personal items go in the bag."

"I want a goddamn lawyer," the prisoner demanded. He even stamped his foot petulantly. "And I need to piss. I need to piss real bad."

"When such time as the crisis is over, a court-appointed lawyer will be supplied to you," the Sergeant stated. Reece figured he'd be saying that hundreds of times as the day progressed. "If you need to piss go right ahead. Or you can wait till you are in the cell."

"Looks like you're expecting a lot of guests," Rodriguez quizzed.

"The facility interior is set up to take five thousand," the Sergeant informed. "So far we've been getting dribs and drabs. It will get chaotic when they bring them in from the processing centres though. First bus is due in an hour." Reece handed the Sergeant the clipboard back. There wasn't much of worth in the bag.

"Some buses followed us in," Reece added.

"Good to know." The Sergeant didn't seem to want to give any more information away. He shouted to one of the MP's to come over. All three came together as if the prisoner was some item of fascination.

"How come I don't get to have a mask?" the prisoner slurred from under his spit hood. Everyone ignored him. The Sergeant passed the first MP the clipboard, and the MP scanned one of the barcodes with a reader he held.

"We are linked to your system," the first MP said. "When you get back to 1200, just log on and you can write your report. It will automatically update our records so we can keep a track of your prisoner."

"Wow, I didn't know the National Guard could do that," Rodriguez prodded. He didn't like what he was seeing here. The first MP seemed to not hear his comment, instead he took a hold of the prisoner who tried to wriggle out of his grasp. Difficult to do with hands cuffed behind his back.

"Are you seriously going to give me trouble?" the first MP asked, exasperated.

"Might do," the prisoner stated proudly. "Might just shit in my hand and throw it at you when I get the chance."

"Do that, and you and I aren't going to be friends. Trust me when I say you don't want that."

"Fuck you Army," the prisoner roared.

"Can I tase him for you? I really don't mind," Reece offered.

"Hey now," the prisoner said suddenly softening, "no need for those negative waves. I'm cool."

"So you're cool?" the second MP added, mischief in his voice. He was stood behind the prisoner and took something off his belt that looked like an injection gun.

"Hey, what the fuck's that?" the prisoner said warily straining his head to look over his shoulder. He tried to move away but the first MP held him tight. The prisoner was wiry and thin, so he was unable to pull away from the stronger grip of the soldier. Without asking permission, the second MP pressed the gun against the man's bare arm and pushed a release trigger.

"Hey man, that hurts. What the hell are you doing to me?" The second MP placed the injection gun back on his belt, and the first waved the barcode scanner over where he had injected. There was an audible beep.

"All processed. He's in the system now. You can get back to the streets, deputies."

"Did you just microchip our prisoner?" Rodriguez demanded.

"Yes. Easier to track and process them."

"Hey man, I've got rights," the prisoner insisted.

"Martial law has been implemented. The only right you have is to do what the fuck we tell you," the first MP said, educating the prisoner who was really starting to wish he had stayed in bed that morning.

Reece and Rodriguez looked at each other. Reece saw the alarm in her partner's eyes and knew that this time he might actually have a point.

21.09.18
Hounslow, UK

The first indication that Major Pickering's scorched earth policy wasn't going to work was when the still burning zombie came running at the soldier's defensive line. The left side of it was on fire, the hair on its head long since charred away. The napalm fluid stuck to the zombie's flesh, slowly consuming the outer layer of fat and muscle, but regardless, the zombie came at them. Tod had the honour of ending its miserable existence, his shot accurate enough to obliterate the brain stem. He got a pat on the back from Whittaker for that shot. The rest of his section who he had gathered and brought up to the roof just watched in amazement as the city around them burnt.

If it had just been the remnants of human zombies, they might have had a chance, but nature had other animals that the virus could play off. On his retreat back to the command base, Whittaker had seen something that hadn't registered with him at the time. His eyes had witnessed it and had even passed it through to his brain, but his mind hadn't recognised it as the threat it represented. When he saw the raven land on the building's TV antennae, his neurons made the final connection and his blood turned to ice.

There was no way that bird should have landed like that with the amount of noise they were making. Plus, the way it flew, it was as if it had lost coordination.

"Sergeant," Whittaker shouted, catching the man's attention. The Sergeant came over, his face stern and unforgiving. Not for Whittaker in particular, just for anyone who failed to do their duty.

"What is it, Corporal?" the Sergeant asked, noticing that Whittaker wasn't looking at him, but up above his head. As he approached, the Sergeant followed the Corporal's gaze.

"When I came in earlier, it occurs to me now that I saw birds feeding on the bodies outside." The raven sat there seemingly inspecting the array of humanity below it, its head lolling from side to side almost methodically. The bird moved strangely, almost robotically, and its left wing kept going into spasm.

"Shit," the Sergeant said under his breath. A hacking cough suddenly ripped through him, the Sergeant's body rocking with the force of it. Whittaker noted his superior's skin was looking awfully pale.

"Tod," Whittaker said urgently, "you think you can shoot that bird?"

"Fuck yes," Tod said and didn't wait for anything more to be said. An easy shot for any of the men. Lining up, he took the raven out, the bird rocketing off its perch as the bullet ripped through it. Seconds later it fell with a wet thud to the rooftop.

It was not hard to tell that the bird was one of the undead. There was a visible hole running right through the centre of its chest, and yet it still flopped about on the ground. It made no noise, another indication that this creature was no longer in the realm of the living. To date, nobody had witnessed a resurrected creature making any kind of deliberate sound, be that former man or beast. The Sergeant stepped over and crushed the bird's head under his boot heel. That ended it for sure.

"You mean we have to deal with random wildlife now?" Tod said amazed.

"Sarge, what else feeds off the dead?" Whittaker asked.

"Any carrion consuming species. Hell, even dogs and cats if they are hungry enough. Corporal, get downstairs and make sure the Major understands this." Whittaker nodded and headed off the roof, a light mist of rain starting to fall as he did. For the first time he'd managed to see the name of the Sergeant, the name patch uncovered.

Wallace. A man you wanted behind you in times like this. Just a shame he was in the latter stages of the viral infection.

The MP's were still outside the office, and Whittaker told them he needed to see the Major. He briefly wondered if perhaps they would be better serving on the front line with the rest of the lads, but the twinge of resentment didn't form any roots.

"Corporal Whittaker to see you sir," one of the MP's shouted through the open door.

"Send him in," came the response. Whittaker walked in to find Pickering on the radio, a finger in the air telling the Corporal to keep quiet and not interrupt.

"General, I need more men," Pickering demanded.

"That may be, but we presently have no means to reinforce you. Heavy armour is the only thing that can navigate the streets of London now and that's all tied up." The voice was coming over the radio, and Whittaker had a notion he didn't want to hear any of this.

"What about helicopters? Surely some can be spared?"

"I would love to send you a whole air squadron of them Major, but we don't have any to spare."

"There's nothing left for us to defend here," the Major almost begged. "The infection has decimated the civilian population all around us, and the undead are massing. It's only a matter of time before they attack in force. I've ordered aerial bombing of the surrounding streets, but I'm guessing the Americans can't keep that up indefinitely."

"Correct Major, they are stretched to the limit and are, as they like to say, getting out of Dodge. They have given the order to pull whatever personnel they can out of Europe. The best they can do from here on out is let us have access to their ordnance stockpiles."

"Shit. Sorry, General." It didn't do to swear at Generals.

"Understandable Major."

"Do I have your permission to try and make a break for it back to barracks? I've got some tracked vehicles that can gouge a path through any jammed traffic. If I leave soon, I reckon I can get my men out of here."

"Then do it Major," the General said. "I'll try and arrange some more air support for you. We keep losing helicopters though."

"Losing them, how?" There was desperation in the Major's voice.

"Bird strikes sir," Whittaker interrupted before the General could answer. The General gave the same response as the agitated Corporal.

"Give us what you can General. I'll aim to have us out of here in the next two hours. Pickering out."

"Sorry for interrupting Major."

"Nothing to apologise for Corporal. What do you think you know?"

"We just shot a bird on the roof, sir. Came in despite all the noise the snipers were making. Myself and Sergeant Wallace think it was undead sir. It never occurred to me at the time, but when I was coming back in from my patrol, I saw some ravens feeding off the bodies lying in the streets. Sir, if other animals can be infected by this virus, how the hell do we combat it?"

"I don't know Corporal. I really don't know."

"There's something else, sir." Whittaker didn't know if he should be saying anything because there was no real precedent for this sort of thing.

"Well, what is it?"

"Sergeant Wallace, sir. He doesn't look well. It's possible he might be infected."

21.08.19
Manchester, UK

Susan lay on the bed of the room that was more luxurious than her mind had been able to comprehend. If it wasn't coated in marble, it was chrome and glass, the en-suite bathroom like something out of a Las Vegas Presidential suite. Did people actually live like this? The bedroom was bigger than the ground floor of her own bloody house, and it was clear to her that it was rarely used.

The Queen size bed was a monster of unsurpassed luxury. She wasn't certain, but the sheets felt like they had been freshly laundered, the clean smell of the fabric reassuring to her. It was a stark contrast to the medical shower she had been forced to take, her skin still itching in parts from its caustic effects. And then there had been the needle that bitch had stuck in her arm, a bruise forming where she had been injected.

But this…she could get used to this. Even the service was second to none, a butler having taken her order for food which had been delivered thirty minutes ago, the culinary delights left outside her door for her to collect. The remnants of that meal rested on the table at the side of the bed. Who the hell had a butler these days? More than that, who had a butler that was bigger than Brian?

She remembered Clay well. He was an arrogant, overbearing self-important little man who used his wealth to get his way with people. She almost felt disappointed that Clay had a sense of style, the tacky crassness of people with new money would better fit his image. Susan remembered that he always dressed well, and had that confidence about him that so many women found attractive. She broke through it all though and saw him for the violent gangster he was. The fact that he employed men like Brian just reinforced that.

Brian. What was she going to do about that? She didn't want him in her life, and yet she had rushed to him as soon as the reality of that life smacked her. Admittedly it had hit her hard, in the guise of potential gang rape, but she resented having to rely on him. Even more, she resented the coldness and distance she detected in him. It was obvious that he had been helping her these last few years more out of a sense of duty than from any feeling of compassion towards her. It was visible in his eyes. He clearly considered her an annoying chore that he felt forced to endure.

Since the death of her daughter and the suicide of her husband, it was true that she had fallen to pieces. Without Brian being there, it was likely that she would have ended up on the streets, alone and afraid. Part of her had wanted that, the self-destructive part that wanted to blame herself for everything that had happened.

Her precious daughter had died because Susan hadn't been there to protect her.

Her beloved husband had chosen suicide because his wife wasn't enough for him.

Foolish thoughts she now realised, but they had been so pervasive, so consuming. How could she function in society with that failure hanging over her? Twice she had even been on the brink of suicide herself, the pills in her hand, the whiskey ready to wash them down. It would have been so easy to drift away into oblivion and let the world continue without her. She wouldn't have been missed, all those she had thought of as friends seeming to disappear like mist when she really needed them.

The only person who had been there for her was Brian. And she hated him for it.

Stepping off the bed, she walked over to the larger of the two chest of drawers and helped herself to the vodka that had been left there. She hadn't asked for it, it had been present in the room as if the person who had prepared her sleeping quarters had known that it would be required. Had Brian advised them of that? Unlikely, he didn't approve of her drinking even though he had been her primary source of the money she needed to ensure a steady supply for her habit. That was another rung in the ladder of her hate. Even in her self-destruction, Brian had tried to exert some control, not trusting her ability to supply the tools required to drink herself to death. And the fact that he had been right just ground that pain into her soul even more.

A man who didn't care anything about her had kept her afloat and had ultimately saved her life. And all the time those who she thought had cared for her had abandoned Susan. Her friends, her husband. How could he do that? How could he have been such a coward? Why hadn't he been strong, like Brian? Had it ultimately been a mistake to choose the brother over Brian? The end result had been nothing but pain and misery.

The vodka flowed into the glass, the sound exquisite to her ears. She poured two fingers worth, and then thought fuck it and poured another two. She was a hardened drinker, she didn't need to concern herself with any form of dilution. There was ice in a bucket next to the assortment of drinks, but there would be none of that. Not tonight, not ever. This was her third drink since entering the bedroom and it wouldn't be her last before sleep finally took her. The events of the past twenty-four hours required copious amounts of liquid anaesthetic.

On the wall opposite the bed, a large TV with the volume turned down dominated the room. Presently the news channel she had picked was playing a rerun of Bangkok footage. Was that how everywhere was going to look, weeks from now? Was that the fate of her city and her country? Susan didn't know if she even cared. She had resigned herself to the fact that her life was pretty much over. Why should everyone else survive whilst she descended into a pit of despair?

21.08.19
Bangkok, Thailand

Strange how your dream holiday could turn into a nightmare.

When the violence had struck three days ago, Natalie Fields had fled to her hotel, thinking it was just a local political disturbance. It wouldn't have been the first time politics had caused civil unrest in the Thai capital. Standing in the hotel foyer minutes after her return from the chaotic streets, she had watched in disbelief as a bellboy had locked the front doors and had point blank refused to let anyone in or out of that entrance. One of the other hotel staff had tried to get him to change his mind, but the man had screamed in unintelligible Thai and had clearly threatened violence. If Natalie had made her decision to seek refuge just five minutes later, she would have been out there on the street when the undead unleashed themselves.

All she could do was watch as the tsunami of death washed down the street. A small child had run up the steps at the front of the hotel and had tapped timidly on the glass of the locked door. The bell boy had looked down at the child, whose shoulder was smeared with blood. With a manic jabbering of words, he had yelled at the child, probably telling her to go away. Fear had obviously cancelled out any form of compassion. The child didn't run because she never had a chance to. One of those with the black eyes had come up behind her and snatched her off her feet.

The small child's body was flung back down the steps, where three other fiends attacked her mercilessly. Natalie hadn't wanted to watch that, but how could she have turned her head away? The zombie directly outside had then attacked the reinforced glass but had been unable to break through despite the impressive red rendition of death it had left behind in its attempts. By the time its assault on the door was finished, the child was nowhere to be seen. There wasn't even a bloody smear to see on the road, a crowd now existing where the slaughter and the defilement had occurred.

That had been the beginning of it all. Most of the time since then, she had stayed in her room, the lights occasionally flickering nervously. From her bedroom window, Natalie had watched the city burn on the horizon, explosions occasionally lighting up the night's sky. Repeated attempts to use her cell phone came to nothing, the city's cell network having been shut down, the landline in her room just as useless. So Natalie was unable to get in touch with her friend who she had lost on the Metro underground system. The flood of people when the panic had first hit had swept them along and they had become separated. Natalie still remembered the look of horror on her friend's face as they had been parted. Guilt welled within her, but Natalie knew there was nothing she could have done to help. Not against the power of the panicking masses.

Natalie had been to her friend's room down the corridor three times, each in the hope that somehow her companion had made it back to safety. Each time her knocks went unanswered, the corridor eerily silent around her. There was hope still that she would make it to safety, but that hope was slim to non-existent. Natalie was slowly resigning herself to the reality that she was alone in a country she didn't really understand.

The morning after the slaughter of the child, Natalie had woken up still fully clothed. There was bottled water in the room's fridge, and she showered and dressed, the clothes she had slept in sweat-stained and pungent. With some hesitation, she had ventured back out into the body of the hotel in search of some semblance of humanity. What staff she saw looked tired and restless, few of them giving her their usual wai greeting. None of them spoke to her, some even scuttling away when she approached them.

On reaching the ground floor, she found the restaurant and the small shopping arcade all closed. With no other way to get food, Natalie resorted to taking what she could from a vending machine she found, some of her currency being swallowed up by the machine. There wasn't much left in the machine, most of the food having already been taken by people who had perhaps woken up to the reality of the situation earlier than her. Holding the precious morsels in her shaking hands, Natalie suddenly became nervous that someone would come and try and take the food from her and she had rushed back to her room taking the stairs. For some reason, the elevator seemed like a bad option. *What if the power went out?* she kept asking herself. She had visions of herself dying of dehydration, trapped in a metal box suspended mid floor. She had claustrophobia at the best of times. That wasn't a way she wanted to die.

As that day progressed she realised the daily replacement of her complimentary water supply wasn't going to happen, and she had rung housekeeping, only for the internal line to ring out relentlessly. With the tap delivered water supply reportedly not fit for human consumption, she was forced to leave the sanctity of her room yet again. Taking a rucksack with her this time, she closed the door behind her as quietly as she could, paranoia telling her that it was not good to announce her movement around the hotel anymore. The place just seemed to have a sense of menace where once it had an air of luxury.

Downstairs there was a commotion. Two tourists were arguing with a hotel security guard. One of the men was big and had dreadlocks, which she thought peculiar for a Caucasian. The second was stockier and with an almost shaved head. They were yelling in German and the guard was shouting back in Thai, so Natalie couldn't understand what the hell it was all about. It gave Natalie the distraction she required and she slipped her way through the lobby and into the hotel bar which seemed to be deserted. In her bag she carried the used water bottles that had not been disposed of, and checking around her, she slipped behind the bar and began to fill the bottles up from the beverage taps there. When nobody came to admonish her, she went one step further and half emptied one of the fridges, the rucksack feeling heavy but manageable. A bottle of gin was acquired for good measure. Adding some nuts she found there as well, Natalie slipped back into the main lounge of the bar.

But she hesitated. This wasn't right. Could this be classed as theft? Before she left, she dropped five thousand baht notes onto the bar in form of compensation. That was surely more than enough to cover what she had taken, although it confused her that she felt guilty in her attempts to survive. She kept expecting an accusatory voice to come and berate her, but it never did.

All her life she had been susceptible to the opinions of others, often allowing herself to be manipulated by those who claimed to have her best interests at heart. Little did she realise that the majority of the hotel staff had fled the building, leaving only those who felt compelled to continue to perform their duty out of some noble sense of honour. Some also stayed at work because it was the only life they knew.

Returning back to the foyer, the Germans had gone. But they had left a warning for her that reinforced the perils she now faced. The body of the Thai security guard lay on the ground, his neck at an obscene angle. Panic began to rise in Natalie which wasn't helped by the lights going out for several seconds. They came back on, but their brightness felt dimmer. At that moment in time her breathing had been the only sound she could hear, and it had filled her soul with a sense of dread that stayed with her till the end.

There was nobody at reception, so Natalie was forced to leave the body knowing her only option was to retreat to her room. She briefly contemplated trying to find a sheet to cover the body, but what if the Germans came back? Anyone who could kill a man like that wasn't someone she wanted to be around.

Being in the lobby and despite the evident dangers that were building around her, curiosity insisted that she take a look outside, and Natalie had quickly made her way to the front entrance, the doors there still mercifully intact. The street outside seemed empty, although it was strewn with carnage. A burnt out taxi smouldered and a strong wind blew the remnants of a newspaper stall along the road. A single child's shoe rested on the top step of the short flights of steps that led down to the pavement. Natalie lingered longer than she knew she should, the urge to open up the doors and fling herself outside crazily hitting her out of nowhere. She retreated from the door, not noticing the twitching hand of the dead guard. She ran up three flights of stairs and, slipping the key card into her door, pushed her way inside, being mindful not to slam the door behind her.

Most of that day was thus spent lying on her bed watching whatever TV she could find. Most of it was in Thai, but there were three English speaking channels that initially didn't tell her much.

Late in the night, there was the sound of violence from down the corridor. She couldn't see what was happening through the spy hole, so she carefully opened the door as silently as she could. Fifteen or so doors down the corridor, the two Germans were attacking a hotel room door with a fire axe. They didn't see her, and she didn't say anything to draw their attention because she knew there was nothing she could do to help. All she would achieve would be to make herself a target. As silently as was humanly possible, she closed the door and double locked it. Resting her back against its coldness, she had curled her knees into her chest and listened to the sounds that only got worse as the woman who was obviously the attacked room's occupant started to scream. Somehow, Natalie fell asleep in that position.

Natalie slept through most of the twentieth. When she wasn't sleeping, she drank prodigiously from the bottle of gin. It was enough to keep her sane.

On the twenty-first she woke up to oppressive heat. It was late in the morning, and the familiar hum of the air conditioning unit was clearly absent. When she tried the light to the bathroom, she quickly realised that the power was out. So not only was she in an alien country, alone and short of supplies, but now she was hotter than was comfortable. A feeling of isolation started to creep up on her, the walls to her room increasingly too close. She couldn't even open the window to get some less than fresh air into the room.

When she found there was no water pressure to work the shower or the toilet, the floodgates in her emotions fully opened and she realised she could no longer stay here. With the streets outside visibly calm, it seemed to her the only choice now was to try and get to the US consulate. Fortunately, the paper guidebook of Bangkok would work in that regard where her electronic devices failed. Rucksack on, and the last of her food eaten, she knew now was the time to leave the hotel. It was only a matter of time for her to run out of water, especially with the heat rising. She reckoned she had enough to get her where she needed to go, and she had brought what was left of the gin for good measure.

When she reached the foyer, the first thing she noted was that the dead body of the guard was gone. So mesmerised was she by this revelation that she didn't hear the man sneak up behind her. When he spoke to Natalie in German, she spun around to see the buzz cut German man from the other day. It wasn't even noon yet and it was clear that he was drunk.

"Please, leave me alone," she said. She tried to put some authority into her voice, but all she seemed to come out with was fear.

"Ah, you are American. Go Yankees," the German slurred, giggling to himself. He pumped a fist in the air.

"I'm just going to go," Natalie insisted, taking several steps back.

"No, don't go. We shall party. Yes, will be good. Stay and talk, I am lonely."

"Your English is good, and I'd love to chat, but I can't stay, sorry," she said, continuing her subtle retreat. The German matched her movement.

"Yes, I learn at school. I learn many things at school. We will show you," the German said, eagerly nodding. Natalie's nerve broke and she turned to run only to find the other German, the one with long dreadlocks, stood behind her. Both of the Germans were big men, and dreadlocks grabbed her by the arms, his fingers like vices. The stench of alcohol wafted from his mouth, and he belched loudly in her face. For some reason, his lips told her that he found this all highly amusing.

"Please, don't hurt me," Natalie squirmed ineffectively.

"My friend here, Hans, he does not speak English," informed the first German. "My name is Karl and I am very pleased to meet you." A hand started to caress her hair, and she was surprised when shame blossomed in her with regards the fact she hadn't washed it. Natalie knew she couldn't let these two trap her.

In desperation, she brought her knee up into the groin of Hans, allowing her to slip through his grasp as he half went to the floor. Karl made a grab for her, but the alcohol he had consumed had affected his coordination. If he'd managed to grab the strap of her rucksack, this would have all been over. The Germans cursed at her as she fled out of reach of their fingers.

"Bitch," Karl shouted. He came after her, but he was slow and lumbering. Hans just knelt on the ground, head turned to watch the pursuit, agony still spreading through his lower body. Natalie had clearly delivered a killer blow and glancing back, she realised there was a good chance she was going to make it.

She hit the main door running. A small voice was telling her she had missed something vital, but it was only when she saw the small keyhole at the top and bottom of the door that she realised the trouble she was now in. Turning, she put her back to the warm glass, knowing it was too thick for her to try and break. Karl was walking slowly towards her now, a stern look on his face. Hans gingerly picked himself up off the floor, an evil smile spreading across his thin lips. Neither of them would be taken by surprise like that again.

"Why are you not being nice to us?" Karl demanded. "We weren't going to hurt you. We are just going to have a little fun." He stopped just out of arms reach from her. "But you hurt my friend and now you must be punished." Reaching behind him, Karl pulled out a flick knife. Natalie didn't wonder where he got such a weapon, every night she had witnessed dozens of stalls selling worse than that in streets all across the city.

"Just leave me alone," Natalie begged.

"No. It is, how they say, the end of the world. All that's left is to drink and be merry."

There was a movement in the corner of Natalie's eye, a blur and she looked over to her right, Karl suspiciously following her eyes. Like a force of nature, the zombified body of the security guard came crashing out from the hotel's reception area, storming towards Hans. The German was too slow to react, and the zombie bundled the big German to the floor, snarling teeth biting whatever they could get to, its fingers wrapping themselves up in Hans's dreadlocked hair. The zombie took an ear as it easily overpowered Hans who was significantly larger than his attacker.

"Get off him," Karl roared. All interest in Natalie was lost, and he charged the zombie who didn't pay a blind bit of notice. Not until Karl grabbed the zombie by the shoulder. Without even turning its head, the zombie freed one of its hand and smashed Karl in a sideways swipe. The stocky German fell to the floor hard but scrabbled back to his drunken feet. He still held the knife and with it he lunged fruitlessly at the zombie. Natalie didn't see what happened next because Karl was blocking her view. She didn't see Karl push down on the back of the zombie's head, pushing its face into Hans's shoulder, which received a howl of pain from the teeth that were already embedded there. She didn't see the knife get slipped into the base of the skull. Natalie saw the zombie go limp and knowing the undead's intervention would only give her a limited amount of breathing time, she reached into her rucksack. She had brought the gin bottle because at the time it had seemed the right thing to do. It took her eight paces to reach the intertwined trio.

When it came crashing down on the skull of Karl, he went limp as consciousness left his body. Falling sideways, he flopped off the now truly dead zombie, landing face up next to his dying friend.

Natalie stepped over, noticed the blood pouring through Hans's desperately placed hand, witnessed the look of utter panic in his eyes. She also saw the keychain on the back of the guard's belt. Unclipping it, she gave Hans one last pitying look and spat defiantly in his face.

"Fuck you," she roared. "I hope you die and eat your friend's cock." She still possessed the rucksack, and the keys allowed her to escape the prison the hotel had become.

In the distance, a car alarm blared, but with the exception of the wind that was still picking up, no other sounds seemed to meet her. It took her a few moments to orientate her position on the map, and with the desire for safety burning through her body, she started to walk. Natalie believed that, with luck, it would take her at least two hours to reach the US consulate. Unfortunately, the universe had other plans.

Unseen, the undead child with one shoe crawled out through the shattered window of the abandoned foot massage parlour. It watched Natalie as its meal hugged the shadows. Even with its injured leg and missing arm, it began to stalk its prey, the saliva pouring from its mouth at the prospect of the meal it was about to indulge in. The wind wafted the odour of flesh to it, and the remnants in its mind became agitated with the coming excitement.

Natalie never saw the child until it was too late and she never had a chance to fight off the creature that was a third her size. Perhaps she should have stayed in the hotel after all.

21.08.19
Tristan da Cunha Island, Atlantic

The Four. Mother, Father, Brother, Uncle. Only Mother was absent now, choosing not to join the hierarchy of Gaia at the recently, and somewhat hastily, constructed base deep into the side of the volcano on Tristan da Cunha Island. In truth, Mother wasn't even aware the base existed having never been told.

It was perhaps better that Mother was not here. Even though she was the founder of their organisation, its ideals had moved passed her naivety, the three men that joined her at the top of the hierarchy certain that the creation of Lazarus was the ultimate weapon to combat the scourge that threatened the very planet they all lived on. With its accidental release, they had perhaps been gifted with the outcome they had planned for years to bring about. Too early perhaps, and too out of their control, but things were happening better than any of them could have hoped. They didn't know how wrong they were.

Humanity was a disease, and Lazarus was to be a cure. Even though it had escaped long before it had been perfected, the Three, as they were now known, assured themselves that it was all for the greater good of mankind. This base that they had constructed out of sight of the island locals would be their hideout whilst the world around them burned. They could stay here with their families and their most trusted acolytes for years if need be, the subterranean structure filled with food water and fuel.

Powered by generators and the ever-present Atlantic winds, they could survive whilst the bulk of humanity died. Then they would rise to take up the dominance of man, guiding whatever was left to create a self-balancing society that was at one with nature. No more hunger, no more inequality, no more bigotry or war. Just total ecological harmony with a planet that had been on the brink of destruction.

That they didn't really know what would happen with Lazarus long term seemed to be actively ignored. They had all been vaccinated against it, a cure they would share with the worthy and those who showed merit come the new world. This was the same vaccine that had been shared with a select few of their agents across the world, many of them ex-Soviet sleeper agents who had infiltrated many aspects of Western government, although Britain and parts of Europe had been all but stripped clean of them by the relentless actions of MI13. Then there were the assassins, Azrael, Gabriel, Lilith, just names to represent lives that had been moulded, shaped and manipulated to do the will of powerful men who cared not for the welfare of those who sacrificed so much.

There was one pressing problem that they were now free to correct. Their base was heavily defended and as close to impregnable as one could make such a facility. Against laser-guided bombs and heavy ground assault, it would definitely fall. But nothing like that was envisaged, the very presence of the Gaia headquarters a secret to the nations of the Earth. Just getting to the island would have been struggle enough. The problem that needed addressing was the island's population. Two hundred and fifty strong, they were an irritation that needed to finally be dealt with. The solution was simple, and just as with

Beijing, they would use drones. Only this time it wouldn't be Lazarus that would be seeded into the air.

Henry Carpenter had been born on the island and had grown up knowing only island life. His schooling had been adequate, and it had been a natural thing for him to follow his father into the fields. The locals called it Utopia, outsiders never allowed to settle or buy land on the island. Despite that, everyone remembered the fateful day the huge ship had moored unannounced offshore, carrying helicopters that descended on a remote part of the island. Those who lived in the community with Henry had been outraged, especially when the smaller boats had started unloading men and machinery totally against the express wishes of the people who were supposed to have a say about who did and didn't live on Tristan da Cunha. The voices of complaint were pointless though because it soon became common knowledge that the construction had been given Royal authority by the Governor of St Helena. Protests did nothing to stop the newcomers. It was just a research station they were told, well away from any arable land and would be no burden on the people or the ecosystem of the island and the seas around it. *Don't worry, the station will only be used intermittently.* When the construction crews left and the huge ships stopped coming, the islanders began to relax.

As Chief Islander, Henry was still upset by the imposition. They had made a formal protest to the Crown, which had been acknowledged and basically ignored, greased palms and secret money transfers back at Westminster responsible for allowing Gaia to go about its business.

With the facility seemingly abandoned and locked up tight behind wire fences and razor wire, it slowly slipped from the minds of the Islanders. Until the night before last that was, when the sound of planes descending became unmistakeable over the placid quiet of the island. Four planes had landed in total at the short runway that had been built as part of the research station, and none of them had seemingly left. People had arrived, and not the tourists that were tolerated due to the cash they brought into the island economy.

Villagers had gone out to the facility, a hard trek over volcanic rock in the ripping wind of the Atlantic. As during the construction, the soldiers were back, only this time they reacted with hostility rather than the polite dismissiveness that had been previously experienced. Several of those who ventured out to see just what the hell was going on never came back to the village, tales of snipers and land mines brought back by the few who survived. When Harry had tried to contact the authorities on St Helena, he learned that the UK government had fallen and that the world was at war with the dead.

Rumour began to speculate as to what the facility was really for. Some wanted to raise an expedition to storm it, but calmer minds patiently outlined how foolish such an action would be. Whoever they were they were heavily armed, dug in deep and prepared to use lethal force as a primary measure. Better to just leave them to their own devices, the stories of the zombie apocalypse seeming to grow to overtake the interlopers when it came to what the Islanders talked to each other about.

It enraged Harry, however, his wife noticing how his mood had shifted and how poorly he slept. Lying in his bed, his wife asleep by his side, he listened to the ocean, the human population mainly still and asleep. It wasn't right that people should be able to do this, there was still a thing as the rule of law. The thing was, he wasn't really sure what he expected from those who held the reins of power. The islanders prided themselves on their independence and their ability to keep the island for themselves, and that pride had been defiled. Was it unreasonable then for him to expect the British Crown to send armed men to deal with the invaders? No direct threat had been made on the village, those who had been killed choosing to walk past numerous signs that stated they were entering private land and that lethal force had been authorised.

Something had to be done though. Harry just didn't know what that something was, and that enraged him even more because as island leader, people were looking to him to fix this.

Sometimes when you lie awake at night, an irritating noise can seemingly come out of nowhere. Be it the drip of a leaky tap, or the nearby beat of a neighbour playing their music too loud, the presence of the sound can seem like a subtle kind of torture. Such a sound reached Harry's ears now, and as it grew louder he found he couldn't determine what it was. It had a high pitched quality that was alien to him. Nobody on the island had ever seen a drone before, so what he was listening to was out of his experience. It wouldn't be an irritant for long though.

There were four drones in total, all running on pre-set paths. This was the ideal hour for such a thing to be done because the majority of the people would be in one place rather than scattered out across the fields and out at sea fishing. Each had a canister slung beneath it that began to release a fine mist low over the village. The wind would pick up the fine particles, blowing them into every nook and every cranny. Through open windows, chimneys, the deployed agent would contaminate everything in the small community. Every external surface would witness its wonder, and wherever it could get ingress into people's homes, it brought its gift with it.

Substance 33.

At the fall of the Soviet Union, Mother had gained much of the wealth she used to finance the early days of Gaia by acting as an intermediary between high ranking Russian military officers and a smattering of international arms dealers. With warehouses full of a mind-boggling array of weapons, and empty bank accounts due to the failure of the new fledgeling Russian State to actually pay anyone, many of those with the rank of Colonel and above found themselves becoming very rich. Some of those stockpiles however, Mother purchased for herself, locking it away for when it might come in handy. Substance 33, similar but considered deadlier to the American made VX, was one such stockpile. Now here it was, decades later, being sprayed on the unsuspecting islanders.

Despite the cold Atlantic night, Harry often liked to sleep with his window open, deeming fresh air essential for health. A gust moved the curtain slightly, the nerve agent circulating around the room, minuscule droplets landing on his face, a lethal dose inhaled by his lungs. Perhaps it was only fitting, as leader of the island, that Harry would be the first to die. It started with a tightening in his chest, which worsened as he found it difficult to breathe. As the symptoms brought distress, such concern was only made worse by further symptoms, shooting pains ripping through his abdomen, nausea building. Wrenching himself from his bed, he turned to see his wife writhing in her sleep, not yet woken by the promise of death that was descending on her.

About a third of the islanders would die that night, the rest contaminating themselves when they left their homes the next morning. By the time the "survivors" started to discover the bodies, many of them found they were sweating profusely, eyes watering as the body did what it could to wash the poison from itself. Twenty-four hours after the nerve agent had been sprayed, there was not a single soul left in the village, pets and livestock also joining the fate of their masters. And there the nerve agent would lie, a constant threat to anyone who should choose to enter the village, the men and women of Gaia safe within their walled and fortified compound.

The island was now theirs. Now all Gaia had to do was wait and let time play its wretched hand.

21.09.18
Hounslow, UK

The undead had come at them in waves, spread out to limit the impact of the ordnance that was being laid into them. Whittaker had seen so many of them weather a barrage of bullets only to just keep on coming. Hundreds if not thousands came at the last defenders of Hounslow.

He wasn't on the roof any more, the ground floor defensive line being broken by the fourth wave. One last glimpse over the edge of the roof had shown his fellow soldiers engaging in hand to hand combat, only to be engulfed by a force that seemingly couldn't be stopped. It was a sight he would never forget. The decision had been made to abandon the roof and flee the building.

Sergeant Wallace was ahead of him, the rest of his section behind. They moved with purpose through the building's interior, having reached the ground floor without any kind of resistance. The sound of violence filled the air around them, the sheer weight of the zombie's numbers too much for the soldiers that in hindsight had foolishly been deployed. Whittaker didn't know it, but the losses here would be a valuable lesson for the generals who were monitoring developments via the satellites in the air. Even Major Pickering was unaware that he and his men had been initially sent in to contain the problem, only for the overall mission brief to change. As they fought for their lives, the soldiers on the ground didn't realise they were being used as pawns to truly understand the capabilities of the undead.

Those watching learned a lot that day. It was just a shame that the virus was worming its way through what was left of the military's high command.

Gunfire could be heard further down the corridor, and Whittaker turned a corner to see fellow soldiers retreating towards him. He recognised the red cropped hair of Major Pickering who was firing his service revolver. With the narrowness of the corridor, the Major and his two MP's were managing to keep the undead at bay, their slow retreat towards Whittaker's position painful to watch.

"Take three of your men out the front entrance, and cover the retreat," Wallace ordered Whittaker over the chaos. "The rest of us will save the Major." The stinging smell of cordite filled the air, mingled with blood and the corruption of the dead. Whittaker nodded and picked three men, Tod one of them. They ran off to secure the front entrance, where armoured personnel carriers hopefully waited.

Wallace came up behind Pickering, the men with him taking up the fight against the undead who were coming down the corridor three abreast. Most of the shots didn't end their progress, but many of them fell from leg wounds as well as the impact from the bullets. It meant that the rest of the undead army had to try and climb over the downed bodies of their necrotic comrades.

"Sergeant, you're bleeding," Pickering shouted over the ruckus. The Major pointed, and Wallace wiped blood away from his mouth.

"Think I might have a dose, Major," Wallace replied, suddenly being racked by another cough. He spat on the ground, the blood invisible on the darkened floor, most of the lighting in the corridor destroyed in the firefight. "Front entrance is being secured sir," Wallace added. "Go now so I can hold them whilst I'm still able." Pickering looked at the Sergeant, realising what he was trying to say. Pickering nodded and left Sergeant Wallace to hold the defensive position. The MP's went with him, only a cursed order forcing the rest of Whittaker's section to do likewise.

"Get the fuck out of here lads. Some of us have to get out of this."

Fortunately for Whittaker, there were no zombies present at the front of the building. Two tracked armoured personnel carriers stood motionless several meters away from where he stood, and he ordered two men to get the vehicles ready. There were dozens of soldiers here, some firing off towards the main road, others retreating from where their positions had been overrun. The rest of the men with him spread out, ready for whatever might descend upon them, their position secure for the moment.

Whittaker couldn't believe how quickly everything had fallen apart. He had hoped the firebombing would have cut the undead numbers down considerably, but there had been thousands engaged in the subsequent attack. The new enemy ran with a ferocity and a speed that was beyond his comprehension. It was as if the virus had taken the human body and moulded it purely for battle. Whittaker didn't understand that this was exactly what the virus had been designed to do.

There was a rumble to his left, and the Warrior fighting vehicle that had been defending the rear of the Civic Centre came into view. It was swarming with undead, many clinging to the sides and riding on top. Some were tearing at the camouflage netting that covered the front of it, others attacking the portals to try and gain entry. The men inside were safe from attack, but until the threat outside was removed, they wouldn't be able to exit the vehicle.

The Warrior went over a steep curve, the sudden jolt sending two zombies flying off the back. They landed and rolled easily, quickly getting back to their feet so as to renew their pursuit of the vehicle which was so tantalising to them.

It was about fifty metres from where Whittaker stood, and he looked in horror as a further swarm of undead rounded the same corner.

"Where the hell is the Major? We need to go, we need to go now."

"I see him, Corporal," one of his men shouted from the Civic Centre entrance. Moments later, Pickering and the rest of his entourage came barrelling out of the building. Whittaker noticed that Wallace wasn't with them.

***

With every shot Wallace managed to expend, the undead seemed to be getting closer. Despite the barrier their bodies made, those that followed seemed more than able to climb over, even if they were clumsy in their motion. To make matters worse, the cough that Wallace had was getting worse making it difficult for him to fight. Twice now he had actually had to stop firing while he expelled whatever substance his lungs were producing. That was where the blood was coming from, a constant flow now beginning to reside in his mouth.

"*You don't have to do this anymore.*" The voice came from inside his head, but even so, he looked around, before firing off another half a magazine. The bullets flew from his L85A3, his left hand caressing the underslung grenade launcher. He was going to use that as a last resort after the rounds he was firing were depleted.

"*Stop it and just give up.*" The voice again, insistent and getting louder. Through the haze of battle, it cut through the noise and made its presence heard. He recognised the voice now...it was his own. His one mind was rebelling against itself.

He emptied another magazine, seven bullets needed to down just one zombie. Wallace didn't know it, but the undead were pushing at the bodies blocking their way now, trying to free up the path, those trapped behind eager to get past, the logjam unacceptable. The obstruction was only thigh high, but it was enough to slow their progression down to Wallace's advantage. In the brief respite, a severely damaged zombie crawled over the barrier of corpses, pulling itself along with bloodied hands. As it propelled itself along the ground, one shattered leg trailing behind, it gave Wallace the perfect target.

"*DON'T!*" the voice insisted, and the Sergeant even paused, his hands trembling with the fever that was now rushing at him. An hour ago he had felt pretty rough, but nothing like this. It was almost as if being in proximity to the undead sped up the progression of the virus through his system. He slammed another magazine home and shot the zombie in the top of the head. Was it possible to kill what was already dead? Whatever the result, the thing stopped moving.

"*There is no point to this,*" the voice persisted. "*Why don't you just accept what you have become.*" He was fading fast, he could feel it. As healthy as he had been, that was actually working against him now, his immune system going into a cytokine storm. Another zombie leapt over its downed companions, and with his wavering aim, Whittaker took five shots to bring it down. His hands were shaking now, the intricate processes that kept his body going rapidly unravelling.

Time seemed to slow, the enemy almost moving in a frozen snippet of time. He could see everything with increased clarity, sweat now dripping off his forehead in a river. Wallace was well aware he was sacrificing himself, and he revelled in the moment despite the illness that was coursing through him. In the quiet moments when he would lie awake at night, he would sometimes think about going out in a hero's death, facing ridiculous odds. In those moments, that fate seemed so compelling, so enticing. Now here he was, fulfilling what his heart had wished for so many times. He could almost taste exactly how death would be, a curious desire that couldn't be shaken.

He knew his time left on this planet could be measured in minutes now.

The magazine ran dry, and his hands scrambled for the last one, ripping it from the pouch on his webbing. The trembling in his fingers caused him to almost drop it.

"*Seriously. And what happens when you fire your last bullet?*" The voice was almost mocking him now, getting stronger, Wallace feeling the pull as it stripped his resistance. It wouldn't be long now before the voice BECAME him, filling his mind with its siren song. He had no way of knowing the words he heard were just a form of auditory hallucination, a mechanism for the virus to break his will, to make him compliant.

"Fuck you," he demanded, suppressing a cough that threatened to completely engulf him. Two zombies vaulted the wall, one slipping on bodily fluids, the smooth corridor floor now a complete health and safety hazard. The other came at him, and then the cough hit, some of his shots going wide. It was more luck than aim that his third bullet entered under the zombie's chin, destroying everything that was keeping it moving.

Tears filled his eyes, and with brain splitting agony, he fought through the torture in his lungs and finished the second zombie off as it thrashed about on the floor.

"*Sleep now. Just lie back.*"

"Shut the fuck up," Wallace roared. Now out of bullets, he fired the grenade down the corridor and watched, mesmerised, as it sailed between four approaching zombies before hitting a fifth square in the chest. The explosion rocked through the corridor, flinging Wallace backwards from his kneeling position, his back hitting the wall behind him. Something inside him seemed to break, he actually felt it. His gun lay discarded and useless on the floor well out of reach.

Dazed, he lay sat against the wall, smoke filling his lungs, making him retch. Taking him completely by surprise, he threw up in his mouth, the vomit dribbling down his chin to further stain his already heavily soiled army fatigues. Part of the ceiling in the explosion damaged corridor came down, a burst pipe spraying water onto the zombies as they picked themselves up from the shockwave that had engulfed them. Most were missing limbs, several didn't get up due to their heads being detached from their bodies.

"*Are you done?*"

"Never," he managed to insist, more vomit coming from his stomach. He suddenly found it difficult to breathe, as if his chest was being compressed under a terrible weight. Tension pneumothorax, the words floated into his mind, a memory of his combat first aid training. Most likely a result of the concussion waves from the grenade and the trauma already being wrought on them by Lazarus. Without urgent medical intervention he was done for...but then he was done for anyway.

That was when his vision gave out, the endorphins now flooding his system, a great feeling of peace filling his mind despite the horror he was experiencing. The very end was often blissful for some infected with Lazarus, and all insight into the world around him dissipated. Wallace no longer cared that there were zombies all around him, and they ceased to care about him. No longer hindered by his dogged defence, dozens of zombies began to file past, his virus infected body no longer a threat to them. They would leave him untouched so that he could join their ranks, his meat by now of little interest. Like so many before him, those in the latter stages of the infection were rarely of interest to the undead. They preferred not to eat their own.

Wallace almost gave in, almost let the voice inside become him in his final moments. But even though the chemicals of his body did everything they could to calm him for what he was to become, resistance persisted there. It was the sheer stubbornness of his character that won the day. As if in a dream world, his right hand drifted down to the Glock 17, pulling it from its holster. One of the zombies passing him paused, detecting the threat the gun posed, but when no shots came, it carried on regardless.

The gun was heavy in his hand, metal cold against his hot flesh. It felt as if it was somehow magnetised to the floor. It took everything he had to just raise it, the muzzle placed casually under his chin, his body swimming in pleasure. Why was he denying himself?

"No need for that mate. Just drop it and enjoy the ride."

Wallace didn't listen to the voice, realising it for the siren song it truly was. He would not become one of those things, the determination suddenly rushing back into his consciousness. The fog began to clear, and as the lungs finally gave up in their attempt to inflate, he fired a single shot right into the base of his own brain. In a moment, all that he was ended. No more pain, no more anguish. No more dark images and flashbacks to the horrific things he had done in his life.

The last thought to hit him was the futility of it all, and then his mind was gone, destroyed enough so as to be useless to the virus that craved it. Now nothing more than dead meat, several of the passing fiends diverted from their original goal. Kneeling down, four zombies began to rip at the clothes that covered their new meal, the virus rapidly dying away in the body now useless to it. Wallace's body became tasty again. Might as well let the boys feast. No point letting perfectly good flesh go to waste.

Ripe pickings.

Whittaker sat silently in the back of the APC. His whole section was with him, the Major in another vehicle. Except for Tod. Where the hell was Tod? They could hear the undead clamouring on top, trying to rip their way inside, but even their strength was no match for armour plated steel. They were safe, but only so long as they stayed inside the cramped confines of the armoured transport.

Nobody spoke because there wasn't anything that needed to be said. They had been beaten, and had lost dozens of good men in the process. Outside, Whittaker could hear machine gun fire and wondered if it was helicopters covering their retreat. He wasn't in a position to see out of the vehicle, and had to hope the guy driving knew how to handle the metallic beast.

How could this have happened? How could they have been so thoroughly trounced? Their enemy didn't come with tanks and bombs, but merely with the remnants of the human body that the virus crafted for its own ends. And by abandoning their position, they had condemned the people of Hounslow to a horrific death. A quarter of a million people utterly defenceless against the viral menace, many of them probably already turned. Likely there were scenes like this playing across London, across the whole country, cities rapidly falling to a foe that attacked without mercy and which was relentless in its ferocity.

Worse was the fact that even now, the virus was burning through the population where the zombies had yet to manifest. Whittaker looked around the interior of the cabin and wondered who here was infected. He had seen first-hand how the strongest of them, Sergeant Wallace, had fallen to Lazarus. What hope did any of them have? Any prospect that they could survive this abandoned him to be replaced by despair, a great weight bearing down on his shoulders.

And then out of nowhere that familiar sensation formed in his sinuses, and he caught the sneeze in his gloved hands. Every man with him turned their heads, their eyes filled with a fear only a soldier could understand. He sneezed again, and he realised there was no real chance for any of them.

12.08.13

Top Secret

From: Klaus Gruber, Psychiatric division
To: Sir Nicholas Osmond, Head of Directorate of Military Intelligence 13
Re: Psychological analysis of candidate Major Nicholas Carter

After thorough analyses of the test subject, I am happy to recommend Major Nicholas Charles Carter for recruitment into the field ranks of MI13. Service record aside, he has many of the qualities that are required for work under the agency's remit and has the emotional temperament to carry out any and all tasks that such a posting would demand. An in-depth analyses of the Major's psychological profile can be seen in the attached video files, but this document acts as a summary.

- The Major displays a disdain for romantic attraction without showing any tendency to sexual deviancy. There will be little or no likelihood of him falling victim to third-party seduction and blackmail.
- The Major shows the prerequisite respect for authority and a love of country bordering on pathological patriotism. It is this clinician's opinion that he would do anything and everything to protect the integrity of The Realm.
- The Major shows a high pain tolerance and an ability to accept suffering as part of his role in the agency. He is one of the few recruits never to break under SAS RTI training and has withstood prolonged pain in combat situations.
- The Major values loyalty and duty as his most important characteristics. He will follow orders, even if he finds them distasteful.
- He is a born leader, but we do not believe he is right for the MI13 command and control structure at this time. His use by MI13 should be initially limited to the field. However, should an event threaten the integrity of MI13 itself, the Major may well be the kind of man needed to combat such a threat.
- It is clear that he will kill, without question or remorse, anyone he deems a threat. At the same time, he lacks the sociopathic tendencies that could make such a trait dangerous.

- There is no sign that he has any predilection to addiction. In fact, there have been multiple occasions where he has refused narcotic pain relief for the injuries he has sustained.
- The Major will complete his mission or die in the attempt.

I therefore recommend that Major Carter be enrolled in the ranks of MI13, as per my remit under Regulation 7(4)a of the relevant legislation. It is also recommended he be advanced in rank.

Professor Klaus Gruber, OBE, PhD, FRCPsych, MBChB

22.08.19
Preston, UK

They had left him in chains, his limbs manacled together so as to restrict his movements. Not that there was anywhere he could run to without the restraints, the thick steel cell door and concrete walls saw to that. Even if he could escape the cell and his bonds, there were dozens of armed soldiers in the buildings around him. Then there were the fences and the watchtowers. Escape was thus a hopeless pipe dream, an idea he had already abandoned.

This did not bother him because the only place he now desired to be was here, close to the woman called Jessica. The stranger who he could not remember meeting and yet who he knew more intimately than himself. Just in their brief conversation, she had already unlocked memories that were both haunting and revelatory. Azrael was well aware he was more than willing to die, any purpose for his existence now gone. All that he asked was that she help him unlock the secrets of who he actually was first. When they eventually put a bullet through his skull, he at least wanted to know the true extent of his crimes. Under the truth drug that had been administered to him, the one called Natasha had asked him what he truly feared to which he had answered: "Discovering who I really am."

Azrael found he no longer held that fear. Seeing Jessica had unlocked something in him. The truth about himself was now everything he craved.

His sleep had been eerily peaceful. Again, the nightmares had failed to descend upon his helpless mind, any dreams he had experienced forgotten the moment his eyes opened. Part of him felt there was a reason the terrors of the horsemen had not defiled his slumber, but the answer to that riddle eluded him. He suspected it would come eventually, along with the other disclosures that were brewing in his churning consciousness. Azrael, so familiar with the night terrors had forgotten that they had not been with him every night, intermittent in their nature. As horrendous and vivid as the sleeping visions were, he found he kind of missed them. They were familiar to him.

He needn't have worried, they would return.

Azrael sat on the bed of his cell, the cuffs around his wrists already starting to chafe. They were tighter than they needed to be, but compared to what the MI13 agents had already inflicted upon his aching body, the discomfort was almost a luxury. The torture was over now and there was little in the way of hardship to be found for him here. Despite the deficiencies of the standard issue army cot, it was actually too comfortable for him. As for what else had been done to him, there would be no more of that. There would be no more interrogation and torture, for anything he knew he would share willingly. Azrael had realised this as soon as they had transferred him from the secluded house. If he was honest with himself, a part of him was saddened by this. The more he learnt about himself, the more broken and depraved he realised he was. Normal people did not relish the slaughter of strangers. Normal people did not kill their own children. Azrael knew he was guilty, worthy of whatever punishments were deemed appropriate. He deserved to pay some sort of penance and strangely craved the opportunity to suffer for his sins.

Ever since he had been reborn, he realised he had always known the two children he had killed in the house of blood had been his own offspring. He had denied it to himself for years, casting the thought away into the deepest recesses of his mind, but the knowledge had always lurked there, merely waiting. He had effectively been lying to himself ever since Mother had created the man that he was.

A mindless killing machine devoid of passion or mercy.

Despite the knowledge of what he had done, there was no remorse within him. The children were just two bodies in a whole list of humanity that had died by his hands. He had no memory of raising them, of watching them walk and talk for the first time. The development of their young minds was a mystery to him, as were the fears that had stalked their tiny minds. Their faces were just phantoms intermingled with the audience of carnage that he had gathered. The dead were simply that. It mattered not that some of them were his own flesh and blood. With what was facing the world, perhaps killing them had been the ultimate mercy.

There was nobody outside the cell, one of several in the barrack's prison building. All the other cells were empty, and no guards were posted because none were needed. Every able man and woman was now involved in the fight against an enemy that struck without mercy. These walls, normally containing drunken and miscreant squaddies, had likely never encased such evil as they did now. That evil was diminished, however, Azrael slowly realising the lies that had been told to him. There was a bubbling resentment in the way he had been manipulated by Mother. She had somehow created him, but not for the purposes she originally claimed. To ask him to kill Jessica? How could she do that? Justice demanded there should be a reckoning there, but Azrael knew Mother was far outside his reach. She would be dead soon anyway, old age reaping its untimely reward on her sagging flesh.

Out of his sight, a door opened. Footsteps, forceful, measured. A man of focus and training was coming. An equal in skill and brutality. Azrael knew before he saw him that his visitor was Colonel Nick Carter. The hatch in the door flew open and Azrael saw that his captor looked solemn, as if he had the weight of a thousand worlds on his shoulders. The door creaked as it was opened.

"Comfortable?" Nick asked. He was wearing an army NBC suit minus the helmet and gas mask. Nuclear, Biological, Chemical, the only thing that could hopefully protect him against the invisible virus that could be residing in anyone, anywhere. With red eyes depicting a lack of sleep, Nick peered through the open door, keeping a wary eye on his captive. Azrael noticed the caution in the man, the apparent respect that Nick held for his captive. It wasn't fear he saw in those eyes. Men like Carter had no fear left in them.

"This is luxury to what I'm used to," Azrael confirmed.

"Yes, I've seen pictures of your London residence," Nick informed his prisoner. An assault team had raided the address Azrael had freely given the day before. They had found nothing that could lead them to the woman known only as Mother, or to the organisation she worked for. Despite giving the address up freely, Azrael suddenly found that he felt violated by the intrusion into his sacred domain. "Jessica has agreed to speak to you again. But we are going to need something more from you this time."

"Anything," Azrael almost begged.

"You haven't heard what it is yet."

"I'm already on a death sentence, I know that. You've already tortured me with an efficiency and skill even I am impressed with. There's nothing more I really could object to."

"You might be surprised," Nick countered. "Colonel Smith thinks he might be close to perfecting an antiserum from Jessica's blood, but he will need someone to test it out on."

"That someone being me?"

"Yep," Nick nodded. "It will mean exposing you to the virus, which means your next conversation with Jessica may be your last."

"Why are you even asking?" Azrael was genuinely surprised. "There is nothing to stop you doing this to me anyway."

"True, but I think you have the right to at least know what is going to be done to you. With or without your consent, these tests will be performed on you. It would just sit better with me if you gave your permission."

"Then you have it," Azrael replied. It was only a matter of time before the virus ravaging the world killed him anyway. "I have nothing to lose."

"Thanks." Nick turned and made to walk away.

"How bad is it out there?" Azrael enquired.

"Bad." With that, Nick stepped back into the corridor. "Time to go Azrael, we are ready for you now". Before Azrael could stand, Nick was already putting the gas mask on. Azrael wasn't a viral threat, but there was no telling what threats waited in the cool August air.

People often forget the blessed moments that are around them every second of every day. Not Azrael, he savoured everything he could now. When you knew you might soon be facing death, you cherished what little there was left of life. Walking into the open air, Azrael stopped briefly and took a deep inhale. The breath coursed into his lungs, fresh and invigorating when compared to the stale air of his cell. Normally he preferred the cold, the dark and the grime, but not at this moment. Right now, he craved the sensation of life.

"Get your arse in gear," Nick's muffled voice said behind him. Four soldiers strolled passed, all similarly dressed as the MI13 man. The only difference would be the rank and name that was handwritten on a front panel on their suits. They gave Azrael a curious glance, the assassin's reputation now a story for the squaddies to tell each other, a distraction from the terrors that they would need to face out on the city streets and in their hearts. The rank and file of the army personnel didn't really understand who these newcomers were, nor did they comprehend why Nick and his team seemed to have free reign to wander throughout the garrison. Their commanding officer had not hidden his hesitation and irritation at the presence of the MI13 team, and yet the man who ran it all showed these people supreme deference. The orders had clearly come right from the very top.

That told the soldiers volumes. Nick and his team were people to be respected...and perhaps feared.

Azrael moved forward, his naked feet cold against the paved ground. He didn't react to the chill in the air, despite the thin paper-like boiler suit he wore. It was difficult for him to move in anything but a shuffle, the chain binding his ankles too short to move with a healthier stride. It was a ridiculous form of motion, there for the protection of anyone he might choose to attack. Even without the chains though, Azrael wouldn't have tried anything. He might have been able to overpower the likes of Nick, but only through luck. It wouldn't have been any different if he had held one of his precious blades. With a knife he was anyone's match in hand to hand combat. But then Nick and his team all carried guns.

The only thing Azrael could do was what his captors told him to. Virtually the entirety of his newly formed life had been spent following the orders of other people, so why should now be any different?

It was a short walk to where he was being taken. Two more men stood waiting for him at the entrance, both fully clad in protective clothing. One held the door open for him, the one called Brodie, the man so effective in his torture methods. Azrael had no hate in his heart for the man. In fact, he had nothing but respect for the skill displayed when the secrets in Azrael's mind had been almost effortlessly extracted.

A sign beside the door announced that this building was the barracks infirmary. There would only be a few medical personnel inside at present, the majority of them out in the field where they were needed, or at the hospital helping Dr Patel with his research. This was the same building they had previously brought him to speak to Jessica...how Azrael craved to see her again. If not for her, he likely would have ended his own life rather than be taken alive. Even now he could snuff himself out with barely a thought. Such a thing wasn't hard when you knew how.

Azrael walked through the open door, Nick and his companions making up the rear. Now in a short corridor, Azrael was guided to the room at the far end where an eager Colonel Smith stood waiting for him. Azrael wasn't sure, but he detected a look of malevolence in Smith's face. This was the first time he had encountered the man, and already he could tell there was something not quite right with Smith. As Azrael moved closer, Smith donned a face mask and pulled some rubber gloves out of his pocket before stepping back into the room that would be Azrael's new home. Azrael followed him inside, noticing that his escorts stayed outside close to the door, not encroaching into Smith's domain any further than they had to. It was obvious to Azrael that Smith was infected.

When evil dwelled in your heart, you got rather adept at seeing it in other people. Azrael walked on regardless, passing into a well-lit, substantially sized room which housed a whole host of hospital equipment as well as a hospital bed. Azrael wasn't surprised to see ankle and wrist straps attached to the bed frame. With the limitations of his present restraints, he hopped up onto the bed before anyone told him to. Might as well just get this over with.

The room contained a long observation window. He recognised it now, this was the room they had kept Jessica in. Was she now free to wander?

"I assume I can trust you not to try any bullshit," Smith said warily. "Carter has told me what you are capable of."

"I won't give you any trouble," Azrael insisted and held up his wrists to be unshackled. Smith produced a key and worked the manacles off him, only to then re-restrain Azrael to the bed. The captive did as he promised, lying back and freely allowing himself to be strapped down.

"The straps aren't to just stop you going anywhere. We have no idea how your body will react to the antiserum. Unfortunately, we haven't had time to do any trials on it. They are thus just as much for your own protection. We don't want you hurting yourself." Azrael saw through the lies flowing from Smith's mouth.

"That may be true, but be honest. Part of you is relishing what you are about to do." Azrael kept any hint of mischief out of his voice. He was merely stating exactly what he detected in the soldier.

"Don't be absurd," Smith admonished him.

"You need to work on your poker face," Azrael said with a smile. In the corner of his eye, Azrael saw Nick give the Colonel a wary glance. *Yes Nick*, thought Azrael, *you need to watch this one for his heart is like mine.* There was definitely an air of menace around Smith. He was clearly ill as well, his face pale and covered in a sheen of dripping sweat. Occasionally the man would pause as waves of dizziness washed over him.

"Just keep your mouth shut, killer," Smith ordered. Azrael felt cold on his arm and he looked down to see the disinfectant swab being run across his flesh. How strange to be worried about an infection when you were about to inject an untested formulation into someone's bloodstream. And then there came the needle. Smith had no problem finding a vein, not with Azrael's athletic physique. Before he injected though, Smith connected him up to the various machines scattered around the bed. The pulse oximeter went on his finger. Without any concern for Azrael's dignity, Smith cut away at the boiler suit over his chest so he could access the skin there for the placement of the ECG tabs.

"Does this mean we're engaged?"

"I said shut your mouth," Smith said coldly. He turned to Nick. "You can leave now, I've got this."

"I don't think so," Nick answered.

"I said I've got this."

"Yeah, I heard what you said. But try not to forget I don't take orders from you. I've agreed to let you use my prisoner for your little experiment, but please remember he is still under my jurisdiction. This is not a man I want out of my sight unless he's locked up." Smith seethed below his skin. Who the hell did these people think they were? That hadn't been thoroughly explained to him, the existence of MI13 not in his need to know. Smith was thoroughly confused why these men, who clearly weren't in the military, seemed to be running the show. Smith knew they had captured Azrael, but why were they also now in charge of protecting Jessica? Why were they being allowed to walk about as if they owned the bloody place?

The needle was inserted into the vein, and Smith wasn't gentle with it. Even so, he was surprised when Azrael didn't even flinch. Instead, the test subject just looked at him with cold, calculating eyes. Smith was shocked when a subtle wave of fear rippled through his body. Perhaps being unprofessional in his manner with a man such as Azrael wasn't wise, even with the restraints and the armed guards.

"Sorry about that, if that hurt I mean," Smith conceded. "I'm not myself today." Azrael merely shrugged, the warmth of the liquid almost pleasant as it flowed up his arm.

"No need to be. Your doctoring is like a soothing massage compared to what I've recently experienced." Smith chose not to investigate that line of inquiry. Now they just had to wait and see if the antiserum did its thing. At this stage, Smith would merely be happy to know the antiserum didn't kill the patient.

Azrael felt the drug flowing further into his system, the warmth spreading past the arm as the liquid was carried by the bloodstream. There was a prickly sensation that accompanied it, but it was not unpleasant. Behind him, Smith had started talking into a microphone.

"Subject 1 is now receiving the antiserum XV1. No sign of allergic reaction."

"When will I see Jessica again?" Azrael asked Nick.

"When the good doctor here has decided his medicine either works or is a failure."

"How will he know if it works?"

"Because once I've given you the full dose, I will be injecting the virus right into your system," Smith said almost casually. "So you better hope I'm as good a scientist as I think I am." The plan was simple. It had already been determined that the rate of contamination from the precursor virus was different than when passed on through bites, the theory being that the zombie's saliva acted as some sort of catalyst. This had been confirmed by animal testing on the first of the zombies acquired from those captured at Wythenshawe Hospital. The sample that would be used on Azrael would be the virus mixed up with collected undead saliva, little concern being given for the presence of other blood borne pathogens. This was desperation, and Azrael was expendable.

22.08.19
Birmingham, UK

Control the food supply and you control the population.

One of the first things the military commanders did was shut down the country's chain of supermarkets, most having the ability to shut up shop behind barriers of roller shutters and steel grills. Many of them had already been picked clean, their shelves stripped of all perishable goods, the canned produce strangely the last things to go. Even when their own survival depended on it, people were still stupid enough to choose bread and milk over something that could be stored for years. Humanity was no longer capable of survival without the luxuries of its technology.

The challenge facing the UK was its "just in time" food distribution network. Already, the chain was breaking down as HGV drivers phoned in sick and the planes bringing in produce were grounded. The country's main ports, now under control by the Royal Navy still accepted the goods that were steaming towards them, but already some container ships had turned around, preferring the safety of the open waters rather than risk their crews contracting contagion. Better to drift out at sea and watch what happened to the world.

The Royal Navy itself had already put all its available ships to sea in the hope of salvaging what they could. It was inevitable that some infected individuals would find their way on board those ships, especially the supply ships that were essential to allow the fleet to stay out of port. Over the coming days, a fifth of the fleet would be lost to the undead.

With the supermarkets closed, the army was initially put in charge of food distribution to a populace that was yet to experience the ravages of hunger. A city as large as Birmingham would have several dispersal points, food ferried to them from the central warehouses under armed convoy. This only took soldiers and officers away from the fight that was already erupting in parts of Birmingham. Thus, some military strategists were already considering the UK population to be an obstacle to containing the rapidly growing rates of infection. Behind closed doors, radical methods of population control were discussed in hushed tones. The undead recruited from the living. Reduce the population and you reduce the army the military would face in the coming conflict. Sacrifice the many to save the select few.

Saner minds won out, the plans for nuclear decimation and nerve agents rejected by the Military's high command. As noble and as humanitarian as such decisions were, they would be seen, in hindsight as the wrong decisions to make. Killing the bulk of the populations in the country's major population centres would have been an horrific act to surpass any of the outrages of humanities past, but it would have saved the country. At that moment in time, the spread of the virus through the UK's rural communities was almost non-existent. Had the voices of slaughter been listened to, a vestige of the UK could have likely been saved allowing the country to rise from the ashes. At least there would have been a chance. Nobody with the authority to make that decision could stomach being responsible for the slaughter that was necessary.

Some countries, like Russia, did take such actions. CIA intelligence reported the mass roundups of anyone who had travelled to the country by air and land in a designated timescale. The forced isolation and detentions also included all people those individuals had day to day interactions with, whole apartment blocks being emptied by soldiers in protective clothing. Once emptied, the buildings were sterilised by fire. At night the flames could be seen scattered across Moscow.

Across Russia, thirty-seven thousand people found themselves locked behind wire fences in what many deemed a return to the old days of Stalin and the Gulags. There was little in the way of revolt in the population, the hard-line seen for what it was…a necessary measure for the protection of the people. Those that did complain just found themselves locked behind the wire with infected individuals. This further silenced any potential dissenting voices. Later the Russian State would take further action, offering financial reward for every dead bird and rat that was brought in for incineration. Russia, North Korea and the Island states of the Pacific were thus able to weather the initial storm well.

The UK, as a liberal democracy, didn't stand a chance.

Somehow, Rashid had missed the fact that the world around him was falling apart. Working hard on his dissertation, he had shut himself away so as to concentrate on the most important thing in his life. So invested was he in his project, that he had rarely even left the house over the past few weeks. For a month straight, he had been trying to get fifteen thousand words to make some sort of sense, and on the morning of the twenty-second, he reckoned he was about there.

Yesterday had needed his entire focus, so even his phone had been switched off, and the landline unplugged. Living alone as he did, he would abide no interruptions for what was then the culmination of his life's ambition. Today, he gave himself the liberty of switching his phone back on, and the world told him that his PhD was now meaningless.

Frantic phone calls. Text messages. A mad search of the online news channels. How had he missed this? How had the zombie apocalypse arrived without him even realising? He had sat in his living room, stunned, unable to comprehend what this all meant. His mother and father insisted he come back home to Pakistan, but it quickly became evident that there were now no flights that anyone could take. Separated from family, and with little in the way of friends to count on, Rashid knew he could only fend for himself. As a Muslim, he had for a while now ignored the callings of his faith, so he didn't even feel that he had the community of the local mosque to call on.

The first act of business was food. He had some, but most of the cupboards in his student flat were bare. The flat was self-contained, two bedrooms with its own kitchen and living room. His family were not poor, and they had been more than happy to fund his living costs whilst in the foreign land. To have a son obtain a doctorate was the prize that his family sought, and Rashid had come so close. Staring at the file on his computer, he cursed the life he had wasted on getting to this point. So many sacrifices, so many opportunities lost just to excel in his chosen field.

And now it was all for nothing. Rashid suddenly felt like a fool, a fool with no skills to survive in the world that no longer needed him. The closest thing to survival gear was a rucksack, so at least he had something to easily carry supplies in should he be able to acquire any.

The streets outside were almost empty, and he walked to the supermarket that was ideally situated for him, a faint breeze caressing the worries as they percolated around inside his head. Ten minutes later, he stood in amazement at the empty car park and the shuttered windows of the building he had visited dozens of times. Walking up to the main entrance, he found a laminated sheet of A4 duct taped to the protective grills. The store was closed, most likely abandoned, the message giving directions to the nearest food distribution site all written down. Someone had even hand drawn a map. Rashid took a picture of it with his phone and saw that, unlike earlier, he now no longer had any kind of reception.

Rashid looked at the drawing, saw the childlike desperation in it. How much food was left in this building? Was he so close to everything he needed only to be denied? The store was big, and he wandered the length of one side, looking to see if there was any way in. Some of the windows weren't protected, their vulnerability showing that all the lights inside were off. Nobody home.

For a moment he contemplated forcing entry, but he knew he couldn't do that. Even with the evidence in front of him that this was likely the end of all things, his own conscience couldn't allow him to commit such a violent act. It was theft, and theft was an evil deed. If he had been hungry, his belly empty for a week or more, things might have been different, survival instincts kicking in to take over the human code of ethics he presently lived by. But he wasn't even close to hunger yet, and although he saw the wisdom in taking what had likely been left to rot, Rashid just wouldn't allow himself to go down that path.

It was then that he heard the truck.

Stood outside the huge building, it finally dawned on him how isolated he was. There were no houses that overlooked where he stood, and what would have been a common day occurrence suddenly sparked a threat warning through his neurons. Who was in the truck? What were they doing here? Caution caused Rashid to back away from the building, and to start making his way towards the car park's pedestrian exit.

The truck came into the car park and headed straight for him. It was a white pickup with an open back. There were two people in the truck's cabin and one riding shotgun. Literally. As the truck got closer, Rashid noticed that the man in the back was actually holding a double-barrelled shotgun. He picked up the pace, but so did the truck, stopping in front of him menacingly. Everything inside Rashid was screaming danger. Here he was, a Pakistani national alone in a car park with three armed white dudes. What on earth could go wrong?

"You're trespassing," the man in the back said. He was lanky with a buzz cut head.

"I'm sorry, I'm just leaving." The driver's window wound down. The driver had a cigarette planted firmly in his mouth, a look of complete disgust etched across his face.

"This isn't the place for you shit head," the driver reiterated.

"You're right, I realise that now. I will get out of your way so you can go about your business."

"Make sure you do," Buzz-cut said, aiming the shotgun at Rashid. "This store is under our protection."

"I understand," Rashid said, starting to move again. "You have my word, I won't come back." The driver revved the engine.

"Better hadn't," the driver ordered. "Your type aren't welcome here." Three sets of eyes watched Rashid as he navigated past the truck. He didn't run, but walked briskly towards the way out, the back of his neck itching where he kept expecting the shotgun blast to hit. Nobody fired, and upon reaching the exit, he turned to see what he had just escaped from. The truck had moved, and two of the men were now attacking one of the rear doors of the supermarket with crowbars. Even if the building was alarmed, Rashid didn't think anyone would bother responding. It would appear that in this land now, might was right.

That had actually been a first. From all his time in the UK, that had actually been the only time he had feared for his safety. He didn't even think there was any racism involved. If he had been a blue-eyed, blonde haired Caucasian, the result would probably have been the same. He was the unknown infringing on someone else's claimed domain.

His options were limited now. The food distribution point wasn't far, just another fifteen-minute walk away, so he made his way there. A car would have been better and safer, but that was a luxury he didn't possess. Hell, he didn't even own a driving licence. Whilst he knew how to drive due to the teachings of an older brother, there was no way he could legally do so in this country. Walking was fine for now, so long as it got him what he wanted.

He saw about a dozen people on his journey, most of them possessing a harassed wariness in their eyes. Some openly carried melee weapons, and Rashid wondered if that was for protection from the undead or to fend off the brutality of humanity that was starting to come to the surface. Perhaps some of those weapons were meant for evil intent, so Rashid kept his distance from everyone he encountered. He also passed by a smaller chain food store, but the front of that had been shattered, another gang piling up food outside. Rashid kept on without drawing attention to himself. Where the hell was law enforcement?

Whilst he had expected people to be at the distribution centre, he hadn't expected so many so soon. People were lined up through a snaking series of metal barriers, intimidating looking soldiers wandering around the peripheries to ensure some sort of order. At the front of the line, five army trucks lay parked, their backs opened. About a dozen soldiers were unloading the truck and handing out bags of food. Joining the back of the queue, Rashid engaged in that very British pursuit. Waiting.

There were murmurings amongst the crowd.

"I bet the army don't have to wait for food."

"This isn't right, why should I wait?"

"They aren't giving much out."

"Why are there so many foreigners here?"

Rashid ignored the people around him, trying to blend in as he moved steadily down the procession of people, wary of being so close to people due to the risks of the virus. Occasionally there would be a commotion at the front of the line, but it always calmed down when guns were raised and threats voiced. This could so very easily turn nasty, the barriers trapping several hundred people into a pre-determined path.

What if he got to the end and they had run out of food? Would the trucks be here tomorrow? And the next day?

Halfway there now, the empty rucksack on his back a surprising irritant to him. It occurred to him that his feet were aching, walking not something he had particularly engaged in for several months. The university campus was an easy bus ride from where he lived, so the use of his legs was pretty limited. Rashid wasn't one to waste his time with something ridiculous like exercise.

He was regretting that sedentary lifestyle now, knowing the trip back was mainly uphill and so potentially arduous. People like him were designed to live in a world of convenience and comfort. He'd never really witnessed hardship, his life one of privilege and excess. It had made him soft and weak of mind and body. His intellect was all but useless when it came to surviving in the world he presently saw around him. His PhD wasn't even in anything useful like engineering or chemistry. It was in fucking theology for pity's sake.

How was he going to fight off a zombie horde by reciting the finer points of Martin Luther's treaties?

The thoughts that had wrapped him up dissolved into the sound of the gunshots that suddenly echoed across the crowd. Stuck in the middle of the human mass, it was difficult to see what was happening. The people around him surged, panic spreading from around them, the volume of their voices converting into screams and roars.

"Contact, we have contact," a voice shouted, cutting through the cacophony. More shots were fired, and Rashid was swept along, his slender frame no match for the fury of the mob. Someone fell behind him, but Rashid did not turn to help, feet stamping down on the felled victim. That was a fate that could so very easily happen to him, hands grasping at his shoulders, people trying to forge their way past. Some tried to climb over the barriers, but that just added to the madness. Rashid was propelled around one corner, then another, his legs moving to try and keep pace with the rush of bodies that was now unstoppable.

From the corner of his eyes, he saw the soldiers jumping onto their trucks, the vehicles starting to pull away. One truck passed by the crowd, only for Rashid to see that it was being chased, the person pursuing running with a strange, jerking motion, her white t-shirt stained with the reddest of blood. More shots and the pursuer jerked as bullets ripped through its torso.

There would be no more food deliveries. Not today, not ever.

Somehow, Rashid found himself free of the crowd, those around him fleeing in all directions. Gunshots still sounded, but they seemed further off, almost not related to this bedlam. Then he saw it, the pile of food that had been unloaded, several people diving into it, filling their arms with whatever they could. He knew what he had to do, but was too hesitant to engage in the full force required, so instead of pushing, he wormed his way between the people, his hands latching onto a precious box of soup sachets. The box was ripped from his fingers by someone stronger and more desperate.

At first, there was resistance, and then he felt those around him melt away, the pile suddenly his for the taking. Kneeling down, he flung the rucksack off his back and started to fill it with his future. Only Rashid really didn't have a future because, oblivious to him, one of the creatures now stood behind him.

He sensed it, he couldn't explain how and his head turned to see the thing just standing there. It didn't even seem to be looking at Rashid, its head cocked to the left slightly as if mesmerised by beautiful music. With his hand around a tin of beans, Rashid slowly stood, his bladder opening as fear totally engulfed him. The switch in his brain that told him how to react went to fright, and his body was half turned towards the zombie when his knees locked into place. His whole being just seemed to freeze.

The zombie, still wearing the hijab of its former owner, took a shaky step forward, a whimper escaping Rashid's lips. Rashid knew to be afraid because the zombie's eyes were totally black, the nose missing from the centre of its face where it had been bitten clean off. The face looked like a skull, the muscles of the mouth retracted to reveal teeth coated in blood and gore.

Predators sometimes hunt by motion, but not the undead. Without warning, it pounced on Rashid, his arm acting by some innate survival mechanism, smashing the can across the zombie's face. It didn't even seem to notice, a fragment of tooth flying off to the side. Powerful hands grabbed Rashid, the fingers digging into his shoulders. He was too fragile to resist, too weak to fight it off, too pathetic to even really try. All he could do was squirm, his arms pretty much held fast, the skeletal face coming closer.

The stench from the creature was unbelievable, and Rashid felt himself retch, his whole world starting to swim. Before he could pass out the broken teeth descended on his vulnerable neck. The violence of the attack was almost as surprising as the fact he was being assaulted by a monster that had returned from the dead. As the assault quickly resulted in life-threatening injuries, Rashid's mind was rapidly swallowed up by the virus that didn't care how intelligent he was. All it needed was for him to walk, run and fight. Released so he could fall to the floor, Rashid lay upon the mound of food he had risked his life for. It would only take him minutes to die.

There would be no more food distribution from this point.

22.08.19
Washington DC, USA

Jessy Whitethorn, the newly made President's Chief of Staff slept the sleep of ages. There were only a limited number of beds in the Whitehouse's Emergency Operations bunker, so she took a small couch in one of the side rooms and made it her own. It was far from ideal because her six-foot frame stretched longer than the seating provided. It was better than nothing, and her body rested for the battle it was presently fighting.

In reality, she hadn't expected to fall asleep, but exhaustion had overpowered her and she had reluctantly succumbed, giving her nose a final blow before putting her tired head down onto the cushion. Whilst she slept, her nasal fluid had run almost freely, the mucous carrying the virus out of her body and onto the soft material that supported her head. Within, there was a secret in her body that the virus had so rarely encountered.

Already, Jessy's immune system was rallying to fight the invader, and unlike most people, her army of white blood cells would be victorious. Jessy was one of the rare ones immune to the virus, a freak genetic accident that left her a beacon of hope for the human race. That was a discovery for later though and for now, she dreamt a disturbing dream. Occasionally she moaned restlessly, her legs slightly twitching as the nightmare took on a life of its own. It was a dream she had never experienced before, and would wake her with a scream caught in her throat. The horsemen and the desert, the red sun high in the sky baking her damaged and flayed hide. And all around her, thousands walked, never stopping, the relentless march of those marked for damnation.

The dream would be the least of her concerns over the coming days. Unfortunately, she had inadvertently infected nearly everyone in the Whitehouse bunker. With the President of the United States dead, the Vice President had been sworn in as acting President. The problem was, he wasn't immune, which meant the virus was working its way through the American administration as if it was ticking off a list. With no Vice President yet appointed, the next in the chain of succession was the Speaker of the House of Representatives, a man who had met with the President two days before. All it took was the shake of a hand.

The Speaker had then passed Lazarus to the President pro tempore of the Senate, so when the virus worked its wonders on him, the leadership would drop down a notch on the list. With the Secretary of State presently struggling to recover from an operation for his life and death struggle with bowel cancer, the next in line was the Secretary of the Treasury. A man good with numbers, but not someone you would want to run a country. He also wasn't an American born citizen, so he was out of the running.

Following on came probably the best candidate for what was needed. The Secretary of Defence was a five-star general who the troops respected and who the press adored. He was plain speaking and able to deal with the political whims of the idiots in the Senate and the House of Representatives. A combat veteran with a brilliant strategic brain, he was a man made for war, a man made for the kind of battles that were coming over the next few weeks and months. Just the man's presence in the office he held had allegedly prevented two armed conflicts due to the absolute certainty that there was someone in charge of the world's most powerful military who knew exactly what he was doing. Regrettably, he was also down here in the bunker, presently chatting to now President Ryan.

So when the smoke cleared and the virus had demanded its toll, the ensuing candidate was the US Attorney General. And that was going to be a problem. Presently the Attorney General, Jacqueline Fairchild, had fled Washington for the relative safety of her weekend retreat. She was an extremely competent lawyer, a woman who knew the ins and outs of the American constitution almost as well as she knew the inside of the King James Bible. Whilst Jessy slept, Jacqueline sat in front of a roaring fire in Montauk west of the Hamptons, the lights dimmed low, her mind fully engrossed by the divine teachings in that holiest of books.

Jacqueline knew what she witnessed in the world around her. It was written for anybody to see in the Lord's message. She didn't know that she was destined for the Office of President, so she sat, fearing that the End of Days had arrived but also excited that the time of truth was most likely upon them. She needed guidance though, and her memory didn't fail her. She easily found the chapter that she knew had prophesied the recent events.

Isaiah 26:19-20

Your dead shall live; their bodies shall rise. You who dwell in the dust, awake and sing for joy! For your dew is a dew of light, and the earth will give birth to the dead. Come, my people, enter your chambers, and shut your doors behind you; hide yourselves for a little while until the fury has passed by

She had left Washington, for had the Lord himself not commanded that she do so, which meant she had escaped the initial infection and would be safe to take command when the opportunity presented itself. When this knowledge was bestowed upon her, there was only one thing she could possibly say in response...

Praise be!

22.08.19
New York, USA

The assassins of Gaia did not want for luxury, some just chose to reject it. Whereas Azrael would sleep in a fetid pit hidden in his plush London townhouse, Gabriel chose the path of sterility and cleanliness. The rooms he slept in were immaculate, the sheets for his most recent bed freshly laundered each day and left outside his New York penthouse apartment. Whilst he was in residence, no other person was allowed access to his hallowed sanctum. He stayed here rarely, this just one of several other residences scattered across the Continental United States. As with the other apartments, Gabriel let no speck of dust gather on the many surfaces of the bedroom he slept in here, his ritual cleaning unhindered for the shelves and furniture were bare of everyday human trinkets.

The assassins differed in other ways too. Azrael liked the barbarity of the life, of prolonging the pain of those he was sent to kill. The thrill of plunging the knife in and feeling the warm blood wash over his skin had, until his capture, been a large part of who he was. Gabriel too preferred the surgical precision of ending life by the blade and with as much bloodshed as possible. The difference was that Gabriel preferred to get the job done quickly, favouring efficiency over artistry. He too had a knife with the same engravings, also given to him by Mother. He was adeptly skilled in knowing how to slice and stab the life out of a fragile human form. This didn't mean he got to use the knife very often.

Many of Gabriel's kills had to be attributed to accidents or natural causes, America's law enforcement ever on the lookout for any hint of a serial killer. His planning was meticulous, his performance in the service of Gaia exemplary. Without question, he did what he was told to do. Why then had they abandoned him in a city where the dead were starting to rise? Sitting on his penthouse balcony, the usual thoughts that afflicted humanity absent due to his previously sterilised mind, Gabriel waited patiently for his next set of instructions. It made no sense to him that they would just leave him here, but without the instruction of Mother, there was nowhere for him to go. He wasn't to know that the release of Lazarus had been accidental, well before The Three had planned, the virus still in the testing phase.

Gabriel did not have the blessing of someone like Jessica to unlock what had been taken from him, his former life a phantom that he could sense but never touch. The forgotten memories of the life he had once led tantalised him, only to deny their knowledge, leaving a void that Gabriel tried to fill by being the best killer he could be.

Thirty-seven people had so far died as a direct result of his actions, only three of those up close and personal. This was not to say he was not adept in hand to hand combat. There were few who would be able to match his skill, the three hours he spent training and maintaining his fitness everyday proof of his dedication. Thirty-seven people removed from the world because they threatened the balance of the sacred Earth. Nobody had really explained how those he killed actually threatened everything, Gabriel just accepting what he was told.

He even allowed himself to indulge in the finer things, sensation a poor replacement for human experience. But it was all he had, and he knew the limits he was forced to put on such indulgence. Some people had control of their sins, others became consumed by the very things they craved. Gabriel, with no real limit to the money he could draw on, ate the finest foods, drank the finest wines and once a month engaged in the services of the most adept prostitutes. He did not indulge wilfully though.

Limit your pleasures so that they do not become your hell.

All this whilst living an invisible life, the everyday people he was forced to interact with barely remembering Gabriel even existed. Like Azrael, Gabriel was a ghost, rarely leaving the apartment except on Death's orders. He would happily sit for hours meditating, his mind an endless void of blankness, so eager to be filled by the humanity around him, and yet denied by the reclusive code that Gaia insisted upon.

Very few people in this apartment building had ever met him, his spacious apartment never victim to the parties it was so ideal for. He had no friends, the women he used, with Gaia's reluctant permission, often refusing to see him again despite the high fees they charged. Whilst he never hurt or abused them, there was a blackness in his heart that they all saw, his emotionless form threateningly robotic in its actions. Perhaps they witnessed in him their future selves, their identities damaged by the oldest profession they chose to join. Some women revelled in trying to fix a broken mind, but those who had true life experience would look into the deep fetid pits of Gabriel's eyes with growing alarm. Rarely did they wish to repeat the experience. None of the women ever spoke of Gabriel, even to warn others of their kind.

Down below, the sounds of the city were alien, the cacophony of carnage and gunshots replacing the early morning hum of traffic. Two blocks over, an apartment building was on fire, thirty floors of steel and concrete burning with a ferocity made worse by the death that was likely occurring inside. It wasn't the only one, several spirals of smoke visible across the city's skyline. And that is what confused him. If the city was dying, as it so clearly was, why had he not been warned? For the first time a new emotion began to grow inside of him, one he didn't know how to process.

Betrayal.

He felt betrayed by the people he had dedicated his very essence to. The chord on the landline was pulled taught as he tried his best to keep the phone by him at all times. Presently, it rested on the table by his side. Unlike the phone Azrael kept in his pit, this one was as clean as the day it was made, treated with reverence to reflect the power the messenger who used it possessed.

Gabriel was actually surprised when the phone finally rang, the first shrill tone almost hidden by the explosion that rocked a building not one hundred metres away. Gabriel lifted the handset, the sweat on his palm an affront to its purity.

"Gabriel." The word sent a flutter through his heart. Here was her voice, his saviour, the woman who had dragged him screaming into the light. Mother, the one who had trained him, had given him his mission.

"Mother, I prayed you would call."

"And your prayers were answered." She sounded amused, but also tired. The sound of the line felt different as if missing something, and Gabriel quickly realised there were none of the mechanical sounds of the great machines and the clanking chains that always came with a phone call of this kind. It felt wrong, to just talk like this, not understanding that those sounds had been hypnotic triggers to reinforce an assassin's commitment and dedication to the voice on the other side of the phone. There was no need for such now.

"I feel lost. I did the tasks as ordered, but am I to stay here?"

"Tell me what you were asked to do?" Mother enquired. Gabriel frowned, for how could she not know? The courier had dropped off the package with the instructions that surely came from her. Still, Gabriel told her of the errands he had done. Breaking into people's homes and contaminating the toothbrushes with the amber liquid in the vials in the dead of night.

"I see," Mother said.

"Was it not you that gave the order?"

"No," Mother said. She was tired and now so very alone. She could have gone and joined the other heads of Gaia, but what was the point with her sickness and her utter aversion to what the other three Gaia leaders had done. "That was done without my knowledge. Do you know what it was you were being asked to do?"

"I assumed at first poison, but now I think a biological agent," Gabriel answered.

"Yes, it was what the media call Lazarus. I suspect you guessed as much."

"The timing did seem too coincidental," Gabriel admitted. "So I am the cause of the chaos in New York?"

"Only partly. The original release of the virus was a mistake. If I had known you would be used to exacerbate that mistake I would have acted." Mother clearly had not been aware of the delivery he received on the seventeenth of August and chose not to share with him how she subsequently found out about his mission.

"I see," was all Gabriel could say in answer to that. He had known there were other people at the head of the organisation he served, but he had always assumed that Mother was the ultimate leader. Had she also been misled?

"Have you ever received any other packages that didn't fit with your mission?" Gabriel thought about the question, searching his memory banks. There had indeed been a time.

"Once. Again it was a package, its contents similar to the last one. Only I was asked to inject myself. Was that something you were aware of?"

"No," said Mother sadly.

"Then perhaps we have both been betrayed."

"So it seems. You were always one of my favourites, Gabriel," Mother said softly. She held great affection for the men and women she trained, despite the horrors she made them do. Mother had never had children, the indoctrination by

Mother Russia taking most of her nurturing years before she stumbled upon the truth. And then the cause of Gaia took its feverish hold. Children would have not just been a distraction…they would have been a mistake, a curse upon an already crumbling world. Thus, she saw the assassins she made as her offspring, for did she not strip them of their fake identities and bring them afresh into the world?

"You humble me, Mother." A rare flowering of affection formed in his heart at the words.

"I am ringing to say goodbye." The words did not shock Gabriel, they were almost expected.

"What do I do now Mother?"

"I don't know Gabriel. The world I free you to is not what I wanted. I always sought an orderly demise of the human population, not this necrotic chaos. I have one final instruction for you before I release you from your oath." He had made a promise to Mother, to serve her until his death.

"Can I survive without your guidance?"

"Yes, because that is all any of us can do in this new world Gabriel, survive. It is ideal for a man like you."

"What is your instruction Mother?"

"I want you to live Gabriel," came the response. With that, she put the phone down on him. Gabriel knew there would never be another call from that landline. Standing, he pulled the chord as hard as he could, ripping the phone out of the wall. With a flick of his wrist, it went hurtling over the balcony. He doubted it would offer much of a threat to the people below, not when half the city was on fire.

22.08.19
Preston, UK

Azrael was asleep. The only side effect of the antiserum Smith had injected into him was apparently to make him doze off. The machines had hardly changed in their rhythmic monitoring, and Nick noted that Smith had almost seemed disappointed that nothing monumental had happened. Nick had started to dislike this Smith, but he hid this revelation behind an external veneer of professionalism. The fact that the gas mask hid his face also helped.

There had been other people watching the experiment via video link but Nick had no idea who they were and had no desire to know. Smith for his part had answered the questions that had come over skype and the consensus was that the lack of any real side effects was a good thing. Evident that Azrael wasn't going anywhere, Nick had told Carl and Jeff that he was going outside to stretch his legs.

Nick wasn't thus there to see Smith inject his test subject with a healthy dose of Lazarus so as to verify the effectiveness of what could be a cure. It made sense to do a large degree of the research into the cure away from Manchester which was likely now becoming a hive of infection. Hours before, the decision to move everything to Porton Down had been put on hold due to a sudden uprising of undead in Southampton. If that growing army couldn't be quashed, it was merely a ten-hour march to the UK military's premier biological research facility. The humans were running out of places to hide.

Stepping out into cool morning air, Nick kept his gas mask on. He never bothered with the helmet because he wasn't facing an enemy that would be shooting at him. There weren't many soldiers visible on the parade ground now, most of them were out keeping order on the streets of Manchester. At night they enforced the mandatory curfew. During the day they helped keep the violence from the streets, ready to move on any reports of zombification. Such reports were building as the hours passed, the population slowly turning on itself.

There were also increasing numbers of zombies that needed engaging. Fortunately, nothing yet like the rotting legions marching through some parts of London. It looked like Peter Dunn hadn't been the first person to bring the virus to the city of chrome, glass and depravation after all. He had just been the warning to the country that the politicians had largely ignored.

The soldier's ranks were also dwindling because of Lazarus. Despite the protective gear, there were already dozens suffering symptoms of the virus. They had been quarantined in one of the barracks, stripped of their weapons and kept under constant guard. Then there was the other major problem regarding the filters to the gas masks. They only had a finite life and there were only so many left in the Quartermasters stores. By the end of the next day, they would be all used up, meaning everyone but the SAS would be at the mercy of whatever this pathogen was. Word was there were unlikely to be any replacements any time soon, recent department of defence cutbacks meaning that stocks at the main army depots had quickly become depleted. Somebody needed to be strung up for that, though likely the person responsible was already dead. When the SAS had arrived, they had brought their own equipment, and they had stocked up specifically for what they now faced. They had even requisitioned themselves a couple of armoured personnel carriers, one of them loaded and ready in case they needed to bug out. Nick reckoned he could blag a few filters off Haggard should the need arise.

Captain Haggard had isolated his SAS troop away from the general army population. Now they merely waited to see how things developed. Nick knew there was a degree of resentment amongst the general army squaddies that the elite soldiers weren't pulling their weight, but with only fifteen of them here, what exactly were they expected to do? Nick also knew that Haggard didn't give a stuff and that his tactics were sound. It only took one infected man to doom the lot of them, and until some sort of effective and quick test for the virus could be established, they were best holding back.

There was a developing backlog with the blood tests. What made the backlog worse was that the tests were now being done daily on every man and woman on the base. The last courier they sent out hadn't arrived at his destination. Nobody seemed to know what had happened to the man, meaning three men teams were now being sent out, which just strained the limited resources even more. Although Fulwood Barracks had a military facility, it still wasn't equipped to do the necessary testing.

"Boss," Natasha's voice came in over his radio coms, "I'm patching you through to Central. Sir Nicholas wants to speak to you." Natasha was their acting coms officer, relaying all the information that was being acquired to and from the huge supercomputer called Moros as well as keeping them in touch with the MI13 Central Command.

"Put him through." There was a pause, and then a slightly wheezy voice came on the radio.

"Lieutenant Colonel," Osmond said, "how is sunny Manchester?"

"Rainy," Nick answered truthfully. The morning's light drizzle had cleared up, but the skies were threatening to give the ground a thorough drenching. "What can I do for you, Sir Nicholas?"

"Sir Nicholas! How pointless all that pomp and circumstance now seems."

"Sir?" Nick said, concerned by the tone of his boss voice.

"I always secretly hated it you know. I never could stand all the bowing and scraping we were expected to do with those leaches that lived off the state. Did I hide it well?" He had always loved the country but detested the institutional corruption it clung on to. Half his time as head of MI13 had been spent challenging and combatting the idiots who came to power.

"Yes sir, you did. And I'm sorry." Nick realised almost instantly that this conversation was to say goodbye.

"Decent of you to say so, Nick. And yes, it would appear I am contaminated by this frightful virus. Tough wicket that one, never thought I'd go out like this."

"There's still a chance," Nick said. "Colonel Smith is testing his antiserum as we speak."

"And if he perfects it in time, I will buy you a cold one." The radio call was filled by Osmond's hacking cough. "But as I'm presently coughing up blood, I'm not too hopeful. But to business. Nick, I'm putting you in charge of the remainder of MI13 assets. There are men and women more senior to you, but most of them are out of the country or facing the same predicament as myself. So you're it I'm afraid old boy. Sorry to lay that on you."

"I'm surprised sir. Is there anything you want me to do specifically?"

"Just survive. I've suspended all operations, and I've put the Orphanage into lockdown. Our best and brightest will survive, at least in the first wave of this. They have enough provisions there to last two years without external help."

"How bad is it in London sir?" Nick had read the reports, but he wanted to hear it from the horse's mouth.

"The centre of the city is lost, as is much of the area around Heathrow. The virus has apparently mutated, those bitten turning much quicker than the earlier reports we've seen. It's reaching the point where it will become unstoppable. If there were any politicians left, they would undoubtedly be talking about nuking the capital. But that won't happen, because there isn't any point. I've also seen worrying reports of the virus passing to non-human agents. Rats and birds. That's a game changer, that's one of the reasons it's spreading so unpredictably. I have given Natasha full access to Moros. As long as the power stays on, you should be able to utilise its capabilities."

"I'm sorry it had to go down like this."

"Me too. But perhaps it's all part of some ornate plan we don't understand. I did my best to hold back the decline of this country, but every year we lost ground to the incompetent bastards who only had their own interests at heart. The only reason MI13 escaped unscathed for so long is that so few people knew about us."

"I can try and get some of the antiserum to you," Nick said. "It's not been fully tested, but it might give you a fighting chance."

"Have you got enough for three hundred people?"

"No sir, not even close." Three hundred, the staffing level of Central, the heart of MI13.

"Then I will have to decline. Wouldn't be right for me to be saved whilst everyone else dies around me."

"That's always been your weakness," Nick said, "you have always been too selfless." It wasn't a criticism, but a statement of respect. Osmond's laughter brought on another coughing fit.

"I do what I do for the Realm. It's all I know." There was a pause in the conversation that Nick felt obliged to fill somehow. He knew this was likely the last time he would speak to Osmond. They weren't friends, but Nick had a great deal of respect for his superior.

"Any word on Campbell?" Nick asked.

"Your arch nemesis has been picked up by a US Delta team and is already on his way back to the States. I regret not letting you retire the man to be honest."

"There's always the chance his own side will put him down."

"I doubt it," Osmond said. "If they didn't want him back the Yanks would have just given us the retirement green light. Another example of our political masters getting things wrong." The line crackled. "Listen Nick, I'm going to hang up now, there are so many people I need to…need to say goodbye to. It's been an honour working with you."

"And you sir." The line dropped, rain starting to come down in a significant downpour now.

Nick turned and walked back to where Azrael was being experimented on. This was not turning out to be a very good week.

22.08.19
RAF Northolt, UK

Whittaker sat on his bunk in the hastily constructed isolation block, resisting the urge to cough. He knew where he was, a requisitioned building in RAF Northolt. There were seventeen other men in the room with him, and most of them sounded a lot worse than he did. Apart from a mild irritation in his throat and a headache that could almost be ignored, Whittaker didn't feel too bad at all and he had yet to manifest the tell-tale skin lesions that looked like someone had injected black ink into the veins. Not like the guy in the bed next to him. Whittaker had watched with growing disgust as his fellow soldier had spent the last ten minutes throwing up into a bucket.

The toilet facilities provided in this building would normally have been adequate, but not when half the inmates were running to the bathroom every five minutes. The toilets were at the end of a long hall that had been filled with beds. If everyone here did have the virus, then it was clear to Whittaker that it seemed to present differently in specific individuals. The doctor looking after them had apparently come to the same conclusion, before leaving the room and locking the door behind him.

Whittaker had been here for twelve hours, and he had watched several of his fellow soldiers rapidly deteriorate. What worried him was what happened when someone in here finally died. He had no weapons of any kind, having been stripped down to his basic uniform by Military Police dressed for the end of the world. He had also noted the thick bars that had been placed over the windows. There was no way out of here unless someone opened the door for him.

All because he had started sneezing and coughing in the back of the armoured personnel carrier. How did they know he had this bloody virus and not just the common cold? By sticking him here, they could be condemning him to death. If only the snake-like tendrils were an early presentation, then they would have a better visual way of knowing. But for those with Lazarus who remained unbitten, that particular symptom frequently only came towards the end. He needn't have worried. His blood test had come back positive.

They had fled from Hounslow, their numbers severely depleted. Cavalry Barracks where the Irish Guard were housed in Hounslow had been abandoned on orders from someone much higher up than Whittaker, the army retreating away from the primary sources of the zombie outbreak, regrettably taking the virus with them. Whittaker didn't know how to take that. He understood the military had to regroup and re-assess the situation, but it also meant that the population of London was now pretty much defenceless. It wasn't just the Irish Guard that had retreated. There were men from several different Regiments here, suggesting that the retreat had been on all fronts.

The death of Wallace (and others) had filled the top Brass with the need for caution. How could you fight a war if your soldiers were dropping like flies and becoming the enemy? There was a rumour that the army was working on a cure, but Whittaker knew how rumours worked. Most of them were rarely true.

The door to the barracks unlocked and a fresh face was escorted in. There were still plenty of beds free, but Whittaker wondered how long it would be before they all filled up with the sick and the dying. The young arrival looked around, terror and suspicion in his eyes. There was something else there... betrayal? The newcomer picked the bed furthest away from everyone sitting down dejected, a sense of resentment rolling through his every motion. Most of the people in the room ignored him, too wrapped up in their own misery to even care. Whittaker didn't get to be a Corporal by ignoring the plight of his fellow brothers in arms though. He stood and went over to the man.

"What's your name, private?" Whittaker asked. The young man was a Grenadier Guard, probably from the battle to hold Central London.

"Stone, Corporal," the private said warily. When Whittaker stuck out his hand, Stone looked at it as if he had just been offered a venomous snake.

"If you haven't got anything, you soon will by being in here. Might as well make a friend whilst you can," Whittaker stated matter of factly. Reluctantly, his hand was grabbed for a brief pump, before the hand withdrew. Whittaker sat on the bed next to him, noticing the way the Private flinched slightly. He was clearly struggling to deal with whatever he had recently been through.

"Have you seen them?" Stone enquired. There was a nervousness in his voice that Whittaker had encountered before. The lad was barely nineteen, and it was clear he had witnessed shit that most people couldn't even imagine.

"Yep, I was at Hounslow. They rolled right over us like we weren't even there. You?"

"I was guarding Parliament when hundreds of them just came out of nowhere. No matter how many of them we put down, more just kept on coming. I overheard a Captain say the whole government was infected." That didn't bother Whittaker at all. He'd never seen a politician he could trust.

"Did many of you make it out?"

"I think about half of us. We escaped by river," Stone said. His voice was close to breaking. "I saw things…"

"We all did," Whittaker added. He was no counsellor, but he could see this kid needed help. Sticking him in here to rot wasn't going to aid with that.

"My mate he…he got taken down by a child. A fucking child."

"Let it out son," Whittaker said. "Sometimes it's good to talk." There were tears in the private's eyes now, the thousand-yard stare developing nicely. A hacking expulsion hit his guts, and Stone doubled over, vomiting onto the floor. There was a groan from behind Whittaker, but he ignored it to concentrate on the person who needed him in the moment. The smell of sick was already strong in the room, a few more litres wouldn't add to it. Even so, Whittaker pulled a bin from under the bed he was on and placed it strategically for the next load.

"There were five of us guarding the East end of Westminster Bridge," Stone said, his voice suddenly wheezy. "We didn't think you know, that being near the Children's Hospital would be a problem. Why didn't anyone tell us?"

"I don't think anyone knew mate. Nobody could have planned for this."

"Everything was quiet where we were. We could hear gunfire in the distance, and we were on edge, but there were still people walking around as if it was just a normal day. I still can't believe that bit. I remember some tourist walking up and asking me if I could hail him a taxi. There was a raging battle going on around Parliament Square, and he wanted to go fucking sightseeing."

"Tell me about the children." Whittaker watched the Private's face, noticed the body go all tense. That was where the trauma was, that would be the thing that would haunt the young man in the small hours.

"The sergeant said there were reports of loads of kids getting sick. He said the virus had spread round the schools. You know what kids are like, they pass everything to everyone, like little virus factories. Well, they got sick alright. They came at us, dozens of them, pouring out of the hospital like little demons."

"How did you get away?"

"I don't know for sure. I remember looking at them, looking at their little faces all warped and enraged. The eyes so black that they didn't even look human anymore. My Sergeant was shouting at them to get back, and then he started shooting without any real warning. Others joined in. But it didn't stop them, not really. I tried, I really did."

"Tried what?" Whittaker pressed.

"I tried to shoot them. But I couldn't…they were just kids, man. But they were so quick and so goddamn strong."

Whittaker didn't press him any further, the tears coming now, the shoulders starting to shake, not from the virus, but from the misery. A lot of what Stone was suffering was coming from the guilt he felt, the guilt at letting his pals down. Instead of firing as his Sergeant had ordered, he'd froze, as so many soldiers and police would do in those early hours. Trained as they were, nobody could prepare the average soldier to combat an undead army that could just as easily be comprised of children as it was adults.

As he had turned to run, a child had jumped on his back, clawing at the body armour he wore. Despite wearing a gas mask, that had been ripped off his head by a hand too small to have been considered a threat in normal times. Moments away from being bitten, a bullet had taken the head off the creature, showering the back of Stone's neck with infected gore. That was how Stone had been exposed to the virus, its nature rapidly penetrating the skin.

The vomiting he was experiencing was from the psychological trauma of everything that had happened. The virus was working away within him, still in its early stages. It would be a day at least before it would present as symptoms. The reason Stone was locked up was simple. He had admitted being exposed to the bodily fluids of the undead child to an officer. His honesty, also a reflection of his shame, had earnt him a one way trip to quarantine. With no quick test for the virus, it was the only card the military could play. With the hasty retreat from London, the commander of this particular barracks was struggling to find somewhere close by and reliable to get the blood tests done. It's not like they could just drive them to the local hospital. The blood taken had to be sent miles away.

There was more commotion behind Whittaker, and this time he turned.

On the bed closest to the barracks toilets, a soldier was fitting violently, the arms and legs thrashing. None of the room's other residents were doing anything other than staring in fascinated horror.

"Restrain that man," Whittaker shouted. Several heads turned towards him, but if anything, people started to back away. "Goddamnit," Whittaker cursed under his breath. Standing, he briefly squeezed Stone's shoulder and rushed over to the door Stone had been deposited through. Whittaker slammed the side of his hand onto the door several times.

"Hey, we need some help in here." He didn't hear any response from the other side. "Can you hear me?" The fitting man was getting worse, his head jerking violently in a sideways motion. With no help coming, Whittaker did the only thing he could.

"For Christ's sake, restrain him," Whittaker ordered, retreating from the door towards the ailing soldier. Faces glared at him, some showing hostility, some disbelief. Was this what awaited all of them. "You," Whittaker said pointing at the nearest private, "grab a leg and hold him down." He gave similar commands as he reached the bed, only half the people commanded doing as they were told.

"I ain't touching him," a frightened voice said.

"For fuck's sake, help me here."

"But he's infected," another voice insisted.

"We all are you dumbass. Now help me you wankers." That broke through, each arm of the now violently epileptic individual being grabbed, Whittaker taking charge of the head, holding it to one side in case the soldier decided to vomit. They got control, but each person couldn't fail to notice how strong the writhing soldier was. Whittaker managed to get a reading on the man's heartbeat, the veins in his temples visibly pulsing wildly.

"Stone," Whittaker roared, "Stone, I need you." From the corner of his eye, Whittaker watched the young private jump off his bed and come running.

"Yes Corp?"

"Bang on that door until someone gives you a response. We need help in here." The Private did as he was instructed.

"What now?" someone asked.

"Now we hold him until help comes. I need sheets, belts, anything. We need to tie this man down in case...in case he doesn't make it through this." Unfortunately, Whittaker's intervention came too late. The sick man gave a final heave, his whole body seeming to lift off the mattress of his bed, and then it stilled, the limbs all going loose. Out of desperation, Whittaker felt for a pulse in the man's neck, noticing for the first time how slimy the skin felt there.

There was no pulse. Shit.

"Get back," Whittaker insisted. "Get to the other end of the room." Everyone followed his orders without hesitation now and they all went to stand near Stone who was still slamming his hands and feet into the door. Over a dozen men defenceless in a locked room with the undead possibly about to rise. Every one of them had been warned that the dead could resurrect within seconds, sometimes hours.

At first, nothing happened. Whittaker suddenly felt like a lab experiment, locked in a cage to see how they would react to the pending threat. The surveillance cameras that watched them from the corners of the room only seemed to add to that feeling.

A minute ticked by, and the body remained immobile, hope beginning to form in the hearts of some of the men that perhaps they weren't about to face the threat of the zombie menace. Most of the soldiers had faced them in the field and could attest to what the undead were capable of. Two minutes, three, some of the men now clearly starting to relax. Whittaker had not yet witnessed the conversion at death, and he too began to ease to the prospect that the danger was passed. Perhaps not everyone came back. Then one of the men clutched his stomach and made a run for the other end of the room, his bowels betraying him.

"Get back here you maniac," Whittaker ordered, only for his command to be ignored. The man made it to the toilet door, just as the dead man's fingers twitched. Even from this distance, everyone saw it.

"Shit," Whittaker said.

Thrombo. That had been the nickname given to him when he arrived at basic training. The Sergeant had taken one look at him and decided that Thrombo was a much better name than Kevin Kennedy. Thrombo, short for thrombosis, a slow-moving clot.

Well today he wasn't slow moving, the churning in his guts overriding any danger that the dead body might represent. He had held it as long as he could, and as much as it would have been forgiven to shit his pants, he just couldn't face that humiliation. So he had gambled that the dead man would remain dead, a gamble he was about to lose. Not once did it occur to him to use one of the buckets scattered about the room.

Past the dead body, Thrombo never saw the movement, his entire being focused on getting to the toilet stall. It was an act of supreme will that he got his britches down and his arse planted just as the dam gave way. Heat rushed through his whole body as he almost passed out from the effects of the expulsion. As painful as it was, it was also blissful in the relief it brought, the stench engulfing him in its loving embrace. He'd not even had time to close the stall door, not that it would have helped save him.

A fresh knife sliced through his lower abdomen and a further stream of rusty water ejected from what now felt like a completely ruined anal sphincter. He actually saw stars, his vision fluctuating in and out as the void threatened to take him. Deep breaths helped keep him conscious, but in hindsight, it would have been better if he had blacked out.

He heard the bathroom door open, but he didn't register it, barely heard the shuffling footsteps that inched across the bathroom floor to him. There were five stalls in all, and he had gone for the second one along because it already had an open door, saving him a precious second. Plus, he knew from previous visits that the first toilet was blocked, probably unable to cope with the volumes that had been forced down it.

At first, he didn't recognise the figure standing before him as the dead soldier, the feet and lower legs all he could see in his hunched over position. It hurt so much to lift his head up, but he did so anyway, Thrombo finally gazing into the black eyes that gazed down sightlessly.

"Oh crap," was all he could say before the zombie fell upon him. Thrombo felt himself pushed off the toilet, his body slipping down the side, more shit spilling from him as fear now took complete hold. All he could see was the ravenous creature that came at him with bloodied teeth bare. Thrombo was not weak, but he was able to hold off the zombie for mere seconds before his arms folded under the weight of the attack. Steel talons grabbed his head, an immense weight forcing his chin down onto his chest. Pain shot down his spine as something there began to give way, then the pressure eased, only for the blows to rain down on his face. Thrombo felt his cheekbone crack, teeth shattered, his eye sockets imploded, and then he was pulled up off the ground as if he wasn't the thirteen stone that to most men would have been formidable.

There was no resistance in Thrombo now, his mind just a black wall of pain. He was almost lifted to his feet, only for the zombie to pull him out of the cubicle and fling him as if he was nothing. Landing sprawled on the floor next to the urinals, Thrombo could only moan and endure the fresh torment the universe had somehow deemed him worthy of.

The zombie kneeled down next to him. Bending down it began to lick Thrombo's face as if he was the most delightful thing it had ever tasted. Then the lips pulled back, and instead of a lover's kiss, it bit down and pulled the lower lip from Thrombo's face in a violent, tearing motion. From his one good eye, Thrombo saw the zombie rear its head back, chewing frantically on what it had removed from him. The undead creature's body seemed to ripple as if in some orgasmic turmoil.

Thrombo coughed up blood, inhaling some of his own fluids which caused his lungs to revolt even more. This seemed to attract the zombie's attention again, and this time it went for the neck, biting deep, some of its own teeth breaking in the assault, a full mouthful of flesh being sectioned away. Thrombo saw his own arterial blood spurt into the air, the blood supply the last thing keeping him going. He didn't live long after that.

Stone continued to pound on the door, more frantic now that the zombie had risen. Nobody went to aid Thrombo, not even Whittaker. What was there anyone could do? They watched and waited, knowing perhaps that the conclusion of their lives had finally arrived. The man's pitiful screams washed over them sending a chill through Whittaker's bones. When the first zombie eventually re-emerged, they knew it was the end, a conclusion reinforced when the second zombie stepped out after its creator.

The door behind them opened.

"Move away from the door," an agitated voice shouted, the owner's face hidden by the protective gas mask. Whittaker threw himself to the side, the other men doing the same as automatic fire ripped into the two zombies. Round after round entered their upper bodies, several shots snapping the heads back. With enough damage done the now decimated zombies crashed to the floor, where they stayed motionless, their usefulness to the virus now over. More men entered, and Whittaker tried to get up, only for a boot to step firmly on his back.

"You need to stay down, Corporal," a sympathetic sounding voice advised. Multiple soldiers kept the quarantined under armed vigilance whilst men in hazmat suits came in with body bags to remove the bodies. A single individual followed, on his back a large container with a spray gun attached. The strong stench of bleach hit Whittaker as the zombies' bodies and the ground around them were sprayed before they were encased in Death's own plastic shroud. The boot on Whittaker's back didn't relent until the zombie carcasses had been dragged out of the room, the man with the bleach spray even venturing into the bathroom area.

"Sorry Corporal," someone above him said, "orders." The pressure released and the last of the armed men backed away from him slightly.

"For Christ's sake," Whittaker begged. "At least give us something to defend ourselves with." The man who had restrained him had Captain's bars on his shoulder, and he turned to leave. Then he paused, obviously mulling over the request, pulling something from his belt.

"I'll probably get into the shit for this," the Captain said. Whittaker would later find out that his name was Beckington because Beckington would end up saving his life.

"The Colonel isn't going to like that," someone said from outside the room, concern etched all over the voice.

"Then we better make sure nobody tells him," the Captain responded. He bent down to Whittaker, a bayonet extended in his gloved hand. There was a faint tremor in that hand, a sign the owner was perhaps not happy with the job he had just been asked to perform, adrenaline leaving the system, the body coming down from the need to kill. Whittaker dragged himself to his feet.

"Sir!" Whittaker snapped to attention and saluted before accepting the offering from his superior officer.

"You keep that hidden. You keep that safe. I'm told inserting it into the base of the neck does the job when such deeds are required." The Captain backed away as if suddenly realising he was exposed and vulnerable. "If you try and use it against my lads, I will personally kill every one of you. Am I understood Corporal?"

"Yes sir."

The Captain pulled back fully and fled the room, the door locking behind them. So that was how it was going to be. Whittaker had suspected it, but this now proved everything he had feared. He and the rest of them had basically been put in here to die. At least now they had a chance to fight the undead as and when one of them turned. But how long before more than one of the soldiers here died at the same time?

Walking over to his bed, he slipped the knife under his pillow, conscious that most of the men were watching him now. Any hope they still held had likely evaporated when their fellow soldiers had stormed into the room. One by one they were going to turn into those things, and there seemed nothing that anybody could do to help them. Whittaker sat down and gazed at the surveillance camera in the corner of the room. Knowing that there was nothing anyone could do to worsen his present position, he gave the electronic eye a prodigious display of his middle finger.

22.08.19
Preston, UK

When Stephanie Benson had been rung by Public Health England to tell her she might have contracted a very nasty contagious disease on the horrendous flight from Dubai, she had become paranoid that she was going to die. The "useless bastard on the phone" as she liked to call him had frightened her half to death to the extent that she had not been willing to wait around in the vain hope that some doctor might turn up at her door and do a blood test. The threat of Lazarus had at that point been mainly hypothetical, and the overstretch and underfunded health officials had moved at about the same pace as a glacier in dealing with the crisis that they didn't really believe was about to unfold.

It was unacceptable for her to have to wait. She had witnessed Peter Dunn grow steadily sicker on the flight and had even experienced him barging in front of her whilst she was waiting to use the restroom. His rudeness, now explained, only increased the fear and irrationality that grew within her almost as quickly as Lazarus was spreading through her system. Instead of waiting for the NHS to do its job, she had taken matters into her own hands and had driven down to the walk-in medical clinic in Manchester city centre.

Not understanding the situation that she had been babbling about, the staff there had been unable to reassure her with her demands and her concerns that she might be infected with Ebola. Sat there waiting to be seen, having already infected three people, her nerve began to give way. An hour after she had turned up, growing panic caused irrationality to mushroom within her, and before she was called through to see someone, she left, bumping into a man who at that moment was coming through the clinic door. That was all it took for her to pass the virus onto him as well. He was the man who would later infect Stuart on the tram going to a job he hadn't realised no longer mattered.

Because she hadn't given her real name, her turning up at the clinic kind of got forgotten. The notable thing about Stephanie was that she was particularly susceptible to the cognitive altering effects of the early virus infection. Her paranoia grew, and withdrawing as much money out of the ATM as she could, she abandoned her car and travelled halfway across the city by a taxi whose driver grew to wish he had never taken that fare. There, spurred on by the virus that was compelling her to hide away so it could feed upon her unhindered by the miracles of modern medical science, she booked herself into a small hotel she had previously used for an illicit affair that had ended six months earlier. This was not a plush establishment, it was primarily designed for people to meet up and fuck, the receptionist somewhat surprised that she was on her own and that she wanted to pay for several days.

The selling point of this particular hotel was that it allowed rooms to be booked without the use of a credit or debit card. Stephanie, a fan of US cop dramas, was well aware that her credit card could be used to track her movements, and thus had dropped the thing down a grate in the street. The hotel was thus ideal for her means, just pay in advance, and you could have the anonymity you craved. By handing the money over, she had infected the receptionist, who then went on to infect seven more people. When hunger finally drew her out of her room and around the corner to the nearest off-licence, she infected the shop owner there as well, a path of contagion left in her wake. He went on to pass Lazarus onto thirty-seven more people, helping to spread the coming zombie pandemic across the city of Manchester.

Stephanie had retreated to her room, closed the curtains and laid on a bed you would never want to shine a black light on. As she grew steadily sicker, the paranoia rose to pathological proportions, meaning that every sound she heard were the agents of Satan coming to get her. By the twenty-first of September, she was in dire need of hospital treatment, the virus ravishing her physiology, her distrust of all things human now encompassing something as simple as tap water which was undoubtedly full of mind control toxins. When the TV started talking to her, a sign that her Lazarus induced madness was complete, she shut off everything electrical in her room and hid herself under the covers so that she could slowly die in a bliss of endorphins that flooded her system.

For some, dying from Lazarus became a form of ecstasy. For Stephanie, those brief hours seemed to last an eternity, ultimate pleasure filling her heart as everything about her was stripped away. It was the greatest experience of her life, and when the final breath left her lungs, she couldn't even remember her own name. When she finally died, she was quick to be reborn. With cheap and weak doors, Stephanie(Z) made short work of the few hotel residents and staff she found.

She was not alone in her response to her infection. Hundreds in the first days retreated away from the world as if to ensure they would fail to seek medical help and thus resurrect unhindered. Even more would present at hospitals and doctors' surgeries, only to spread the virus to the very people who would be at the forefront in the attempts at defeating it. By the evening of the twenty-second, thousands of people in Manchester alone were infected, and they methodically began to die by their dozens.

22.08.19
Manchester, UK

Dr Moneel Patel had gone another night with very little sleep. He was living off caffeine and amphetamines that he had persuaded the hospital pharmacy to supply him. It didn't take much in the way of coaxing, the fact that he was on the forefront of battling a virus that threatened the entire human race was reason enough to acquiesce to his very reasonable demands. Even so, the pharmacist had refused to give anything out without a proper prescription. It seemed the wheels of bureaucracy still kept grinding, even when the armies of the dead were at the door.

With the recent attempted abduction of Jessica from the Northern Manchester General Hospital's infectious diseases unit, the hospital was under military lockdown to protect the research Patel was involved with. Still, there were fewer soldiers present than he would have liked. With an anticipated influx of the sick and the dying, routine operations had been cancelled to free up as many hospital beds as possible, the army bringing additional beds to fill the spaces. That did not initially concern Dr Patel, for he was primarily focused on creating as much of the antiserum XV1 as his laboratory could with the eventual hope of finding a way of synthesizing it. What they needed now were positive results from the field trials being done by Colonel Smith. Patel needed to know that his frantic research would bear fruit, despite the shortcuts he was having to take.

It was perhaps an understatement that he was not happy with the way this was being done. A serious scientist, he understood the importance of thorough testing before medicine could even be considered for human trials. And yet here they were injecting a "volunteer" with a drug derived from Jessica Dunn's immune blood. He had made his protests and had been informed by Colonel Smith that his objections were noted. But the military was in command now, the civilian authorities and even the police under their jurisdiction. They even had couriers on standby to ferry stuff between the hospital and the army base. There wouldn't be a great deal of antiserum, they were presently limited by the amount of blood they had been able to take from Jessica. They were also inundated with the numbers of blood tests they were being asked to perform, presently the only effective way of testing for the virus.

There was no denying the urgency of the situation though. Yesterday, Patel had sat in awestruck silence as he had watched the broadcast by the Queen from Windsor Castle ordering the dissolution of Parliament and martial law. Did she not realise the recent cuts to the country's armed forces meant that there weren't enough service personnel for this to have a chance of working? He wasn't aware that the reservists were all being called in, and active measures were being taken to "invite" anyone who had left the military within the last ten years to re-enlist. Even those held in the military prisons on lesser charges were being let out to help fight the zombie menace. All complete acts of total desperation.

What troubled him now, more than anything, was how those infected were being treated. Whole wards had been set aside to "care" for the sick and the dying, but it had been deemed unacceptable to just leave people lying around so they could turn into those things. Based on previous experience, that was a road to disaster. Those who arrived at the hospital with symptoms of Lazarus were being taken up to the wards by people who cared, only for them to be quarantined by people who perhaps didn't.

Against the advice of the doctors and hospital administrators, the military had decided that the only way to contain this was through the use of forced restraint, with sedation for those who protested and objected. Catheterised and fed through IV drips, the now mainly chemically comatose patients where shackled to beds and left to deteriorate. In a way, it was to be a merciful death for some, but even more were also denied the bliss that often came in the last moments as the virus took control. And people kept arriving at the hospitals, social media shut down to civilians to stop the word getting out. Mobile phone coverage was becoming sporadic at best.

Even with those measures word got around. The problem was, there was no benefit to the individual to seek medical care for your infection, it was more a means to try and control the spread. Across the country, thousands who could have sought care chose not to, dying in their homes where they were free to join the rabid hordes.

Patel guessed the only reason the military brass didn't just order forced euthanasia was through the hope that they might uncover another Jessica Dunn. So far, no other immune individuals had surfaced to Doctor Patel's knowledge, making Jessica a unique and valuable resource. Stuck in his laboratory, Patel had only learned of the extreme methods being employed by the quiet words of a friend, a Sister on one of the wards.

Apparently, each ward of the infected had a pair of willing soldiers who worked in shifts. Their job was clear. When an infected individual died, when they started thrashing in their bindings with their eyes like pitch and the skin crawling with the darkened tendrils, the soldier on duty was to put an end to the threat they posed. Porters would then come and unstrap the body so it could be added to the pile forming in a secluded part of the hospital grounds.

"The men they use, they seem to enjoy it," the Sister had cautioned under her breath. It was as if sharing her secret would put her in peril. Perhaps she was right, there was no telling now how far the military and those that controlled them would go to try and maintain order.

Patel had to forget about that now. He was in charge of producing the antiserum that they were making from the discoveries in Jessica's blood, and the soldiers seemed to be happy to leave him to his own devices. He had so little to work with. The whole idea of the antiserum was to create short-lived passive immunity, a month's protection tops. It was also hoped that the antiserum would kill the virus in those already infected. Long term it wouldn't offer any kind of protection, only a vaccine could do that. And with only one immune individual to harvest blood plasma from, this was at best a stop gap to a devastating disease. What they needed were more immune individuals and the ability to synthesize the antiserum on a large scale. And time, the most precious resource of all. If they ran out of time, Patel feared what that meant. Not only would the virus run out of control, but those thought to be infected might find themselves facing summary execution. That would be the act of desperation that would tell Patel the battle was lost.

They desperately needed more of the immune to volunteer their blood. That was why so many of the infected were being brought to the hospital. They also needed an ability to isolate the specific antigens from the Lazarus virus so that antiserum production could be done on an industrial scale, and they would probably need animal trials for that. Then there was the ultimate goal, the creation of a vaccine after discovering the secrets to Lazarus.

They had sent their first trial batch of antiserum to the barracks where Colonel Smith was conducting his risky field trials. Two doses, no more, created from several days of blood harvesting from the "volunteer" Jessica Dunn, all sent by armed courier, helicopters being deemed too risky due to the growing risk of bird attacks that they had been seeing around London. There was more, but it was locked away in the laboratory freezer, armed guards keeping watch in the corridors outside.

The antiserum was totally untested because the rules, it seemed, no longer mattered. His hospital laboratory was not an industrial medical facility. The amounts his people could create were totally insufficient for even the hospital's demands. They could only hope that one of the pharmaceutical companies could take their findings and somehow get to work on widespread production. This needed the full weight of human scientific wisdom behind it. But that would mean synthesising what naturally came from Jessica's blood. And that could take days, weeks even.

Hopes of a vaccine were months away, maybe even years.

The pharmaceutical representatives were also being unhelpfully obstructive. Patel had felt like he was constantly on the phone to them. He was still amazed that one or two of the people he had spoken to had objected to the proposed salvation of humanity due to the cost of what was being discussed. You couldn't just start producing this sort of stuff on an industrial scale at the drop of a hat, he had been informed. There needed to be trials, government approval, health and safety checks. Patel had almost screamed at those who resisted. Fortunately, that was out of his hands now, his contacts now dealing with the military who were threatening to nationalise whole industries and arrest those who didn't cooperate.

Sat at his desk, he watched again the computer simulation they had created showing how Jessica's blood killed the virus. It fascinated him, a prime example of why he got into this particular field of research. For some reason, Jessica was able to completely annihilate a pathogen that was fatal for the majority of mankind. Patel knew she wouldn't be the only one and was surprised when he had been told that Peter Dunn had not been immune. It was not unusual for such resistance to pass through families.

Patel had been there when Colonel Smith had asked her where her other brother lived, but Jessica had point blank refused to give such information.

"He's safe where he is. I'm not having you drag him into danger on the off chance he might give you a cure," she had tenaciously stated. *"With the way you have treated me, I wouldn't trust you for a second."*

Patel could understand her hesitancy. He himself was not overly fond of Colonel Smith's methods and had quickly grown to dislike the man. But what could you do? These were unprecedented times, there was nothing in his life that could even compare to the hardships and the terrors that his species now faced. Moving the computer image of the virus with his mouse, he gazed at its simple complexity, knowing that it represented perfection. Patel could readily believe that it had been designed, and despite the evil behind such an act, Patel couldn't deny the genius that had created it.

Its structure was perhaps the most amazing thing he had ever seen.

It was when that thought hit him that he realised he could smell burning. It was faint, but yes, something was definitely on fire. Not electrical in nature, almost like meat cooking. There was a harshness to it as well, the unmistakable odour of charred hair. Was there a human on the planet who didn't know what that smelt like? No, they couldn't be doing that.

One of the windows to his laboratory was open and as he stood and stepped closer, he could tell that this was where the stench was coming from. Looking down, there in the courtyard below, a mound of bodies was on fire, piled on top of each other. The sight horrified him. To just openly incinerate the dead like that screamed of desperation. And this was only a temporary solution. When the dead started piling up in greater numbers, they would have no choice but to start digging pits, huge tombs to encase the disease in the scorched earth. There would be no traditional mourning, not any more.

Everything that marked human civilisation was being torn up and replaced with a clawing, crazed instinct for survival. And Patel had a very strong notion of what that would result in. Whilst he struggled to help save the human race, he found himself wondering if he wanted to live in such a saved world.

22.08.19
Peak District, UK

Tom Dunn was happy for his mother to be here with him and was even happier that she spent most of her time sleeping, her way of dealing with the stress of what was occurring. It wasn't that he found her tedious, it was just that he needed to be alone so that he could think. As much as it pained him, Tom had insisted his mother temporarily stay in the farm's spare cottage, just to ensure that she wasn't a carrier.

"It's only for a few days," Tom had insisted. His mother had driven here, and with those words had visibly deflated before his eyes. She said she understood, but deep down she saw it as a form of coldness and detachment that she had come to expect from him of late. They hadn't even hugged yet, Tom's paranoia now fully justified and entrenched. He was more than happy that

Jessica's friend Stuart hadn't shown up, because that would have layered another level of complexity onto a scenario that merged his dreams with his nightmares.

For over a decade, Tom had been persistent in his belief that the end of the world was coming. Whilst he could never have believed it would be a zombie hell that would cause the downfall of man, much of the preparations he had made were strangely adequate to meet the tasks ahead of him. His farm was secure and so well hidden it had taken his mother an hour longer than it should have just to find the entrance of the poorly maintained road that rarely saw traffic other than the occasional farm vehicle.

That his satellite phone and the internet still worked displayed that there was still time for Jessica to get here, the added bonus being that she was apparently immune to whatever was causing all this. Or at least, that was what she said. Could he believe her in that regard? And what if she were to bring others with her? Tom didn't think he could accommodate too many people, especially with the need for them to be quarantined.

This wasn't his most pressing worry. As much as he realised it no longer mattered, he was distressed to see that his stock portfolio had dropped in value, along with the stock market overall. So bad were things that the markets weren't even trading at present, the exchanges closed indefinitely. Tom really hadn't considered how that would affect him, and even with the precautions he had taken, he had only managed to unload about half of his digital holdings. He'd made a fortune online, and had invested wisely in his property and his resources, but he had gained a strong sense of identity by his ability to adequately invest the profits to bring even greater returns. But that money was now sat there, useless as the economy creaked and moaned under the weight of the zombie menace.

And now all those shares he hadn't been able to sell were likely just useless digits on a computer screen, just like the money in his bank accounts. If the markets never opened again, then all that effort would have been for nothing. He thought he was prepared, but think how much more he could have bought for this farm if he had just trusted himself a little more. With the millions he had, he could have stocked up enough food and supplies for several decades instead of mere years.

Secretly, his belief in TEOTWAWKI had always been tempered by the further belief that humanity would ultimately prevail. A year, maybe two, and then humanity would re-emerge as the dominant species on the planet and rebuild. Ironically his latest attention had been on the world falling to a pandemic, but not one of this nature and not one that spread so quickly. He had believed that the economy would still keep ticking over to some degree. Even Tom was taken aback with what was happening, and now that Armageddon was here, he found no comfort in the fact that he had been pretty much right all along.

The good news was that he could now freely communicate with Jessica. The bad news was that she was still being held in a military facility at least an hour's mad drive from here. Would they ever let her go to join him? As much as he had affection for his family, there was no way he was leaving the safety of his compound, not now. If that made him selfish and a coward, then so be it, but what would anyone expect him to do anyway? Was he going to take one of his shotguns and drive into a packed army camp all guns blazing?

No, he wasn't going anywhere. If Jessica wanted sanctuary, she would have to come to him. He might be persuaded to meet her halfway, but even then he knew he would waver. This place was now everything he was, and he would forever be loath to leave it undefended. There was no part of him that wasn't in some way ashamed by those thoughts, but he had never considered himself a brave man. Why else had he decided to cower away in the middle of nowhere rather than enjoying the wealth he was able to create.

22.08.19
Beijing, China

They had all been infected together due to the actions of Lilith, an assassin of the same creed as Azrael. Over ten thousand had received Gaia's gift, and each one of them had passed the virus onto dozens more. By the last hour of the twenty-first, there were three hundred thousand infected with the virus, spread all across the huge teeming metropolis. Beijing, home to twenty-one million people, was already dead.

There had been earlier infections, which the Chinese military had stamped down on ruthlessly. But on the morning of the twenty-first, with the hospitals swamped and people collapsing in the streets, the Communist government knew they had to act, sending the army in to try and contain the situation.

When the dawn rose on the twenty-second, there was no stopping it, the dead rising from where they had fallen. Hospitals, streets, beds, tens of thousands of zombies took to the streets, overpowering the troops and the police. An unstoppable force that required decisive action. The Chinese Premier was able to take that action, although the result was a rebellion amongst the people of China who couldn't comprehend the threat the country had faced. His decisive act ended up being his undoing.

The troops on the ground who were fighting for their country were never warned that the Dong Feng-5 was on its way, and their only hint was when the bright flash blinded some of them with a brightness that even surpassed the sun. Everything at the centre of the blast was completely vaporised, even the bricks and the stone that made the city what it was. Ground zero had a radius of nearly two kilometres. By the time the mushroom cloud was forming, the centre of Beijing had been reduced to atoms, buildings in a radius of twelve kilometres completely flattened. Above ground, everything alive or undead was utterly destroyed within the core of the explosion.

Outside and below was where the problems started. At a radius of twenty-five kilometres, the survivors suffered horrific third-degree burns, even when in the false protection of buildings. Further out still, deaths from flying debris were horrific, glass acting like lances, piercing flesh and severing limbs, chunks of masonry acting like missiles, bludgeoning skulls and shattering bones.

The problem was, outside the radius of the air blast, most of the zombies survived, their bodies weathering the radioactive storm. Spread across the city as they were, more than fifty per cent of their numbers carried on their assault, the humans now weakened and dying, easier prey for a creature that cared not that its flesh was charred and missing limbs. Wherever the zombies could walk, they attacked the survivors with a fury that was unsurpassed.

There was yet another challenge that the military planners had completely forgotten about.

Over the previous decade, China's economic miracle had lifted hundreds of millions out of poverty but had also sent the price of housing through the roof, making it unaffordable for large swathes of the population. These people needed somewhere to stay, so where better than the nearly ten thousand underground nuclear shelters that previous regimes had built in Beijing alone. With no real present-day threat of nuclear conflict, the bunkers had taken on another purpose…unofficially housing China's poor. Despite the government's efforts, nearly a million people called these sometimes forgotten structures their homes

One out of every twenty-first person lived in structures designed to protect them from nuclear bombardment. Whilst those constructions were obliterated at ground zero, thousands of them survived across the city, nearly five hundred thousand residents sheltered from the worst of the first blast. Being home to those on the lowest strata of society, many of the people in the shelters had been on the street that day when Lilith had used her drones to release the virus. As the second bomb fell, those below the surface waited to die from the infection that was ripping through them.

Three bombs in all were dropped, and if anything, the progress of the virus was only stalled. As the survivors above ground moaned from their injuries, many trapped under debris, the undead emerged to once again take control of the streets. Although collapsed in parts, the Beijing underground had harboured thousands of them, and they re-emerged, the radioactive dust that coated them as they wandered the rubble-strewn streets of little concern.

Another form of the infection came from underground. Hiding in sewers and basements and the very nuclear shelters that saved so many, the rats arose, feeding off the shattered zombie corpses, the virus quickly spreading through their ranks. Two billion rats survived the atomic blasts, two billion tiny soldiers to be converted to the cause of Lazarus. Across the world, the surviving governments watched on, horrified by the actions of the Chinese military and their leaders. With so few countries in possession of nuclear weapons, many looked on enviously, deprived of a means to control the spread through their own populations. Disgusted as they were, you had to respect the force of will that could take that kind of action.

Shame it didn't do anything to stop Lazarus.

Ironic really, for the Chinese had not realised the nuclear death would only make the situation worse for China. As the undead began to crawl out of the underground bunkers, the radiation began to work on the virus within them, altering and mutating the creatures that already defied all medical logic. As the hours ticked by the radiation worked its magic, some of the those wandering the earth with no discernible heartbeat beginning to change.

And Lilith? Waiting for instructions that never came, she died in the first atomic blast, her body reduced to atoms. Mother never did get to speak to her.

22.08.19
Manchester, UK

Brian surprised himself with how relieved he felt about being given the all clear from his blood test. He hadn't believed he was infected, but to receive an official negative result, even from a doctor as unlikeable as Florence, was a weight off his shoulders. He hadn't really realised he was concerned about the prospect until it was removed from the equation.

The test result was accompanied by him being invited into Clay's opulent bedroom so that they could have breakfast together, an honour that Clay rarely bestowed on anyone. Clay was not holding anything back with the banquet being served, the two place settings of full English breakfast indicating that Clay was determined to enjoy life even with the coming adversities. Clay's butler stood silently to one side, ready to clear the dishes away once the feast had been accounted for.

"Tuck in Brian, you might not see the likes of this for a while."

"Yes Mr Clay. You said there was something you might want me to do today?" Brian asked.

"Indeed there is Brian, indeed there is. But first, eat." From the corner of his eye, Brian watched the Butler, a man said to be utterly devoted to Clay and almost as ruthless. He was Clay's close protection bodyguard as well as his occasional servant. He outmatched Brian in both height and bulk. Brian had never seen the man in action, but he was aware of the man's ability when it came to hand to hand combat.

They both ate, no further words shared until every last morsel was cleaned from the fine china plates. If he was honest, Brian wasn't a great fan of mushrooms or black pudding, but he made no complaint and just forced it down coated in ample portions of ketchup. Rarely was it wise to refuse something Clay offered, the gang boss was sometimes easy to take offence. Still, Brian had to admit, that was a damn good meal.

The Butler stepped forward and filled both their mugs from the teapot on the table they shared. Mugs didn't really fit with the rest of the expensive crockery on display, but Clay liked to drink his tea in bulk. Brian couldn't complain about that. Once the tea was poured, the now empty plates and cutlery were collected, and the Butler left the room. Clay waited for the door to close.

"Best investment I ever made finding him," Clay said nodding after the Butler. "Never speaks unless he's spoken to and does what I tell him. A bit like you in that regard Brian."

"If you say so, Mr Clay."

"I do say so." Clay sat back in his chair and crossed his hands across his lap. "Does it annoy you that I make you nervous Brian?" There was no warning about the question, which Brian knew was some kind of test. He'd suspected for a while that Clay had a streak of paranoia in him, which was why he was so ruthless in dealing with those who betrayed him. Brian also suspected that that streak had perhaps now grown to a five lane motorway, causing his employer to begin to question even the most loyal of his soldiers.

"I wouldn't describe it as nervousness Mr Clay. More a healthy level of respect."

"And loyalty?"

"I think I've shown my loyalty is without question." Brian kept any kind of displeasure out of his voice so that he was merely stating a fact.

"Good," Clay suddenly said clapping his hands together. Clay's eyes had been prodding, searching for weakness and deception, and now that he apparently hadn't found any it was time to get to the matter at hand. Brian let himself relax a fraction.

"Even with the warning I was given by those who have grown rich under my watch, it's only a matter of time before external help for my operations evaporates. Have you seen what has become of London?"

"I saw some of it, Mr Clay, but much of the news isn't covering it."

"London has been lost Brian. The dead own it now. No more Piccadilly, no more Leicester Square. I'm told the army is in full retreat. It won't be long before Manchester goes the same way." Clay almost sounded like he was reminiscing about times gone by.

"I still find it all hard to believe."

"Don't we all Brian. But the proof is there for everyone to see. Which is where we get to the little jobs you will be doing for me today. How do you fancy a nice drive with some of the lads?" That was where Brian learned he would have to leave Clay's mansion for most of the day.

***

So much for the safety of Clay's residence, thought Brian. He had stopped the convoy of four vans a safe distance from the guarded gates. Through the binoculars, Brian could see that there were three soldiers guarding the entrance of the distribution warehouse. With the high wire fences all around its grounds and limited road access, it was easily defendable from ingress by unarmed civilians…if you had the men and if you had the will. The same went for assaulting the place, and Clay had both.

He noticed the sergeant's stripes on one of the soldiers, which meant to Brian that there were likely more men inside the huge building. Whilst Brian's team could probably overpower the military presence here, the casualties would likely be high on both sides. He had ten men with him, all heavily armed, and some of them were even army veterans. This wasn't some gang of youths they were facing though. Soldiers were trained, they knew their shit, so he figured he had to try another way. Word was that these were also Para's, some of the best soldiers there were. They would normally be dedicated to their orders. However, with most of the British government dead, and the streets of several major cities already becoming swamped by the armies of the damned, the chances were that these men would be open to negotiation. Brian felt he had to at least try.

"Hold your positions. I'm going to try something," Brian said to the man in the van with him. "You might not want to be with me when I attempt this…in case it goes south. Get the sniper rifles out and set up under cover. That's our leverage." His minion looked at him through the portals in the gas mask he wore, and nodded, quickly unfastening his seat belt and climbing out of the van. With a fist slammed several times on the side of the vehicle, the two men in the back got out also. Putting it into gear, Brian slowly drove over to the front gate. This was a risky move, but it was worth taking.

The soldiers had been watching them warily, and now two of them retreated behind the sandbag enclosure they had created. The light machine gun one of them was wielding worried Brian. That could do devastating damage, and he would prefer it if this could all be resolved peacefully. Why fight when you could negotiate?

Stopping the van a reasonable distance from the soldiers, Brian switched the engine off and stepped out of the vehicle. Whilst the sergeant didn't point his weapon at Brian, the other two men did. The soldiers also wore protective clothing to fend off the virus. The guns they carried were needed to protect against the likes of Brian and the end result of what that virus brought.

"That's far enough," the sergeant said. "You need to get back in your vehicle and leave."

"You see there's a problem with that," Brian said, lifting the respirator up off his face so he could be heard better. Alone in the middle of the road, there was little chance of the virus getting at him. He kept his hands visible at his sides, moving deliberately so as to show he wasn't a threat. "My boss has asked me to start emptying this warehouse, and I really can't disappoint my boss. He has a bit of a temper you see."

"That's not my concern. Leave now. This facility is under military protection authorised by Her Majesty." The food distribution network in the UK was a fragile behemoth. So long as the food kept being shipped and moved and grown, then the shelves in the supermarkets stayed full and stocked. But any disruption to that supply would see those shelves run empty within a matter of days, which had already happened in most supermarkets that had foolishly stayed open.

The military had initially hoped that by controlling the distribution warehouses, they could somehow keep feeding the population once order was restored, but they had already seen that this plan was turning into a logistical fuckup. Even without the zombies attacking the massed gatherings of people already desperate for food in the cities, there were further problems with the plan. Firstly, stability wasn't being restored in many of the desired areas, the army and the police just spread too thinly. And secondly, the international inflow of goods was going to be cut to nothing as world commerce began to break down. Even with the warehouses secured, the country would run out of food within a week. Even if the farms kept producing, there would be no labour to pick the crops out of the ground or drive it to where it was needed. The majority of the people would either thus fall to the virus or die from starvation. It was a calculated bet which would claim the most victims, and military strategists were already suggesting that the available food supplies should be requisitioned for the Military and civilian authorities. The average Joe on the street, well he would just have to fend for himself.

"Your government's dead mate," Brian informed the sergeant. He saw one of the soldiers nervously moving his gun, and past the gates near the huge warehouse, three more soldiers could be seen.

"Leave now."

"Have you thought about it though?" Brian asked. "You all have families right? Wives, parents, girlfriends." This was Brian's leverage, and he saw the two squaddies glance at each other. "If you are here protecting this, who's there protecting them?"

"Military families are being moved on base," the Sergeant lied.

"Well that's very cosy," Brian admitted. "But who's defending those bases? Most of the police are probably dead or fled. And I bet your ranks are depleted with desertion." It was true. At least thirty per cent of military personnel from the Sergeant's regiment had so far abandoned their posts. "So let's make a deal."

"I'm not here to make deals. We are authorised to use lethal force to protect this warehouse."

"Mate," Brian said taking a step forward. "I don't want the warehouse. I just want what's in it."

"Not going to happen." The sergeant's voice was stern.

"Look I will do you a deal," Brian persisted. "I've got four vans here. You let us fill those for say three trips, and we will be on our way never to return." Clay had considered occupying the warehouse itself, but he realised that would spread his men too thin. He had decided to turn his home into his principle stronghold. Its high perimeter walls and thick iron gates were enough to keep the undead out. Brian knew that Clay had ideas of becoming some sort of warlord, and to do that he needed men. And men needed to be fed.

"Time to go," the sergeant warned.

"One way or another we are getting in that warehouse."

"Not today," the sergeant advised. Brian backed up and put his hands up in mock defeat. He turned and made to walk away, only to pause and look back.

"I'm sure you are familiar with the L115A3 sniper rifle?"

"Leave. I won't tell you again."

"Only there are three aimed at you right now." The two privates ducked down slightly. "My men are good shots. Ex-military. One of them used to be a para, like you. Perhaps not as good as you guys, but good enough. Your position is wide open. If we don't kill you, we can keep you pinned down and outflank you. And then we will kill you, and I don't want to do that." Brian really didn't want to kill these men, even though he was prepared to. They weren't the threat. The undead were, and the more soldiers there were able to fight, the fewer zombies there would be to deal with.

"Sarge?" one of the privates said. "Maybe we should consider what he's saying." Ah, the first fracturing in the ranks, thought Brian. The sergeant spoke to the private without looking at him.

"Carson, now would be a good time for you to keep your fucking mouth shut."

"But Sarge, my wife's pregnant. I need to be with her."

"Listen to him," Brian said, "and think about it. We will nip in, fill the vans and be on our way. Nobody will know or care. We aren't the enemy sergeant, the dead are." Brian looked at the sergeant who returned the gaze. There was steely resolve there but also doubt. Brian was someone you never wanted to play poker with, he could read people like a book. Here was a man conflicted, the breathing and the way he held his head told him a lot. On the one hand, there was honour and duty and on the other the threat of death and the very real risk that presented to loved ones. The sergeant's shoulders sank.

"I've got ten men and there's six of you from what I can see. Do we cooperate or do things get unnecessarily nasty?"

"For fuck's sake," the sergeant said, probably more to himself than anyone else. "Carson, open the gate."

22.08.19
Houston, USA

Reece hadn't gone home. What was the point? With most of the prisoners being diverted to the Astrodome, she took the opportunity to sleep on one of the beds in the vacant cells in the Sherriff's Department, a place that was usually filled with the drunk, the violent and the unruly. Its holding cells were now one of the quietest places in the whole Sherriff's Department. Ideal for someone who needed to get some sleep.

The silence did not mean untroubled sleep, unfortunately. There she dreamt of the desert and the horsemen, a terror that was very recent, this only the first time it had occurred. She had no idea why her mind brought her a frightening reality of decay and torment and it caused her to toss and turn with the ravages of her own imagination. So vivid was it that sweat poured from her skin, the smell of charred flesh almost real in her nostrils. It wasn't those horrors that woke her up but the banging of the baton on the cell bars.

"Morning Reece," her Sergeant said. He looked at her with a measure of concern. As usual, he was immaculately attired, which was more than Reece could say. She looked at him, noticed the lack of the usual jovial smile that he was known for.

"Morning Sarge," she said, the sleep still in her system. How many hours had she got, two, three? She noticed the Sergeant was holding a piece of paper. He was also wearing a mask and gloves.

"Reece, your blood tests came back. I'm…I'm sorry, but they came back positive."

"Shit," Reece said. She felt the bottom fall out of her world. She liked the Sarge, he was always fair with her even when she went too far and busted his balls. It wasn't fair that he was having to give her this news. The Sergeant stepped back, clear of the cell door. Reece suddenly felt like she was about to throw up, a coldness spreading through her at the thought of what this all meant.

I'm dead, she thought. There was no way around the truth of that.

"I don't like it, but we are going to have to ship you to the Astrodome. The feds know you came back positive. If we don't send you there, they will just come and take you."

"Any chance that the test was wrong?" Reece asked. Foolish question she thought, but she had to ask.

"No. The CDC guy said it was pretty accurate. Obviously they will check it again at the Astrodome, so you never know they might just send you straight back here."

"And Rodriguez?" They had shared a car together, so it wasn't looking good for her partner.

"Came back negative, but it doesn't mean much because he went home and hasn't come back." The Sergeant sounded almost accusatory. He had a job and he should be here to do it.

"I can't blame him," Reece admitted, "he cares about his family too much." She wouldn't lie to herself and say she wasn't disappointed in him. She could understand it, but it didn't mean she accepted what he had done.

"If my wife wasn't a goddamn witch I doubt I'd be here either," the Sergeant lied. Reece laughed, thankful for the respite the humour brought.

"Can I at least go under my own steam?" Reece implored. "I don't like the idea of being shipped there in a bus. With me and Rodriguez gone, you won't need our patrol car. I can go there without wasting any resources." She saw the doubt in the Sergeant's eyes. "It will give me chance to deal with this."

"I know you Reece, so I know you are as good as your word. Do you promise me you will go straight there and not fuck about?"

"Cross my heart and hope to vote Democrat," she stated making the mandatory hand gestures. She felt sick, the thought of what this meant churning the acid in her stomach.

"Ouch, you really mean it. OK, but remember my butt's on the line if you don't turn up. So go now before I change my mind." Reece began to rise from the bed, her body stiff from the mattress that was more lumps than it was soft. The Sergeant took another step back, staying what he deemed a safe distance even with the protection over his face.

"How many have we lost?" Reece asked.

"Twelve per cent of the roster has gone AWOL. Five per cent came back positive. And we lost three good men last night in a firefight."

"It's all going to shit isn't it Sarge?"

"You got that straight Reece."

22.08.19
Manchester, UK

Sometimes the nicknames soldiers were given seemed particularly apt. Private Renfield had picked up the nickname "Delmonte", because no matter the task, he would always say yes and volunteer, so eager was he to prove his worth. Nobody was really surprised therefore when he stepped forward to accept the role nobody else really wanted to take.

He had to guard the patients on the ward he was assigned and "end their suffering" when one of them passed over.

It didn't matter that those that needed ending were already dead and a danger to everyone around them. Shooting them at a distance was a lot easier than getting close and personal and sticking a knife in the base of their necks, the most effective way the scientists had now determined that zombies could be killed. Bullets though, at such close range would produce blood splatter, bits of flesh being propelled from the body. Plus, the sound, in such a confined space would not be conducive to a seemingly orderly hospital. It was therefore decided that the knife was much more efficient. That made finding volunteers even more difficult.

The thing was that, with the exception of his dear mother and one particularly insightful Sergeant who had spotted something in Renfield's eyes, the Private had hidden a truth about himself from most of the people he met. That truth was that death fascinated Renfield. Most mothers have a certain degree of nervousness when their sons tell them they have decided to join the military. The thought of the apples of their eye coming home in body bags, or with pieces missing from their bodies and minds a harrowing image that was haunting because of the truth it threatened.

Renfield's mother was relieved when her son gave her the news. She saw it as the only safe path for her son. His fascination with death clearly needed an avenue to express itself, and if not for basic training and an acceptance into the Duke of Lancaster's Regiment, his mother reckoned that prison or death were the only real future for the boy she had pushed out of herself eighteen years before. Whilst she had never even seen him commit a violent act against another person, sometimes a mother just knows these things.

To the staff on the ward he was stationed at, he was like a morbid Guardian Angel, watching over them, ready to act should he be needed. Without even a constant supply of tea brought to him by the depleted nursing staff, he sat vigilantly over the sedated, bored, terrified and sleeping bodies that were packed into the room around him. Difficult to drink from a mug when you had to breathe through filters and keep your face covered.

Every hour, hospital staff seemed to bring more people and more beds to be squeezed onto the ward, some now being left in corridors. There were other soldiers on this floor of the building, all tasked with the same essential job as Renfield. Despite the knowledge that hospital personnel were glad to have him around, he also saw the wariness in most of their eyes. To do his job here would have to go against everything that medical ethics protected, the doctors themselves pushing the limits of what the Hippocratic oath even allowed. But then Hippocrates never had to worry himself with a global zombie pandemic that threatened to wipe the human race from the history books. Renfield's job was to simply destroy what the doctors and nurses couldn't save, which was likely to be everything in the room.

He had placed his chair at the end of the ward by the closed double doors which allowed him to keep an eye on the whole room. Without even the luxury of a toilet break due to the military issued diapers he wore, he did not waver in his task until his relief came. Sitting there for six-hour shifts, with little to entertain the mind except for the quietly moaning forms that filled the room's beds would have left some people bored. Not Renfield. The process of death fascinated him, and every ten minutes or so, he would rise from his seat and wander up and down between the two rows of beds to check that the patients had not yet converted. He was always disappointed when the relief soldier stepped through those doors giving Renfield a chance to decontaminate himself and get something to eat.

Whilst regrettably none had yet passed on his shift, Renfield had been shown videos of how the undead were born from the living. The convulsions and the writhing death throes were not difficult to spot. The videos had been made from the last remaining survivors of the outbreak at Wythenshawe Hospital, not all those zombies having been dispatched in the name of medical research. If the military doctors who had briefed him were competent in their observations, the Private was certain he wouldn't be mistaking the dead for the living.

Psychologically it helped that the patients were all strapped down, although he had been advised, in the strongest terms, not to rely on that. The undead were strong, much stronger than when they had been alive, bonds and restraints that could hold an adult human faring poorly against what some of his fellow squaddies were now calling "Dead-heads". The Chinese whispers that filtered through the army ranks had told him that Dead-heads could smash their way through doors and take a shotgun blast to the chest. There were other tales that were surely exaggerations, of zombies working together to overwhelm armed defensive positions, of men ripped apart, limbs being torn clear out of their sockets. Renfield didn't know what he was supposed to believe, so he kept a healthy level of scepticism from anything he didn't hear from the lips of his Sergeant and his superior officers. His fellow soldiers could sometimes be full of utter shit.

Renfield did have a distraction though for there was one patient in the room that almost mesmerised him. Whilst the other people in the room would get an almost cursory examination by his eyes, Renfield had found the most beautiful woman in the world in the midst of all the chaos. He would often linger by the end of her bed, mindful of how that would look should a member of the nursing staff make one of their infrequent visits to check on the patients. The patient's name was Lucy, and she slept with a peace that would make Sleeping Beauty appear restless. Renfield wasn't sure, but he thought he might be in love. Not a romantic love, the concept being alien to him. The thoughts that formed in his mind dwelled more on what he could do to her, myriad ways he could use and abuse her body dancing through his mind.

How strange that this should happen when there was no chance such molestation could blossom. It was almost as if God himself was taunting the hapless soldier.

Standing for the umpteenth time, Renfield walked slowly down to the end of the ward, watching the slow steady breathing of those who mainly had no awareness that he was even there for them. About a third of the patients had accepted the restraints willingly, and the awake ones followed the soldier's progress with wary eyes. Most had objected to being tied down, but none of them were given a choice, sedation forced on those who objected. Of those who were induced into slumber by drugs, the sedative heaven occasionally wore off or was not enough to fully knock them out. Renfield had no idea what was being used to keep the majority of patients sedated, and he had overheard one doctor's concerns about such mass medication. There weren't enough electronic devices in the hospital to monitor so many individuals, and there was the worry that the drugs might speed up someone's demise. Still, the sedatives were used. Even some of those who had seen the wisdom of restraint chose chemical sleep when they were told they would also need to be catheterised.

He stopped by the end of Lucy's bed, and for the first time he noticed that her eyes were open. Her face told him he was deemed a threat by her.

"It's okay," Renfield promised. "Nobody here will hurt you." A lie so easily spoken.

"Who are you?" she almost begged. Her gaze kept flitting around the room, the restraint making it difficult to raise her head off the pillow. She was spread eagle, two sheets covering her legs and lower torso. The hospital gown hid the swell of her breasts well, but Renfield's eyes still lingered there, the gas mask hiding his perversions from her. She was just absolutely perfect. He would like to take that from her.

"Just a soldier ma'am. Here to keep you all safe."

"Why am I...?" Lucy asked, struggling slightly with her bonds.

"Do you not remember being brought in?" Her chart, which Renfield had spied a look at several hours earlier, stated she had been admitted five hours ago after being reported as infected by her parents. Her own parents had watched as the paramedics had come under police escort to take her away. Amazing how quickly fear could unravel the chemical love of Oxytocin. She had not come willingly, forcing the paramedic to dose her.

"It's a blur. Why are we all tied up? What the hell is this?" It wasn't just a question, it was a plea for sanity.

"Everyone here is infected. You need to be restrained in case one or more of you dies and..." For some reason, he couldn't say the words, not to that face. His heart was already in his throat, the blueness of her eyes like heroin to him. He was suddenly glad he was wearing the gas mask for it hid the nervousness that was coursing through him. She let her head fall back onto the pillow, resignation and exhaustion seeming to seep out of her. The medical chart didn't state what the paramedics had sedated her with.

Renfield didn't know how he would react if he woke up in her situation.

"Can I get you anything?" he asked impotently. The intravenous fluids being poured into her meant she wouldn't be dehydrated and it wasn't like he was able to rustle her up a sandwich. He could have kicked himself for asking such a stupid question and fortunately she just shook her head. Lucy gave the bindings on her right wrist a final pull, and then she just started to cry.

"Hey, it's going to be okay," he tried to reassure her.

"Just leave me alone," Lucy demanded. He was going to say something more, anything just so he could keep looking at her, when the person in the bed behind him started to shake.

Renfield turned at the sound, the old woman was one of the latest patients to have been brought in, and she had not been one of the ones needing sedation, dementia seeming to deal with that aspect of her care. Even without that, she was so frail that she would have been unable to offer any kind of effective resistance. Looking at the old woman now, Renfield was surprised by how she was able to contort her body so violently, the entire torso lifting off the mattress, the sheets that had been tucked in offering nothing in the way of resistance. Her arms and legs seemed to lock into place, and then they relaxed, the bulk of her falling back down onto the bed. As he watched, her head began to thrash wildly, as if she was trying to shake her own head loose.

"What's wrong with her?" Lucy pleaded from behind. Renfield didn't answer, too engrossed by what he was seeing. This was exactly how it had looked on the video he had been shown, and his right hand fondled the handle of the knife he knew he was shortly about to use. It was a stiletto blade, just right for slipping into the reptilian part of her brain. All the men guarding the patients had been supplied them, the thinness of the blade ideal for what was required.

Renfield took a step closer, froth now foaming at the old woman's mouth. Not long now, he thought, not long at all. His eyes were wide, and he noticed several people watching what he was doing. The privacy curtain would be useless here, the beds having been pushed too close together to get the maximum number on the ward. It looked like Renfield was about to free up his first bed.

At that moment a nurse pushed her way through the swing doors, the noise drawing Renfield's gaze. Her timing, although pure fluke, was impeccable.

"Get the porters," Renfield ordered, his voice calmer than he could have expected. The nurse just stared at him for several seconds as if he had grown a second head. Truth hit her, the moment she had come to dread that was now commonplace, then she turned tail and ran out the way she had entered.

"Why won't you tell me what's happening?" Lucy demanded. She was now fighting against her restraints again, panic starting to set in. Renfield didn't even look at her. Instead, he moved down the side of the bed he stood by, the patient nearest the old woman chemically oblivious to what was occurring.

He watched her death struggles, eager to help the old woman on her way. Not from any sense of compassion you understand, he just wanted to feel it again, the rush when he took someone's life. Even though he had never been in active combat, Renfield had taken life twice before. That was what his mother sensed in him, the murderer that lurked below the surface. A serial killer in the making, but one that was able to control his impulses and bide his time.

The old woman began to cough up blood. Inside his glove, the knuckles of the hand holding the blade were turning white.

"Not yet, not yet," he mumbled softly under his breath,

"Tell me what's happening, you fuck," Lucy roared. Renfield couldn't ignore that, but he didn't take his eyes off his pending prize.

"You need to be quiet now Lucy. It would be better for everyone if you were quiet."

"Don't tell me to...." she tried to counter, but then the finger shot out, pointing directly at her heart.

"Shut the fuck up." The words were cold, not how he wanted to speak to someone so stunningly attractive, but her interference was spoiling the moment. Objects like her needed to know their place in the world.

The doors opened again and the nurse returned, a male porter in tow. Still pointing at Lucy, Renfield issued an order with a voice that commanded authority. He was in his element here, he was in charge. The people present were to do as he said and they all knew it despite how repulsive what was coming was to them. The knife in his hand, the handgun on his hip and the supremacy of the Lord Almighty were all the legitimacy he needed. Although as for the latter, God could lick his balls.

"That patient needs sedating."

"You sick fuck," Lucy screamed, realising the soldier was referring to her. Her outburst actually cemented the nurse's wavering mind and moments later she was there with a readily loaded syringe.

"Don't you fucking touch me," Lucy exploded, her face red with anger and desperation, her mind close to hysterical now. The nurse didn't even try to console Lucy. Any empathy the nurse possessed had been used up by the dozens of people she had seen die on her shift. This wasn't the only ward she was helping to run. The drug was easily administered by Lucy's IV line, and a troublesome patient rapidly drifted off into narcotic compliance.

The old woman had stopped convulsing now, the raspiness as she inhaled suggesting the end was close. With his non-dominant hand, Renfield pushed the woman's head to the side, exposing the base of the skull. He did it gently, savouring the moment. He wanted to take his gloves off, to feel the skin with his own, to feel the heat and the power coming off his next victim. There was a twitch in the woman's right arm, the fingers clawing at the air as if trying to grasp something that only she could see. Then came the death rattle, the air expelling itself from the lungs which this time did not inflate. Underneath his mask, Renfield was smiling.

"Is she gone?" he asked the nurse. She came next to him, placed a portable pulse oximeter on a withered finger. It was a small thing, almost inconsequential. But in its cheap battery driven circuitry, it now had the power to determine who met the ultimate fate. The device registered nothing, the body soon to grow cold and rigid. At least, that was what would happen in an ordinary world. A second porter entered, this one pushing a trolley with a squeaky wheel, a portent of the death that was to descend upon the rest of the ward's inhabitants.

Someone in the room whimpered.

"She's gone," the nurse said, Renfield pulling the knife clear of its scabbard. But he hesitated, his hand wavering over the corpse. "What are you doing?" the nurse pleaded.

"I need to see it," Renfield insisted pulling the old woman's head so that he could see the eyes. They were still open and initially they kept their whiteness, but as he watched, the darkest of reds began to creep from the peripheries, the lips of the old woman's mouth starting to curl into a sneer as the resurrection process began. Renfield was lucky, the first zombie he was about to kill was a fast changer.

"Seriously dude, don't fuck about," one of the porters begged, true desperation and urgency in his words. *What has this man seen to make him so afraid* Renfield thought? As the Private pushed the old woman's head back onto his side, he felt resistance forming there. So it was true, everything he had been told that he would have thought unbelievable was the God's honest truth.

The blade slipped easily into the zombie's flesh, and he moved the blade around inside as he had been shown by the Sergeant who had given them a brief but thorough tutorial on the best way to kill the undead. *How many of them have you killed?* Renfield had asked the Sergeant. The only reply he received was a look of pity.

The zombie seemed to slump into the bed as if gravity itself was pulling down on every muscle with increased force. He knew he should have felt elated, just as he had those times when he had killed in secret, the victims not being attributed to a lanky fifteen-year-old boy. But there was nothing. Renfield had discovered that killing had been the sweetest thing, and yet his actions now gave him none of the rush he had so feverishly needed.

If he was alone, he would likely have screamed.

With the knife still present, the blood flow from the wound was limited. His waterproof gloved hand would need decontaminating, and the nurse would help with that. But first Renfield would need to help move the body. Another corpse for the fresh pyre being built outside. He should have felt on top of the world, but all he felt was malignant disappointment.

22.08.19
Houston, USA

With the permission of her Sergeant, Reece ended up walking out of 1200 under her own steam. She was still a Sherriff's deputy, they couldn't take that away from her. When she left the cell, a janitor had appeared and sprayed it down, the bleach hitting her nostrils even through the mask she wore…a mask that was now more for the protection of others than herself. She had even been allowed to keep her sidearm, which surprised her. Perhaps things were getting so bad that nobody cared anymore.

She knew what she had to do and she wouldn't fail in her duty due to the threat she posed to everyone around her. There were some things she needed to do first. Now sat in the cruiser she had shared with her partner for many months, she rang Rodriguez, not to rip him a new one, but instead to just say goodbye. They were friends, and that's what friends did.

"Reece?" the voice said.

"It sounds like you're driving?" Reece answered.

"My wife is. We are heading out of the city."

"I heard you didn't turn up for work today."

"Don't bust my balls Reece, I'm doing what I have to." She could picture him in the car, probably still wearing his uniform to give him some sort of authority when it was needed. His wife would likely be looking at him nervously, concerned perhaps for the emotional turmoil going through her husband's mind. The woman would know the confliction he was facing between protecting his family and doing his duty.

"Didn't call for that," Reece insisted. "I think mainly I'm just calling to say goodbye. My test results came back... I have the virus." She could picture his face as she told him the news.

"Shit," the voice came back. "Maybe they are wrong you know. Maybe..."

"No, the tests are right." Reece was surprised by how easily she had accepted this. Perhaps when the symptoms really started hitting her, then the anger would come. But right now, she felt resigned to her fate.

"I'm sorry Reece."

"It's okay, at least you got your family out. I hope your father in law doesn't become too much of a twat." She heard him laugh nervously. In the background of the call, she was surprised to hear someone coughing.

"Use a tissue honey," Reece barely heard the words of advice from the wife to one of Rodriguez's daughters, and it made her heart grow cold. He had two girls, the cutest things you would ever meet. Were they infected? If they were then it was all over for Rodriguez too.

"Listen Reece," he started to say, only for the call to suddenly cut out. Reece looked at her phone, saw that there was no longer a signal present. The phone told her she could now make emergency calls only. What was the point of that though, the 911 service was likely swamped.

The fucks. They had cut the cell service, most likely to the whole city. The phone had cost her two week's wages and now it was a useless piece of junk. That was it, now the anger came like a storm out of nowhere, the eruption surging up from her guts. Reece considered smashing her phone on the dashboard of her car, but instead she calmly put it on the seat next to her. It was only then that the violence came to match the anger, the steering wheel experiencing the full brunt of her assault, her hands slamming down onto it with frustrated ferocity.

It took her five minutes to get it all out of her system, a brief moment of insanity that was perhaps justified. Her hands were sore and red, likely bruised in places. Who would criticise her with what was going down? Who could possibly admonish her for her justified frustration at the way her life had changed? Taking some deep breaths, she didn't bother mopping her eyes which streamed with tears. Fortunately, there was no mascara to run. That would have made her look a picture. As it was, she was content to let anyone who saw her know the distress she was in, perhaps more because it increased the chances of them staying away from her.

Don't go near the scary lady with the gun and the nasty infection.

The key caught the engine first time, and she carefully drove out of the underground parking garage so as to discover what the last days of her life would hold.

Reece wasn't surprised to see the streets virtually empty. There was plenty of military traffic, but nothing really civilian. There was the occasional work van, essential personnel having to go places to keep the city running. Houston was like a living organism, it needed feeding, it needed energy and it needed its waste dealt with. For any one of those essentials to stall, the whole city could easily die. It had already lost the ability to talk to itself.

With the number of buses Reece was seeing, she reckoned the city was dead anyway.

Her route to the Astrodome had to be detoured due to a whole block being sectioned off. As she drove past, Reece saw Houston Police engaged in a firefight with armed civilians in a large warehouse. Already the resistance to martial law had begun as she knew it would. Texans did not like being told what to do, and a large proportion of them were going to be highly dubious of what the government was telling them. Calling out the state militias had only been partially successful. Some had chosen not to heed the call, and there was no telling what they were planning. Reece resisted the temptation to help her fellow law enforcement officers. This wasn't her fight anymore.

Perhaps the most surprising and surreal thing she discovered on her final drive was an open fast food drive through. When she got closer and saw all the first responder vehicles parked up outside, the logic of it came clear to her. Those battling lawlessness and the growing zombie menace still needed to be fed.

"Why the hell not," she said to herself, and she pulled in to the queue that had formed. In front of her, a National Guard Humvee bristled with armed soldiers who didn't look old enough to be out of school never mind fighting a war. She envied them their naivety, just young men who probably knew nothing about the world. Days from now, if they were still alive, they would have likely aged mentally by a couple of decades.

It took five minutes for the line to deplete enough for her to be able to give her order. The place wasn't that busy, but she reckoned the staff inside the place were depleted in numbers. She didn't know how right she was. It was a franchise chain drive through, owned by a married couple. They and their teenage daughter were the only people running it. It wasn't even for the money, the food being given away for free to anyone in a uniform. They just felt it was their patriotic duty to help those fighting the zombie outbreak, and it had earned them the right to be given blood tests which had come back as all clear. The military was still willing to look after their own and those that helped them. With a constant flow of soldiers and police moving through, it also gave the owners the illusion that they were safe in the midst of all the madness.

A big handwritten sign duct-taped to the outside of the building stated, in big bold red letters, that they would be serving anyone in uniform until the food ran out.

"What can I get you?" the friendly and somewhat harassed sounding female voice said over the intercom. Reece gave her order, more food than she would ever eat, just feeling the desire to gorge. With her fitness regime, she rarely got to eat crap like this, and she needed the indulgent hit. Something perhaps to remember in the coming days…or was it hours? Something to remind her of the good things in life, which seemed to be largely absent the last twenty-four hours. Reece tried to ignore the gunfire that appeared to be constantly in the distance.

At the serving hatch, Reece wasn't surprised that the bag holding her food was delivered on the end of a pole. Why risk it right? With the logistics, it made sense that only canned and bottled drinks could be supplied, the sugar laden milkshakes totally off the menu.

The smell of the food filled her car and made her mouth begin to water. It suddenly struck her how hungry she really was, and parking her car up in a free car park space, she let the air conditioning bring the scents from the bag to her nose. So many times she had denied herself this kind of mouth pleasure and for what? It wasn't like she had extended her life any.

Reece knew the food wasn't good for her, but just by unwrapping the first of the burgers she had ordered, it dawned on her that she should never have cared. With death staring her in the face at such a young age, it all seemed like a game that she had played wrong. There was so much Reece could have done that she hadn't, so many experiences that she had denied herself because of bullshit rules she had set out for herself.

Looking at the bun she was surprised at how juicy and delicious what she was about to eat looked. Normally when you ordered this kind of food you got a sorry, squashed affair, but not here. Taking her first bite, she almost died with delight, not caring that liquid dribbled down her chin onto her uniform. It was probably the greatest thing she had ever tasted, and she greedily took another chunk with her teeth. Reece took her time, concentrating on every bite, every mouthful nectar to her. The peak of human civilisation had come down to this.

Yesterday, towards the end of her shift she had killed her first zombie. Down a side alley, they had uncovered what had once been a homeless person eating the remains of a large cat. Kneeling on the ground, the creature had turned its head to them as they cautiously approached on foot, the cat's carcass quickly becoming irrelevant now that more acceptable flesh had arrived. Reece had even heard its joints clicking as it stood up to full height, the bare emaciated face hidden by the blood that coated it. There was no mistaking what it had been, and Reece had ended it in three shots. She reckoned that was the moment Rodriguez had truly lost his nerve. Her partner hadn't even pulled out his sidearm, instead he had just stood there, horrified as his belief about the world was turned upside down. To finally see it was more than some people could bear.

Reece had no idea how she had contracted the virus. In the great scheme of things, it probably didn't matter. At least she hadn't passed it onto Rodriguez, so that was some comfort she could take from this.

The burger finished, Reece unwrapped another one. She didn't care about trans fats or cholesterol anymore. All that bullshit was past her. There were probably four thousand calories in the bag, and she didn't care about that either. As it was, she was already on a death sentence, so wasn't she allowed the right to one last meal? Reece doubted there would be anything this good in the place she was going. Her food from now on would likely be crackers, MRE's and at the end, needle delivered fluid from a bag. Was that the way she wanted to go? Was going to the Astrodome the right thing to do?

As good as the food was, Reece had never felt so alone. The knowledge that Reece had nobody truly close to her came at her like a revelation. An orphan, she had joined the force because of the injustice she had seen in her childhood. Her last five years had been a whirlwind of work and failed relationships, mostly from people she worked with, all of them ultimately a disappointment. None of them could compare to the one man who had meant everything to her. Nobody even came close. She fell in love with him knowing it was a risk, knowing that he would be away for days on end. Those were the perils of falling for someone who worked undercover. The ultimate peril was when that undercover work turned south fast, her reason for being getting his brains blown out in a drug bust gone bad.

It had devastated Reece, putting a considerable coating of ice around her heart. From that moment on, the job became an all-consuming passion rather than just a way to pay the bills. And now even that was going to be stripped away from her. Mid-bite, the food seemed to sour in her mouth, but she forced it down anyway. What was the point? What was the point in any of this?

That was the moment she almost gave up like so many others would in the coming days. It would have been so easy to put the car in gear, drive to somewhere secluded and just put a bullet in her skull. An escape from everything the world had to offer was there waiting at the short length of a barrel. Reece had even pictured herself doing it, knowing that nobody would likely even be there to clean the blood off the upholstery. Would that be an acceptable end to her though? To slowly rot in the Texas heat, bloating as the flies found their way into her flesh.

No, she wasn't giving up so easily, she still had a life to cling on to. As long as she was breathing there was still hope. There would be no suicide, not today.

22.08.19
Manchester, UK

Sitting around, doing nothing was not something Stuart could easily do, especially not with what was happening in the streets and the houses outside his window. He needed to get out, to feel the air on his face.

It wasn't really him saying this though. In the complex chemistry of his mind, Lazarus was working away to manipulate him, causing him to seek the presence of others. The streets were relatively quiet at present and he reckoned it would be safe for him to go out and…and what exactly? Have a walk? Why did he want to go strolling around Manchester when it was safe right where he was?

His lawyer's brain valued logic, so it was confusing to him that the urge just kept growing. Twice now he had even put his coat on, only for him to swear at himself that to leave the flat would be a bloody insane thing to do. He had witnessed violence in the streets below, did he really want to risk being caught up in that? Whilst he was a big man who could handle himself in many an altercation, his size was unlikely to help against someone armed with a knife or a gun. Best to sit down and try and fill his mind with one of the many box sets of unwatched TV series. If things got any worse, this might be the last chance he would get to see them.

Are you seriously thinking about watching fucking TV? It's the end of the world.

He had to do something though, the need to leave and seek humanity like an insane itch that just couldn't be scratched. Perhaps if he just went for a short walk? He was out the door to his flat before he could stop himself.

What the hell?

Standing by the lift he had used so many times before, his finger wavered over the call button. No, this was insanity. He should just go back to his flat and try and calm down. Millimetres away, his finger seemed to be frozen in space. And then it moved, impacting the button, the green circle of light appearing around it. Stuart heard the elevator start to move, ascending to come and get him.

He had his phone on him and it was at that moment that it rang.

"Stuart? Why haven't you been answering your phone?" Jessica said on the other end. The call felt broken, patchy, only one bar at best on his phone. Looking at his phone he noticed that she had tried to phone several times.

"Jessica, something isn't right."

"What do you mean?" The elevator stopped and the door opened before him invitingly. Stuart resisted, partly because he was scared of what he was doing but also because the reception might cut off.

"I have this urge that I don't understand. It's like I have to go outside for some reason, to leave the safety of my flat."

"But it's not safe out there Stuart," Jessica said stating the obvious.

"I know. And yet I still want to leave. Just for a walk. Why do I want to do this?"

"I don't know Stuart. Do you feel okay?" He could hear the concern in her voice.

"I think so, although I'm a little light headed and I think I might have a fever. My thinking is a little fuzzy as well."

"Where are you now?" Jessica asked. The elevator door started to close, and Stuart found himself stopping it with his foot.

"I'm stood outside an open elevator. I don't know why I'm here." Desperation started to creep into his voice. "What's wrong with me?"

"Go back to your apartment Stuart," Jessica said sternly.

"But I feel like I can't breathe in there. Even here, the air feels like it's getting thicker." It wasn't, the virus merely pushing buttons to try and compel him into this action. Anxiety was building within Stuart, a claustrophobia he had never experienced before, the virus randomly demanding that he go out and spread his gift to the world. Suddenly the idea of entering the elevator filled him with unexplained dread. This time he let the door close.

"You need to breathe Stuart. Just close your eyes and take deep breaths."

"Okay, I can do that." His heart had started to race, the beat all over the place. It felt like it was fluttering in his chest. He was starting to have a full on panic attack.

"Breathe in for a count of four," Jessica's calm, reassuring voice said, "and breathe out for four. Concentrate on my voice." He did what she said and felt the calm start to return to him. When he opened his eyes though he found he had walked several steps and he was standing by the door to the staircase.

"I don't understand what's happening. I need to get out of here." Stuart pushed through the door and began to frantically descend the steps.

"Stuart? Stuart?"

"I can't stay here Jess. I need to get out." He was four flights down now, stopping briefly to speak the words.

"And where will you go Stuart?" That question cut through him. Where was he going to go? What was the point in just walking around?

"I...I don't know. Somewhere, anywhere. Maybe I can still get out of the city." Was that it, was that what was driving him? He began to run again, the phone almost forgotten, this time even more frantic. His feet began to skip steps, taking two or three at a time, his athleticism more than a match for the task. Until it wasn't.

He missed his footing at the top of the second to last flight and went hurtling down the concrete steps, his bones crunching and his skull cracking as he did so. The phone flew off, its screen shattering as it hit the wall. Stuart landed as a fractured heap on the landing, his hip broken and a bone in his right arm sticking out of the skin where it had shattered. Blood poured from his left ear due to the head injury and he lay motionless, unconsciousness threatening to descend. A groan escaped his lips as delirium set in.

Nobody would ever come to his aid, his fall unnoticed by everyone in the building he shared. It took an hour for the brain haemorrhage to kill him, the zombie born from his death relatively unhindered by the injuries sustained. The hip fracture gave it a slight limp when it walked, but Stuart(Z) was able to drag itself from the ground so as to go in search of the juiciest flesh its former apartment building had to offer.

Jessica never would learn what happened to him. She would beg Nick to go and help her friend. He would listen calmly and respectfully, only to logically pull apart her emotional request. They couldn't risk the lives of the depleted number of soldiers to go after someone who was just one man amongst millions.

"*But he's my friend,*" she would beg.

"*And you don't think the soldiers here have friends and relatives they care about? Some of them are on the brink of bolting. What message do you think that would give them? As much as I understand how difficult it is for you to hear this, your friend is on his own. The only thing I need to concern myself with is your safety. That's my priority. I'm sorry if that upsets you, but your friend Stuart can't be helped.*" He would remove his gas mask when in her presence and there, in his face, she saw the coldness again. Jessica learnt to hate him that day, but she knew that he was right.

She would still do what Nick said, at least for now.

22.08.19
RAF Northolt, UK

Fifteen more soldiers had been deposited with them and in that time two more had died. It had fallen to Whittaker to do what was necessary before the bodies opened their eyes and became more dangerous than rabid wolves. The newcomers looked on in unrestrained horror at the sheer brutality of what was being done, the resigned acceptance of those in the room seeming to seep into them. There was no objection though, the logic of the act seemingly reinforced by what they each had personally experienced over the last day or so.

Whittaker wasn't the most senior soldier in the room, but the only person of a higher rank was a Colour Sergeant who just lay there moaning deliriously. The rest of them were privates, some of them just young kids in the Territorial Army. It was starting to look like the army hadn't sent their best into battle. What was the old phrase for it…cannon fodder?

They all looked to Whittaker to tell them what to do. Ultimately, he was the guy in charge and he accepted that without complaint. The bodies, they left by the door to make it easier for those outside to collect and dispose of what were now thoroughly dead soldiers. It left a sour taste in the mouth, but the more Whittaker thought about it, the more sense it all seemed to make. What else could the army do than what they presently were? Nobody could have planned for this. It was never something that could have even been envisioned, despite the countless films and books that had been made on the subject. Fiction was exactly that, make-believe. It wasn't supposed to be real. It was there to entertain and then be forgotten. It wasn't supposed to be instructional.

He was worried about the Sergeant though who was likely the next one to go. There just wasn't anything any of them could do to prevent it. Sitting there, watching the men deteriorate, there was also a level of confusion in Whittaker's mind. Since his arrival, he hadn't become any sicker. In fact, if anything, he was starting to feel better. Should he tell someone? That was laughable, who was going to believe him? He would just be some squaddie who, out of desperation, was trying out any lie to give himself some sort of fool's chance. There was also the added confusion caused by what had happened an hour ago. The medical captain had entered and had taken Whittaker away to one side. In a voice louder than was perhaps needed the Captain had explained that they needed to do Whittaker's blood test again due to a lab error.

He was seconds away from having other things to worry about.

The door to the barracks opened and another soldier was dragged in, someone Whittaker recognised instantly. This one wasn't coming willingly, his shouts a sign of outright rebellion. If he wasn't infected, the guy would have undoubtedly ended up in the glasshouse for his belligerence. Flung in with a kick to the backside, the level of aggression by those guarding the infected showed just how much trouble the newcomer had been to them. Up until then, those outside had treated the men locked up here with muted respect. With his hands cuffed behind his back, the new arrival fell to the floor hard.

"Fucking bastards," Tod spat as he dragged himself off the floor, difficult to do when you didn't have the use of your hands. Perhaps for the first time, he noticed the men around him, most staring at Tod like he was in possession of three heads. Tod made to attack one of the guards, but the pistol aimed at his head put paid to that. The guards withdrew, the door once again being locked, a set of keys thrown to the ground just beforehand. There was blood leaking from Tod's nose, most likely a result of someone punching him for his idiocy.

And there stood Whittaker, the man Tod had thought dead or AWOL. "They got you too then Corp."

"What the fuck was that Tod?"

"I should be out there killing these things, but I started throwing up so they marched me into a truck and brought me here." Tod wiped at the blood on his top lip as best he could, the lapel of his uniform soaking it up greedily. "When I said I didn't want to they got persuasive. Cunts."

"What the hell were you fighting them for?"

"Are you kidding? I don't want to be put in some room to die."

"Oh Jesus," someone behind Whittaker almost begged. Casually, Whittaker stepped over and picked up the keys. They fit Tod's handcuffs perfectly, allowing the man to finally relax his hands. Tod gripped his wrists one at a time, the soreness there probably exaggerated by the cuffs being too tight.

"Christ man, you don't have a choice. You should have just accepted that," Whittaker informed him. Tod looked genuinely taken aback.

"Jesus Corp, who rammed a pole up your arse?" He was going to say something more, but Tod suddenly doubled over and started dry heaving. Nothing came except for a stream of spittle, little left in his stomach to regurgitate. Whittaker took a step to the side and kicked a bucket over to his subordinate just in case. This one was empty, Whittaker having set up a rota to at least drain the buckets down the toilets so that some semblance of dignity resided in the room. Tod didn't end up needing it, not that time.

"Tod, you're infected. This is the only place you can be."

"I don't agree," Tod argued. "I can still shoot. And it might just be food poisoning."

"Mate look at you, you can barely stand," Stone pointed out.

"Who the fuck asked you?" Tod looked around and was enraged to see pity in most of the faces. He didn't want their sympathy. He had killed so many of the undead, he had become hooked on it. His first real engagement as a soldier and it was everything Tod knew it would be. And now he was being denied. It wasn't right.

"He's right Tod. You aren't well. Take a bunk and get some rest. You ain't going anywhere."

"We will see about that," Tod mumbled, but he took Whittaker's advice, picking a bed that clearly hadn't been slept in yet. Whittaker sat down on the bed next to it, looking at the private with genuine concern.

"Calm down and tell me what happened." Whittaker could see the fury in Tod's eyes, but a sigh of resignation settled over him. He was looking around, noting the bars on the windows, noting the ill-disguised blood stains on the floor and the now ever-present smell of bleach.

"What's the point? None of it matters."

"You were with us, what happened?"

"I decided to take some pot shots at Dead Heads on that Warrior, help the boys inside a bit. Ended up in Major Pickering's APC. He was the one that had me dragged here after I started throwing up." *And likely infected everyone inside*, thought Whittaker.

"Well, what's done is done. It's time to stop being a dick and accept where you are." Even as Whittaker said the words, he could tell they were being rejected.

"Whatever you say Corporal." Whittaker had met enough squaddies in his time to know trouble when he saw it.

Outside the locked barracks, Military Police watched the infected soldiers. Each of the people in the room had all had their infection confirmed by blood tests, but they were likely the tip of the iceberg. Already talk of how people were being isolated was spreading throughout the ranks, Chinese whispers distorting the reality of what that meant. Many of those who were showing the early symptoms hid their condition as best they could. Others went absent without leave, deserting their posts. Several of those accused probably didn't even have the disease due to the way it mimicked things as basic as the common cold.

Spread across the country, the military didn't have the time or the facilities to determine with one hundred per cent accuracy that everyone they isolated actually carried Lazarus. The ability to take and test a person's blood was actually a luxury. They weren't even able to test all the troops fighting on the front line, or the soldiers working logistics. That resulted in infected individuals being missed, still walking around shedding the virus.

Mistakes were made, some of the soldiers being quarantined when in fact they were no kind of threat. Nobody said anything about those cases. Nobody talked about the innocents who were doomed to infection by being confined in a room teeming with the virus. They got quarantined all the same.

Captain Beckington was one of those watching. As a member of the Royal Army Medical Corps, he was here to monitor the infected in the hope that one or more of them would turn out to be immune. He considered it a futile task because with every hour the front line of the fight against the disease got closer to them. Presently the RAF were bombing areas of London in an attempt to cut down on the undead numbers, but their enemy's influence was constantly expanding. With so few planes, the RAF's impact was limited, the air force of the United States being shipped home rather than joining the battle on British soil. At the barracks Whittaker was being held at, plans were already being made to evacuate and move further north. One of the only saving graces they had was that zombies only travelled by foot.

Beckington had considered his job a hopeless one...until he had noticed that Corporal Whittaker didn't seem to be getting any worse.

The men under the Captain's care were deathly sick. Except Whittaker. He had been in quarantine for nearly a day, and he hadn't really shown any signs of deterioration. Normally, once the symptoms came on, people started to go downhill fairly rapidly, often the fittest showing the fastest decline. Beckington had read the memo written by Colonel Smith about what to look out for and reckoned the Corporal might be a viable candidate. If he did turn out to be immune the orders were to ship him to Manchester where the trials were being conducted. This was why he had personally ordered Whittaker to have a second blood test.

Beckington just hoped they didn't get the command to ship out. Because in such an event, the standing orders were to abandon those in quarantine. At least he hadn't been ordered to murder them, although it would only be a matter of time before that became standard operating procedure he feared. How long would the rank and file put up with the wholesale slaughter of their infected brothers in arms?

22.08.19
London, UK

Colin thought that he had witnessed it all. Since venturing out of his flat, he hadn't slept, the window overlooking the street his new intermittent entertainment system. Whilst he kept the TV on in the background, the number of channels broadcasting had gradually depleted. The BBC was no longer broadcasting from London, Broadcasting House evacuated early on into London's undead uprising.

After he had plundered the corpse, Colin had sat in his window with growing wonderment. The zombies that had chased the woman were long gone, but more of their kind occasionally appeared in small groups, sometimes alone. He had yet to see the vast numbers reported on the news which was reassuring for the plan he was concocting. The world of Westminster was far away from him, this part of London still relatively under human control. Twice he had seen army patrols drive slowly down the road, and throughout the night the sound of gunfire and explosions could be heard intermittently.

At three in the morning, the gang of youths had returned to try again to raid the off-licence. This time they came better prepared, their crowbars making hard and noisy work of the metal barrier that had separated them from Nirvana. Their foolishness had attracted the undead, two running at them down the street with their usual deathly silence. After an initial and very brief display of bravado, the gang had all scarpered, perhaps finally abandoning the madness of their alcoholic desires. Colin wondered if they made it to safety. He hoped they hadn't, their kind not deserving to live in his opinion.

As the dawn rose on a new day, about a dozen zombies ran with speed down the centre of the street, the sound of a helicopter growing louder. As unbelievable as it was for Colin to see, the zombies were fleeing death from the skies, and several of them were chewed up by the bullets from the Vulcan cannon that was able to make short work of them. That just strengthened Colin's resolve. He didn't like seeing the agents of change struggling in their task.

By then he had already carefully loaded the pouches of his bomb vest with the nails and the ball bearings that he had coated in the gore of the undead. He had taken precautions to protect himself initially, but then the foolishness of that struck him. He was prepared to blow himself up for the cause, and soon. What did it matter if he contracted the virus or not? As sharp as the nails were though, he had managed the task without inflicting any kind of wound on his hands. He was of the opinion that luck was smiling on him this day.

By ten o'clock in the morning, he was still trying to figure out how exactly how he could deliver his glorious gift to the maximum amount of people when the TV gave him his answer. The advice to "stay in your homes" and "await further instruction" wasn't being followed. People were fleeing, trying to get out of London and who could blame them? There were camera views of large crowds gathering in areas of North London as they tried to escape the undead. All the time, the newscaster admonished those selfishly thinking of themselves. Any one of them could be spreading the virus to the people around them.

Nobody seemed to care about that, self-preservation becoming an overriding concern.

Colin had thus decided to join the exodus. It wasn't doing him any good staying around in his flat. This was why he was now on the street heading north.

The vest felt bulky and uncomfortable, but it was reasonably well hidden under the poncho. It was a crude device, made from explosives he had put together from simple household chemicals. He had no training in such, it was just stuff he had found on the internet through numerous anonymous visits to internet cafés. A simple USB stick allowed him to download such information without fear that the agents of the state were watching him. When most of your social life was spent online, you soon learnt the things you could get away with.

He was well aware that such information was not freely available on the visible web, so had needed to delve into the murky depths of the deep web. Even with the anonymous TOR browser, this wasn't something he was prepared to do at home. The last thing he wanted to have was the Met police or MI5 kicking his door down and carting him off as a suspected terrorist. That wouldn't have done his plans for revenge against humanity any good whatsoever.

Paranoid by nature, he had even visited different stores for the ingredients required, paying cash that he really couldn't afford. It was all for a good cause though, the explosive device becoming an obsession that took up weeks of his free time. During the day, when his menial job failed to occupy his time, the visions of what he would create filled his mind. He would drift off into a daydream of slaughter, his soul sacrificed to the martyrdom of a cause very few would understand.

All that had led him here. He was fortunate that rain was now forming, giving him an excuse to wear the poncho that adequately hid the intricacies of his homemade contraption. In his left hand, he carried the trigger, connected by wires to a detonator that he had put together himself. That had probably been the hardest bit of the whole thing to create.

His free hand held his phone, Google maps guiding him to his destination. He didn't need to know exactly where the masses were gathering. All he needed to do was follow the largest road he could find north, and eventually, he would come across a group of humanity big enough to make an impact.

His progress so far had taken him towards the Brent Cross. There would be people there and the proof of that was already evident. For the last two miles, the roads had been clogged with abandoned vehicles. So many people had stupidly tried to flee by car. What were they thinking? Some of the unoccupied vehicles were still packed full of suitcases and material wealth that had needed to be forsaken, the flow of human traffic on the pavements gradually getting thicker.

An hour ago, he had felt vulnerable, an isolated soul wandering deserted streets. Now there were dozens of people around him, all heading in the right direction. Soon there would be hundreds, then even walking would become difficult as the choke points and the crowds made progress difficult. That was what Colin was looking for. That was when he would strike. But not yet, oh no, not yet.

Around him the people travelled either alone or in small groups, separating themselves as much as possible, perhaps fearful of what anyone could now represent. Colin noticed that along with the haggard looks on most of the people's faces, eyes nervously flitted around seeking the inevitable danger. Most of these people had never faced anything but luxury. Even some of those on the lowest rungs of society had plasma TV's and smartphones. They didn't understand true hardship, most probably never having to walk this far in their lives. They amused Colin and it just reaffirmed why he needed to act in the way that was planned.

Humanity had come to the end of its run. They had been given wardenship of the planet and they had been negligent in their management of her resources. Perhaps with the bulk of humanity removed, the species could once again find its true place, creating a technological Eden in balance with nature.

Wishful thinking, Colin realised. More likely, if mankind survived, they would go right back to raping the planet. *Let's see if we can help stop that from happening*, Colin thought.

22.08.19
Manchester, UK

There was a knock on her door. Susan hadn't felt comfortable leaving the bedroom because she was doubtful that the house's owner actually wanted her here. She held a very reasonable fear that she might encounter someone that would suddenly decide she wasn't welcome after all. The end result would be her ejection from the building onto the now lawless streets. Whilst she had been hesitant about staying here, Susan had decided she didn't want to be outside those walls, not with what she had witnessed on the TV playing in this room. As much as she didn't like the thought of being around gangsters, it was a better proposition than being alone and vulnerable. She would soon learn that she was very wrong about that.

There was another knock, slightly more insistent this time. Wrapping the provided dressing gown around herself she cautiously went over to the door, mindful that she was still somewhat hung over. Susan opened the door, the Butler patiently standing on the other side.

"Good afternoon madam," the Butler said respectfully. "Mr Clay would like to express an invitation for you to join him for a late lunch." He spoke with a thick Eastern European accent that had at no time been spoilt by the fifteen years he had spent around English people.

"Really?" She was genuinely surprised.

"Yes madam. You would need to be suitably attired of course."

"Of course," Susan responded. She felt like she was suddenly in a dream.

"If I can have your dress and shoe size, I am sure I can find something to accommodate you. Mr Clay has a stocked wardrobe for just such occasions. Would that be agreeable?" Susan didn't think she had ever met anybody so polite, whilst at the same time being so potentially menacing. She could see what was underneath. This was no mere house servant. There was power under that immaculately pressed uniform as well as a bubbling malevolence. This was not a man you wanted to upset so Susan gave the man the information he had requested with exaggerated willingness.

"Very good madam. I shall make some suitable selections and return shortly. You will find a full makeup bag in the drawer below your bedroom mirror." He made it sound like a suggestion, but it was clear to her that this was a requirement.

"Thank you," she said numbly. The Butler actually bowed slightly as she spoke, before walking off with a grace that a man his size shouldn't possess. Susan watched him until he turned at the end of the corridor before closing the door.

It felt thick and sturdy, but she knew it would offer her no protection should somebody want to get through it. Was she actually a guest here, or was there more to this than she had originally expected?

The Butler's name was Viktor Patsiuk and he had worked for Clay for well over a decade. It was the perfect job for him. The pay was good, the tasks minimal and it presented him with a place to hide from his past. The past clearly didn't matter now, but he had pledged his service to his paymaster, and Viktor never broke a pledge. A former Ukrainian Spetsnaz, he had left the failing state to seek his true worth having discovered a growing realisation that his skills would be in great demand on the free market.

Working freelance had put him on Clay's radar as well as made him many enemies. Clay saw a man who was calm under pressure and who also had an enviable bearing and character. Viktor was also ruthless and hard as nails. So Clay had offered him a job, and soon found another use for the Ukrainian. The butler aspect was actually Viktor's idea. What better way to hide a vicious killer in plain sight than to masquerade as a simple servant? Several of Clay's enemies had fallen for the trap when presented to them. Viktor only masqueraded as a butler, he rarely actually performed the role. When he did though, he played the part perfectly having even taken instruction in the various tasks butlers performed.

There were other aspects to his employment that only a man like Viktor could carry out.

As he walked through the maze of corridors Clay's house represented, he assessed his opinion of the newcomer called Susan. She was a reasonably attractive woman despite her age, Clay normally requiring Viktor to acquire them much younger. She was thin which was not through exercise, but more likely borderline malnutrition. Viktor couldn't help but notice the half-empty vodka bottle on the sideboard, the smell of her room very telling. Viktor knew the knowledge of her alcoholism would be a powerful tool for Clay to use in the coming manipulation.

Viktor now understood why Clay had agreed to allow Susan entry to his home. It would be interesting to see how Mr Metcalf reacted when one of the lesser known truths about Clay was revealed to him. Viktor was looking forward to hopefully going toe to toe with Brian, his reputation as a hard man well earned. It was important for people like Viktor to constantly test their own abilities, and Brian would hopefully be more of a challenge than the last three people Viktor had been asked to kill.

There was always the chance that Brian would just accept what was about to happen to Susan. Viktor was just as happy for that eventuality to occur. Competent soldiers would be worth their weight in gold over the coming months.

At the end of the corridor, Viktor ascended a short flight of steps, taking a key out of one of his front jacket pockets. The door was innocuous, a passer-by likely considering it to be the boundary of a storage room. In a way it was, and a casual observer would think the contents belonged to the lady of the house. Inside there were several racks of elegant dresses, all wrapped in plastic, all delineated with exact sizes in ascending order. An impressive array of shoes, again all separated into various sizes and styles took up several shelves.

The problem with such a room was that there was not, and never had been a lady of the house. There weren't any closet transvestites living here either. These garments were present for another purpose. Viktor picked one dress that matched Susan's size, the one he knew Clay would want her to wear. The other dresses he picked were deliberately too small so as to give the illusion of choice.

All part of the game. All part of the trust that needed to be developed so that Clay could have his fun. What Clay did was of no concern to Viktor, he had seen things ten times worse on the back streets of Kiev and you had to give powerful men their allowances for their weaknesses. It was just that perhaps there were more important things for Clay to be concerning himself with at present than getting his dick wet.

***

Stuart(Z) had been relentless. Despite the injuries it had inflicted upon itself there was nobody that could stop it doing what the virus demanded upon it. Staggering from the stairwell, it had emerged onto a corridor that led to a dozen apartments. It had stood there for several moments, smelling the humanity that dwelled behind those doors before moving over to the closest one where it began to pound with calm fury.

Humans are a strange creature. Often in the horror films out of Hollywood, they are depicted as idiotic, doing things that are clearly counter to their own survival. As infuriating as this can be to some people, it was actually a true reflection of how mankind acted when faced with stress and impossible situations. People do stupid things due to a type of brain fog that descends in emergency situations.

Some people freeze in place, unable to react or save themselves, even when an opportunity for such presents itself. The brain kind of locks due to its limited ability in processing new information. Flooded with feel-good hormones, the prefrontal cortex shuts down, the part that is responsible for higher functions such as strategy and memory. Just when you need to be at your best, the brains of some people actually go against them.

The person whose door Stuart(Z) attacked first should have stayed cowering away in the hope that the undead creature would go away. But as the door shook in its frame, the fear that the door wouldn't hold grew. It would have, a single zombie unable to smash through what was effectively a fire door. The relentless pounding though, the almost rhythmic, endless assault seemed to go on without end.

The apartment owner got it into his head he could fight off the zombie, and armed with a large kitchen knife, he stared at the mindless assailant through the fish eye security viewer. Alone in the flat, there was nobody there to talk him out of it. When he finally opened the door, Stuart(Z) made short work of him. One zombie became two.

With the noise temporarily ended, some curious souls, perhaps not really believing what they were hearing about zombies on the news, decided to be all neighbourly and see what all the fuss was about. Two zombies became four. With one of the apartment doors left open, a zombie wandered in to find an elderly man sat on a sofa smoking a cigarette. He didn't even have chance to get to his arthritic feet before the zombie was upon him, the cigarette falling from his fingers onto the fabric at his side. If the apartments had been fitted with a sprinkler system, what happened next might have been prevented.

As the fire began to grow, a select few of the residents on that floor began to grow concerned with the noise they were hearing outside in the corridor. When the smoke billowed into the corridor through the open door, the fire alarm was triggered. With so many floors above this one, the result was a foregone conclusion. In the event of a fire, it was advised that residents stay in their apartments to await rescue by the fire services. But what chance was there that the fire brigade would even come? People made the only choice they could. They fled, the zombies going with them.

As the residents of Jessica and Stuart's apartment building began to descend the smoke-filled stairs, they would arrive in the entrance lobby to find the undead waiting for them. Many of them saved themselves from the fire only to be cut down by the dead guardians who blocked their way to freedom. Because one man chose to open his door to fight instead of hide, ninety-seven people were given the gift of resurrection. That was the start of how the city centre of Manchester eventually fell.

22.08.19
Houston, USA

Reece pulled up short of the military checkpoint and let the car idle. A yellow school bus passed her and pulled into the side road that led to the Astrodome. Nobody stopped it, the bus' arrival obviously expected. Reece wondered if it would ever be used to ferry children to school again. She had no idea who was on the bus because all the windows had been painted over which itself was somewhat odd.

She was hesitant to go any further. Reece was well aware she had made a promise, but really, did she owe anything to anyone other than herself? She could just drive on past and keep on going, couldn't she? Or would she eventually hit some checkpoint where her name and car registration would be flagged up? Even a Sherriff's deputy would be unlikely to have freedom of movement in the world that was forming around her. Better to perhaps just get this over with. It was at that moment that her thoughts were drawn to the sound of vehicles approaching fast. In her rear-view mirror, she saw three of them.

The pickup trucks shot past her and came to a screeching halt in front of the army checkpoint. The trucks were packed with men sporting an array of weapons. Doors opened and angry, riled up men piled out, others jumping from the backs of the vehicles. In response, the army corporal who Reece had encountered on her last visit appeared from under cover to see what the problem was.

Whatever these "Good Old Boys" were up to, it was damned stupid. They weren't just facing off against a few soldiers manning road barriers. From where Reece was parked, she could see the Bradley fighting vehicle, the guy in charge obviously aware of the commotion because the gun turret swung itself around. This could get ugly very fast. Whilst she couldn't hear what was being said, the fact that guns were about to be pointed at all and sundry meant this was likely only going to go one way. She wouldn't be surprised if there were snipers somewhere nearby getting very itchy with their trigger fingers.

"This is how you get yourself killed Reece," she said to herself as she put the car in gear and drove the fifty metres that separated her and the commotion. She was hoping her credentials still had some clout here, so she set the lights flashing and gave her siren several blasts just to let everyone know that the cavalry had arrived. Completely outmanned and outgunned cavalry. She parked and got out of the car, only some of the red necks even giving her a glance.

"You have my wife in there you son of a bitch," the obvious leader of the new arrivals was demanding. He was clearly the big swinging dick of this group, with the emphasis on big. Six foot four at least, an intimidating figure. Someone men would fear and who men would follow. From the corner of her eye, Reece saw soldiers running, the Bradley revving its engine.

"Sir, this is a restricted area," the Corporal shouted louder than perhaps he needed to. There were the same soldiers Reece remembered behind him, one manning a mounted machine gun behind an array of sandbags that had also been there when Reece had last visited. Security was being taken seriously, the number of civilians arriving increasing with every passing hour.

Reece sauntered over, deliberately putting a swing in her hips. She had a good figure and had never been afraid to use it to her advantage. She would use anything she had to give her a strategic edge when she needed it. Now she was catching a few eyes, most likely the nervous ones of Big Dick's group. She was already starting to see which of these men truly wanted to be here, and who felt they had no other choice less they lose face in front of their friends and peers. They were the dangerous ones to be wary of, not Big Dick and his inner circle. It was always some young punk close to wetting himself that caused situations like this to kick off. One of them would either feel they had to prove something or would take a shot just out of pure stupidity.

She had seen it all before. Men, sometimes they were just pathetic.

"Boys, can't we play nice," Reece chastised them from behind her surgical mask. She kept her hand on the grip of her pistol, but she knew drawing it would be a mistake. Strategically she put herself slightly in between the Corporal and Big Dick, who she now thought she recognised. Rupert Clayton, head of an unofficial militia that rarely gave the Sherriff's Department any trouble. They just liked to hang out in the wilderness at the weekends, shoot guns and, as their website stated, "*get ready for when the commies and the libtards try and take over the country*". They had no love for the Federal Government, but she was hoping that the Sherriff's badge on her uniform might mellow them somewhat. It still had to mean something.

She also knew she had to take her mask off for this. That was fine, Clayton and his men were all wearing some form of protection, although she wasn't sure the stars and stripes bandana one of them wore over his mouth would be particularly effective against a virus that turned people into the undead. She pulled her mask free.

"Mr Clayton isn't it?" Reece asked in a voice that said she already knew the answer. Clayton tipped his Stetson to her.

"That's right ma'am."

"What do you boys think you're doing driving around scaring folks?" Reece admonished them. She looked a few of the younger lads straight in the eye, very few of them able to keep her gaze. Yeah, these weren't troublemakers. They were scared people faced with what they thought was a legitimate problem, and they were intent on fixing it the way some Texans liked to.

"This isn't any of your concern, deputy," Clayton stated in a respectful tone. "These maniacs might have my wife in there, and I've come to get her out."

"If she's in here it's because she has been quarantined," the Corporal stated. The Bradley stopped at the other side of the barrier. Reece looked at the Corporal.

"Is there any way of finding out if Mrs Clayton is in your fine establishment?" Reece asked. What amazed her was how calm she felt. Normally the adrenaline would be going with so many guns around, but not now.

"Yes, but that's against regulations," the Corporal obstructed.

"Honey," Reece said playing the part she figured would have the most effect, "You aren't from Texas are you?"

"No ma'am," the Corporal added. It was clear from the soldier's accent, even behind the respirator.

"Why don't you help this gentleman know if his wife is in there." Reece pointed at the Astrodome. "Such a little thing to stop people shooting at each other."

"I just want my wife," Clayton insisted. "I'm not here for trouble." The Corporal seemed to mull it over and then talked into his radio.

"What's your wife's date of birth?" the Corporal asked finally.

"Eleven, two, seventy-four," Clayton added. He had dropped his gun now, as had most of his men. One of the worrying ones hadn't and Reece turned to him.

"Sweetheart, why don't you point that thing somewhere else before you hurt yourself." The worrying one looked like he had been ripped out of a trance, glanced around himself and saw that everyone else was now pretty much relaxed. He lowered his gun. "Bless your heart sweetness."

"Your wife was brought in two hours ago," the Corporal reported.

"Well you go and get her and we will be on our way." Clayton took a step forward as he said it, the tension ratcheting up again.

"Mr Clayton, did you receive the call this morning?" The call that Reece was referring to was the call for help by the Governor.

"Yes we did, deputy, and we were all willing to do our part until my wife fell ill at the hospital where she works. That's where she needs to be."

"What job does she do, sir?" Reece asked. She moved closer to Clayton, her hand now no longer on her gun.

"She's a nurse. She had sniffles last night and insisted on going into work this morning even though she felt unwell. We all rise to the challenge, her more than most. Then I hear she's been shipped off to this infernal internment camp. Betrayal is what I call it."

"Those infected have been brought here for their own safety," the Corporal said. Reece just wished he'd stop speaking.

"Bullshit," one of Clayton's men shouted. It got a murmur of approval from the crowd. Reece spoke again, she had to calm this because now she was, perhaps foolishly, right in the middle of it.

"She's a nurse, which means she would have been tested yesterday. Just as I was." Reece put her hands on her hips. "So if she was infected, she would have got the results today...just as I did."

"You're infected?" Clayton's body language actually told her he looked upset about the news.

"That I am. That's why I'm here, because this is the best place for me." Reece unbuckled her gun belt and held it out to the Corporal. "If these boys have no objection, I'd like a room with a view please." The Corporal took the belt off her.

Reece knew that without her intervention this thing would have devolved into a shouting match. Then the bullets would have started flying. Men were just so goddamn predictable. She helped diffuse the situation, but only because the anger was drowning out the good in these men. It didn't take much for Reece to persuade the Corporal to get Mrs Clayton on a radio so her husband could talk to her, especially with the subtle hint that Clayton's militia was nearly three hundred strong.

It was good to see the husband's tears as he clung the radio to his face, all the tension melting out of him as his wife calmly told him that her being here was for the best. Likely she told him off for being the loveable dolt he was. In this place, she could help as many people as she could whilst getting the treatment she needed. As big and as scary as Clayton was, Reece knew the mother of his children meant everything to him. That was the kind of relationship Reece had almost had once. Both of the Claytons would have been willing to die to save the other. Good people caught up in a shit situation. Fuck whatever God allowed this to happen.

"Thanks, deputy," the Corporal sounded relieved as the pickups drove away, a lot slower than when they had arrived. Reece had already joked about letting them all off the speeding tickets they were due.

"Things are getting hairy out there," Reece said. "You need to remember people are scared and unpredictable. Next time, be a bit more understanding."

"Yes ma'am. Can I say, you didn't look scared during any of that." That made Reece chuckle. She was talking to just a kid it seemed.

"Christ man, I'm already under a death sentence. What else is there for me to worry about?"

22.08.19
Manchester, UK

Only one of the dresses properly fitted her, and Susan wasn't stupid enough to consider that this had been a genuine error. The outfit was black and elegant, the dress just reaching the floor. But it exposed much of her back and would only work if she went braless. The plunging cleavage made that a challenge for her until she found some tape to hold things in place. There was a long slit down the side of one leg as well, meaning she would need to be very careful when she sat down. The butler had also brought her some black lace underwear which she was hesitant to wear. With the makeup, she had done what she could to hide the bruising on her face and neck.

The heels on the shoes were higher than she was used to also. Even so, the whole outfit was probably worth more than she had been able to earn in a month when she had been working. It was also very flattering to her figure, as if the dress had been made for her. The jewellery she wore in her ear was not even close to matching the finery of her attire, but there wasn't anything she could do about that. She looked at herself in the full-length mirror one final time and mulled over the prospect of what she was getting herself into.

Where the hell was Brian anyway? Why hadn't he come to see her? *Probably*, she told herself, *because of the way you keep showing him you don't want him around.*

Opening the door to her room, she wasn't surprised to see the Butler standing there again for her. Had he been stood there ever since he dropped the clothes off? He must have been, how else would he have known she was ready? There was no way for Susan to know about the surveillance cameras covering every angle of the bedroom she had been given.

"Madam looks radiant," Viktor said blandly. "If you will follow me." The heels were difficult for her to walk in and she struggled to keep up with Viktor who seemed to glide rather than walk.

"Are you a dancer?" she asked him.

"I have many talents," Viktor said, not really answering her question. The corridor led to a marble-lined landing, and he led her down a flight of stairs, slowing her progress even further. On the ground floor, Viktor waited for her to descend, no hint of any emotion detectable in his face.

"The kitchen is this way, madam." She could already smell the food, fantastic aromas filling the air around her.

"Smells wonderful," she observed, finding a need to make small talk.

"Yes madam." Viktor reached a large oak door and held it open. It led into the biggest kitchen Susan had ever seen, and she walked inside, Viktor closing the door behind her. There was a dining area, the open plan square footage probably larger than her house.

Inside, Clay was stood by one of the stoves, depositing freshly cooked food onto a pair of plates. He had on a tailored shirt and slacks, a cooking apron covering his substantial belly. The apron was black and had white letters saying *I'll get spicy if you get saucy.* The attempt at humour didn't really seem to fit the surroundings.

"Susan," Clay said enthusiastically. "So good of you to join me."

"I didn't realise you would be cooking the meal," Susan said. Behind her, Viktor poured a glass of red wine and handed it to her. She took it absently.

"For a guest as stunning as yourself, I would be foolish not to. Please, sit down." Susan looked around and saw that Viktor had pulled a chair out for her at the head of a table. The table was long, able to seat at least twelve people, and was positioned by a panoramic window that gave a delightful view of the ornate gardens. Clay pulled his apron off and lifted two plates up in his big shovel-like hands. The apron was left casually on the kitchen work surface, its presence almost an affront to the immaculate condition the kitchen was in. Walking over, he set one plate down in front of Susan, and the other on the placemat next to hers. Clay sat down not needing any assistance from Viktor who stepped back to a respectful distance.

"This smells wonderful," Susan said. She was nervous about what this was all about, but she was strangely reassured that Brian wouldn't bring her anywhere where she was in danger.

"Wait till you taste it," Clay bragged. He was bigger than she remembered, both in terms of muscle and fat. He wasn't grossly obese, but he could have done with losing a stone or two. Susan cut a piece off the salmon she had been served and popped it into her mouth.

"This might be the best thing I've ever tasted."

"I'm glad you think so," Clay said. He seemed genuinely pleased, and as he dug into his own meal, Viktor appeared over his shoulder as if on some unheard command. The empty glass on the table quickly filled with the same wine Susan was drinking. *Well at least the wine isn't drugged*, Susan found herself thinking. She stopped eating to drink a healthy mouthful.

"I'm not really used to this kind of elegance," Susan admitted almost embarrassingly.

"Very few people are. Even those who get it rarely enjoy it." Clay took a gentle sip of his own wine. "Me, I relish the finer things in life."

"I'm surprised you had time to do all this," Susan noticed.

"Susan you are my guest. It is important to me that you are looked after. Especially with what's happening outside the walls that surround us." He put his fork down and lightly gripped the top of her hand where it rested on the table. Her fingers seemed so tiny and delicate when compared to his sausage-like appendages. "It's important to me that you fit in here." The gesture seemed genuine, but she still felt uncomfortable with the physical contact. She didn't break it though.

"I was surprised you let me stay." The hand finally withdrew.

"You are Brian's family. He seemed concerned about you, but I don't want you thinking I'm being all altruistic here. I need Brian's mind on the prize, I can't have him getting distracted by you being at risk on the outside world." Clay took a larger swig of wine, Viktor on hand to refill the glass. "He's spent a lot of money looking after you the past few years, you should be thankful.

Besides, this house is empty without the presence of at least one beautiful woman. I'm not sure Viktor would look too good in one of my dresses. Isn't that right Viktor," Clay laughed.

"Very droll sir," Viktor commented without even the hint of humour. Outside a man walked past the window. He carried a machine gun and a gigantic German Shepherd was unleashed at his heel. Neither paid Clay or Susan any attention.

"How many men do you have here?" Susan asked.

"Forty-two. I'm a little understaffed because I had to give the maid the day off." For some reason, Clay found this immensely amusing. Susan took the last piece of salmon and slowly placed it in her mouth. "Every man has been specifically chosen for his worth. They are here because they are loyal and because they realise I offer them the best chance for their long-term survival. Even now your faithful Brian is on his third supply run to bring me the provisions I need to keep everyone safe." Clay pushed his plate aside. "You do want to be safe, don't you Susan?"

"Yes of course." The back of her neck itched a warning to her. Here it comes.

"Good. Because everyone here has to earn their keep." Clay looked at Viktor and nodded over to the oven, the butler leaving his post so as to deliver up the next course. The itch got stronger, danger signals going off in her head. Clay must have detected concern on her face. "Do not be alarmed my dear, there are several ways you can be useful to me." Viktor extracted a sizzling joint of lamb from the oven.

"What would you need me to do?"

"Susan, I am a businessman. Whilst I have been known to engage in acts of charity, that has always been with the understanding that such acts benefited me primarily." Susan found herself distracted by the way Viktor was carving up the meat. She nervously finished the wine in her glass.

"I'm not sure I understand."

"Then let me spell it out. To stay here you will be expected to pay your way. How you choose to do that I will leave up to you. Obviously, you are not equipped or trained to help defend my mansion so we need to find a position more…" Clay paused as if mulling over the words, "more suited to your talents."

"My talents?"

"You are an attractive woman with no specified skill set that I have been made aware of. You have no medical training that I know of, nor are you proficient in the use of firearms. I'm sure you can work the rest out for yourself." Susan sat there in shock, her fears finally realised. Part of her wanted to explode in outrage, to shout at Clay and chastise him for his arrogance. But the part of her mind that craved survival stopped her. These were not men you could insult and scream abuse at lightly.

"Would that mean having sex with…" She couldn't get the words out.

"With me? Of course. And frequently too." She looked at him, close to tears. A plate of the most delicious looking lamb she had seen was placed before her, but any appetite she held had long since disappeared. "You're shocked, that's understandable. Know that I would never force myself upon you, as I find such things detestable. So if you were to decline my offer of protection, I'm sure we could find you a roll more agreeable." Susan was blushing now. She had only met this man on a few previous occasions, and she had never expected him to be so forward with her. "As I said, my maid is no longer under my employ, so I will be needing someone to keep my house spick and span." He sat back as his main course was delivered. "All house staff work under the direct supervision of Viktor here. What do you think Viktor, do you think you can whip her into shape?" Viktor said nothing.

"Can I... can I have time to think about it?" Susan found herself asking.

"Of course you can my dear. Why don't you sleep on it and let me know in the morning? Know though that servants don't live in the main house and you will be on survival rations. No more luxury, no more access to the alcohol you so obviously crave." There it was, the final knife into her gut. Was he really prepared to use that against her? Damn right he was.

"Do you promise never to hurt me?"

"My dear, why would I want to harm a hair on your head? The only violence I ever use is against my enemies and those who betray me. You would never betray me now would you Susan? You would never dream of disappointing me?" It was all said with a smile, but the threat was there floating just below the surface. "Now eat. We have to keep your strength up." Susan forced herself to consume her second course despite the knot that had formed in her stomach.

"Think of what it would mean to you though Susan. As a mere maid, you would be the least useful person here, looked down upon by everyone. But as my lover, you would experience wealth and power that you could only dream of." As Viktor refilled her glass, she caught him with his guard down, a look of utter contempt etched across his face. Or was that done deliberately, just to empathise the alternate fate she could choose?

This was insane, but was it any worse than being one of those faced with survival on the streets? Susan's mind swam with the implications of it all. Oh Brian, what have you done bringing me here?

22.08.19
Leeds, UK

Andy Burns had filled his house up with food two days ago and hadn't left the house except to go to the garage a few times. Neither time had he encountered his psychotic neighbour Iain, which was something he was thankful for. He doubted his neighbour would be an immediate threat, but at no time now did Andy leave the house without his loaded shotgun sitting in the crook of his arm. The gates to his driveway were closed and locked with a large padlock he had never thought he would need to use.

One of the things he hadn't bothered buying on his shopping spree was water. A few years back he had purchased himself a dozen five-litre plastic containers, which had all now been filled via his house's outside tap. They were now carefully stored in the upstairs bedroom, with the bulk of his food, most of which was chosen because it wouldn't need cooking.

His mind was still telling him that the government would somehow get everything under control, even though the ever decreasing news channels were painting a dire picture of desolation and hopelessness. The British terrestrial channels were still giving the old "stiff upper lip" version, but most of the foreign broadcasts told the news for what it was. Riots in a burning Paris. Bangkok lost. Nuclear devastation in China. Forced deportations in Hungary. Mass executions in Russia. And all under the enveloping cloud of the undead who were on the march across the world.

With the bathtub full, Andy reckoned he had enough water to last about two months. But he didn't need it yet, the taps still freely flowing. Even with how much he had purchased, he was likely to run out of food first, so he had been briefly tempted to go out and get food from one of the distribution centres the army had set up, but that really was only going to be a last resort. Andy just didn't want to leave the apparent safety of his home. The virus was only just unleashing itself on Leeds, so he was sure it would be days before Hell's Armies came knocking at his door. Maybe, just maybe, the powers that be might be able to actually get this area of the country under control before then.

Last night had been briefly intense and Andy had barely managed to get any sleep. His detached house was on a hill and on the edge of the estate that the affluent moved to so as to escape the pollution and gridlock of the city centre. His back garden was guarded by a fence and thick trees that were virtually impassable. The only way onto his property was via the front driveway or over the fence he shared with that cretin Iain. Being on a hill, he also overlooked much of the middle-class estate as well as the main road that for much of the night had seemed deserted. For a ten-minute period though, the road, which was probably only a hundred metres from his front door, had been the scene of carnage. A gang of about a hundred had fled before a line of riot police. If he hadn't known better, Andy would have sworn the police had been firing live rounds. It had certainly sounded like it.

The only way to defeat this enemy was for people to resist the call of anarchy and chaos.

Tiredness weighed on him, but he felt relatively secure. The ground floor windows were all protected by security shutters that he had drawn down, and the doors were sturdy and specifically designed to withstand home invasion. His house was important to him as was his ability to keep it secure. A trained locksmith might have been able to defeat the front and back "drug doors" he'd had installed but each door was guarded with a motion alarm. Entry wouldn't go undetected. With what was happening, it was clear that he wasn't in the slightest bit paranoid with the precautions he had taken. His plan now was to wait it out and keep his fingers crossed. Could you wait out the apocalypse?

It was towards the afternoon when he heard the commotion outside. His house was on a cul-de-sac of ten, his being the largest and probably the most secure. So much so that any observation of outside had to be done from an upstairs window. It was one of those windows he now looked out of in complete disbelief as he watched Iain attack another neighbour's front door with an axe.

What the fuck was that maniac playing at? The door he was cleaving into was wood, and it clearly wasn't faring well under Iain's assault. Those particular neighbours were elderly, they wouldn't stand a chance against Iain's angry and muscular bulk should he get in. Any illusions that there was a shred of decency in the man who had casually assaulted a complete stranger two nights ago were quickly dispensed with.

Iain was dangerous, and sooner or later he would become a threat that would need to be dealt with. Would the police be there for that? Probably not, they were useless at the best of times but he was still willing to give that option a try. Andy's first port of call was thus the mobile phone. It would only allow emergency calls due to most of the network now being down in this area, but even then only a recorded voice answered telling him that his call couldn't be answered at this time. The irony was he could see the local police station from this very window. If anyone was going to help his neighbours, it would have to be Andy, and better to do that before Iain made his way through the door.

Was this a risk he was willing to take though? There was no telling how volatile Iain was at present. Nobody had been able to understand why he was so belligerent all the time, and with his unpleasantness people had actively tried to avoid Iain wherever possible. That likely just increased the nutter's paranoia. Andy seriously thought there was something mentally wrong with him because normal, well-grounded people just didn't act like this. Even if this was a life or death situation, they were a long way from the point where raiding houses was needed for personal survival.

Andy made his decision and ran downstairs where the shotgun rested against the front door, already loaded. The cartridge belt hung from the door handle, and Andy flung it over his chest. The last thing he wanted was to be outside without ammunition.

Keys in pocket and door locked behind him, he stormed over to his gate.

"Iain," he shouted angrily, at first not getting any kind of reaction. The front door Iain was assaulting was almost done, two more hits from the axe would probably finish it off. "Iain, fucking stop that." Iain seemed to finally hear him. Ten metres away, Andy's neighbour turned, brandishing the axe in both hands.

"You want some do you?" Iain screamed.

"What I want is for you to leave those people alone." The lock on the gate came off easily and Andy rested it on the ground. Passing through the gate, he levelled his shotgun at his adversary's chest, closing the gap until he could see the manic look in Iain's eyes.

"What does it matter to you?" Iain roared. His face was beet red, veins sticking out on his neck and temples. Even from this distance, Andy could see he was likely high on something. Was that what this was, some drug fuelled madness? Iain stepped away from the shattered door.

"It matters to me because you are scaring people." Andy was in effective range now. If he fired from here, Iain was in serious trouble. Even a blind man couldn't have missed from this distance.

"Scaring people? I have a right to defend myself."

"Defend yourself against what?" Andy had no notion of what this conversation was about.

"Against all of you," Iain almost screamed the words. "Ever since I moved in you've all been out to get me." Iain took another step forward, Andy matching it with a backwards motion.

"If you kept a civil tongue in your head there wouldn't have been any problems."

"Ah you say that, but I hear you all whispering about me."

"I've told you this before. Nobody is whispering about you Iain."

"Don't lie to me. You," Iain said pointing the axe at Andy, "you are the worst of them."

"I'm done putting up with you," Andy finally said. "Get back to your house and stay there."

"Or what?"

"Or you won't like what happens next." Andy didn't know if Iain believed the threat, but in that moment of exasperation, if Iain had rushed at him there was a very real chance that the trigger would have been pulled. It was in that moment that Andy realised he had it in him to kill another human being. Perhaps Iain saw this in his saner neighbour's eyes. Perhaps it was the voices echoing around in Iain's crazy head. Whatever it was, Iain dropped the axe and ran off back to his house, screaming incoherent obscenities as he did so.

Andy had a feeling that wouldn't be the last problem to arise from Iain. He noticed a few concerned faces from the surrounding houses, the neighbours he was protecting waving their thanks through one of their property's windows. Andy nodded back and returned to the safety of his gate. Perhaps he should have offered them further assistance, but he wasn't willing to help them more than he had, his community spirit all used up by the fear that was welling within. As for the elderly couple, they would have to repair their own door and fend for themselves from now on.

There was no telling who, if anyone, was infected. That was a fear that just wasn't going to go away. Also, the fact that nobody else had come out to help told Andy everything he needed to know. It was every person for themselves now. He couldn't rely on any one of his neighbours for any kind of help. Part of him was wondering if perhaps it would have been better if he'd let Iain do what he wanted. Might he have then got the madness out of his system? Or would it have just fuelled him on to greater acts of barbarity?

22.08.19
Manchester, UK

The early evening light was already threatening to fade, not that he had sight of that from the room he was in. Smith would have preferred to do this in privacy, but he knew that people would need to watch and record what was about to happen to him. He was thus no longer at the army base, the experiment too important to be done away from a fully staffed medical facility. Smith was back at the hospital, several rooms from where his Sergeant had been murdered by those bloody Americans. In fact, if he wasn't mistaken, he was in the very isolation room that had held Jessica.

On the army base, there had been no fellow scientists or doctors who knew enough about virology or genetics to help him. Here, the prying eyes gazed at his every move through an observation window and over the webcam he had set up. The room he was in was locked, his presence here now mandatory even with his standing and rank. On the army base they had not put him with the other quarantined suspected infected, for his knowledge and skill were too valuable to be put at risk by the premature risk of death should one of those other quarantined die and turn. Plus, it was bad form for officers to be cooped up with enlisted men, the latter making up the bulk of those who had become infected.

If this experiment didn't work, his last days it seemed were to be away from direct human contact. Azrael didn't count, Smith considered the assassin more of an animal than a member of the human race. When Smith had left the Preston Barracks, Azrael had been asleep, still restrained to the bed that was his new prison. The monitoring machines there had still confirmed that the assassin was in good health which gave Smith hope. What he was about to do was probably Smith's last chance at life. By Smith's reckoning, if this didn't work, he'd be dead this time tomorrow.

He had taken blood from Azrael before he left and had asked Patel to personally run the tests himself. From what they could see, the antiserum did give the appearance that it could kill Lazarus if administered pre infection, the virus giving indications that it was dying. Smith would have liked to have waited so as to do more thorough testing, but that was a luxury nobody could afford now. Now they needed to see if XV1 could cure an infected individual.

The screen of the laptop at the foot of his bed was split into four, three of the boxes representing concerned and anxious faces. In the bottom left, Michael Perry, the Director of the Centres for Disease Control, looked on, eager to see if there was some hope to help calm the building storm. The news out of the USA wasn't great, with multiple US cities reporting outbreaks. New York was the worst apparently, Gabriel's seeding of the virus having the desired effect. Containing the growing army of the undead wasn't the initial problem, the armed populace had that pretty much under control…when they weren't fighting amongst themselves. The problem was the virus that had started all this was ripping through the people like wildfire. With the US containing over ten cities with populations greater than a million people, the chances of any one of them becoming a teeming necropolis was too great. Consensus stated that, at this rate, it wouldn't matter how many guns there were, because there wouldn't be anyone around to shoot them. To date, the Americans had not encountered an immune individual on home soil.

Smith let Perry in on the observations due to more than just a courtesy. There was always the chance that at some point in the future, the Americans themselves might uncover the key to defeating Lazarus. Smith would want to be there at the front of the line if that happened.

On the other side of the observation window, Dr Patel looked in with a concerned expression. Patel was worried not just for Smith but also for himself. He too had started to show the early symptoms of the viral contagion. If the blood test results came back positive, he would also need to be isolated, and it would then be all but impossible for him to do the job required of him.

Smith for his part was now clearly unwell. He was sweating profusely, and was finding it difficult to keep food down. So nauseous was he that his life was now being sustained by an intravenous drip feeding him precious fluids. Smith was also finding it difficult to breathe, the high doses of antibiotics he was injecting into himself to fight off what he knew was bacterial pneumonia seemingly having no effect. He figured his life expectancy could now be measured in hours rather than days.

All this medication had been self-administered, which had been a challenge because sticking a Venflon needle into your own arm when your hands are shaking was not the easiest thing to do. Several of the army medics had offered to get suited up and do it for him, but Smith didn't want to put anyone else at risk. A needle stick injury was death, plain and simple. He might well have been considered a cold bastard by many, but he wasn't willing to put another soldier's life at risk unnecessarily.

"The time is nineteen twelve. The date is the twenty second of August, two thousand and nineteen. I am Colonel Wilson Smith, head of microbiology at the Defence Science and Technology laboratory at Porton Down. This is the second live trial of the plural antisera manufactured from the blood of the immune individual Jessica Dunn. This trial is to test the effectiveness of the antiserum on an infected individual." Smith spoke loudly, knowing everything was being recorded.

"Are you sure about this?" Perry asked genuinely concerned. "I still think we need to do more tests. The lack of any notable reaction by the initial test subject actually concerns me."

"Test subject one is stable and blood tests confirm he is fighting off Lazarus, despite my injecting the virus directly into his system. And I don't think I have much choice." Smith was about to add further comment, but he was overcome with a violent coughing fit that left him breathless and wheezing. That seemed to say more than words ever could. Lurching over the side of the bed, he vomited into the bucket he had strategically placed there. He hardly noticed the smell anymore.

Finally, he was able to gather his resolve and sit back up, having fallen out of the view of the webcam. "I'm running out of time. Extrapolating from other subjects, I'd say I have a day at most." Smith picked the pre-loaded syringe off the surgical metal table that sat at the side of his bed. The amber fluid inside didn't look particularly threatening, but he knew there was a strong chance this wouldn't work. He was dead anyway though, so what was there to lose?

"I would advise introducing it in increments," Patel interrupted over the room's intercom. "I too worry that you are rushing into this." Smith noted the doctor's concerns, and completely ignored them. Introducing the syringe to the Venflon that was already in place, Smith threw caution to the wind and injected the whole lot.

"I am administering ten millilitres of antiserum XV1," Smith said as he pushed down on the plunger. With the contents deposited, he removed the syringe and placed it on the metal surgical table that stood by his bed. He almost dropped it due to the shaking in his hands, and with the job done, Smith rested back against sheets that were already stained with his skin's secretions. Beside him, medical machines beeped and clicked, monitoring his vitals, all the data being sent over the internet to the concerned parties.

The back of his hand felt warm, and Smith held it up to get a better look. The dark, worm like tendrils had only started to show on his skin within the last hour, and he watched those around the injection site eagerly. The warmth spread up his arm, the antiserum quickly being pushed along by his bloodstream. No allergic reaction yet, thought Smith, at least that's something. The warmth spread to his chest.

Smith's heart skipped a beat.

"There is a slight lessening in the discomfort in the injection arm," Smith reported. The true test would be when the fluid he had deposited finally worked its way to his brain. Wouldn't be long now. His heart fluttered, the heart rate monitor sounding a temporary alarm. It felt like he suddenly had gas trapped in his oesophagus, and he tapped his chest to try and clear it.

"There is a marked decrease in the level of skin tendril pigmentation," Smith reported. "It feels like…" The words were stripped from his mind as his body suddenly went into a violent spasm. The virus did not appreciate the doctor's attempt to kill it, and it made its displeasure known.

"Colonel, are you alright?" Perry almost begged. One of Smith's feet struck the laptop a glancing blow. Whilst it didn't get knocked off the bed, the screen and the webcam were pushed so that Smith was no longer visible. The three people looking in over the webcam watched on helplessly as the room they were looking at shook violently, the laptop being buffeted by the gyrating of Smith on his bed.

They couldn't see him, but they could hear him scream. Patel was able to witness it all and he was horrified.

Smith had given strict instruction that nobody was to enter the room, no matter what happened to him. So violent did the seizure become that Smith fell off the side of the bed onto the floor. The IV stand went with him, the bag of saline bouncing slightly as it hit the vinyl flooring. A flailing hand knocked the half full bucket over, blood infused vomit sweeping across the ground.

"Colonel, can you hear me?" Patel asked through the room's intercom. He got no answer. Miraculously, Smith was still connected to some of the machines which told the world that the infected Colonel was still alive. But for how long? Patel could see that he was still breathing, so they had that. Zombies, like former US presidents, never inhale.

Smith thrashed on the floor, his hand striking the side of the bed so hard that it broke the skin. For Smith, none of this mattered. His world was pain, his mind an all-encompassing agony. There was no other perception detectable by him, the world around him meaningless. The battle with the virulent virus had begun.

His skin flushed, redness spreading across its surface. He should have been restrained during this, his movements actually propelling him across the floor. Smith ended up with his back pressed against the wall, a red smear left to mark his journey. So far had he gone that the pulse oximeter was ripped off his finger, the leads to the ECG pulling taught. If the wall hadn't been there to stop him, Smith would have likely pulled the trolley with the cardiac monitor across the room.

As quickly as the fit had started, his limbs quietened. The head still gyrated from side to side as if to some unheard music, his right temple resting on cold linoleum, but the bulk of his body stilled. That didn't mean it wasn't moving, the muscles under the surface, even the tiny ones that controlled the hair follicles, rippled and flexed making his skin look like it was alive. None of the cameras picked that up though, but Patel witnessed it with morbid fascination.

The storm in Smith's brain dulled slightly, and a thought popped in there, breaking through the static of torture that the antiserum had wrought.

You shouldn't be defying it.

He didn't understand what he was telling himself.

The virus is the next stage. It is who you are meant to be.

Smith tried to open his eyes, but it was as if they were welded shut, the thick pounding in his skull now matching his accelerated heartbeat.

It is who WE are meant to be. Why would you deny yourself that?

"Shut up," he managed to whisper, the lips burning as they moved. That was a new sensation, heat throughout his body.

This won't end well you know.

"I said shut up," Smith ordered, louder now, loud enough for the watchers to hear. The voice in his head was his own, and yet completely alien.

"Colonel Smith, can you hear me?" Perry insisted.

You should embrace it. Why try to fight? You really don't know the damage you have done to yourself...you will learn.

What was his own mind trying to tell him? With exaggerated effort, Smith tried to lift his head off the ground, a wave of dizziness ripping through him just from that slight movement. When he persisted, nausea was added to the equation, and even though there shouldn't have been anything left in his stomach, his body still managed to eject a fair volume. Blood, so much blood.

"Somebody's going to love cleaning this up," he joked to himself, the words virtually incomprehensible with his delirium and confusion. Through double vision and a cloud of confusion, he looked at the skin of his left hand, bringing it close. The skin seemed to dance, as if something was crawling under the surface, but Smith was too far gone to be concerned about that. His body twitched slightly, and he had one more thought before the blackness of unconsciousness took him.

The black tendrils...they were gone.

22.08.19
London, UK

Night-time and the crowd no longer moved forward. Whilst he couldn't see it, up ahead Colin could hear the orders being shouted through a bullhorn.

"Return to your homes."

"There is nowhere for you to go."

"You risk spreading contagion."

That last one was true enough. All around him people were coughing. On his travels, he had seen dozens of people doubled over in the street as they threw up. How quickly Britain had collapsed, spurred on by panic and the death of those who were supposed to be running the show. The army and the police couldn't fight a war and control the population at the same time, there just weren't enough of them. Even what they had was being whittled away by Lazarus which spread amongst them, unconcerned by rank or experience or age.

People had piled into their cars, intent on driving to motorways. But then where would they go? When the cars no longer became viable, they set out on foot, following the same plan, desperation and the faint hope of safety their only guiding light. As many people as there were here, even more still hid in their homes, listening to the advice given, hoping that some sort of order could be restored before the lights went out. Before the food was all consumed and before the taps ran dry.

Before the horde came.

On his way here, Colin had passed by a supermarket car park that had been signposted as a food distribution area. There was no sustenance to be found there, only dead bodies littering the cold asphalt. Colin didn't get close enough to find out if those were the bodies of the undead. Perhaps they had been alive, dead as a result of a riot or an attempted insurgent action against those handing the food out. None of that mattered, only the creation of more undead was of concern to Colin. Two dozen out of billions that needed to draw their last breath were of little consequence.

He had also seen a young child's body with its head caved in, the bloodied baseball bat that had been used to commit the foul deed abandoned and left as evidence by the side of the body. The killer would never be found, and truth be told there was no crime. It was clear that the child had turned and its body dispatched by those with the will to survive.

The crowd surged and pushed, concerns about contagion seemingly now forgotten. All they wanted was to get away, to forge forward, to clear the blockage that stood in their path…even though most of them didn't know where they were going. What was there for them past the boundary of the M25? The more people that fled into the suburbs and the countryside, the more they would be like locusts, stripping the land of any kind of life sustaining nutrition. It was as if a kind of collective madness had overcome them, their minds overtaken by a force too strong for their will.

Colin didn't realise how right he was.

Whereas many infected with Lazarus hid themselves away from the world, others felt compelled to interact, to spread the virus throughout their community. Many in the crowd were now displaying this characteristic, most blissfully unaware that their brain chemistry was being manipulated by a genetic aspect that tweaked thoughts and fired neurons. An addict would know exactly how they felt, because it was the same mechanism that was being manipulated, endorphin rewards being released the more those infected touched and caressed the human world around them. In this way Lazarus maximised its spread and its survival. Some carriers would circulate the disease, whilst others hid away so they could be guaranteed to transform into the virus's ultimate creation.

Several people over from Colin, a young man collapsed to his knees so he could vomit, the stream splattering across the floor. People tried to back away, shouts of abuse and distress rippling through the mob. Because that was what they had become, turning on the hapless youth, feet suddenly descending on him in a rain of merciless kicks. Colin, unimpressive physically as he was, managed to position himself to witness the desperate act of self-preservation. All the victim could do was curl into a ball and accept the blows that fell on him relentlessly, some of his attackers grinning madly, their minds swamped by the madness of what they were doing.

Colin thought he heard bones breaking. The sound was fantastic.

A hefty kick got through the defences, smashing into the man's temple. The villain of that particular assault was wearing heavy work boots, and the mob seemed to part to give him more room. The villain kicked again, this time stepping back to put more power into the effort. The fallen man's face exploded, his defensive hands falling away, resistance now gone. Then the throng renewed their attack and Colin turned away, bored now of what he was seeing. Civilisation was being stripped away with every second so Colin wormed his way to the edge of the crowd, knowing that this was the best way for him to move his way forward.

Still the cacophony from the megaphone ordered and pleaded for the people to go home. Wasn't it clear to the speaker that there was no going back for most of them? Colin knew he had to act fast, for it would not be long before guns were used to quell the pack. He suspected that this would be an epic mistake, because this was a herd, and they were not intent on going anywhere but forwards. There weren't enough bullets to stop what was inevitable.

Colin slipped into a side road, the crowd almost pulsing as the numbers continued to grow. Ten metres down this smaller road, he saw a woman being gang raped by a group of three men. A second woman, one with the rapists, sat on top of the car the victim was being held against. She shouted encouragement to her companions, mindless of the damage that was being inflicted to a fellow woman. Somehow Colin caught her eye, and she beckoned him over, a bottle of some nameless cleat spirit gripped firmly in one of her hands.

"Come and stick your dick in something sweet," the vile woman yelled at him.

There was no temptation to join in such unthinkable abuse. Colin was here to end such atrocities, not engage in them. Ignoring the drunken woman and shutting out the plight of the men's prey, Colin turned and forced his way back into the crowd, the finger on the trigger he held itching to be used. He would stop this, he would stop it all.

By the time he got into the centre of the mass, his ear was swelling and he thought it a strong likelihood he was now the proud owner of a black eye. Elbows and fists had been thrown, some by accident, some deliberately as people objected to his intrusion. Standing there amongst people compressed into four people per square metre, jostled by everyone around him, Colin knew the violence humanity was capable of. People were dying here as well as infecting each other. Some fell through sheer exhaustion only to be trampled underfoot.

Others were singled out and killed by a group mind that seemed intent on removing any perceived threat.

Any apparent slight was no longer met with a verbal exchange, but by instant physical retribution. Now was the time before those present descended into a primal version of themselves. Here and now Colin would make himself known to the world, and with his death he would do his part in bringing forth the new order. He was not unique in the desire to kill himself, thousands across the city already having done so. Very few however had the desire to cause such mass carnage.

Colin pressed the button.

His concerns that he had created a dud were to be unfounded. The bomb detonated at the rate of twenty-eight thousand feet per second, the surrounding air pressure spiking to over two thousand pounds per square inch. Those within the initial blast radius were ripped apart, organs rupturing, eyes liquefying, limbs stripped clean off. The shockwave turned the nails into lethal projectiles travelling at over a hundred miles an hour, shrapnel thrown out into the crowd. Ball bearings passed through pliant flesh like it was tissue paper. Within seconds there were over a hundred dead, hundreds more maimed and mortally wounded. Broken limbs, ruptured ear drums, shattered organs, flesh pierced by shrapnel, some of it from the very bodies closest to the blast.

Colin's torso was completely obliterated, his head hurled into the air, landing within the maimed crowd several metres away. He would never have to worry about the plight of humanity again.

Those killed directly next to the blast would be useless to the virus, others damaged too badly to be of any worth. Many of those killed outright died before the virus could get a grip on their system, the blood streams already dead so as to prevent the transmission of Lazarus to the brain. But enough were left to resurrect, either due to already being infected, or maimed just enough that it took them time to die. Others with less serious wounds were victims of the shrapnel, the virus forced into their system by the piercing of the flying knives.

Colin did his part that day, and within minutes, dozens of the undead were rising up to attack what was left of the living. Within an hour an undead horde had formed that numbered into the thousands which moved north to the M1, the country's primary motorway. With so many people congregated in one spot, a new battalion of the damned formed. And with its many feet it would head out north expanding the war that was already being lost.

22.08.19
Preston, UK

To look at him, people would think that Azrael was asleep. Still on the bed that Smith had shackled him to, his body was immobile but his mind raced. Once again the dream had come, and now it was more intense than ever. To think that Azrael had somehow missed this ordeal. Even he wasn't guilty enough to suffer such cruelty.

A thousand times he had been here, but the world of his nightmare had never felt this real. This was true pain. The sky above burned with the heat of hell itself, the sun red and baking in the sky, the very air moving as the ground was scorched beneath it. Azrael looked at what was left of the flesh of his hands and saw only a blackened crust. Every movement caused the surface to crack, blood and pus seeping from the wounds, only for it to boil away into the atmosphere.

His ability to see confused him for he remembered that his eyes had been plucked out long ago. There was a new sensation here also, one that he had never before suffered. A hunger so terrible it felt like his innards were being sliced apart by the finest of razors, thousands of them meticulously and surgically altering the lining of his intestines. He needed food, and there was only one thing that would satiate him...human flesh. The need for it almost brought madness, but he wouldn't be spared by that mercy.

Around him hundreds of bowed and decimated figures walked as he did, the feet never stopping despite the toes now being reduced to blackened stubs. It was as if the floor below was coated in a myriad of needles that pierced into his calves every time he took another faltering step. Yet still he walked, the agony there almost irrelevant, hidden by the purgatory that seemed to encase every cell of his being.

To his right somebody fell, only for them to pick themselves up out of sheer force of will. Never before had Azrael seen someone so close in the wasteland, and what was left of his sight became drawn to the form. A female who had suffered damage, but nowhere near the torment inflicted on Azrael. Had he been here longer than her? And why was she so familiar?

In the distance the great mountains called to him as they always did. They towered on the horizon, guardians against the storm that swept the dust off the ground to contaminate even the smallest of wounds. Again, the woman staggered, her nakedness hidden by the dirt that caked her, burning away the top layer of her epidermis, changing her.

Over the sound of the wind, Azrael heard her weep. Then she turned to look at him...Jessica?

Never had he deviated off the path, but he did so now, turning towards her, steam rising from the ground where her knee rested. Stumbling, he reached her, helping Jessica from the parched earth, the very contact with her flesh sending lances through the palms of his hands. He cared not, and he held her so that together they could move forward.

"Thank you," the words came from her cracked and desiccated lips. Why was she here? What did this mean? Azrael did not speak, merely urged her on because he sensed the true danger was close. Others felt it too, the lost souls picking up their benign pace as the dust rose high to their rear. The horsemen were near and they were getting closer.

"Why are we here?" Jessica asked. "What have we done to deserve this?" Azrael knew his own crimes, but had no knowledge of the sins of Jessica's flesh. He urged her on, better to be away from this place. There was no escaping the horsemen, but at least there were others in their path. They still had time. They still had...

"TIME," Azrael shouted to the room as his eyes opened. The space around him seemed to retain the heat of the desert, but only briefly, the sun vanishing to be replaced by the overhead halogen. The bindings held him, the room locked and empty of anything sentient. His captors would be outside, unwilling to leave him somewhere he could even remotely escape from. How little they understood about him now, Azrael wasn't going anywhere. The fact that he had pissed himself meant nothing to him.

"Carter," he demanded loudly to the room knowing that there would be people listening, "It's time to uphold your end of the bargain. Bring me Jessica. Bring me Jessica now."

22.08.19
RAF Northolt, UK

As they were under observation, the men in quarantine would have to sleep with the lights on. Many here no longer had any set sleep patterns. They spent their time in their beds or by spending torturous hours walking to and from the bathroom. Every time the door opened, everyone expected another soldier to be unceremoniously deposited. Not this time.

"Corporal, I need you to come with me." The door to the barracks had opened and Captain Beckington had walked in flanked by two Military Police guards armed with pistols. Several of the quarantined men closest to the door cowered in their beds, wary of the guns the two MP's were brandishing. They had seen what those MP's had been willing to do.

Whittaker stood up. He didn't know that the evacuation order had been given due to multiple zombie outbreaks north of London. A series of defensive lines were being set up across the country, and if they stayed here they risked being on the wrong side of the battle. Most of the army personnel at the base would be relocated to Northwood Command, the military headquarters facility of the British Armed Forces. Military strategists had deemed it an essential facility to hold. The RAF were preparing to abandon the base if necessary.

"What about the quarantine?" Whittaker asked. The knife he had been given was now thrust into the belt at his hip. With the volatile reaction he had witnessed in Tod, he was wary about not having it on his person.

"You let me worry about that, Corporal." Whittaker stood, but so did Tod.

"Hey, why does he get special privileges?" Tod objected, stepping forward from where he had been sitting. His breathing was laboured, but he resisted the irritating temptation to cough.

"Sit down private," one of the MP's said menacingly. He didn't raise his gun, but the arm holding it tensed.

"Or what? You going to shoot me are you? Might be better, put me out of my misery."

"That is presently a strong possibility," the MP countered.

"I'd rather not leave these men," Whittaker pleaded.

"That's an order, Corporal," the Captain insisted. Whittaker looked around at the men and simply shrugged his resignation. It was at that moment the Sergeant chose his moment to begin his final death spiral. Going into violent spasm, everyone in the room was distracted by the event.

Whittaker turned, one of the guards stepping forward into the room further than he should have. Tod was thus partially obscured from the MP's sight.

"Restrain that man," the Captain shouted indicating the Sergeant who was very close to drawing his last breath. Several of the men followed the orders, but not Tod. Even though he was shaky on his feet, he sidled up beside Whittaker who was momentarily engrossed with the Sergeant's impending death. Whittaker wasn't expecting Tod to be so stupid until he felt Tod rip the knife from his belt. With desperation, Tod gripped him by the back of his collar, the knife pressing dangerously into Whittaker's back.

"Easy now, private," Beckington said. Any lunge at the man risked Whittaker being impaled. Both MP's raised their weapons.

"You know I've always thought you were a cunt," Tod almost whispered in Whittaker's ear.

"Feeling's mutual." Whittaker tried to crane his head to look at the idiot holding him captive, but that just got the knife pushed into his back a little bit more. It was yet to break the skin. This just proved what he had always suspected about Tod. Unstable and unworthy of anyone's trust.

"You don't want to do this Private," one of the MP's stated calmly.

"Oh yeah? Why does he get to leave and the rest of us get stuck in here?"

"Because Corporal Whittaker is immune," Beckington finally relented. He hadn't wanted to tell anyone, hoping to just spirit Whittaker away and leave the rest of the dying men to their own devices. But there was always one ready to spoil your best laid plans.

One of the MP's, the one who had been forced to punch Tod, had strongly suggested the best course of action would have been to shoot the petulant private. Beckington was kind of wishing he had taken that biased advice. The martial law powers given by the Royal prerogative would have probably allowed for it. Even if it didn't, who was going to put him before a court martial for acting in the best interests of his men? The country's civil liberties were disappearing faster than cheap lager on a stag do.

"Fuck off with that bullshit," Tod said dismissively. He didn't believe a word of it.

"His test results came back. Your Corporal is one of the few who is able to fight off the disease." The Captain let those words hang in the air for several seconds before adding, "which means with his blood we can provide a cure to everyone in this room."

"I'm seriously immune?" Whittaker asked. Even with a knife in his back he felt overwhelmingly relieved.

"Yes." The knife eased in his back. As yet, the Sergeant was still not an immediate threat, but that wouldn't last long. "So private, if you harm your Corporal, you pretty much sign the death certificates of everyone in this room." The hand grabbing Whittaker's collar slowly released itself. "Including yourself."

"There's a cure?" Tod asked. He was almost crying, his actions most likely fuelled by rage and desperation as well as his own inherent idiocy. Nobody rushed him, none of the men in a position to had the energy. The knife dropped out of Tod's hand and Whittaker moved away from him after picking the blade off the floor. He was very tempted to punch Tod in the face to add to the existing injury, but when he looked at what was a broken man, all he had was pity.

"I'll take that," one of the MP's said and Whittaker handed the knife over. The other MP stepped up to Tod and pushed him sprawling to the floor.

"Now that the stupidity is over," Captain Beckington couldn't hide the exasperation in his voice, "let us deal with the more important business. You men," the Captain said to those holding down the Sergeant, "step back there." Looking at one of the MP's, Beckington indicated what was required. The MP took five steps forward, and without a second's hesitation, shot the ailing Sergeant in the head several times. Clearly there was no time for the usual finesse, blood splatter coating the wall behind the bed. Why was it so much worse to shoot someone so close to death rather than just after?

"Corporal!" Beckington indicated to Whittaker that now was the time to leave. Whittaker felt relieved that he was free to go, but at the same time he had an overriding sense that he was abandoning the men. He was also shocked by how the Sergeant had been mercy killed. Were they at that stage already?

Whittaker left the room where more soldiers were waiting for him.

"When will we get the cure, Captain?" Tod begged. He still lay on the floor, his stupidity clearly taking the last of his strength. Whoever was in a position to help him had stayed well away. Two soldiers with a body bag pushed past Whittaker and went over to the now dead sergeant, the sick soldiers backing away further, still wary of the fact that there were guns being pointed.

Tod never got his answer. Outside, Beckington caught up with the men spiriting Whittaker away. The Corporal didn't know it, but he was now one of the most important people in the country, perhaps the whole world.

"So you can use my blood to help those men?" Whittaker asked.

"We can use your blood, but it won't be for those men. Those men are lost, Corporal. The sooner you understand that, the better it will be for everyone involved."

"You're just abandoning them?"

"Yes, because we don't have any choice. There is a vast undead horde less than an hour away. We have to leave, and all we can do is save what we can."

Whittaker wanted to protest, to insist that more be done for the men, but he didn't, instead accepting what the Captain had told him. He would always wonder what ultimately became of the men he had shared his quarantine with, not knowing that they were all to be killed before the evacuation, just as the Sergeant had been. The pressure of fighting the enemy was straining the humanity of the defenders to the limit.

22.08.19
Manchester, UK

Renfield had needed to kill two more in the last hour alone...and neither of them had given him any kind of buzz. Sitting there, his previous optimism and excitement had worn off rapidly. He'd hoped to at least have an opportunity to safely feed the evil that lurked in his soul. Instead it left him feeling like his very essence was being starved. It was becoming more than he could stand.

Even the thought of Lucy did nothing to help this. She was a delightful creature, but her presence was a distraction at best, the dissatisfaction of his present situation overriding her allure. Also, he found the gas mask stifling, his whole body hot and uncomfortable and he discovered that he was constantly fidgeting, almost nervously. The soiled diaper he wore annoyingly chafed him. Killing the undead had given him nothing in the way of satisfaction. It was like being in the best restaurant in the world, only to suddenly find you had lost your sense of taste. Renfield wasn't prepared to put up with it any longer.

At the end of the ward, he had noticed that one of the beds was more isolated to the extent that the privacy curtain could be drawn around it with effort. The notion of what that meant kept crawling up at him, nudging his conscious thoughts along a path he knew all too well. In his youth he had learnt to control the compulsion to kill, to bottle it up safe in the knowledge that there would be a time when it could be released. His own sense of self-preservation had beaten the animalistic urge that was always there, suppressed beneath the surface. His successful dances with death as a child had taught him a lot about how difficult murder was to get away with, luck playing a big part in why his miniature killing spree hadn't been discovered.

Here though, the urge now became unbearable, unleashed by the total frustration of the situation. He knew he had no choice, his desires needed feeding. It was all he could think about and Renfield finally stood up and walked what he had overheard one nurse call his "death march".

The bed in question held a middle aged man who was barely conscious. He was still clearly alive, but Renfield had already decided that this was an error that needed correcting. Why prolong the inevitable? Nobody seemed to care when he pulled the privacy curtain around the man's bed, the sound of the runners almost hypnotic.

Renfield wasn't surprised by the erection that formed as he stood over the still form. This was a moment to be savoured, perhaps the defining point of his life. He was about to kill a man, out in the open where he could easily be discovered and he knew he was going to get away with it. He had the ultimate alibi, the perfect reason for fulfilling his passion. It was perhaps not the way he wanted to go about the killing, the knife too quick, almost merciful. But you had to take the chances life gave you.

The first victim he had ever killed as a teenager had died by fire. That was where he had learnt how easily your act of murder can attract the attention of others.

He peeked his head outside the curtain and checked that he was still the only person in the hospital ward who was presently standing. Briefly his eyes passed over Lucy whose bed was half way down the ward. She was clearly watching him, the expression on her face unreadable due to the distance. That was not something he needed to concern himself with, he told himself, and Renfield brought his presence back to where it was needed, the curtain falling back into place from where he had briefly parted it.

Cautiously he got close to the head of the bed and laid a gentle hand on his soon to be victim's shoulder. The patient didn't stir, the breathing shallow and rhythmic. Renfield matched that breathing, letting his own chest rise and fall to the flow of life that still coursed through the man. Memories flooded back to him, images from his childhood that delighted and inspired him. Now was the time to make true everything he knew he was. And if he got away with it, Renfield knew this would only be the first.

Renfield's hand moved to the patient's forehead so he could push the head to one side. A low murmur came from the parched lips of the near sleeping man, but there was no real protest. Was there even a crime here? This man was dying, there was no denying that. There had been a briefing saying that there were "immune individuals", but that information was clearly either false or overly optimistic. He didn't care either way. As far as Renfield was concerned, as many as possible now needed to die by his hand. It was as if some switch had been flipped in his head. He would not let the virus rob him of his true calling. The challenge was that one death would not be anywhere close to enough for him.

There was a potential problem though. If this man was going to die anyway, could Renfield's mind reject the upcoming act? Would it be seen as a gift of mercy, negating the rush that he hoped would flood his system? There really was only one way to find out.

Renfield withdrew the knife from its sheath, a jolt of power rippling up his arm. Inside, he felt the pleasure building, the expectation of what was to come. None of this had happened when he had killed the zombie. Carefully his free hand slid down the patient's face until the fingers lightly covered the patient's mouth, the thick glove preventing him from feeling the hot breath that would be escaping there. Such a shame, Renfield would have liked to have experienced that. His protective clothing spoilt some of the sensation for him but it was essential for his own protection. In truth, he would have preferred to be naked for this, skin to skin contact needed for the full force of the transference. It mattered not the sex of the person he was killing.

The second person Renfield had killed as a teenager was with a knife slicing open the throat. That was where he had learnt the danger of your victim's blood, the way it sprayed, the way it corrupted everything you wore. It was also where the belief that he could absorb other's life energy occurred. That was what Renfield pretty much now believed. By ending the life, he was going to draw the person's spirit into himself. There was no telling why this madness had developed in the neurons of his mind, but it was there, a belief as strong as the knowledge that the sun would rise every morning. Even though he saw the effects of what the virus did, the pull to disrobe, to just let go and experience the fullness of the act was strong. Renfield resisted, knowing he had no choice but to compromise.

He couldn't let this just be a single act.

His fingers pressed down harder over the sedated man's lips, no real objection there either. Renfield drew the blade closer, pushing the tip against the base of the neck. There he paused, pressing slightly, readying himself for what he hoped would come. It was so easy to push, the force steady and strong, the sharpness of the blade breaking easily through skin and muscle, the path of the weapon slipping easily between the bones. That was when the dying patient came back into the world, his eyes shooting wide, the limbs suddenly thrashing in the bonds that held them. Giving one final shove, Renfield circled the knife in the man's brain, destroying everything there, severing nerves and blood vessels, slaughtering the thing that separated mankind from the animals. Memories, gone. Consciousness, gone. Never more to hope, dream or fear the world that could create such a thing as Lazarus.

The body slumped on the bed, now totally still. Blood poured, soaking into and corrupting the pillow.

Renfield nearly fainted, the power flowing into him almost toxic. As it was, he staggered on his feet, almost falling into the curtain, the knife left in the skull momentarily forgotten. This was it, this was everything he remembered. And more, oh it was so much more, the ever present threat of discovery heightening the sensation. He was relieved that his soul rejected the idea that this was an act of charity. No, this was savagery, and Renfield revelled in it.

He climaxed, his orgasm almost going unnoticed in the other sensations that stormed through him. Renfield realised that he had almost forgotten what this feeling was like, his child's brain not really able to fully appreciate it. Any control over his addiction was thus instantly lost. He knew he needed this now, his wise abstinence almost confusing to him. There would be no more waiting for the dead to become dead. No, everyone here would die by his hand because it pleased him to make this happen. He would help every one of them on their way, but perhaps he would save Lucy.

Or at least leave her to the last. The thoughts about what he could do to her sexually were nothing compared to what it would mean to have her inside him. When he finally sucked up her life force, she would be with him till his dying days.

It was several minutes before he emerged back from behind the curtain so as to shout the nurse. His story about how the patient had rapidly died and had thus needed instant action on his part was easily believed by people who were now becoming numb to the horrors of what the hospital represented. It was no longer a place of healing, but a place of death. The nurse and the porters, they too would join the list of the dead eventually.

Renfield saw it all now, saw what he needed to become. He had a legacy to build.

Lucy saw it also and knew the truth in it all. But her mind was delirious with the effects of the sedation that had been forced on her so perhaps, she told herself, it was in fact all in her imagination. Still she would watch the soldier as if her life depended on it.

***

"Do you dream of the desert and the horsemen?" Azrael was sat up, still shackled, the back of the bed raised for him and pushed closer to the observation window. Jessica sat on a stool well out of his possible reach behind the glass, her guardians with her. Nick and Jeff looked at each other, both confused by what was being said.

"But how did you…"

"I saw you there. I saw you marching towards the mountains."

"That's impossible." Jessica looked at him as if he had gone mad. And yet, how could he know about her dream? Whilst it had only occurred a few times since being bitten, it had become more intense this last occasion. Normally the images she dragged from sleep dissipated and blended into obscurity, but not now. She could remember much more of the nightmares, and their memories sent a chill down her spine just to think about what she had witnessed in the realm of sleep. Fortunately for her, she didn't really remember the suffering, just the imagery.

"And yet here we are. Perhaps we are connected."

"I don't believe in such things," Jessica insisted. She knew she was lying to herself, but there was no need to reveal that to this man. Not when the evidence of what he had done was so great. Her lawyer's mind had always tried to hide her yearning for what so many called a soul mate.

"That's not what you said when we first met. You looked me in the eyes and told me you felt we had a deep connection."

"You…you remember that?" That was why she had originally fallen for him, and fallen hard. Even with his betrayal and the witnesses to his murderous character, she felt the old pull forming. Being here with him was dangerous. Perhaps that was why she had told Nick that at no point was she ever to be alone with him.

"I told you, I remember some of it. Being with you brings more things back, recollection flooding into my mind. I'm just not that man anymore, it's like I'm remembering someone else's life." Just being around Jessica also caused him to have a headache which he easily ignored.

"So you don't have any feelings for me?" Jessica blushed at the question.

"I'm not even sure what feelings are." There was a sadness in his face that threatened to melt her heart. With the knowledge of what had been done to him, she found it was difficult to hate Azrael. She tried hard to find that emotion, but it was annoyingly elusive. "I think any part of me that can feel affection was killed off when I was reborn."

"What do you think the dreams mean?" Nick asked. Nobody had been expecting him to speak, including Jeff. Jessica welcomed the interruption.

"I can only speculate."

"I ask for nothing else," Nick reassured him.

"I think we will know for sure when you uncover more immune individuals."

"You think it has something to do with the virus?" Jessica asked. She looked at Nick, but it was difficult to tell what he was thinking. His face never gave anything away.

"I do. I have a memory from last year that comes to me now. I had been told to expect a delivery, a parcel dropped off by the usual courier. Only this time it was an injection gun with an attached vial. I was ordered to inject myself with it. The dreams started shortly after that. Nothing like that had ever been ordered before."

"What, you are telling us this now?" Nick was clearly exasperated.

"I told you, it only just came to me."

"Thin ice my friend, thin ice," Nick warned his captive. He flipped a switch which activated his radio headset. "Natasha?"

"Yes boss," her voice came over the single earphone he wore. Nobody else could hear her.

"I need to ask Moros a question. Can you do that for me?"

"Easily," Natasha stated. "I have full access."

"Here's what I want you to ask."

Everyone but Azrael seemed shocked by the question.

22.08.19
London, UK

Sid(Z) marched at the head of the horde, street lights creating shadows that just increased the feeling of their malevolent presence. Now thousands strong, the horde moved slowly and meticulously attacking any residence that held the smell of humanity. Sid(Z) did not concern itself with such distractions. It still held the half eaten remains of the baby it had acquired hours ago. Occasionally it would lift the limp body up to its mouth and rip a chunk from the soft pliant flesh. No longer able to swallow, it just chewed the meat relentlessly, the taste an essence of pleasure and frustration. The flavour was a delicacy like nothing a human had ever experienced. The frustration because the hunger within it could never be satiated. But it knew of nothing else it could do, the virus forcing it on to a never ending circle of denial.

The only way to end its ceaseless torment was to destroy the part of the brain that now caused the dead body to defy the laws of nature. So far it had escaped that fate.

There were bodies strewn about the street, not the result of a zombie attack however. These people had been alive, their torsos so less resistant to bullets than the sons and daughters of hell who now stepped over them. Occasionally a zombie would bend down and begin to feast, fulfilling the demands of the hunger. Most followed Sid(Z), some mechanism temporarily making it leader of this particular pack. They needed to move, to spread, to enrich their ranks with fresh carcasses. The bulk of the mob marched thus on, their feet the only sound to escape their massing ranks. Across the city, more such groupings occurred, each accumulation separated into clumps. The zombies had somehow learnt that there was a very real risk from the humans who flew in the sky.

If it could still read and see, Sid(Z) would have seen the sign that said A40, would have observed the bridge they travelled under. The piecemeal conversion of humanity to their army was a success, but the virus now drove them on to where the people really were. Better to attack larger numbers now so as to really swell the ranks, which meant chasing the human flight. They could all smell where their meals were, the scents blown by smoke filled winds from miles around. Perhaps there was a semblance of memory left in its brain. Perhaps it was just some uncontrollable intuition, but either way, Sid(Z) led them to the hotel where the Sid before death had spent time in the embrace of a woman she had loved. Such passion was dead to it now, a mere shadow of the yearning that drove it ever forwards.

With nearly five hundred rooms, most of the residents had done what the military had told them to do. Stay where you were and wait for help. Cut off from their normal communities and with the transport network either shut down or clogged, the only other option was to set out on foot which most were ill equipped to do. The fact that any military that might have come had long since fled this part of the city did not escape most of the people left in the hotel. The absence of the police and the army on the surrounding streets told them everything that they needed to know. This resulted in many people cowering in their rooms, watching the ever dwindling selection of TV channels to try and get some understanding and some hope for what they now faced.

There was little in the way of either.

Stopping in the centre of the road outside the hotel, Sid(Z) turned and set its sightless eyes upon the building's main doors. With the whole front of the hotel comprised of glass windows, it was perhaps uniquely vulnerable, and without warning, the horde swarmed at the building, leaving Sid(Z) standing, buffeted by the many who rushed past it. As a unit, dozens impacted the windows and the doors that had wisely been locked. Inside, frightened faces looked on in disbelief as the undead hurled themselves at the strong, yet exposed glass. The attackers spread themselves along the hotel's front, pounding with their fists, even mashing their skulls in the hope of forcing entry. It was clear that the windows might be able to hold, but perhaps not indefinitely. All it took was one crack, one breach.

Despite their efforts, the accumulated zombies couldn't get in. Even over the noise, a sense of relief replaced the initial shock of those hapless souls in the hotel lobby. Not all stayed to watch the spectacle, nearly half of those present when the zombies arrived fled to the upper floors. *They can't get in*, was the overriding assumption. *But what if they do?*

Stepping off the road, Sid(Z) almost stumbled over the curb. The zombies were a dozen deep now, and Sid(Z) couldn't get anywhere close to the doors. Instead it made its way around the pack, passing down the side of the hotel where more windows presented. And more doors, only a few of its kind following behind. Then it stopped, listening to the skies, its brethren doing likewise. The whole horde seemed to pause in their assault, their cacophony cut off in mid strike. True death was coming.

There was that noise they had encountered so many times before, and the zombies began to scatter. The hotel could wait, now they needed refuge and as many of them ran across the road, the bullets from the heavens began to chew them up.

Man and his relentless flying machines. The problem with Gatling cannons though…they aren't particularly accurate, and as the bullets ripped up the asphalt the helicopter aimed its tiny missiles at the largest concentration of undead. It was therefore inevitable that some of those bullets would penetrate and shatter several of the hotel windows.

With nearly a hundred still pressed against the glass, they poured in through the freshly created portals, the humans who had stayed to bear witness suddenly realising their stupidity. Sid(Z) ignored it all, its sense of smell taking it further towards the back of the hotel, the helicopter noise irrelevant. A side fire door opened and half a dozen hotel guests (who had been trapped in the building from the start) tried to flee. Only some of them made it, Sid(Z) there waiting for them, its speed equal to theirs. You don't have to run faster than a zombie. You just have to run faster than the slowest human being chased.

The remnants of the baby now discarded, Sid(Z) grabbed and held the frightened woman in its arms, the weakness in the meal's muscles making it an easy target, Sid(Z) bit down into her face, one of its incisors snapping off at the gum line. The tooth fragment got buried in the screaming face, becoming a permanent fixture there. Sid(Z) let the weeping and destroyed woman fall to the floor and stepped through the still open door. Inside, it could hear the tantalising screams of those who were already dead in waiting.

The helicopter had done little to thin their ranks, only a couple of dozen zombies now useless to the viral cause. But there were other weapons the humans could drop from the heavens, and the zombies spread throughout the surrounding buildings and the hotel. There were also ways for the undead to fight back.

Sid(Z) was not there to hear the small flock of birds attack the helicopter, their viral infused flesh striking the most vulnerable parts of the flying monstrosity. With the tail rotor now destroyed, the flying marvel came crashing out of the sky, exploding amongst some houses several streets away. The different types of zombies weren't coordinating, they just seemed to have a link that helped spread the virus and protect the army that was being built. The birds were a momentary advantage. It wouldn't be long before their wings decayed to the extent that flight was impossible.

The zombies renewed their attack. Each door in the place they now invaded represented a potential banquet, the zombies attacking each in turn with a relentless methodical approach. As usual, Sid(Z) led the way, the first to find the staircase which led to the upper levels, the first to feed on the hapless human who was caught in one of the corridors. It could hear hundreds of hearts beating, its auditory capabilities getting stronger with every passing hour. Every one of the hotel guests would meet an unenviable doom.

On the first floor, Sid(Z) stopped outside a room. The smell there was stronger than she had ever encountered, several other zombies gathering behind her. Some filtered past to other rooms, but this door seemed to be the focal point of many. With no conscious minds they went purely on primal instinct, and that instinct told them that the human in this room needed to be destroyed.

The Hounslow mutation had developed a worrying aspect. The immune were so rare as to hardly be worthy of mention. Normally, when the undead encountered them they were treated as just another source of food. Not so with the Hounslow variant. Sid(Z) felt pulled to the room's occupant. Here was someone the virus couldn't defeat and something in Sid(Z)'s dead mind seemed to know the threat this resilient human represented. It attacked the door with an aggression it had never before displayed, the other zombies following Sid(Z)'s lead, the wood actually splintering as fists broke through. One of Sid(Z)'s hands was rendered useless by the barrage, the door lasting mere minutes as it was reduced to mere fragments.

The woman inside was dispatched with unstoppable ferocity, only for the freshly created corpse to become a banquet of carnage. The flesh of the immune, it seemed, was the sweetest taste there was, and the zombies fought each other to get just the smallest piece of such a delicacy, dozens of them forcing their way into the room. By the time Sid(Z) stood up from the carcass, nearly thirty zombies were trying to get at what was left. No trace of this true enemy could be left.

It was as if Lazarus had recognised the threat the immune posed and had started to evolve to deal with it.

22.08.19
Preston, UK

"That's an interesting hypothesis," Dr Patel said into his military issue phone. Natasha had called him and patched Nick's radio into the call. "I'm not sure how such a thing could happen though."

"If I'm not mistaken, you would have said the same thing about zombies a few weeks ago."

"Very true," Patel admitted. "Still you are talking about some kind of telepathic link. You are also suggesting that this Azrael has been given a vaccine against the virus. These are, some would say, preposterous presumptions that are difficult to defend."

"There is something you need to understand," Nick said patiently. "This isn't me putting this forward, but an acquaintance of mine. We call her Moros."

"Moros?" Confusion now in Patel's voice.

"I ask Moros questions, and the answers given are usually correct."

"I'm not sure who this Moros is..."

"Not who, what. Moros is a multi-billion-pound quantum super computer that has more computing power than either of us could even fathom. It states that there is an 83% probability that the immune are telepathically linked somehow. With the information provided, it has also given a 58% chance that Azrael has been inoculated. Might such an individual be of use to you?"

"We will run some more tests on his blood," Patel responded. Nick assumed that was all the answer he needed.

"OK, keep me in the loop. If he is as useful as he claims to be, we will be shipping him to Porton Down with Jessica. Manchester is already showing dangerous signs of being unstable. There are too many military personnel either infected or deserting. You need to be ready to leave as well." Plans were already being made to relocate any and all research from Patel's laboratory to the Preston Barracks. Order was still there, but it only seemed to be a matter of time before things finally fell apart.

Despite being a military man himself, or perhaps because of that, Nick couldn't blame any soldier for deserting their post when their country needed them. Especially this country. There was an impossible task being asked of the young men and women of the UK's armed forces. It wasn't as if the country and its political masters had looked after them, something Nick was well aware of. The military had been underpaid, underfunded and often left in squalid conditions. And then when their service was deemed complete, they were often abandoned on the scrap heap, many with a host of psychological conditions that the criminals in Parliament cared little about.

However, even in such a broken system, there were forces at work trying to restore some sort of balance. MI13 had been one of those forces, working tirelessly against the country's enemies, both foreign and domestic. Ever since Thatcher had been ousted by a coup within her own party, those domestic enemies had seemed to multiply like mice. That was the period when the rot had truly started. MI13 had held much of the damage at bay, but it had been losing the war. The realm that it was there to defend had started to feed upon itself.

Even when the military went to war, they were shat on. Nick had been there, in the second Iraq war. He was special forces then, so was exempt from many of the problems much of the military faced, but that didn't mean he wasn't witness to the insanity of it. And even with the barely edible food and the shortage of ammunition, the British had still been considered by many the best soldiers in theatre. He would freely admit that he was biased in his assessment and was more than happy when the USAF came hurtling out of the skies to give much needed air support when it was called on. And it had been called on often. It also didn't matter how good the British soldiers were, the Americans would always be the dominant military power.

That was all in the past. Whatever it was that had made the British squaddie so formidable, part of that seemed to be lacking in the modern day British forces. The UK military had been decimated to the extent they were not up to the task being asked of them. Was it a generational thing? Nick didn't know the answer, but he understood why so many of them were running for the hills.

Was he being disloyal? Just because Nick worked for the most secret government funded organisation in the country, didn't mean he couldn't state the truth about how that country was being run. Osmond had said it best. Over the last twenty years, MI13 had spent a considerable amount of its time cleaning up after bureaucrats and members of the political classes who seemed intent on destroying the nation. There had been a similar situation in the nineteen sixties, but that was a direct result of communist infiltration at the height of the Cold War. It had almost been successful, communist sleeper agents infiltrating all the main political parties as well as the civil service. Osmond had spent his early years with MI13 removing as many of the undesirables as could be uncovered. This was before technological marvels such as Moros. Back then it was all hard graft and field work. The British public never learnt just how close they came to being a Russian vassal state where the orders would have come directly from Moscow. It was almost ironic that it was the remnants of the old Soviet system running amok that had caused the present crisis.

To this day, it still confused him whenever he saw left wing protestors carrying the Hammer and Sickle flag, seemingly oblivious to the horrors that had been perpetrated under that symbol. Millions dead in the gulags. Tens of millions dead by forced starvation. Assassination, wholesale slaughter. The communists made Hitler and his fascist cronies seem almost like amateurs at times.

There would be little in the way of concern for a person's political ideology in the world that was coming. All that would matter was your ability to survive and your usefulness to any group that managed to come together. Hopefully, that meant the politicians would die out, but Nick wasn't too hopeful. They always seemed to find a way of sticking around.

As for the theory on telepathy, Nick had no idea what it all meant. That was for minds much smarter than his to figure out. They wouldn't even know for sure until they got more immune subjects to examine. Would that even happen though? Admittedly, the more that became infected, the greater the chances of another immune individual cropping up. But conversely, more infected also meant more zombies and a greater threat that the whole infrastructure would collapse around them. Without the hospitals, the laboratories and the scientists, there would be no vaccine. Even with the best equipment, a vaccine would take months to create and produce.

Humanity didn't have months. At this rate, it probably didn't even have days.

22.08.19
Isle of Man, British Crown Dependency

Trevor Hughes had lived on the Isle of Man for twenty years. He liked the relatively sedate life the island represented, as well as the extremely favourable tax rate. His job at Douglas Harbour kept him busy, but for over a day the ferries hadn't been running. Stood on the edge of the docks, he watched the two Royal Navy frigates patrol on the horizon. There had been many ships visible over the last few days, a great exodus from the two countries that sandwiched the Isle of Man in the Irish Sea. None of them had been permitted to land on the island's shores, the Royal Navy helping with that embargo.

It was no rumour that the Isle of Man was under naval quarantine, signs being placed in ever street to report any sighted boats trying to land. Only this time the quarantine was to keep something out rather than to contain it within. The worry was that people fleeing the British or Irish mainland's might bring the infection with them, and as the island was apparently disease free at present, it was hoped that it would stay that way. The hotels were full of those who had fled before the quarantine, so who could say what had been brought over. There was the chance that islands such as the Isle of Man could become bastions of humanity, allowing mankind the prospect of rebuilding, to start again should the countries of the world fall.

Unfortunately, the island wasn't free of Lazarus. One of the planes to arrive on the nineteenth had carried a single infected individual. That had let the virus spread throughout Douglas so that there were now nearly a thousand viral carriers on the island. Trevor wasn't one of them, but even now his beloved daughter was being infected in her primary school. She would bring Lazarus back to the family home and spread it to himself, his wife and his other three children. By the time Lazarus became apparent on the island, there would be too many already carrying the disease for it to be stopped. It was already too late.

For much of humanity the need to flee was thwarted by the invisible and highly contagious nature of their microscopic enemy. There was no way for people to know where it was safe to hide.

Even without the virus, there would have been problems. The island was far from self-sufficient and it couldn't survive without the modern capitalist system that brought in goods every day of every week. With a population of nearly eighty-five thousand, as well as thousands of tourists, it would take a lot of work to feed itself. Theoretically it could be done, but only with a massive dose of science and a huge infrastructure building project to rival the agricultural marvel of the Netherlands. Nobody had bothered with that though. Nobody had previously considered the island any kind of possible haven except from the terrible terror of taxation.

It was a problem many such islands would face over the coming weeks and months. Some would survive unscathed by the virus, only for their populations to slowly start to starve, air travel and international shipping lanes shutting down the deliveries of goods essential for human life to continue. The things that would be done in the name of survival would be reminiscent of the worst of humanity's many atrocities. Ranging from forced euthanasia to cannibalism, the will of man would gratefully accept barbarity over extinction when given the choice. Such was the new world that would start to form, civilisation replaced by a new merciless order.

Mankind had spread himself across the globe, getting into every nook and every cranny, placing himself firmly on every continent no matter the hardships faced by extremes of climate or nature. Most wouldn't escape the virus though. They would die and rot as the dead rose up from the earth to seek and consume the flesh of the living. For those that escaped the virus, their fellow humans would become the new enemy.

22.08.19
Houston, USA

Reece hadn't really known what to expect, but she was shocked by what she saw once she was past the fences and the check points. When Clayton and his men had left, the Corporal had given her back her weapon. Although she was infected, there was a standing order that first responders could fulfil their existing roles within the facility for as long as their symptoms allowed. So infected doctors and nurses cared for the sick, and infected law enforcement helped keep order.

As she had already witnessed, the Astrodome and the surrounding area had been separated into two zones. One was for infected, and the second was for those who were dragged off the streets for their criminal actions. Those taken to the new jail were initially going to be screened for the virus, but after a few incidents it was considered problematic to force blood tests on the violent and the often drug addled. With each of the new cells housing several people, they would just have to take their chances like everyday folk did on the street. Reece had no idea what plans were in place for when one of the prisoners died and came back. She made subtle enquiries but nobody seemed willing to tell her, an umbrella of secrecy already descending over the Astrodome's operations. There was a natural side effect to that of course, because secrecy causes gossip, whole generations addicted to the internet and reality entertainment. When the majority of a population had developed an almost insatiable need to know the ins and outs of other people's business, the addiction to gossip wasn't going to be cured by going cold turkey.

Reece had only been here a few hours and she had already heard the rumours. It wasn't just criminals they were bringing into the new prison. There was speculation that the Federal Government was using the crisis to round up as many political agitators as they could. Reece wasn't in that part of the facility to confirm or deny such a conspiracy theory, and she told herself that her government and the government of Texas wouldn't engage in such activities. It was against the constitution, and that sacred document was what made her country great.

There was a strong chance however that she was simply deceiving herself. Why would people in power want to let a good crisis go to waste?

The sick were being housed in the Astrodome itself, the main sports field sheltered under the huge roof that covered it. The number of sick were only in the hundreds so far, many of those still being processed in the array of tents that had been set up outside. Even now, work was still going on to install the facilities needed. The Astrodome had ample washroom facilities for tens of thousands of people, but you couldn't ask hundreds, probably thousands of sick patients to trek all the way from the centre of the field to where the toilets were. Many of them would be suffering from an array of gastro intestinal ailments, so another solution was needed. Chemical toilets were far from ideal, but they were really the only viable solution.

As for housing, a series of wire cages separated by wire tunnels were being erected. People often baulked at the thought of being placed in a cage with little privacy in the sight of strangers, but with the fact that anyone who died would likely return to try and eat all those around them, people still understood that the impenetrable wire was for their own protection. Already, choke points had been established to defend against a mass uprising of undead should the cages fail. The infection was to be contained, and ended on this field if at all possible. Reece was amazed that such a facility could be erected so quickly. She didn't realise everything necessary had all been set aside and mothballed years ago to combat a pandemic, or even to detain belligerent and violent insurgents should civil order begin to break down. There was even a constant stream of trucks that were bringing nearly a hundred thousand plastic coffins that had been simply stored in fields waiting for this very eventuality.

FEMA and the Department of Defence had been planning for a global pandemic and civil uprising for over a decade…and much of that they found they could use to combat the growing zombie menace. Texas was prepared and ready.

Reece patrolled the spaces between the wire enclosures, her accommodation a small office in the administration aspect of the Astrodome well away from any of the uninfected individuals. She was forced to wear a health monitor that was locked onto her arm so as to give warning should she start to go downhill. Once that happened, she would be disarmed and placed in one of the cages like the rest of the populous. Reece wasn't sure she saw the point in her relative freedom, but she was happy to stay out of one of those cages as long as possible. Once she was in there, then her ultimate death was probably certain. As it was, she didn't think she had any real worsening of her symptoms.

Considering she was supposed to be infected, she felt well enough in herself.

She spent her time talking to people, the role she had always enjoyed most on the streets. Let them see you, let them feel safe that there is someone there to protect them. The fact she wasn't encumbered by a facial covering seemed to go a long way to building trust. To many she was one of the THEM, not one of the often tactless soldiers who didn't seem to treat the sick with the humanity they deserved. Some of the people she encountered were hostile to her though. Not all of the sick were pleasant human beings and she soon realised who she liked and who she couldn't tolerate. Some people were scared, others just outright antagonistic towards her because of her uniform and the fact she was on the other side of the wire. A minority even acted as if the whole situation was her fault. Then there were the ones that needed watching, characters that could have done with being placed in the other place with those who chose to break the law. She ignored them, there were other people available to cater to their needs.

Reece had even seen a few cases of faeces being chucked at the guards in open defiance. All that resulted in was a beating and a long march in irons to the cells that held the criminality. All in front of the frightened masses. People soon learnt the importance of towing the line and behaving themselves.

Then there was the other side of the equation, the soldiers who were just abusive because it was in their nature. Reece kept an eye on them, soon learning which ones to be wary around. One private had even pumped her behind with his gloved hand. Perhaps he thought he ruled the roost that he could somehow do what he pleased. Maybe he got high on the thought that he could somehow intimidate her. The lascivious soldier hadn't got the response he expected.

"Honey, do that again and I'm going to get all overwhelmed. I might just have to rip that gas mask off and give you the deepest kiss you've ever seen. You know, plenty of tongue, just how you like it." It hadn't happened again.

What surprised Reece was the high number of children here. Children were kept with one or more parents where possible in a separate section of the facility. Some parents who weren't infected opting to share their child's cell, an example of the ultimate sacrifice. Those without parents or guardians were kept together with those of similar age. There was no way they could be allowed to play together, and the younger ones just cried behind the wire, devoid of any real human attention. Reece stayed away from that part of the Astrodome. She didn't do kids at the best of times, finding her interaction with them awkward and stunted. There was also the fact that she didn't think she could listen to so many of them weeping. That might have broken the wafer thin barrier that was allowing her to keep it all together.

Reece was there to see the constant inflow of the sick and the dying. As the day moved on, an increasing number of those brought here ended their short association with Lazarus as death took them. Trapped in their cages, the zombies were quickly dispatched by the soldiers who finally showed their ultimate purpose here. Sooner or later she herself was going to have to kill a zombie when it resurrected. She was confident she could do that, or so she hoped.

22.08.19
Washington, USA

President Ryan woke up with the worst headache he had ever experienced. He had gone to bed feeling unwell and exhausted, leaving his staff to run the emergency that was sweeping across the country. Sleep was no longer on the usual schedule. You went as long as you could and then got the bare minimum you needed. The thought that he was infected with Lazarus hadn't even occurred to him.

Unlike some in the emergency bunker, he was given the privilege of a bed. Beside him, his wife slept peacefully, oblivious to the world that was rapidly crashing around their ears. She could get the rest the body needed, preferring sleep than to be awake. Sleep allowed her the luxury of not having to worry about how everything was falling apart. Her husband would have little time for her as the crisis unfolded, so she opted to stay out of his way, knowing that he knew she was there for him if he needed her advice. It was something he had done often through his political career, Ryan being of the opinion that he would never have reached the position he had without her guiding hand.

Before retiring through shear exhaustion, he'd been witness to multiple reports that showed the virus was burning through the continental United States at a horrendous pace. He'd always wanted to be President, but he'd never imagined his Presidency would be so potentially short.

Gingerly, Ryan got out of bed, slipping his feet into the slippers that waited for them. For some reason that he couldn't explain, the souls of his feet hurt, an unusual symptom that could be just about tolerated. He'd been a marine major in the invasion of Grenada, a bit of discomfort when he walked he could deal with. His head though, man he needed something to take the edge off that.

The marine outside his room snapped to attention when the President opened the door. Ryan gave the soldier a reassuring pat on the shoulder before heading off to the kitchen area, the men here to protect him worthy of his respect. As if drawn to the President's presence, Jessy appeared from a side room and quickly came to his side. She had the mandatory file of papers in her arms.

"You look terrible sir," Jessy noticed.

"Why thank you Jessy. And good day to you too."

"The New York State governor has sealed off Manhattan," Jessy said getting straight into business, "but they have had reports of outbreaks across the city and the state."

"Can I at least get a coffee before we discuss the end of the world," Ryan jokingly begged. "And I need some painkillers too. I've got a bastard behind the eyes that I need to kill." A concerned hand grabbed his arm.

"Seriously sir, are you okay?"

"My feet hurt, can you believe that?"

"I suppose it's better than other parts of you hurting, sir." It was the only response that seemed to make sense to her. They walked into the kitchen area together which was presently deserted.

"You see, that's why I keep you around, to keep my head out of my ass." Ryan poured himself a large mug of coffee, the presidential seal stating that the mug was just for him.

"Can I talk business now?"

"Painkillers?" Jessy pulled the med kit off the wall, and after a brief search through its orderly contents, withdrew the dissolvable aspirin. With a glass filled from the tap, she presented the fizzing mess to the leader of the free world. The President gulped it down greedily. "Now you may begin."

"As I said, New York is bad. The National Guard are keeping a lid on it, but the infection rates are through the roof. The NYPD has lost most of its command and control structure. Los Angeles is on fire, rival gangs tearing each other apart. The governor of California has decided to just cordon them off and let them fight it out. And there are running battles on the streets above."

"Is there any good news?"

"No sir, not really. Texas seem to have things under control for now, and the rust states haven't reported any outbreaks yet."

"Do you still want to be my Chief of Staff in all this?" It was a serious question. He wouldn't blame her if Jessy decided to just get up and quit.

"Of course, sir. There's nowhere I would rather be." It was true, she had committed a large proportion of her life to the man who she knew to be an honourable and capable leader. "When you are ready, General Roberts would like you in the incident room." General Roberts, the head of the Joint Chiefs of Staff, who had been in the Whitehouse when Secret Service agents had grabbed Ryan and dragged everyone down to the bunker several days ago. That was before they had fully understood what the virus was capable of, the numbers it had infected, and the ease with which it had spread. The Whitehouse bunker was still sealed off, nobody allowed in or out. Even if blood tests had been done on everyone before going down, it would have been too little too late to stop what was about to happen.

General Roberts was immaculately dressed. He stood ramrod straight watching one of the larger display screens, CNN still broadcasting. Rumour was he never smiled.

"General," Ryan said greeting him.

"Mr President."

"How is the military handling this?"

"Poorly, sir," Roberts stated without trying to gloss over the truth. "We're about to lose our base in Okinawa. The infection got a foot hold and cut through the men stationed there like wildfire. Other than that desertion rates are unacceptably high, especially amongst the Guard."

"Can we contain this?"

"We might be able to save parts of it, but we need to be prepared to lose some of the larger cities. In my opinion New York's gone. So is Chicago, Seattle and Detroit. Houston, Atlanta and Dallas acted quickly and seem to be getting it contained, but those are isolated roses in a whole pile of shit. The city above you is on lock down. We don't have the manpower or the resources to come close to stopping this. We need to think about taking more drastic actions."

"I seriously hope you aren't asking me to nuke our cities General."

"Whilst it might come to that, I think other options need to be considered first. We've seen the satellite images from Beijing, the nukes didn't stop a damn thing."

"Thank God for that, I doubt I would ever be able to authorise using nuclear weapons on our own citizens," Ryan said genuinely relieved.

"My alternate solution would maintain the country's infrastructure. We need to use nerve agents on the areas of highest infection." The President looked at the general as if he had suddenly gone mad. Another voice entered into the conversation.

"General Roberts is right," the Defence Secretary stated as he walked over to the pair. A General himself, he could see the wisdom in the action being proposed.

"Are you two out of your mind? Anyway, we aren't supposed to have any nerve agents."

"Destruction of stockpiles is behind schedule," General Roberts stated. "That would have been one of the things I would have briefed you about had you become President under more favourable times. We can blanket the heavily infected areas allowing our troops to go in and mop up."

"No, I will not order the mass slaughter of US citizens." He still held his coffee mug, and it shook in his hand as the cough descended on him. Those painkillers needed to hurry up and work before his head split open. "We don't even know if nerve agents will work against the undead."

"It wouldn't be them we would be trying to kill, sir." Roberts kept a straight face, fully serious with what he was proposing.

"How can you even think this?"

"It's my job to Mr President. I am here to give you all viable options to combat this threat. And in my opinion starving the undead of the chance to recruit further soldiers is a consideration that has to be considered."

"I agree Mr President," the Secretary of Defence concurred.

"No," Ryan said, coughing again. "Such a thing should only be a last resort. Besides, what if you kill infected people. Won't they just come back as these things?"

"A calculated risk based on present infection spread," Roberts stated.

"I will not go down as the President who gassed millions of my own citizens. I'll hear no more about poisoning civilians, not now." He could just see the images in his head, whole streets filled with people clawing at their necks as the nerve agents choked the life out of them. Whole communities stripped of life, the outrage of the survivors deafening. Ryan even felt that if he did what the Generals were asking, he would lose much of the military. It would be their relatives and friends the nerve agents would ultimately be killing. There had to be another way.

"Very good Mr President." Roberts was not about to usurp the command of the democratically elected leader. At least not yet. Standing there looking at a President he actually had some respect for, General Roberts managed to resist the urge to cough.

23.08.19
Manchester, UK

Midnight came and went.

The biggest problem had so far been his need to keep up appearances so that his madness would not be uncovered. Renfield didn't consider what he was suffering as madness, it was just a yearning that could no longer be denied. There was so much he had to do, and none of it could be done if his true intentions were uncovered. The waiting around when he wasn't on his shift was like an addict going through withdrawal. In essence, he supposed that was exactly what he now was.

It was surprising how quickly insanity could descend. Whilst denying the true nature of what he now was, Renfield supposed he could have resisted the rediscovery of his old self. It would have been better for those he killed if he had. But sticking the knife into the zombie's neck that first time had unlocked something within him, drawing forth the desire that had lain dormant for so long. The anticipation had been great, only for his craving to be denied. He thought he had it under control, but that control had only been achieved through denying himself completely. Now he was a slave to it.

What would have happened if he had killed someone in combat? Would that also have unlocked the door? So far his postings had been away from any opportunity to inflict death on an enemy, so perchance fate had been leading everything to this moment. With no satisfaction from ending the zombie's existence, the dam had finally begun to burst, the need for what had been withheld expected but not delivered.

He had no choice but to kill, that much was clear to him. Now the longing grew unrestrained, a feeling of urgency meaning he needed to pick up the pace. Killing one or two every hour was no longer acceptable to him. It just wasn't satisfying the crushing need. Each rush was slightly weaker than the last, each kill less satisfying. He'd found himself pushing the boundaries as well, the last one killed without the benefit of a privacy curtain. The addiction was causing him to take risks without him having yet experienced the true scope of what he could create here.

At this rate, he was going to be discovered for the maniac he was, the world events breaking what was an already fragile mind. The ward kept filling up as well, clear evidence to him that a tipping point was coming. London was reportedly already lost, how long before the same was said of Manchester? How long before these infected were left to their own devices and he was told he was needed elsewhere? That would be devastating to Renfield.

He knew what he needed to do, and it had to happen now whilst he still had time. Having relieved his shift partner, Renfield waited until the man left the ward and headed off down the flight of stairs to the shower room that had been set aside as their decontamination area. It was a bit of a compromise, consisting of a shower that had been set up to release a bleach solution which had been shown to kill the virus. Self-scrubbing the suit would leave it relatively safe to take off, and only then would the soldiers be able to eat, rest and do whatever ablutions were required. Within thirty minutes his fellow soldier would likely be asleep. Renfield would wait that long, his feet nervously twitching as he did so. Fortunately, none of the patients chose to die in that time period so nobody came to disturb him in his deliberations.

This was going to be truly biblical.

At this hour of the morning, the hospital was quiet, even though its wards were likely filled to bursting point. He listened to the hospital breathe, the gentle hum of its heating system, the occasional moan from a patient close to death. The odd external sound broke through the barrier also. A lorry outside unloading supplies. A rifle shot off in the distance. Were the undead getting closer? He even heard motorbikes, not knowing that was a courier escort transporting what would be another batch of three vials of antiserum to the Fulwood Barracks. If anyone was to be saved by XV1, better it be those who could benefit the most from it.

His thirty minutes now up, he rose from his seat one last time. It occurred to him that he would never sit in that chair ever again because there was a good chance he wouldn't even survive this himself. He was about to unleash the dead in a confined room with only two exits. There was no telling what effect such a sustained killing spree was going to have on him. He'd almost fainted once so far with the pleasure that had surged through him and here he was about to take a heroic dose of the narcotic he loved so much. Might such a thing even ruin him?

He really didn't know why he had taken the decision to let the undead rise instead of killing the patients in the proscribed manner. There was just something appealing about it, perhaps a chance for him to slip away in the mayhem. Was that it, a pure act of self-preservation? To kill so many with a chance of living to kill again?

Most of the people in the room were asleep, those that weren't were drifting in and out of one form of delirium or another, either chemical or virally induced. As luck would have it, there was one awake individual, her eyes now constantly on Renfield. Again, fate seemed to be smiling on him. Renfield moved slowly, walking into the centre of the ward, excited by the way the eyes of Lucy looked at him. She was fully awake now, any semblance of sedation long since passed. He sidled over to her bed and sat down on the sheets next to her hip. Despite her restraints she tried to pull away.

"Leave me alone," Lucy demanded firmly.

"Now why be like that?" he admonished. "Why are you so cold towards me anyway?" He had to speak louder than he would have liked due to the respirator somewhat distorting what he said. Renfield realised Lucy had no idea what he looked like. Perhaps that was part of her reticence towards him. The temptation to pull the gas mask off and show her the face of the person who would be her end almost bewitched him, but he held fast and kept his face covered.

"Because you kill them. I've seen you." She sounded like she was shocked that he even asked the question.

"They are already dead. What I do is a mercy," Renfield lied.

"You're still a monster."

"I'm not the one with the black marks all over my skin babe. If you want to see a monster, look at yourself in the mirror in about, ooooh, two hours." Lucy spat at him, but all this did was bring on a coughing fit. She had deteriorated rapidly the last few hours, the final stages of the viral infection coming along nicely. "That's if you have two hours left."

"Fuck you," she finally managed.

"Normally I would oblige, but I don't think a condom is going to cut it. But I have something better for you."

"You're sick." He knew she was about to shout but he acted quickly, placing his hand over her mouth.

"Don't be stupid. What do you think calling the nurse will achieve? You will only be sedated again, and I need you awake and aware for what's about to unfold. You were right about me when you said I was a monster." Earlier when getting back into his suit, Renfield had cut off several strips of duct tape which was normally used to seal the gap between glove and containment suit. With his free hand, he now peeled one of these off his arm where it had been placed, irritated with how it clung to his gloved fingers. He waited though, just in case their conversation had roused any of the other patients. Renfield didn't expect it to, and he was pleased when nobody raised their voices in protest.

"It doesn't look like anyone's coming does it? No rescue for you. No hope. You should have been nice to me. I was thinking about letting you live." Her squirming was irritating as well as pointless and Renfield could also detect the lack of energy there, the drained and weakened body that wasn't up to putting up much of a fight. Even if she hadn't been shackled to the bed, Renfield knew he could have easily overpowered her. It took him all of five seconds to get the duct tape planted firmly over her dry and chapped lips.

Standing, he stripped the bed sheets off her. Lucy's naked form lay beneath the hospital gown and Renfield slowly withdrew his knife, her eyes showing the terror she was now experiencing. Renfield actually laughed at her reaction.

"Don't worry, I'm not going to hurt you. I'm certainly not going to rape you. But we need to have a look at the goods so that I have something to remember you by." The knife was sharp and it easily sliced the thin cloth from her body. It was everything he had expected, although he felt that the skin was slightly soiled by the virus. "You are one good looking woman Lucy. I look forward to having you inside me." That didn't make sense to her. What the hell did he mean?

Renfield stepped back from the bed and walked to the patient at the furthest end of the room. One by one he started undoing the bindings on a single arm and both feet of those who were close to comatose. He worked slowly, methodically. There was no need for haste, he could deal with anyone who chose to interrupt what was now likely his final act. Anyone entering the ward now would face the ultimate penalty.

Each patient was prodded to see if they were anywhere close to being awake. Those that he felt could give him trouble, he gagged in the same manner he had done to Lucy. Those he didn't release from their bonds. Most of the patients though didn't even notice that they were almost free. By the time he was finished only four patients were gagged, and that included his love, Lucy.

"Watch this Lucy, you are going to hate this." He adored how horrified she looked by what he was doing. One by one, Renfield took his knife to the neck of the helpless patients, a single slice through one carotid artery. The first few times he wasn't accurate and had to cut again, but he soon got the hang of it, the little fountain of blood became a clear indicator that he was bang on target. On his third murder, the blood had shot into his face, briefly obscuring his vision until he wiped it away with the bed sheet. He kept stopping to look at Lucy, relishing the utter destruction he saw in her eyes.

"Only takes several minutes to bleed out Lucy, each pump of the heart sending the individual closer to death. Are you excited?" He was taunting her now he realised. It felt like the right thing to do, and the words he spoke were probably barely comprehensible. The rush was hitting him, in waves, building to a crescendo, the lives slowly flowing away to be replaced by the new. "Don't worry Lucy, I won't forget to do you too." He was becoming short of breath with the excitement, adrenaline flooding his bloodstream. Ecstasy didn't even describe what he was feeling.

Half way down the room he had to stop and prop himself against one of the beds. The pleasure was mounting to unbelievable levels, the world around him going into complete tunnel vision. His groin ached painfully with the intensity of it all. It was almost too much, the room around him becoming an unreal realm. Renfield felt that he was moving in slow motion now, each slice of the knife taking longer than the last. His mind was filled with bliss.

It only took him mere minutes to end everyone's lives, but to him it felt like hours. And every second was the ecstasy he had denied himself for so many years. He now didn't regret waiting so long for there would never have been an opportunity to experience such delight before today. This was the experience he had always wanted, and he demanded more. Renfield was almost staggering by the time he got back to Lucy's side, his breathing laboured, his limbs weak. Several of those he had sliced were now already dead.

"Oh Lucy, if only you knew." She didn't say anything of course, how could she. Once again he sat down by her hip, no longer even interested in her nakedness. His mind was flooded with endorphins compromising even his ability to think. It was everything he hoped it would be, death after death sending bolts of bliss to his now fevered mind. As if in an afterthought, he smeared the blood on his knife hand across her breasts causing her to squeal in distress.

"I can feel them Lucy. They are inside me. You are going to be inside me too." She wanted to scream, she really did, but the tape cut off her words. A blood soaked glove grabbed her face, leaving a further streak down her cheek as it forced her head to one side. "I'm going to save you Lucy," Renfield said. He was crying now, perhaps the first time he had cried since being a small boy. "So weak, so vulnerable. I am going to spare you becoming one of them. You don't have to thank me."

With her head forced down as it was, she couldn't help but look at the bed next to hers. The patient there was flailing as it tried to sit up, all life having abandoned the zombie that was now being born. Even if Renfield didn't kill her, that fate was still a certainty. She stopped struggling. Perhaps this was actually the better way. If he left her alive, that would leave her vulnerable to being fodder for the undead.

"That's it. Accept what I am giving you babe." Renfield slid the knife home into the base of her neck, her body jerking as he severed her life. "And to think you called me a monster."

Her whole form seemed to relax as he hallucinated the last of her life energy departing the body. Electricity filled him, the biggest hit yet sending Renfield to a nirvana he hadn't even known existed. The world around him became oblivious, the zombies that were rising up of little consequence to him, most still semi restrained as they were. He did the only thing he could and laid down next to the woman he would carry until the end of his days. Time became irrelevant to him in that moment. There was no telling how long he had lain there.

He barely reacted, even when the first undead hand grabbed at his foot. All throughout the ward, zombies began to crawl from their beds, easily pulling at the weakened restraints, in some cases dragging the beds with them. Some were still to convert, their bodies needing time to adjust as the blood stopped flowing from their grievous wounds. But as they struggled to surround the now only living human in the entire room, Renfield realised through a haze of endorphic bliss that he might well have just made a very terrible mistake.

He stood up from the bed and realised this wasn't enough. He wanted more. Renfield didn't forget to take his knife, slipping it easily from the dead body. Renfield would never forget how peaceful Lucy looked at the end. He was glad he had given her that.

Renfield barely made it from the room alive. One zombie managed to grab a hold of him, but the fingers didn't grip properly, the new brain still trying to work muscles that were already starting to die. He pulled himself free and was out the swing doors at the end of the ward before the first of the zombies finally ripped its restraint free of the bed. That zombie and several others almost went in pursuit of Renfield, but instead they turned to the still warm corpse of Lucy. Fresh meat could not be so easily denied. Even though she had been infected by the virus, the undead, it seemed, could tell a body that wasn't one of them.

The nearest ward where more infected were being held was down the corridor he was now on, and he was about to run there. Instead he almost collided with the nurse who had so often come to his aid. Perfect, who better to bear witness to what he had created?

"You have to see this," Renfield shouted, grabbing one of her arms perhaps not as gently as he should have. His grip was like steel, fuelled by the adrenaline that was flooding his system.

"What are you talking about?" she said trying to escape his grasp. His hands felt slick, and with horror she saw the blood there, the exterior of her biohazard suit now thick with it. She increased her effort to try and get away, but her attacker pulled his side arm and stuck it painfully under her chin.

"Why do you resist? Why would you not want to see the wonders I have created?" He knew he wasn't talking like a working class kid from one of the poorest estates in Luton, but the new him preferred the artistry these fancy words represented.

"Oh my God," the Nurse cried.

"No God here," Renfield advised her. He started to force her back the way he had come, the doors to his new paradise mere metres away. The nurse barely put up any resistance, her future sealed. She was then pushed through the swing doors, Renfield throwing her to the floor.

"Oh boys," he said to the zombies as they turned to the sound. As the nurse began to scream, he shot out her right kneecap. Stepping back, he let the doors close behind him and ran off in his original direction, the nurse now sprawled on the floor out of his sight. The sound of her distress roused him to partake in further acts of destruction.

23.08.19
Moscow, Russia

Claudia Renton had, it seemed, chosen the wrong time to go on holiday. She had landed in Moscow on the eighteenth, and had been woken in the early hours of the twenty first to find masked men storming through the door of her hotel room. In the dark and the haze of her broken sleep she had struggled to understand what was happening, the Russian the men were screaming at her completely incomprehensible.

Dragged naked from her bed, she hadn't even had chance to put on a dressing gown. She was clothed now, but only in a thin blue boiler suit which did nothing to dispel the chill in the large concrete room she now resided in. Claudia had been dragged from her hotel room without her dignity, along the corridor where another hapless visitor to the country was receiving the same treatment. She was forced into an elevator by men in black combat gear. There was a word in Russian written across their backs, and she guessed they were either police or something similar. Removed from the darkness of her bedroom, she had seen that their faces were in fact covered by gas masks. She remembered there had been a smell of disinfectant that had permeated the air.

Despite her pleas that she was just a tourist, they had manhandled her through the large ornate hotel lobby which was teeming with similarly dressed police. Other people, it seemed, were suffering the same treatment, this hotel popular with tourists. Outside in the cold autumn air, she was virtually thrown into the back of a police van with four other people, all either naked or in some kind of night attire. At least they hadn't put her in handcuffs. They hadn't needed to, it wasn't like she was about to try and run off in her birthday suit.

Claudia had done what she could to cover herself up, one of the people sharing her ride constantly looking at her in a leering way, despite the predicament they were all in. None of the people with her spoke English.

Without a means of telling the time, it was difficult for her to determine for sure how long the journey took, but she figured it was around forty minutes. Her extremities had felt like they were frozen, and by the time she had arrived at her new destination, Claudia had been reaching near exhaustion from the shivering that had overcome her body. It wasn't cold enough to cause hypothermia or frostbite, but it wasn't far off. When the doors finally opened, a seemingly shocked female Russian guard had shouted something angrily and a large blanket had suddenly been provided. Claudia never got to see if there was any remorse in anyone's faces because they were all hidden from her view.

Wherever they had brought her, it was well lit, with fences topped with razor wire. She was ushered towards a gate where armed soldiers stood stoically. The freezing ground had bit into the souls of her feet, which were not used to such harsh treatment.

Now she was sat in a corner of her new home, mattresses laid out for ten people, harsh halogens blazing in the ceiling. She had no idea how long she had been here, but she had been served four meals so far, flung through a hatch in the bottom of the door. The first time that had happened, the other women had scrambled to get their portion of the food. They had been almost like animals. Now with a reassurance that it represented a regular supply, everyone had calmed down. No real hierarchy had been established in the room's occupants, her conversation with the few English speakers forced and strained.

There was a single toilet and a sink for the people here, each mattress having an owner. None of them spoke to her, everyone was in the same level of shock. This sort of thing just wasn't supposed to happen in civilised society to people who hadn't done anything wrong.

There was a loud buzzing sound and the door to her cell opened, all eyes warily turning to the door.

"Claudia Renton, you will exit the room and follow the red line," a man said in English over a loud speaker hidden somewhere in the ceiling above. Everyone looked around, finally settling their eyes on her. Stiff from the way she had been sitting, Claudia reluctantly did as she was instructed. There seemed to be nobody that she could talk to or shout at, so really she didn't think she had any choice. There was the very real worry in the back of her mind that if she didn't comply, something nasty would occur to her. Nastier that is than what had already happened.

The cheap slippers she wore slapped off the concrete floor as she did as she was instructed. Outside in the corridor there was a red line with arrows which led down a darkened corridor, doors like the one she had passed through lining both sides. Her door closed automatically behind her leaving her feeling isolated and alone. Claudia noticed her cell had the number 5 almost casually written on it in white paint. All the doors she passed had hatches and she briefly got to glance in one that was open. Like with her cell, this room was also filled with people.

"Hurry up please," the voice said. The red line looked fresh, as if it had been painted recently. What even was this place? It looked like it had been abandoned long ago, only to have been re-opened recently. There was a faint smell of disinfectant in the air, and the walls gave the impression that the building was in an advanced state of decay.

Her journey led her to a door made of bars which opened automatically, the red line carrying on a further ten paces before it led into a small room with a single chair and a desk which was pushed up against a clear partition. There was an officious looking, clipboard wielding woman on the other side of the partition and she motioned to Claudia to sit down.

"You are Claudia Renton, US citizen, is that correct?" The woman's voice was coming from a loud speaker on the wall to Claudia's left.

"Yes," Claudia answered. "Look what....?"

"Please only answer my questions," the woman said sternly. She even had those thick rimmed glasses she could look over.

"But I..."

"Shut up," the woman ordered, slamming the clipboard on the desk on her side of the partition. "And your date of birth is twelve, oh seven, nineteen seventy-nine, correct?"

"Yes," Claudia responded meekly.

"Very good. Our system says you arrived from your New York flight on the eighteenth?"

"That is correct."

"You are being detained because you represent a threat to the security of Mother Russia. Specifically, that you arrived by aircraft which represents an unacceptable risk with regards the virus known in the western media as Lazarus."

"But I'm not infected," Claudia protested.

"So you say. And how do I know this is true?" Claudia didn't have an answer to that. "You will be detained until such time as you are deemed no longer to be a threat to my country. Once that occurs it will then be determined what is to be done with you."

"Why don't you just deliver me to the US embassy?"

"The US Embassy?" the woman almost laughed. "That building is under military quarantine. Nobody is allowed in or out."

"But..."

"You may now return to your cell." The woman thrust her clipboard under her arm and walked out of the room, the lights behind the partition going out. Claudia sat there for several seconds before resigning herself to the fate she now faced. She was sure this was just some sort of bureaucratic mix-up.

There were hundreds of people in the facility thinking the same thing.

23.08.19
Manchester, UK

"We are unable to take your call at this present time as all operators are busy. Please try again later." Brian closed the phone that he had tried to dial 999 with. The whole system was clogged with calls, it wasn't likely any witnesses to what was about to happen would be calling for help any time soon.

Brian waited at the side of the road, the streets around him quiet. He was tired, his day spent running an almost endless array of errands for Clay. Three warehouses had been picked clean, as well as a tobacconist that Clay often bought from. We weren't talking cigarettes here, but some of the finest cigars available to mankind.

Brian reckoned he and the men under him had acquired enough provisions to keep everyone going at Clay's mansion for at least six months, probably longer. And it had all been done without a single person being hurt. In fact, some of those guarding what Brian looted had joined in, possibly realising the stupidity of the orders they were working under. It helped that most of the men with Brian throughout the day had been ex-military because Brian wasn't always the one to do the talking. When your own kind points out how futile everything is, sometimes that information gets through.

This was a different mission however. Although the mobile phones were no longer working, either due to a mechanical failure in the cell phone system or an intentional shut down of everything but the emergency network, Brian wasn't hampered by that. The phone he had been given by Clay for the day's missions was an encrypted satellite phone, just one of the many toys the mob boss sold to clients overseas. It was via this phone that Brian had been receiving his instructions throughout the day.

The urgency of what was required had meant that, although he and his men had made several trips back and forth from Clay's mansion, nobody had really had chance to relax save for an hour just before the sun had gone down. There was little chance that Clay's men had come in direct contact with anyone that could have been infected, so with some basic precautions, most of Clay's followers had been able to keep themselves hydrated as well as taking the toilet breaks they needed.

The non-violent streak was regrettably about to be broken. Clay's text message had told them where and when to be outside the Northern Manchester General Hospital, which is where Brian and five of his men now were. They had witnessed the three army motorcyclists ride past towards the hospital grounds, and now waited for them to exit, knowing the exact road they would take back to the Preston Barracks. The risk of being caught outside of quarantine was strong here, which was why everyone was armed to the teeth. They were far enough away from the hospital so as not to need to worry about the military personnel there, whilst being close enough to be sure the motorbikes they were here to intercept wouldn't take an unexpected path.

You need to intercept a military motorbike courier and bring me what he is carrying.

That had been the text message Brian had received after his destination was outlined. So now they waited, the thin paracord pulled taught across the road between two lamp posts. Motorbikes made sense in that they were fast and were able to traverse most roads clogged with abandoned cars, the latter not actually much of a problem around this area of Manchester, but definitely an issue on the motorways and dual carriageways. They were however uniquely vulnerable to ambush. Brian had no idea what it was they were carrying or why it was so important, but if Clay wanted it, he was going to acquire it.

The man crouching next to Brian was about his size and had been long ago given the nickname Bulldog. It wasn't known how that nickname came about, although the man didn't really possess a neck. It was more of a huge slab of muscle, so it was probably that. Bulldog was one of Clay's debt collectors, a man you sent to acquire the tithe that some businesses were forced to pay to prevent their buildings being torched. He was a useful man in a fight, someone who did what he was told. Bulldog just wasn't the sort of individual you would sit down and have an intellectual conversation with. Not much there between the ears, some said.

This was about self-preservation and keeping Clay happy. Brian had seen how things were going, how discipline in the army was starting to crack based on the soldiers he had interacted with throughout the day. It was only a matter of time before complete civil disorder descended and when that happened, a man like Clay would become even more powerful, especially with the stockpiles he now had. If he could get away with so much in a land of judges and laws, imagine what the likes of Clay could achieve when HE made the rules. Brian wanted to be on the inside of that looking out.

In the distance, the sound of motorcycles could be heard. Of the houses on this street only half a dozen showed lights inside, people either asleep or terrified to show their presence to the now dangerous world outside. What did the cowering populous fear the most? The riots in Manchester were over, but who was to say if the desperate and the dispossessed wouldn't rise up again to bring havoc to the streets. Or was their terror now consuming the thought of zombies invading their communities? Such would not happen this night though, Brian and his men thus able to lurk unmolested in the shadows. Brain didn't fear the mob, but he feared the undead, and he hoped not to encounter any this night.

The motorbikes got closer, their engines the only real noise in the night's sky.

"Get ready," Brian said loud enough for everyone to hear him.

At the end of the street, three headlights came into view, travelling at speed. Quickly, the vehicles advanced, two in front. The riders would likely be scanning for threats, knowing that everywhere was becoming bandit country, but probably still feeling at relative ease. If Brian was in their situation, he would still be feeling secure knowing how close they were to the soldiers back at the hospital. Surely nothing would happen here.

The first motorcyclist took the paracord in the neck, ripping him from the bike and rupturing the disk between two cervical vertebrae. Whilst he wasn't dead by the time he hit the floor, his resulting paralysis meant he was as good as. The second rider was more fortunate, able to get an arm up just in time to take the brunt of the hit. Still, he was flung to the ground, arm broken, body winded as it thudded to the asphalt. Both bikes continued on a distance before veering off and colliding uselessly with cars parked at the side of the road.

The third rider, the courier, took the only option he could, putting the bike into a slide that sent the bike hurtling like a missile into the two men already felled. The courier slid off to the side, hitting the curb, armed men appearing from behind walls and hedges before he even had chance to stop his motion. He tried to get up, but a boot kicked him in the already bruised ribs.

Within seconds, Brian's team had the soldiers secured, knees on backs and chests, the soldiers' weapons being stripped from them. Helmets were ripped off heads because helmets had microphones in them. Nobody seemed to have got a warning off to whoever might be listening. Obviously, such a violation to a man with a broken neck only made the injury worse, destroying any chance that the damage could have been reversed.

Brian stood and watched his men work before stepping forward. Bulldog was already at the courier's bike, stripping out the refrigerated package from one of its satchels.

"Is this what the boss wants?" Bulldog asked.

"Seems to fit the description."

"Do we open it to make sure?" Bulldog further enquired.

"Were we told to open it?"

"Well, no."

"Then there's your answer." Clay was always very specific when he gave instructions.

"This guy's hurt bad," one of Brian's other minions said, indicating the soldier with the broken neck. Brian knelt down by him, saw the shallow way the injured soldier was breathing. Damned shame.

"You won't get away with this," the courier threatened.

"Shut your mouth," ordered the man standing on his back. Brian considered his options. He didn't want to kill these men, but he also knew leaving them alive was a threat. If they lived, they would report back that there were armed men who knew about what they were transporting. That would then likely cause all sorts of problems. Besides Clay had given very specific instructions.

Kill everyone.

Brian stood, Bulldog handing him the parcel.

"Deal with them, and do it quietly," he ordered his men, and he watched grim-faced as guns were replaced by knives. It would be so much cleaner to kill them with bullets, but why take the risk? Gunshots were not an uncommon occurrence, but this close to the hospital they might attract unwanted attention. Before any of the soldiers could object, all three were killed with a ruthless efficiency that meant none of them even had a chance to voice a protest.

"Stick the bodies in the truck, we'll dump them on the way back."

"And the motorbikes?" Bulldog asked. Perhaps the man could think after all.

"Deal with the rope and then move the bikes down the road. Push them if they won't ride." They would hide the truth of their crime in the hope that the fate of the missing courier and his escort would remain a mystery.

This was a dangerous game Clay was playing. As well armed and as rich as he was, Clay was going up against what was now the biggest gang on the block, the British military. This was a gang armed with tanks and predator drones that could blow his whole estate to dust. Brian seriously hoped Clay knew what he was doing.

He felt eyes watching him, probably from different windows. Should he threaten the watchers? Hopefully, the scene of their crime wouldn't be discovered until it no longer mattered. Brian needn't have worried, events at the hospital were about to make the loss of the courier almost irrelevant.

What he didn't know was that the encrypted phone he used wasn't as secure as Clay had been led to believe. Deep in the heart of MI13, the still operational Moros had intercepted the messages and was already logging the communication for human review.

196

22.08.19
New York, UK

Midnight was still to strike on the clock in Times Square, and as much as he would have preferred to be indoors, Gabriel made his way through the city streets, knowing he somehow had to get out of New York. Leaving his penthouse apartment had been the first of his challenges, the fire alarm going off indicating the vulnerability staying put was likely to cause.

Tiredness had yet to descend on Gabriel, sleep to him a mechanical thing that occupied less than four hours of his day. Unlike Azrael, his dreams were not disturbed by the plight of the damned in the barren, scorched desert. Instead, his dreams were boring, sterile affairs, barely a memory or a feeling following him into the waking hour. If he hadn't read about such things in one of the many books Mother had forced upon him, it was likely he wouldn't even know what dreams were.

The streets should have been deserted, but they thrived with life, much of it seeking perhaps one final act of hedonic indulgence. Even with the undead rising up across the Metropolis, the police found themselves having to also combat the living, thousands of them across New York engaged in a frenzy of destruction. Gabriel slipped through the carnage relatively unseen, a lone figure of little threat or interest to those around him. On the rare occasions people had approached him with the intent on doing violence, a display of the dual Glock 17 pistols strapped to his hips had shown them the wisdom of seeking an easier target.

There were no police visible here and it soon became clear that taking Seventh Avenue had been a mistake as it seemed to be a funnel for wherever the violence was spreading. With only chaos ahead and behind him, he broke from his more direct route, still heading for 33rd Street. He had to first get off Manhattan Island, and taking the bridges would be all but impossible, easy choke points for the military to seal off.

To survive he ultimately needed to get out of New York, and Gabriel had deemed north of the city the best direction to head for. South ultimately led to the Ocean, and although he might be able to find a ride on a boat, the chances were that anything that could float was already doing so. West was out of the question because that would likely hit the same level of refugees fleeing Philadelphia as were evidently trying to escape New York. East was where the rich lived, so the roads there would be heavy with blockades. North was the key to getting out of this teeming mass of chaos. The key to surviving the virus was to limit your exposure to those who could be carrying it.

He did not want to have to swim the Hudson River, but he would if no other opportunity presented itself. The swim he could probably make, but there had to be another way. Instead, he headed for his best option, the PATH line which would take him under the river.

The crowds were rapidly behind him, many of them evidently heading for the iconic Times Square. Normally a place of celebration, it was likely now a scene of the worst that humanity could accomplish. With his destination now in sight, a group of ten people loitered ahead of him, their drunken shouts making it evident that these were some of the very people intent on raining destruction onto a city that right now needed order.

The whole of New York sounded insane, the way it breathed mutated by the violence occurring. This was only added to by the sudden screech of jet fighters in the sky. Gabriel looked up, but saw nothing, only for the whole world to seem to shake as the explosion rocked several blocks over. He didn't see the flames, but he felt the hot air as the blast wave washed over him. That had occurred the way he had come. Had he carried on Seventh Avenue, it was possible he could have been turned into prime barbeque. He didn't know how, but he knew the smell of napalm.

Had they just napalmed zombies or rioters? Did the authorities even distinguish between the two anymore? It was time for him to get off the streets and he saw the subway station across the road where the drunks seemed to be celebrating something. They shouted in unison, their attention most likely drawn to the explosion that was still reverberating across the city. These were not friendly good Samaritans. Gabriel looked at them and made his way towards where they stood anyway. There was no threat there that he couldn't deal with.

When you faced an obstruction you had three choices. Turn back, go around it or go through it. Only the latter seemed to make any sense to Gabriel now, and he knew he had little to fear from the cockiness expressed in the mixed-race collection of scum that apparently now felt Gabriel was someone to fuck with. One by one they turned to face him as he stalked towards their position, his destination clearly visible metres behind where they stood. They would either get out of his way or they would pay a steep price.

"What you got in the bag bro?" one of the gang members shouted at him. The rucksack Gabriel carried on his back should have been of no concern to them, and by inserting themselves into his business, all of them had pretty much sealed their deaths. Gabriel considered them children despite their ages. Men would be out there trying to help the city survive. Children went with their primal instincts, their soft brains unable to fathom the morality of their actions. These brutes were an example of why humanity was so unfit to steward this world.

"Yeah give us what's in the bag and maybe we'll let you get home in one piece." The second voice was slurred, either due to alcohol or some illegal substance. The menace they tried to exude was laughable. To an old woman or a metrosexual beta male, their presence would have been viewed as terrifying. To a man like Gabriel, whose very being was the slaughter of the innocent and the guilty, they were barely a challenge.

The fact the men were either drunk or high would mean their reaction times would be off, reflexes hampered, cognitive discipline shot to shit. They were spreading out across the road as he approached, forming a barrier, not realising that they were the sheep instead of the wolf. Some of the boys were clearly armed, knives glinting off the street lighting that still illuminated the city. Would any one of them know how to use those weapons? Gabriel was more than a physical match for any of them individually. There was no need and no time to go down that road though.

Gabriel showed no mercy. Walking towards them, he drew one of his Glocks and stepped into a shooter's stance, firing off several rounds before any of them could even realise the mistake they had made. He aimed for the ones his instincts told him were the greatest threat, another four shots leaving his gun before he was moving for cover behind a mailbox to his left. The biggest threat he faced here was underestimating their capabilities. It only took one to get off a lucky shot for all this to be over.

Seven bullets, seven bodies hit, three fatally, his accuracy lethal. The three remaining should have fled, but instead they froze for the briefest of seconds, amazed at what was happening around them. By the time they too were running for cover, Gabriel was already lining up his next three shots, every one hitting the required target. Of all the assassins Mother had trained, Gabriel had never been surpassed when it came to pistol shooting.

The road itself was pretty deserted when it came to vehicles, so by spreading out as they had, their intimidation tactic had merely given Gabriel plenty of chance to prove how good a shot he was. From the limited cover the post box gave him, he emptied the rest of his pistol magazine into the life forms that were still writhing or groaning on the floor. Ejecting the clip he ripped another one from his belt and slammed it into place. He hated wasting so much ammunition like this. His was likely to be a long journey, and what he had with him in the pouches of his belt and the rucksack on his back had to last. There was no guarantee that he would be able to restock when he needed to.

No shots came hurtling back his way, so he came out from cover and carefully stalked over to the nearest of the downed bodies. This one showed a bullet wound right between the eyes, seemingly obliterating the two orbits into one fatal cavernous hole, the hollow point round he used ideal for its stopping power.

"Still got it," he said to himself. He'd only ever experienced engaging multiple targets in an artificial environment, muscle memory from hundreds of hours on shooting ranges across the country making the difference here. He was highly trained, they were not, and that's what it always came down to when random luck was removed from the equation.

The thugs had clearly not expected a lone target such as him to be so well armed and so thoroughly ruthless. Even more, they wouldn't have expected him to just come out shooting, because their criminal experience would have told them that the people of New York just didn't carry guns. Even the police gave some kind of warning. *Sucks to be you right now*, Gabriel said to himself. Gabriel had more threat in the tip of his little finger than all of these stupid children combined.

One of the thugs still moved, and Gabriel walked over to the dying male, covering his every movement with the gun. The man was about eighteen and Hispanic, bleeding from a sucking chest wound that was likely collapsing his left lung. There would be damage to the heart as well, most likely a tear in the aorta. Blood flung itself from his mouth as he coughed, the pain etched across his young features. Even if the youth miraculously appeared on the surgical table of the city's most experienced thoracic surgeon all prepped and ready to operate, death was most likely certain.

"Who the fuck are you?" the Hispanic demanded through gritted teeth. Gabriel didn't answer. Instead, he stepped on the man's right hand and searched the body, pulling a knife from an inside pocket. Returning his gun to its holster, Gabriel opened the flick knife and slit the Hispanic's throat ear to ear, the cut deep and meticulous. Surgical, precise, just how he liked it. There was no hesitation in response to the dying man's pleas. That was the other difference between Gabriel and Azrael. When Azrael killed, he was a talker. Gabriel liked to make the act of death do the talking for him.

The air around him was suddenly still, the only movement caused by a light breeze that blew smoke and the aroma of burning to him. If idiots like this felt they had free rein to wreak havoc on the streets, then the order that kept the city in check was likely lost. The validity of that thought was proven by one of the dead men sitting up, the black eyes staring sightlessly out at the world. It would seem Gabriel had done them a favour. If one was infected, it would only be a matter of time for them all to be. The zombie didn't even have a chance to get to its feet before Gabriel dispatched it.

At the PATH entrance now, Gabriel descended the steps to find the way into the subterranean network unbarred. The utility belt that held his Glocks and ammunition also contained an array of other useful items. One was a lock pick gun, supposedly only available to law enforcement agencies, but easy to acquire for an organisation with the wealth and reach of Gaia. Had there been a locked gate as on most subway entrances, such an obstacle would have offered resistance for all of four seconds.

The lights below were off, the darkness of the PATH station an inconvenience that was easily dealt with by the tactical torch that was attached to one of his guns. It illuminated the steps leading down to the entry turnstiles that he easily vaulted over. The high-intensity xenon light broke through the blackness, the red laser highlighting the path. Anyone down here was well advised to keep well out of his way.

With the PATH shut down, the tunnels were the obvious way for him to get out of the city by foot. It would avoid much of the mayhem above and see him safely under the river. Using this network, he could hopefully get as far as Newark. Although safer than staying on the surface, this wasn't a risk-free option. In the dark, any danger would be more difficult to spot, so he knew he had to be ever vigilant. It was highly unlikely that he was the only person amongst the millions of New Yorkers to have had this idea. There would undoubtedly be people down here, and he would deal with each eventuality as he saw fit.

The world around him shook slightly, fragments of plaster breaking away from the ceiling above. Another bombing, probably closer than the last. He was glad Mother had called when she had, sharing in the treachery they had seemingly both suffered. Had she not taken the time to pick up the phone, he would have probably sat in the penthouse until the end came. It really hadn't occurred to Gabriel before that he was perhaps expendable. Another incidence of the growing betrayal he was experiencing. A strange desire began to form in his diseased heart that he had never knowingly experienced before.

He suddenly felt the need for vengeance on those who had used and abandoned him.

23.08.19
Manchester, UK

Smith opened his eyes. The noise of the alarm was glaring to him, but also reassuring. At least it confirmed that he was still alive. There wouldn't be a noise like that in the afterlife.

The clock on the wall told him it had been nearly twelve hours since he had injected himself, and he had been out cold all that time. Somebody had picked his body off the floor and had placed it on the room's bed. The gentle beep of the machines he was connected to could almost not be heard over the din of the fire alarm and Smith slowly disconnected himself from the adhesive pads and the clip on his finger. The IV line he pulled out carefully, his body still feeling somewhat fragile from the after-effects of his self-experimentation. Pressing the call button, he waited for as long as he could for somebody to come. But nobody did. All the time the fire alarm was blaring impending doom at him.

He still found it difficult to breathe, but it was obvious to him, almost straight away, that his body felt better. The skin looked healthier as well, any evidence of the virus now gone from its appearance. He wasn't sweating, and the black lines had evidently disappeared. His pulse was mostly steady rather than erratic and elevated as it had been.

My God it had worked.

Had he found the cure? Carefully, he swung his legs over the side of the bed and took his time standing up. There was still a pounding in his skull, but that he could live with if it meant he had survived the plague. Why was the alarm going off though? If there was a fire, why wasn't somebody here? There was nobody visible outside the observation window which didn't make any sense. He should have been under constant observation.

Naturally, the door to his room was locked. Whatever was happening he would have to wait for someone to come and get him. By the door was an intercom panel, and he pressed it in the hope of grabbing somebody's attention.

"Hello? Is anyone there?"

Nobody answered which finally caused concern to well within him. Had he been forgotten? Had he cured the greatest scourge of mankind only to be abandoned, locked in a room in a building that might be on fire?

"Hello," he said again, this time louder. Again no answer, and he moved over to the observation window to try and get a glimpse of someone, anyone, outside. Smith could see the room and the open door that led out into the corridor. A figure ran past before he could react, and then another. Banging his fists on the reinforced glass, he suddenly realised the futility of his actions. It was unlikely anyone was coming for him.

He didn't even have a phone, but maybe he had the next best thing.

His laptop had been placed on a desk by the side of his bed. Opening it up, Smith noticed that it remained in standby mode. People were still likely watching the video feeds, and he tried to skype all the people who had been monitoring the moment he injected himself. Only one person answered the call, and he wouldn't be able to help because he was across the Atlantic in Atlanta. The face of Perry looked bloodshot and tired.

"Michael, can you hear me over this damned alarm?"

"Yes Colonel. What's going on there?"

"I don't know," Smith answered, "but the antiserum seems to have worked."

"Yes, Dr Patel told us. Your latest blood test showed XV1 has all but eradicated the virus from your system. We were just waiting for you to come round."

"I don't have a phone and there's nobody here. Something is clearly happening and I need to get out of this room."

"I can try and ring Dr Patel for you," Perry said, suddenly coughing. "You haven't got any of that XV1 spare do you." It was a joke of sort, to tell Smith that the director of the American CDC was also infected.

"Michael I'm so sorry. Have you had any luck finding immune individuals?"

"No. So far Jessica Dunn seems to be the only one. We have been able to determine a crude test for the virus which we hope can be used in the field. It seems to give a few false positives, but so far hasn't missed any of those genuinely infected that we tried it on." There was the sound of something slamming on the glass, and Smith turned to look at the window.

"Oh no," uttered Smith. There was no mistaking the zombie, the blue nurse's uniform ruined by the blood that had poured out of the shattered neck. It stood there with both hands on the cold glass, the side of its face pressed up as if it was trying to listen to the room.

All the lights flickered.

Smith turned back to the computer monitor, only to see the white snow of static. Any internet connection had obviously been lost, Smith didn't know how. The network was supposed to be secure god damnit. The alarm had also been silenced. At least that was something. It was obvious to Smith that this was some sort of power outage.

He approached the glass, strangely unafraid of what was on the other side. Tapping the glass lightly, the zombie went into a violent frenzy, beating at the window randomly with its entire upper body. It didn't take long for it to smear itself across the window's surface, the red gore a mark of how relentless the zombies were willing to be.

"So you've come for me have you?" Smith said to it. His words were soft, but he was sure the creature could hear him.

"*Isn't it beautiful,*" a Voice suddenly said. It had no direction, instead, it came from all around Smith, filling the words with a sound that was so familiar.

"Who's there?" Smith demanded. The static proved that the sound wasn't coming from the laptop, and he moved over to the room's intercom.

"*Getting colder,*" the Voice taunted.

"Who are you?" Smith demanded. The intercom was quiet, the owner of the words seemingly in his head.

"*That would be telling wouldn't it.*" The Voice even gave a muted chuckle, as if amused by Smith's confusion. "*You didn't think you could get rid of it that easily did you?*"

A horrible thought suddenly struck Smith. Was this a side effect of the antiserum. Had it caused some sort of neural episode, a miniature stroke perhaps? Had he not in fact been cured. The zombie seemed to be enraged by the conversation Smith was having with himself. Sitting down on the bed, Smith watched as a second zombie joined the first.

"I'm going mad," Smith said to the air.

"You could think that I suppose." It was clear to him that the Voice he was hearing was his own, but distorted like when you heard a recording of yourself. *"But no. Whilst you are hallucinating, there is a physiological cause."*

"Am I supposed to have a conversation with myself now?" Smith asked himself. The power fluctuated again, the electronic lock on the door faulting. Smith looked on in horror as the door released itself slightly from its frame. A moment ago he had wanted the door open, now it was perhaps the worst thing that could happen.

"Ooops. Talk about bad timing." Smith watched the zombies intently. Had they heard the door unlock? Frantically, he looked around the room for something with which to defend himself with. There was nothing here that could hurt the undead. *"It's alright I'm sure they haven't noticed."* What the hell was this Voice, and why was it mocking him?

Unfortunately, one of the zombies had noticed, and it slowly stalked out of view until it was able to push open the door to Smith's isolation room. The lights were clearly on emergency power, which gave the scene a stereotypical glow.

"Now you're in trouble."

"SHUT UP," Smith screamed to himself, only for the zombie to explode at him. It collided with where he sat on the bed, both of them toppling over the other side. Smith ended up on the bottom, the creature scrambling to stay above him. This had once been a patient, Smith didn't know it, but it was one of the ones released by Renfield, most of that ward's offspring now running rampant throughout the hospital.

Smith tried to struggle, but the zombie was too strong, easily pinning him down. Over its shoulder, the second zombie came into view. Held as he was, there was nothing Smith could do to stop the tongue licking a bloody trail across his cheek. It was almost as if both zombies were smiling at him.

"Have you had enough yet?" the Voice joked. Smith ignored it, because he felt his only option now was to scream with terror and frustration. The scream never came because the second zombie turned and ran off. The first just seemed to examine him, as if unsure what to do. Smith felt the weight of it on his chest shift, only for it to grab his hand, pulling Smith's fingers towards its grotesque mouth.

"No!" Smith heard himself beg, but the zombie ignored him. He tried to clench his fist, but the zombie wasn't having any of that, violently opening his fingers, nearly ripping two of them off in the process. Perhaps it would have been better had it done so. Holding the index and middle finger of his right hand extended, the zombie placed them into its gaping maw.

"Oh God no." Smith did scream then as the teeth bit down, slicing through the flesh and then cracking the bone. It bit right on the second knuckles, tearing the fingers away with a sweep of its head. And then it was up and off him, leaving Smith clutching his ruined hand. Fire lanced up his arm as the severed nerves signalled their objection to the treatment they had received. Smith almost passed out but he held on through sheer will. In disbelief he watched as the zombie left him, still chewing on the morsel it had selected from the bountiful human buffet that had presented itself.

"Well, now you get to see just how good this antiserum really is."

22.08.19
New York, USA

The darkness that surrounded him felt somehow comforting. Many people had a fear of the dark, but most of humanity didn't have the training and the desire to inflict death that Gabriel possessed. It wasn't that he was without fear, he just knew how to control it.

Not all the PATH line had been in darkness, emergency lighting present in many parts of it, but he had still needed to use the torch to fully illuminate his way. Now on the tracks, he kept well away from the electrified rail. The likelihood was that there was no current flowing through it, but why take the risk?

By his calculations, he was under the river now. And he wasn't alone. Up ahead he occasionally got a glimpse of torches flashing. Hushed voices came to him, but he never heard what was being said. The people never got any closer, they were obviously just using the tunnels as he was. No danger there, not at present.

That all changed when the scream ripped through the air around him. The light ahead seemed to drop as if a torch had been flung to the ground. Gabriel didn't pause, knowing there was only one direction he could go in. Another cry of pain came, louder than the first and male this time. Whoever was ahead of him was clearly being attacked, innocents caught up in a plan for the world they didn't understand. No part of Gabriel yearned to come to their rescue. Live or die, he had little interest in the fate of others. Whatever was ahead of him would be dealt with the way Gabriel dealt with all things.

The guiding light was extinguished making Gabriel the only source of illumination. He had little concern that the batteries in his own torch would fail for they had been freshly placed a week ago. Gabriel was all about preparation and illuminating unexpected variables. Whilst there was a risk that all plans disintegrated as soon as the enemy was engaged, he did what he could to mitigate that well-known rule. Stepping carefully so as not to lose his footing, he heard the sound of footsteps charging towards him.

Night vision goggles wouldn't be ideal down here because there wasn't any ambient light. He had considered wearing thermal which he had packed away in his rucksack, but there was a problem with that. He was well aware that he might encounter the undead down in this underground refuge. Did the undead even give off heat though? Did their core body temperature drop to that of the surrounding air? He had chosen not to risk it, and now with enemies approaching, he knelt down in place and waited.

The light caught glimpses of them first, at least five figures running towards him. It quickly became clear that they weren't human, their speed and movement too fast and erratic, limbs moving in a frenzy as they seemed to compete to get at him. Some were damaged, blood evident on much of the clothing they wore. The one leading the pack was even missing an arm, the injury that had most likely killed the human.

Gabriel fired, not wasting his bullets on body shots, aiming for the heads. Even with his skill, it was difficult, the ungodly motion of the undead making them challenging targets. Two fell, the projectiles doing enough damage in the right part of the brain to end them, but even with headshots, the other three kept coming. A frown appeared on Gabriel's face, a rare show of emotion for a man who was as close to being as dead emotionally as the things he was now trying to kill.

Could you kill a zombie?

He changed tactics, the remaining three now dangerously close. Shooting out the knee caps was an even more difficult target, and he managed it twice, the zombies' legs collapsing under them, the joint ruined. The final one his shot missed, but Gabriel managed to finish it off with a final shot to the head. The two that remained tried to crawl towards him, but they were now easier and slower targets. More ammunition used. At this rate, he would need to seek out supplies.

Gabriel should have moved on, but something inside him wanted to know more about what these things were. He shone his light on them in turn, noticing the clothes they wore and the people they had once been. One had clearly been homeless, the attire a clear give away. Two were dressed in expensive suits, perhaps bankers on Wall Street, their wealth unable to save them from the indiscriminate actions of Lazarus. Moving past the bodies, Gabriel noticed the last two had been women, one a police officer. Her sidearm was missing, but the belt still likely held the same ammunition that Gabriel required. Bending down, he began to search for what he needed in the various pouches. Two magazines were a welcome addition to the ammunition he had so far spent, and he added them to his own belt.

He spotted the movement too late. The officer's body was badly wrecked, much of the scalp missing from the left side of its head. How it got down here, Gabriel would never know and not being familiar with the way Lazarus worked, there were some things even Gabriel could not predict. The ripped shirt over the lower abdomen gave him no hint at the creature that was living inside the zombie, feeding on its innards which the zombie no longer needed. This zombie had been slow to rise, the rat finding the freshly dead corpse and burrowing into it to feast.

The rat crept from the putrefying guts, slipping out from under the bullet proof vest and launched itself at Gabriel's face. Even with his reflexes, he was only able to catch it with his free hand a fraction too late, the rat claw scratching his cheek. Although living off the guts, the rat itself had yet to succumb to Lazarus, the changes still occurring inside it. Why it had chosen to continually feast off a creature that still moved would never be explained, its attack more a sense of desperation than outright aggression.

Gabriel closed his fist around it, feeling it squirm and writhe, the blood and gore coating it making it slick. His cheek stung. Did that mean he was infected? Would such an injury be enough to be the end of him? With one hand on his gun, the only source of light, and the other holding the rat, he had only one real course of action. Gabriel flung the rat at the wall of the tunnel as hard as he could where it hit with bone crushing impact. As it fell to the floor of the tunnel, Gabriel ended it by blowing its head to smithereens.

Likely his tactical glove was now a source of infection, moisture seeping through in parts. Gabriel stripped it off as carefully as he could and flung it down the tunnel in disgust. He should have been more worried about the scratch, but he knew that there was no point concerning himself with that. There were only two outcomes here. He would either catch the virus or he wouldn't, and he knew exactly what he needed to do in case of the former.

His brain at that moment allowed him to remember something he had discussed with Mother. A year ago the package had arrived, the one containing the self-injection gun just as with Azrael. Like with Azrael, he used it on the instructions given, the remnants discarded in the trash. Until this moment he hadn't thought anything more of it.

What had that injection been for?

22.08.19
Manchester, UK

Doctor Patel had ultimately succumbed to sleep, despite his best efforts to hold the sandman at bay. The sound of the alarm was enough to rouse him from the office desk he had collapsed his head onto, and with bleary eyes, he looked around the well-lit laboratory. What was it, a fire?

Dizziness hit him as he stood up, Lazarus now well advanced in his system. The latest batch of antiserum had been sent off to the barracks as per directions from the military. The courier had also been given a complete rundown of all the research done so far on a USB stick just as an added back up. The country's infrastructure was starting to get a bit sketchy, so there was a worry that the reliability of the internet wouldn't be there. Even the hardened military system was becoming vulnerable. Then there was the power supply of course. Already parts of it were failing and there were very few people willing to go to areas that might be swamped with zombies to fix what randomly occurred.

Patel looked out of his window expecting to see people gathering outside. Instead what he saw were people fleeing. Three soldiers came into view and started firing in what seemed like a random pattern. Patel soon saw what they were shooting at, several of the zombies collapsing. But not all of them. Some got through the onslaught, bringing the soldiers down.

How had this happened? How had so many zombies resurrected at the same time? Or was this an external invasion, the true nature of the outbreak finally reaching them? With the night fully fallen, much of what was happening was hidden by the darkness. The pyre of charred and ruined bodies still flickered, recent additions keeping it going, but with no fresh fuel, that would soon die out. What he was seeing was a catastrophe.

Patel had previously thought there weren't enough soldiers on the hospital grounds, and he was being proven right. Just as he was considering his options, the lights flickered and died, only to be replaced by emergency lighting, the hospital generators clearly taking the strain from what was most likely a failed electrical grid.

He had to leave. He had to leave now, but he wasn't going anywhere without his own copy of his research, most of which was stored on his laptop. There were still a few files to transfer from his main office computer, which was rebooting, still able to run off emergency power.

Patel also wasn't foolish enough to leave without the last samples of XV1 which were locked in the laboratory fridge. He had been waiting to ensure its viability on Smith who seemed to be now beating the virus. With his own symptoms now developing, he didn't think he had a choice but to take a dose himself. Having seen the violent reaction it caused in Smith though, he would need to wait until he was in a safe location before taking the hopefully lifesaving medication. Taking it here was no longer a possible option, not with zombies running amok.

Where would he go though? If he could find soldiers, then maybe that meant he could evacuate with them, but would they take him? Most of them wouldn't know who he was. Perhaps the best option was to get Smith and if he could be roused, the pair of them could leave. At least then Patel was relatively certain he could flee to somewhere safe.

That was all assuming there were safe places left...

23.08.19
Leeds, UK

When he finally fell asleep that night, Andy dreamt of oceans. The scorched earth and the baked flesh, the thousands of relentlessly walking souls were all images that were yet to become etched on his psyche. They would come.

He was spared the full bliss of such nocturnal escape because he was ripped from sleep by the sound of violence in the real world. The noise had been loud and brutal, the source completely alien to Andy as his mind tried to reset itself from the fantasy it had been having to endure. Another crash came, obviously from one of the spare bedrooms, the blackness of the night almost total. Jumping from his bed, he heard the sound that sent ice into his veins, the orange flickering quickly illuminating what had just been done.

He didn't have time to think, the spare bedroom was on fire. The smoke was already starting to gather in the upper landing, and he grabbed the fire extinguisher that he had left at the top of the stairs. Andy was fortunate, the room the Molotov had been thrown in was relatively empty. No furniture or beds in there, just a place to put crates of books which were fortunately slow to burn. Still, the flames were consuming the carpet, sticking to the fitted wardrobes, threatening to spread the way fire does. The extinguisher soon made light work of that, the broken window evidence of where the missiles had entered.

There was only one man who would have done this. Iain.

"YOU LIKE THAT CUNT?" he heard the insane neighbour shouting from outside. Instead of going to the window, Andy went back to his bedroom. He was already dressed, having chosen to sleep fully clothed, his reptilian brain warning him earlier that something bad was likely to happen due to his earlier altercation with the axe-wielding maniac.

Andy put on his shoes which would be needed to avoid the newly lain carpet of broken glass. He also grabbed the shotgun which he now kept as close by as possible. Was this it, was it time to deal with this once and for all?

Returning to the scorched bedroom, Andy was surprised to see his building's rear security light wasn't on. Iain again? Most likely he'd climbed over the fence and snipped the power wire. There was the sound outside of someone climbing back over the border fence, only this time there was a wrenching sound. Hesitant as he was to look due to the fear of another missile, Andy peered cautiously outside, the half-moon giving just enough light to show what had happened. The wooden frame of the fence between gardens had collapsed under Iain's weight. Clearly, it was not designed to accept the insult of having such a brute of a man climb over it more than once. Andy could see Iain picking himself up off the floor, and so he lined the shotgun up and fired just as Iain jumped from view.

Andy couldn't tell if his aim had been true, but he heard Iain curse loudly. At the very least, some of the buckshot most likely hit him. Not likely a fatal wound, but hopefully enough to teach him to stop fucking about. Or conversely to enrage him even more. Andy remembered the man who had come round when he had first started getting quotes to have security shutters put on the property.

"Are you sure you don't want the upper windows protecting as well? It's the only way to be totally secure." At the time, Andy had considered the man to be just a salesman trying to earn a bigger commission. Now he saw the wisdom in the words said. Upstairs shutters would have prevented all this. Fortunately, Andy had plenty of ply board in the garage and the tools to fix this up, but now he was going to have to do it to all the windows. Iain was highlighting the weaknesses in his fortress.

"Iain, so help me, the next time I see you I'm going to fucking shoot your balls off," Andy shouted out of the window. As if to answer, a trio of gunshots echoed off in the distance. No other response came. Even with the windows boarded up, Andy realised he would never be safe until Iain was out of the picture. Sooner or later things were going to come to a head.

He was surprised he was having these thoughts if he was honest. Mere days ago this matter would have been dealt with by a phone call to the police. They would have come round, assessed the situation and likely carted Iain off to a cell for the night. Criminal damage with life-threatening arson weren't trifling occurrences. But it occurred to Andy that the days of police assistance were over. Even so, he grabbed his phone from the bedroom and tried 999, just to see.

Again, he got the useless recorded message. It seemed the only law that existed now was the law of retribution.

There was no civilisation anymore. If Andy was to deal with this, he had to take charge of the situation himself. What friends he had were on the other side of the city, or in different cities entirely. They likely had their own concerns to deal with, and even if they could come rushing round to his aid, there was always the fear that they would bring the virus with them. He was alone in a world that was now intent on killing him. Crazy that the biggest problem he was presently facing was down to the living.

He knew he was able to kill Iain, but the remnant of a civilised mind still lurked within, the guilt at breaking the laws that nobody was presently enforcing. Such thinking caused inaction, thousands dying over the coming days because they weren't able to switch off the instructions that society insisted people follow.

Andy wasn't going to let his life fail like that. When morning came he would use the safety of daylight to deal with Iain. He would either kill him or leave him so damaged that he would no longer be a threat. One way or another, this was going to end.

23.08.19
Manchester, UK

Smith had managed to stem the bleeding from the severed stumps on his hands using the medical supplies in his isolation room. There was pain, the initial sharpness turning into a dull throb which had become a constant reminder of his run-in with the undead. The injury made his head swim, his middle-aged body unused to having such damage inflicted.

Smith caught his haggard reflection in the isolation room's window. He had declined hospital attire, insisting instead to remain dressed as an officer of Her Majesty's Armed Forces. His shirt was stained and tattered, his tie lost somewhere in the room. The trousers were caked in vomit down one leg, and he had no doubt that the smell from him was less than palatable. This was not how an officer was supposed to look. The military tunic however was relatively pristine, hanging from a coat hanger by the now open door. Smith put it on, telling himself that it would offer some measure of protection against further bites. Deep down though, he wore it because it represented the identity of who he believed he really was. If he encountered other soldiers, he would need the instant authority the uniform represented. If he encountered further zombies, it was unlikely the fabric would give him any kind of protection.

The compelling temptation had been to shut the door and cower away from the now obvious dangers of the world. As tempting as it was, that would mean surrendering to fear which he would never do. Instead, Smith took the only real path available to him, opting to leave the isolation room to seek anyone who could get him the hell out of here. Escape held with it the chance of safety.

At the end of the day there was no denying that he was a soldier with a job to do, his task undoubtedly more important than most of the people in this hospital.

He wasn't even going to deny that his recent research had been driven by a significant amount of self-preservation. That still didn't change the fact that there were billions of people out there who needed a cure to a disease which threatened to wipe the human race from existence. When it came down to it, he was also a doctor, admittedly one with an ego the size of a small planet. Smith was here to save lives, and if he could get some notoriety out of sparing mankind on top of that, then he would graciously accept such.

The immediate danger would be something he would just have to deal with having survived it once already. The chemical process in his brain chose fight and flight instead of hiding away in a room that would ultimately become his crypt if he didn't leave. That was all depending the recently inflicted injury didn't overwhelm the effects of the XV1 coursing through his system.

In the corridor outside, he found the body of a police officer whose head had actually been severed from the body. What kind of power made such decapitation even possible? The head in question had been placed almost lovingly on a discarded trolley at the side of the body, the zombie mouth trying to chew at the air. It was clear that the building he was in was no longer under human control, blood the new paint for many of the walls and floors.

The cadaver of the deceased officer was armed with a pistol, and Smith took that as well as the spare ammunition, stripping the utility belt off the body with difficulty due to the loss of his fingers. He wasn't sure what good such a weapon would do though. One or two zombies he could now probably deal with, but a mass of them would easily overwhelm him in seconds, especially as he would be forced to shoot with his non-dominant hand. Even the Voice in his head agreed.

"That gun won't do you much good you know." Wherever the Voice came from, why did it persist? Why was he being plagued with this madness? The voice didn't answer that particular question.

The other gut-wrenching question kept coming to the front of his mind. *Would XV1 protect him against the bite he had received?* His own research had shown that the bite delivered strain of Lazarus was much more contagious, much faster to infect and much deadlier than contracting the virus from the way Smith had caught it. Death and reanimation could occur in hours rather than days…minutes if you were condemned by the London mutated strain. If he found himself going downhill rapidly, then at least he knew the gun would be of some ultimate use.

Across the world, millions would choose suicide rather than face what was coming. Like them, Smith was determined not to end up like one of those things.

"Oh aren't you?" the Voice chided him. Why was he talking to himself in this manner? The Voice sort of sounded like him, and it was definitely coming from his own mind, but with every passing minute it seemed to become more alien. Also, standing there with the gun in his hand, he could feel a part of him slipping. That was the only way to describe it, as if bit by bit, fragments of his personality were being removed. He needed to find help and get the hell out of here.

Fortunately, Doctor Patel was still in his lab, a chance finding as Smith passed the laboratory door. Patel wouldn't be much use in the needed escape, but Smith found himself stepping through into the room anyway. There was something that needed to be done here, but Smith found the identity of that task strangely elusive. He shook his head to try and clear the fog that was threatening to envelop his identity.

"How did you get out of the isolation room?" Patel asked, shocked to see the bedraggled figure of Smith in the doorway of his lab. When Smith had entered, the doctor had been removing the last samples of XV1 from the locked medical fridge. Those three vials were hardly the saviour of the human race but they were an important start.

"Must have been something to do with the power outage," Smith said. The words seemed to form shapes in the air in front of him.

"*You need those samples,*" the Voice insisted. Was that why he was here?

"Your hand…"

"I got bitten, but I think that might be the least of my problems. I'm having auditory and visual hallucinations." Behind Smith, a nurse ran past in the corridor, ignoring the two men. Briefly sticking his head out of the room, Smith checked that nobody or no thing was actually chasing her. He thought to shout after the nurse but then thought better of it. She was of no use to him. Further gunshots rang out outside.

"*Now why did you have to tell him about your hallucinations? This was our little secret, and there you go flapping your lips to everyone about it.*"

"Hallucinations?"

"Specifically voices, telling me what to do."

"*Shh, stop telling him our business. What's wrong with you?*"

"Are they talking to you now?" Patel asked. He put the three vials of XV1 into a refrigerated carry case. Smith's eyes followed their progress.

"Yes. We need to get out of here." Had there ever been a truer word said?

"We do, but we also need to get an MRI of you done. We must see if the antiserum has caused cerebral damage. If it's not safe then how can we use it?"

"*Hey, I'm right here you know.*"

"But I feel much better," Smith said. "Even with the bite, I think XV1 is protecting me from the virus. That's the important thing, surely." Smith felt the hand holding the gun twitch as a spasm ran through his whole arm. A strange and slight numbness seemed to be washing over his skin, unfamiliar sensations interrupting his consciousness.

Patel gave a hurried looked out of the window. Half a dozen soldiers were holding the undead at bay, behind them people were being loaded up onto a truck. The whole hospital had become a war zone.

"Investigations can come later then, let's go," Patel insisted. Smith barely heard him due to an unpleasant coldness that descended across his mind. In the brain, the supramarginal gyrus is a part of the cerebral cortex and is approximately located at the junction of the parietal, temporal and frontal lobe. When this brain region doesn't function properly a person's ability to feel empathy is dramatically reduced, if not removed completely. Smith didn't know it, but that part of his brain was presently dying, a tiny bleed wiping it out. Smith had just lost a large part of who he was, the better part.

XV1 had removed the lethality of the Lazarus virus, but not its presence entirely and the fresh surge of infection from the bite had changed the equilibrium of things. Just as at death, Lazarus could alter the structure of the living human mind, so it seemed able to adapt when under direct threat. The voice he heard was the first instance of that manifestation as Smith's brain started to rewire itself, new neural pathways forming. Now it was going one step further, causing a segment of his brain to actually die. Smith barely noticed part of who he was just disappear.

"*Patel is dangerous,*" the Voice insisted. "*He will be the end of us.*"

"Colonel, what's wrong?" Patel was looking at him, concern etched all over his face. Smith stood there rigid, making no indication that he was going anywhere.

"*Nothing's wrong,*" the Voice instructed.

"Nothing's wrong," said Smith almost robotically. It seemed right to follow the Voice's lead. "I feel just fine." That was the truth from a physical point of view. The pain in his hand and head had momentarily lifted, an intoxicating relief seeming to flood his system.

"Really, because you're staring off into space like you are having a petit mall seizure."

Smith shook his head, tunnel vision descending on him, the pain flooding back. A chill ran up his spine, and he felt the gun hand twitch again. Without even meaning to, the thumb flicked off the safety.

"*Enough of this. Just shoot him and take the XV1.*"

"I can't do that," Smith objected. His face looked pained.

"Can't do what, Colonel? Is your hallucination a voice? Is it talking to you now?" Patel took a step back even though he was trapped in between laboratory desks, Smith blocking the room's closest exit. The emotion had drained right out of Smith's face. He looked like he was in some kind of narcotic-induced trance.

"I'm talking to myself, yes," Smith confirmed. "It says I should shoot you."

"Ignore it, Colonel. Please. It's not real." There was alarm in Patel's voice, a dawning fear that something truly bad was about to happen.

"*The cheeky fucker. Of course I'm real. Why don't you show him how real I am?*"

"I'm sorry Doctor," Smith said, although his face gave no indication that he meant it. In fact, the corner of his mouth was turning up into a slight sneer. "If I could help myself, I would. But you just don't understand." The hand holding the gun raised itself, a slight shake evident there.

"Colonel, please, you don't have to do this."

"*But you do.*"

"But I do," Smith repeated. "I'm not myself you see. I'm sure you understand." The finger tightened and Smith shot Doctor Patel in the lower abdomen. Not an instantly fatal wound, but one that would kill without urgent medical intervention. Patel just seemed to grunt as he fell backwards onto his backside, his head smashing off the metal radiator that was behind him. The blow stunned Patel, whose thoughts swam with the desire to pass out if only to escape the pain.

"*I like that, I like that a lot. Why don't you shoot him in the knee?*"

"Why would I want to do that?"

"*Why not?*"

"No, I shouldn't have wasted a bullet on him in the first place." The gun wavered now, the hesitation not from any real concern for his fellow doctor. What if the noise he just made attracted the undead? What if he needed these bullets to save his own life?

"*Didn't you like how I took the pain away?*" the Voice enquired, analgesic peace flooding his system again. "*I can help you, but you have to help me.*"

Smith's vision began to tunnel again. A little bit more of him slipped.

"Oh, okay." Smith fired off a second shot which shattered Patel's right knee cap. This injury caused the doctor to scream. It was the most painful thing Patel had ever experienced, momentarily dwarfing the shot to his gut.

"*Too noisy.*" Smith was surprised the Voice was now complaining to him. "*Shut him up, will you?*" Smith had been right all along, this had been a bad idea.

"Do I have to?" Smith seemed to beg, but still his face remained impassive.

"*Just do it.*" Smith put a third round right through the centre of Patel's forehead as if he was on autopilot, a good shot considering he was firing with his nondominant hand.

"Shit, I shouldn't have done that." Smith felt confused, the loss of his empathic centre meaning he was now capable of almost anything. There was no sense of guilt there, just a general malaise that he was in a place he didn't want to be. He needed to get out of here, so why was he delaying?

Smith looked at the gun he held, as if confused about what he had just done. It was obvious that nobody in the hospital would have cared about the gunshots, but Smith knew it was time to get out of here in case he was suddenly discovered by something less than human. Picking up the carry case, he suddenly realised it had been its contents that had brought him here all along. But why? What use was the antiserum really?

Smith left the room without giving the body on the floor a second look, so he failed to see the muscles start to ripple in Patel's face, the shot enough to kill him but not to stop resurrection from his infected body.

Smith didn't bother with Patel's laptop. The doctor's research was of no immediate interest to him now. There were undoubtedly copies on the military deep web. Everything they had discovered had also been shared with the American CDC.

The lumbering Colonel ran, or at least he thought he did. Was he even in command of his own body anymore? He wasn't sure, everything felt like a daze to him. He had just mercilessly killed a man who had been no threat and he simply didn't seem to care. There would have been more negative emotion attached to scratching his left ear. Down a flight of stairs now and into another corridor, one that smelt of smoke and death. There were bullet holes in the wall to his left and several corpses lying face down. Human or zombie, Smith couldn't tell and he didn't concern himself with them. There would be plenty more by the time he made it to wherever he was going.

"Where am I going anyway?" Smith asked himself.

"*You know where,*" came the response only he could hear.

"I do?"

"*Of course.*"

He was about to make for the next flight down when behind him, a zombie pushed its way through a set of swing doors. It was dressed in a patient gown, blood and vomit staining most of the front. There was no pause, as soon as it saw its fresh prey, it charged. Smith should have been alarmed, instead he almost casually turned towards it.

"NO," Smith shouted. Or was it the Voice? He no longer knew.

The zombie pulled up, a pained expression on its face. It stood twitching in front of Smith as if unsure what to do. There was a restraint cuff on its left wrist, its life ended by the blood that had poured from the wound to its neck. Another of Renfield's victims. Smith stood there as the zombie bobbed its head in front of him, forcing the air into its nostrils so that it could smell Smith's essence. Finally deciding that Smith wasn't a target to attack, the zombie turned around and ran up the stairs Smith had appeared from.

What the fuck had just happened?

"*I told you to listen to me,*" the Voice mocked.

Unnoticed by either Smith or zombie, a lone figure further down the corridor had witnessed the brief exchange.

Having so far survived what he had wrought, the fact that someone could tell the undead what to do fascinated Renfield. The Private had been ready to shoot his superior officer from his point of concealment, but not now, not with what he had just seen. To kill Smith would leave this new mystery unsolved. Perhaps this dishevelled officer was somebody that shouldn't be killed.

Renfield took a risk and stepped forward from his place of concealment, still wearing his gas mask and still armed with both the pistol and the blood caked knife. The pistol he aimed at the newcomer, the first person in the last hour he actually had no immediate intention of killing. Not for the time being at least.

"How did you do that?" Renfield demanded. Smith turned, noticed the gun the soldier was pointing and made no attempt to raise his own weapon which he still held. In fact, he put his finger in the guard and let it spin in his hand so that he now held it by the barrel. Renfield seemed to recognise the gesture. For some reason Smith felt no concern that one of his own was aiming a weapon at him.

"I don't know. I don't think it was even me." That was the only answer he had for Renfield. "You realise, private, that you are pointing a gun at a superior officer?"

"Like I give a fuck," Renfield calmly replied.

23.08.19
New York, USA

Jacqueline Fairchild thought she would be safe from the virus in her weekend home. As the hours passed, however, the FBI Dignitary Protection Detail guarding her became more and more agitated with the news coming out of New York City. The roads leading from the Big Apple to the homes of the rich and famous were sealed off by the army, only sporadic incidences of violence flaring outside the border of the concrete and steel city. The problem was, there were nearly nine million people in New York City, and the infection was stripping the humanity from them at a rate the police and the National Guard couldn't even hope to deal with. Even where the streets seemed under relative control, the high rise buildings just seemed to breed the undead, a constant stream pouring out to play havoc with any hope of getting the virus under control. Combatting that was being hampered by the people trying to flee, and the unconscionable riots that had broken out, people hurling themselves onto the riot shields of the very people trying to stop the plague. As with much of the cities in the world, New York, with its great spirit and noble history, was not immune to the utter stupidity that homo sapiens were known for.

What made matters even worse was the way the zombies were reportedly using the subways to move around the city. Then there was the human uprising that broke out in Queens, heavily armed gangs taking claim to a whole section of the city. With too much to deal with, that part of New York was abandoned by any kind of law enforcement. It was hoped the virus would deal with their rebellion in the coming days. If not, there were some in power who would consider other means to supress the defiance.

Manhattan was the worst hit due to Gabriel seeding Lazarus amongst the hierarchy of the New York Police Department. 1 Police Plaza had been abandoned, a building now riddled with the virus that infused the very surfaces within it, brought by hands, breath and sweat. Wall Street had been forsaken, the stock market closed, probably never again to be reopened in the opinion of those who still had the ability to appear on the nation's airwaves.

As Attorney General, a constant stream of messages was being brought to Fairchild seeking her approval for actions that a week ago would have been unimaginable. The law still mattered, the constitution yet to be stripped of the last of its power. That day would come, but it was not to be this day. It was in one of these messages that she learnt of the bombing of the Brooklyn Bridge and of the napalming by A10 Warthogs of a mass of undead that were charging along Seventh Avenue. New York burned.

An hour ago she had spoken to the President, a man she detested for his liberal-minded ways. She knew she should have been more concerned by how hoarse he had sounded over the phone, but secretly she found she didn't care. In her opinion, he was the wrong man to be in power at this present moment in history. If he was to fall to the virus, it would ultimately only be of benefit to the nation.

Fairchild had already packed herself a bag. She could see the way the wind was blowing, and she knew it wouldn't be long before her FBI protection detail deemed relocation the best and only acceptable option. Not that she would allow any of her FBI detail to come anywhere near her physically. From the time since Lazarus's first awakening, she had become steadily more paranoid about contracting the virus, even taking to wearing a surgical mask around the part of the house that others had access to. She washed her hands with an almost religious ferocity, more out of panic than any overwhelming OCD. The FBI knew to keep out of her way wherever possible, for she had a sharp tongue and had never shown any reticence in using it to berate those who she deemed had fallen below her high standards. There were many who were thankful a woman like her wasn't President.

The other precaution she insisted on was a healthy dose of prayer. It was clear to her that this was Revelation, and with nobody around her even close to being a peer, there was no one to explain to her that this wasn't God's work, but the actions of humans with a warped and sick ideology. Even if such people had been present, it was unlikely she would have listened. How could she deny the truth when the proof of God's will was on every TV channel still running and in every email that landed in her inbox.

When she wasn't watching CNN or doing what her position demanded, her nose was deep in the comfort of her Bible. Everything she needed to deal with this was right in there.

As yet, she didn't know that within the day she would be made President, the long line of people before her in the chain of succession removed due to their exposure to the virus. There was nothing that was going to stop the first true Christian fundamentalist from becoming the Commander in Chief of the world's greatest nation. Jacqueline was a woman who believed in the will of God and the need for men and women to suffer for their sins, men most of all. Penance needed to be paid in this world and the next, and she was more than happy to judge those who defiled the laws of the Almighty via the most extreme interpretations of the King James Bible. She had just never had a true opportunity to relish in the true harshness of her faith. That would change.

It was sad though that she was to face this day of judgement alone, her once beloved husband being taken from her due to his own weakness and vanity. God had tested their relationship and had found him wanting, Dominic Fairchild being ripped from her arms by the siren call of a younger, more attractive woman. Jacqueline had actually laughed when she found out, twenty-five years of an admittedly loveless marriage ruined because he couldn't keep his pecker in his pants.

He could have been here with her, safe from the plague that had been unleashed. Instead, over a year ago, he had run to the arms of that slut, Jacqueline's suspicions verified by the FBI surveillance that had been ordered. If he was having an affair, was her husband not also a security risk to the country? From that moment of indiscretion onwards, Jacqueline had turned his life into shit.

When the divorce papers were filed and the press learnt of who he was sticking his dick into, Dominic learnt just how vengeful a powerful woman could be, especially one who knew every legal trick in the book. She utterly destroyed him financially, safely using New York's divorce laws to extract vast sums from him every month. There was no way he couldn't have known that this would be the end result of his sexual indulgence, for he had married a puritan and had witnessed first-hand the unremorseful way she seemed to take glee in destroying people's lives. He had assured her that he was an equal in his devotion to the Lord Our God but that had all been an act. It soon became clear that his infidelity was worse than it originally seemed, further affairs from the years gone by soon coming to light. The press loved it, and Jacqueline played the injured but stoic party brilliantly.

Some of those women had even been persuaded to accuse him of sexual impropriety, and the Attorney General rabidly encouraged the investigation of those accusations. Jaqueline would have loved nothing more for him to end up in prison as the final act in her methodical destruction of his betrayal. At least the apocalypse saved him that. Shame really. She'd had further plans for him which really would have hopefully driven him over the edge of his sanity. That was her only regret that the apocalypse had arrived…it had robbed her of her ultimate vengeance.

There was a knock on her bedroom door.

"Come in," Jacqueline said testily.

"Sorry ma'am," the FBI agent said. "The army has just informed us there has been an outbreak of the undead in Hempstead. The virus has got past the cordon they set up. It's off Manhattan Island for certain and there's street to street fighting in Brooklyn and Newark. Helicopters will be arriving in about ten minutes. You are being relocated to Site R." Site R, the Raven Rock Mountain Complex, an underground nuclear bunker in Pennsylvania. One of the core bunker complexes to ensure the US continuity of government. To ensure the continued security of the nation, its leaders needed protecting. Its leaders also needed to be strong and decisive, traits presently missing from the present Commander in Chief.

Jacqueline was loath to leave a home she loved but knew she had to listen to those whose job it was to protect her. Some of them might well have been Godless heathens, but they were the best at what they did. She could tolerate a few atheists because didn't God love a sinner who finally saw the error of their ways?

23.08.19
Preston, UK

Brodie was sat in the door to his quarters when the army Land Rover pulled up. There was nobody in the immediate vicinity so he had opted to do without the protective clothing, the threat deemed negligible. He had been unable to sleep and needed to feel the cool early morning air on his face. It was getting beyond cool now, though nothing he would allow himself to be bothered by. There was enough tragedy raging through his head without adding to it by concerning himself with the fucking weather.

Brodie was in turmoil internally. He remembered little of his life before the MI13 Orphanage, the training facility that viable candidates from the young and the dispossessed were sent to. He had been seven when his PTSD afflicted father had tried to kill him, Brodie the only survivor from that murderous spree. The images that stayed with him from the time before were sparse at best, much of it stripped away by psychiatrists who turned the trauma to the advantage of the people training the young man. Broken children could always be put back together for the benefit of the Realm.

This meant that Brodie's entire life had been pretty much dedicated to MI13 and the protection of the United Kingdom and its commonwealth. That had been the time before Lazarus though, and that life was pretty much over now. He wasn't one of those who saw any way out of this for his country, blindness not a condition of his patriotism. Brodie had spent much of his time as an agent developing the ability to accurately judge the outcome of differing scenarios, a skill that had been propelling him towards the top of the secret organisation. When he looked at the dire state of the country now, he found himself gazing into a huge void in his life, not knowing if his presence on this Earth still even had any meaning or purpose. This was a devastating discovery that had rapidly unpeeled in his mind, revealing itself as the country he was sworn to serve had started to collapse. The only scenario that made logical sense to him was the utter devastation of the United Kingdom and its institutions.

What was he for if not to protect the country that had saved him? His whole life plan, the thing he had been aiming for was now in ruins, a shattered remnant of a mind that had been laser beam focused on getting to the top. There wasn't even anything he could do to reverse what was happening. There was no spy network for him to uncover, no agent of chaos for him to kill. The tragedy presented no way for him to personally have any impact against something so small as the damned virus. How could he fight against an enemy you needed an electron microscope to see? How do you adjust to that? How do you adapt when your very identity is stripped from you?

Brodie hadn't told anyone in his team yet of course, although he knew at some point he would have to share it with Nick. That wasn't the sort of thing Brodie wanted to do but his mental turmoil risked impacting his effectiveness, and so Nick, as team leader, had to be informed.

To combat this kind of problem he needed professional help. The psychiatrist who had rescued him from the terrors of his own mind all those years ago would know what he would have to do to cope, but that man was dead, cancer taking his life quickly and mercilessly. With MI13 now all but mothballed, there was no such formal professional psychiatric help available. He was on his own, Brodie realising that this was something he was going to have to work out for himself. It was perhaps the greatest battle he had ever faced, a war against his own thoughts.

Sitting around here doing bugger all certainly wasn't helping matters at all. There was nothing to occupy himself with, so his mind was turning in on itself, all his usual techniques at stress management seemingly useless for this particular task. Normal boredom he could handle with his eyes closed. Death and insurrection he could deal with without breaking a sweat. Fighting zombies, he could even excel at. But coping with a crisis in his own identity was an enemy he had never faced before.

The thought that the other members of his team were facing a similar dilemma never really occurred to him. If there was no realm for him to protect then what was the point of any of it? Why had he spent his entire life with one overriding mission only for the Gods to rip everything up and start again? Never since the night where his father had shot him had Brodie ever felt so alone.

The side door of the Army Land Rover opened and several soldiers stepped out. Only one wasn't wearing the now ever familiar protective clothing, the others just in standard army issue NBC suits. Normally that meant an infected individual being delivered, so Brodie was surprised when instead of being taken to the quarantine building, the soldier was directed towards the building that held Jessica. His salute showed that he was a relatively low rank.

A semblance of something stirred in Brodie, and he slipped back into his sleeping quarters to wake Nick. Could this be another immune individual? Was this hope that had suddenly sparked in the back of his thoughts?

***

Whittaker was tired. It had been a long drive from North London, some of the roads difficult to pass. As amazing as it seemed to him, he had been given a tank escort, his importance expressed by the number of men guarding him. He had asked why not use a helicopter, only for him to be given the somewhat cryptic reply that helicopters couldn't be trusted with someone so potentially important. Nobody told him that the undead birds were making flying hazardous across the south of the country.

The tank had been essential to clear the way on some of the roads that were blocked by traffic, cars often abandoned due to the inevitable congestion fleeing people tend to create. The convoy had basically used the tank as a battering ram, pushing cars aside, even crushing the metal barriers in central reservations on two occasions. At times whole crowds of people could be seen at the sides of the roads, seemingly begging for the military to somehow help them. The military couldn't, there were just too many people and not enough soldiers. Was that how quickly British society could collapse?

The original plan had been to take him to a hospital in North Manchester where much of the research on Lazarus was being done, but near the end of their journey, Whittaker had overheard the radio saying that the hospital was being overrun. So now he was here, in an army barracks in the dead of night. With his journey now seemingly over, he was told to wait by the indicated building and someone would come and see to him shortly. It was as if whatever was happening at the hospital had destroyed any and all motivation for those escorting him. He could feel it amongst them…they were close to just giving up. Morale and duty were the last lines of defence in the war against the undead, and that line was being breached on multiple fronts.

He still felt bad about abandoning the men he had shared quarantine with but none of that had been his choice at the end of the day. Whittaker was still a soldier, and soldiers followed orders. It just didn't feel right though, leaving them like that. Couldn't those infected have been evacuated as well? He had to be realistic, such an idea was ridiculous if he was honest with himself. In the back of a transport truck, any one of them could have died and turned at any moment. How do you defend against that when you are transporting people? Could you really risk the few men you had left to protect those who were already lost?

But hadn't they claimed Whittaker was lost until he showed them otherwise? It made Whittaker wonder just how many immune people there were in the world. From what he was seeing, it didn't seem that there were very many.

As he walked towards what he had been told was this barrack's medical facility, he saw two men leave a nearby building and walk towards him. In this artificial light, they looked ominous in their army-issued protective gear. Was this his welcoming committee? It was clear they were heading toward him, so he stopped and waited for them, wary of the guns they both carried. He knew that was a bad sign when you started fearing the men on your own side.

"Morning," Nick said. His rank was hand-written on the front panel of his NBC suit. Not only had the base commander supplied the suit, but he had also insisted that Nick display his rank at all times whilst wearing it. Nick had understood the commander's requirements and had accepted the stipulations. He had declined however to wear army fatigues underneath, for those days were now behind him.

As tired as he was, Whittaker snapped to attention.

"No need for that lad," Brodie said sounding amused. "Save your salutes for the people who matter." Whittaker noticed this man had no rank displayed.

"Sir?"

"What Mr Brodie is trying to say is at ease soldier," Nick clarified.

"Yes sir."

"I think we can dispense with the sirs as well. My name's Nick."

"Carl." Nobody shook hands, which somehow felt wrong to Brodie. He wasn't a soldier and hadn't saluted anyone in his entire life. Not even as a child. They didn't play such kid's games in the Orphanage.

"Chris," Whittaker responded. He managed to avoid saying sir, even though it was sat in the forefront of his mind dying to jump out. Who were these guys anyway? Special Forces perhaps?

"I couldn't help but notice you were new here." Nick hadn't told any of the other team, but he had been informed that another immune individual was being delivered. The insignia on Whittaker's uniform definitely didn't match the soldiers stationed here. Whittaker was undoubtedly the person he had been waiting for.

Nick also knew of the problems occurring at the hospital. Extra soldiers had been dispatched there about ten minutes ago. As long as Natasha could keep Nick connected to Moros, Nick would be privy to pretty much everything that Moros knew. Not even the top military brass would have his direct intel so quickly. Moros was plugged into everything.

Nick made a point of keeping Haggard in the loop as well. It was only fair.

"I've just been driven up from North London. The barracks there were overrun." Not the best of news, thought Brodie. The undead were gaining ground too quickly. At this rate, the country would be lost in mere days.

"Is there a reason you are heading to the medical facility mate?" Nick enquired, already knowing the answer.

"It was where I was told to go. Apparently, I'm immune."

Inside Brodie's heart, the despair that had been crushing him lightened just a fraction.

23.08.19
Manchester, UK

"I'm considering not shooting you," Renfield stated calmly. He stood with his gun aimed at the Colonel, that act of rebellion increasing his feeling of empowerment.

"Shooting me would definitely be a mistake." Smith had laid his gun on the floor to increase his chances of getting out of this in one piece. He tried to smile but he wasn't sure he knew how anymore. The prospect of getting shot held no real concern for him which he found surprising. Smith felt like he was looking at life through a haze.

"I don't know. You're a colonel," Renfield stated, noting the insignia on Smith's tunic. "I've always wondered what it would be like to kill a colonel."

"I'm nothing special, trust me. Killing me would likely be a great disappointment in fact. Did you..." Smith felt himself hesitate. "Did you do all this?" Changing the subject seemed to be the best and only plan he had available to him right now, but were the words he spoke even his?

"What, release the undead? Of course. I created them first though. They were sticking the sick in rooms to die. I thought why should nature not get a helping hand to speed along the demise of some of the useless eaters." Renfield didn't see what he had to lose by bragging about what he had achieved. The high he was on was barely diminishing, making him feel invincible.

"Nature?" Smith was confused by the reference.

"The virus, Lazarus. Nature's way of sweeping humanity from the Earth." It wouldn't matter how many people Renfield killed, he knew he couldn't match the destructive force of the very planet he lived on.

"Oh no my friend," Smith found his smile at last, although he wondered if it looked genuine or malevolent. "This isn't nature. Lazarus was made by man. A mistake gone wrong." The words he spoke were definitely his own now as the Voice confirmed.

"*I think we both know this isn't a mistake,*" the Voice said, chastising him. Renfield lowered his gun.

"Man?"

"Yes. It broke out of a lab North of Bangkok. Weren't you briefed on that?" They should have been.

"No. Man made? Wow, somehow that makes it even better." Renfield stepped up close to Smith, breaking into his personal space, rank clearly of no issue to the soldier anymore. "Can you do that again?"

"Do what?" Smith asked.

"Stop the dead from attacking you."

"I have no idea." Genuinely, Smith didn't know why the zombie had listened to him. His voice had sounded wrong as well, sounded more like the Voice in his head.

"I have killed all I can kill here," Renfield said revelling in his madness. To be able to freely admit what he had done to a complete stranger, an officer of all people, just increased his excitement at what he had achieved. "Can you get me out of here?"

"Yes," the Voice answered, forcing itself out through Smith's unwilling lips.

Renfield could still feel them all inside him, Lucy more than most. No matter how many he added, he knew she would always be his favourite. He just didn't want to join her in whatever afterlife existed just yet. Renfield still needed time to relish in the fruits of what he had done. There were also still too many lives that needed taking, a whole world left to plunder. Renfield was still on a high, the bulge in his pants hidden by the thick protective suit he wore.

When he had vacated his ward after leaving the nurse to her fate, Renfield had gone to another where the infected were also being kept. The soldier there he knew and his body language had seemed relieved when Renfield had calmly stepped through the doors. That reaction had said volumes, a friend to share the crushing burden the soldier was being asked to bear. That soon changed when the now completely insane Private Renfield had put three bullets in his fellow soldier's unsuspecting chest. With nobody left to stop him, Renfield had repeated the slaughter on fifty more docile and generally compliant patients. Only three gave him any kind of trouble, and that was merely in the way they had begged for mercy. He couldn't abide weakness of character like that. Just accept your suffering. There was no need to make such a song and dance about such a little thing as death. Those he didn't kill, instead leaving them for the undead to feast upon.

The sound of running feet drew both their gazes. A doctor appeared, out of breath having frantically climbed the stairs. He was helping a teenage patient who was desperately trying to stem the flow of blood from the neck wound that had been inflicted upon her, the surgical compress there red with the blood that was so easily soaking through it. In her case, the carotid artery had been spared, the teeth not digging deep enough. The undead were clearly spreading throughout the hospital, soon everyone present would join their ranks, this teenager one of them.

Seeing the military uniforms, the doctor totally misjudged the situation. He should have turned around and run straight back down the stairs. Only he couldn't due to the monsters that were stalking the lower floor. Renfield took a step to the side away from Smith, hiding the gun behind his body so that the doctor wouldn't be concerned by it. Another one to kill thought Renfield, and his head swam with the thoughts of further slaughter.

"Thank God," the doctor pleaded, "you have to help us."

"Glad to," Renfield stated calmly, now stepping casually towards the newcomers. "Which one?"

"What?" With the doctor preoccupied, the patient finally collapsed, blood loss rapidly bringing unconsciousness. She slipped through the doctor's arms, totally distracting him to the impending danger he was now in.

"Which foot is your favourite?"

"I don't understand." The doctor was close to exhaustion and hysterics. Why weren't these people helping him?

"Guess it will be both then." With that, Renfield shot the doctor in the right ankle, the gun whipping out to once again cause destruction. The shot was precise, the blast echoing around the corridor, exemplifying the sound of battle that was occurring throughout the building. The ankle joint was completely annihilated by the impact, multiple bones fracturing, cartilage rupturing as the disc there was all but destroyed.

As the doctor crashed to the ground clutching the damaged limb, the Private stepped closer and shot the other foot, the pistol now held in both hands for accuracy. As much as it was unwise to make loud noises in a building with creatures that partially hunted by sound, the doctor let out a roar that rivalled the cacophony of the gunshots that had stricken him.

"You know, I like this guy," the Voice commented about Renfield, clearly amused by what was happening.

"We should go," Smith insisted. He resisted the urge to grab hold of Renfield, rightly predicting that this would have unfavourable results. Noticing the way Renfield was staring almost mesmerised by his latest creation, Smith reckoned he could have run then, could have left the Private to his new fascination. Smith chose not to, or was it that the Voice wouldn't let him?

"Not yet." Renfield looked down at the bleeding doctor for several seconds and then, as if sensing something, stepped back so that he was stood directly by his superior officer. Did the concept of officers even make any sense to Renfield anymore after what he had done? "I want to see you do it again."

"But I don't know if I can," Smith implored.

"Don't worry, I've got you covered."

"You better," Renfield said without looking at him. "Because if you can't you aren't any use to me." There it was, the threat to his life that could only be cancelled by his performing some sort of arcane magic trick. Smith briefly considered trying to overpower the Private, but that would likely not have ended well. Renfield was younger, stronger, and not weakened by combating Lazarus within his system for days. Plus, Renfield was armed with a knife and a gun. Smith was army medical corps. It had been years since he'd done any kind of hand to hand combat training. He wouldn't stand a chance against the younger man who was at the very peak of his insanity.

At the end of the corridor they were standing in, a zombie charged through a set of double doors. It didn't stop to survey the scene, instead it just went straight for the squealing doctor who was trying to pull himself along the floor away from the fresh hell that had arrived.

"Watch this bit," Renfield insisted, "it's fucking great."

"Yeah, I really like this one. Can we keep him?"

Smith wasn't horrified by what he saw, there was no capacity left in him for such an emotion. He had seen them up close, but the assault on his own person was nothing compared to what he witnessed now. The zombie, a former police officer now missing an ear and with an eye that dangled from a shattered socket, leapt upon the stricken doctor and began to smash its fists into the doctor's face and body. There was nothing the doctor could do to fight it off, the blows too powerful, the energy of the creature relentless.

Within seconds, the doctor was close to unconsciousness, his body lying lazily beneath the being that straddled him. The zombie ripped at his clothes and, seeming to sense the already existing injury, shuffled down the body, grabbing one of the doctor's legs. The one with the ankle wound bled freely, and the zombie seemed to close its mouth over the wound, sucking the blood greedily into its mouth. With his jaw smashed in three places, the doctor was barely able to scream.

"It's like it's drinking from him," Renfield said with fascination, more to himself than anyone else present. The words seemed to float in the air, finally drawing the zombie's attention. It lifted its head before biting down on the ruined joint, tearing into the flesh and cartilage. The doctor passed out, the pain too much for his mind to further endure.

The teenager had stopped moving, the eyes slowly turning black as it began the process of resurrection. The wound itself hadn't been too severe, but when added to the disease that had originally brought the teenager to the hospital a week ago, it was too much for her to ultimately cope with.

"Get ready to do your thing." Renfield moved from Smith's side and stood behind him.

"I've told you," Smith hissed, "I don't know how."

"Then there will be one less wanker Colonel for the squaddies to salute." To emphasise the point, Renfield poked Smith in the spine with the tip of his gun, just under where the case carrying XV1 was riding on Smith's back.

The zombie gave up on eating the leg and stood, still chewing the contents of its mouth. If he ran, Smith knew he was dead. Either Renfield would shoot him or the zombie would catch him. Could he do it again? Could he tell a zombie, a creature without apparent mind or conscious will to leave him alone? It didn't run at Smith, instead it seemed to approach cautiously, head flinching, fingers twitching.

Stopping an arm's length away, it detected the creation of its sister, the former teenager rising up to join it.

"Go away," Smith ordered. He tried to put some authority in his voice, not knowing if that had any impact on the skill he seemed to have acquired. The zombie seemed to shiver, falling back a few steps, pushed by some invisible force. The newer zombie collided with it, eager to get at the fleshy meat that hung on Smith's bones, but it too stopped, not coming any closer. It was like there was a force field surrounding the Colonel.

"*Told you,*" the Voice stated. "*You don't need to worry about the undead. Not anymore.*"

"But how?" Smith demanded to know. It briefly occurred to him that there really wasn't any need for him to talk out loud to himself. But then he realised that perhaps that was the only way he was going to be able to truly distinguish himself from the intruder in his mind.

"I don't know," Renfield answered, mistaking Smith's question as being aimed at him. "But you are my ticket out of here."

"*Do I need to tell you everything?*" the voice admonished him. "*You're a scientist, figure it out for yourself.*" Apparently losing interest, the two zombies turned back to the fallen doctor who moaned as he faltered in and out of consciousness. With unmatched ferocity, they descended upon the doomed body, the teenage zombie punching its hand right into the doctor's guts. They would feast, but enough would be left to resurrect.

"Now we go," Renfield ordered. As fascinated as he was by the horrifying scenes, the Private had realised he had overstayed his welcome in the hospital.

Smith couldn't agree more, although he had no idea what was happening in the confines of his own brain.

23.08.19
Preston, UK

Standing outside the observation window that looked into Azrael's room, Nick called the number again on the satellite phone, his gas mask presently discarded. He had no expectation that Mother would answer, but she did.

"Mother?"

"Mr Carter, I had a feeling you would call back."

"It feels wrong to call you Mother. May I know your real name?" There was a pause at the other end of the line.

"You may call me Maria." Maria Braun, once a dedicated East German member of the Stasi and later seconded to the KGB. A respected intelligence officer managing nearly a dozen illegals who had ultimately become disillusioned by the corruption she had seen on both sides of the Iron Curtain.

At the fall of the Berlin Wall she had formed her network into an efficient clandestine organisation that was now responsible for killing the world. She herself had not profited from this, her body an arthritic mess slowly dying from the cancer that riddled her bones. Medical science had totally failed her and she couldn't ignore the irony that the person who had set out to reduce the human race to manageable numbers would shortly die herself.

"Thank you, Maria."

"What do you want?" She sounded suspicious.

"I never let you talk to Azrael when we last spoke, and I have been thinking that this was a mistake." This had all been before the true extent of what Lazarus meant to the world had been revealed.

"I agree, it was," Mother stated. She sounded tired, almost defeated.

"Would you like to speak to him now?"

"Very much so. I would at least like to say goodbye." She would have liked to say goodbye to all her children, but most of them were now dead. So many had been turned to her whim, their Soviet era pre-programming so easy to manipulate and abuse to her own whims. Azrael, Gabriel and Lilith had been the last assassins she had trained.

"Okay, I can do that for you." Azrael watched Nick from inside his locked room, the assassin's body still restrained. "I have some questions for you first though."

"Agreeable and expected."

"Was Azrael vaccinated against Lazarus? He said he remembers being asked to self-administer an injection about a year ago."

"I don't know," Mother said truthfully. "But another like Azrael has recently told me something similar. Whatever it was, it was unknown to me." How blind she had become to the actions of her organisation. Curse the disease that had made her so weak.

"We ourselves used Azrael as a guinea pig for an antiserum that is being developed which seems to have protected him from the virus, but I have my suspicions that he was already immune."

"How horrific," Mother said. She sounded genuinely shocked.

"Spare me. What you made him do is infinitely worse."

"I did what I did. I won't apologise for that." Even though her actions had ultimately led to all this, she still had to believe it was all for the greater good. The belief was something to cling onto with the tips of her fingernails.

"Were you ever told about a vaccine?" That was the question wasn't it.

"No. I knew about Lazarus, even tried to prevent its creation. But they never told me whether they had a cure," said Mother. *And why was that* she found herself asking? Simple really. Because she was dying and past her usefulness. To give her the vaccine would have revealed just how close to perfecting Lazarus the Gaia scientists had become. The Three had asked her to re-join the fold, but only after side-lining her so they could carry out the plan she had rejected as insane.

Part of her wondered if the accidental release of the virus was in fact deliberate. The only reason she could imagine for her now to be brought back into the organisation was so that Father, Uncle and Brother could gloat over how they had been right all along. The thing was, they hadn't been right. This whole thing was a disaster. She would rather die alone than be forced to see their lying faces again.

"Okay. I'm inclined to believe you. Are you prepared to tell me more about your organisation?" Another pause from Mother as she contemplated her response.

"Yes," Mother said. And she did. She told him everything. Unfortunately, she hadn't been able to tell him the identity of the mole in MI13. Nick didn't know if that individual was even still alive, but only a spy in his network could explain how Azrael had been tipped off at Manchester Airport.

"Azrael?"

"Mother!" Nick held the phone to the assassin's face allowing him to talk to the woman who had created him.

"I'm sorry Azrael, for everything." The apology shocked Azrael more than the phone call itself. "I'm sorry for how I used you."

"It doesn't matter," Azrael heard himself say. "I don't know the person I was before and I don't think I ever will. Even though I have memories now, they mean little to me."

"You remember?" Mother was shocked to hear this, the conditioning should have been total in its illumination of his past life, because that life had itself been a fake imprint.

"I do. With the help of Jessica." He could still sense the hatred and the despair in Jessica's heart. The hurt he must have caused her went deep. "Tell me Mother, why did you instruct me to kill Jessica?" There was a hint of venom in the question.

"I didn't," Mother said and Azrael heard the truth in the words. "There are others in the organisation I never told you about. Three men who now rule in my stead. They betrayed me as they obviously betrayed you. We have both been used to their own ends."

"How could they do that? You are everything."

"No Azrael, I am nothing. And I'm dying which is why I wanted to say goodbye."

"Dying." He repeated the word. He saw the truth of her mortality, even though Mother had been the World.

"Cancer, a terminal diagnosis. I've been clinging on for years, doing my part for Gaia, thinking I was still of use. I never realised that all the time they were working so tirelessly behind my back."

"So it wasn't you who sent me after Jessica?"

"No, Azrael."

"So I am not expendable?" Tears welled in the corner of his eyes. The email he had received on the nineteenth ordering him to assassinate Jessica had stated that Azrael should consider the mission more important than his own life. He had thought it then a penance for his failure the day prior, but now he wondered if he had been at fault at all. He'd had Jessica in the sights of his machine gun and had failed to take the shot. Even with the revelations Jessica had helped him with, that inability to shoot had plagued him with guilt. A conflicted emotion, guilty about defying the person he came to see as a betrayer. But now it seemed that Mother hadn't been the one asking him to do a task that ultimately wouldn't have been in his best interests. He felt washed of another sin. He hadn't defied Mother after all, and she hadn't betrayed him.

"God no Azrael, you were the best I ever trained. So merciless, so skilled." Nick was listening into the conversation and he couldn't help thinking that this was a strange relationship these two people had.

"Thank you, Mother, that means a lot."

"I should thank you for your dedication."

"I had flaws you know, things I never told you about."

"We all do. It's what makes us human." The voice of Mother was soft, caring.

"Am I still human after everything I have done?" Azrael was shocked by the notion.

"Of course you are, perhaps more human than most. That's why I want you to survive. Mr Carter has promised not to kill you. In return I have told him everything I know about our organisation."

"I will be allowed to live?"

"Yes," Mother replied almost in tears now.

"Thank you," Azrael said. With his sense of failure exorcised, Azrael felt a huge weight lift from his shoulders.

23.08.19
Houston, USA

Rupert Clayton was pissed in both senses of the word. Angry and drunk from the Jack Daniels he had been consuming far too quickly, even for his iron clad constitution. His wife had talked him out of storming the quarantine facility and in hindsight she had been right to do so. The place had been too well guarded, the military force there too strong for his rabble. If he had lost control of the situation, it would have been a massacre.

He might have been head of his militia, but very few of its members actually had any kind of proper military experience. It was mainly young men interrupted by the occasional female face. Young men who liked to drink beer and shoot guns, although not necessarily in that order. Clayton had formed the militia because it was his God given right to do so under the Constitution. In times of need he saw himself as the final insurance policy against anarchy and the evils of the Federal Government. Those Goddamn liberal criminals had taken the universities and they had taken Hollywood. They had even tried to take Washington, but it would be a cold day in hell before he let them take from him the Texas he loved.

Clayton could have gone down a very different road if not for the love of his wife who he absolutely worshipped. The very ground she walked on was sacred to him, the thought of someone hurting her precious pale skin enough to send him into a seething rage. There was no denying that she was the better half of him, keeping him out of trouble and tempering the volatile side of his nature. She made sure he kept control of his temper which, in his younger years, had been known to boil over into acts of wanton violence. To this day he didn't know how he was so lucky to find a woman like that, and now she was locked away with the rest of the sick and the dying. It wasn't right that she be taken from him like that.

Earlier he had been all intent on storming the Astrodome to get her out, more out of blind panic than any real distrust for the military's intentions. If not for the intervention of the Sherriff's deputy, things might well have become really unpleasant. So he held a secret thanks to Reece's interference, for his actions had been foolishly impulsive. No matter how many of the soldiers they had killed, there would have been no getting into the Astrodome. To do that needed proper planning.

He still didn't want his wife in there, and when he finally broke her out, Clayton knew she would understand. If she was going to die, he wanted it to be in his arms so that HE and he alone could do what was required to be done to end her suffering. As wise as she had seemed, the Deputy had been wrong about one thing. Mrs Clayton wasn't where she needed to be. Where she needed to be was here with him. If only if to just be able to say goodbye.

The call to arms he had received had told him everything he needed to know to assist in the fight against the zombie menace, his men now helping guard several checkpoints to ensure the flow of people around the city was kept under control and to a minimum. Clayton would have his people do their duty in that regard for now, but he would also do what ultimately needed doing so as to rescue the most amazing woman he had ever met. Clayton just hadn't figured out how he was going to do that yet.

If people were going to die, it should be in the presence of the people who loved them the most. And whilst Clayton knew he could voluntarily go into the Astrodome to be with her, he could not abide spending his last days in a glorified concentration camp. He wouldn't go out that way and would go down all guns blazing if anyone tried to force that fate on him. Instead he plotted, his drunken mind trying desperately to formulate what would ultimately end up being a flawed and grandiose plan to rescue his wife. It would mean storming the wire. It would mean creating a diversion. There were three hundred men and women at his beck and call who would pretty much do what he told them to do.

He had already told the militia sub commanders. They all told him that they backed him one hundred per cent, although he knew he only had some of their loyalty. In his drunken haze, he found himself wondering how many of them he could truly rely on. Clayton was to end up being pleasantly surprised.

***

Reece sat up in the stands eating the MRE she had been given. It tasted as bad as it looked, but she forced it down, her taste buds pretty much shot from the runny nose and the cough that had been forming all day. She felt like she had a mild cold, nothing that she would have taken a day off work for though.

It was deserted where she sat, the cages filling the football field below. Reece had no idea how many cages there were, and quite frankly she didn't want to know. There was no doubt the number would depress her, especially as now they were all starting to fill up. The Astrodome was already at two thirds capacity, neighbours and co-workers undoubtedly reporting suspected infected with increasing regularity. Self-referrals seemed to be a minority when it came to infection reporting. The army were busy out there rounding up what they could and trying to fight what they missed.

It would be getting difficult for them now as well. A program such as this could only work with the willing consent of the population. Already there was talk of armed resistance, of soldiers being fired upon from windows and in the streets. Many of the people who had been labelled as infected were not coming quietly, which meant the army and the police were suffering growing casualties, all whilst their ranks were being thinned from within by Lazarus. Reece wasn't the only infected person in uniform here, many of them much further gone than she was. Most of those in her position had freely given up their weapons when their symptoms became too debilitating. One or two had foolishly resisted. That didn't end well for them.

Those in uniform who carried the infection were easy to spot by the monitors they wore and the fact there was no point wearing any kind of personal protective equipment.

Considering some of the people she encountered here, Reece thought she was coping with the disease pretty well. Her bowels felt fine, and she hadn't as yet needed to throw up, although there had been hints of nausea especially with food of this dire quality. Whilst she was certain it would shortly get a lot worse, she was thankful that she was so far having a relatively easy time of it. Everyone down there was suffering badly, the smell of vomit and human waste reaching her even here. Taking the fork to the morsel masquerading as food, she forced another bite down. If armies were supposed to march on their stomach, Reece was amazed America hadn't been invaded by now. How were people supposed to live off this crap?

But then perhaps it had been conquered, only the invader had no interest in the oil wells and the gold stored in the nation's vaults. The invader in this case cared only for the cells and the blood of the people who called themselves Americans.

Reece heard the person walking down the stadium steps behind where she sat, and turned to see the image of one of the CDC doctors making their way towards her, all spruced up in full hazmat finery. Dr Jee Lee had been there to admit Reece to the facility, and had done Reece's blood tests as well as locking the monitor onto her arm. Reece could tell that the thirty something doctor had been drained and close to burnout with the workload so the Deputy had struck up a conversation with her. As lonely as Reece had often felt before the apocalypse began, she had no problem when it came to talking to people and had quickly learnt that the doctor's first name was Jee.

"*Jee Lee, you can imagine all the fun the kids had with that in secondary school.*"

Jee sat down next to Reece, who jokingly offered to share the delectable meal she was forcing herself to consume.

"Are you kidding? You want me to throw up in this suit?"

"It's delicious," Reece lied.

"Is that how you get suspects to confess? Force them to eat that crap?"

"Hey," Reece countered, "you guys are the ones serving this swill up."

"Yeah okay, I'll give you that. How you feeling Clarice?" Jee didn't need to take Reece's pulse, the monitor told her all that and more.

"Checking up on me now are you?" Reece liked Jee, she had a refreshing honesty in her communication and a way about her that easily instilled trust. She was also prone to smiling, which was a rarity in this place. In a better time, they might even have become friends.

"Totally. I've decided you are my star patient. All the grunts are talking about the kickass babe who helped stop a massacre at the front gate. Rumour has it half the men here have the hots for you."

"Only half?" Reece acted upset at the news.

"The other half are too far gone to even see straight, Clarice." Jee's train of thought was broken by the sound of gunshots down on the playing field. Somewhere in that maze of cages, another unfortunate victim had taken the final step with Lazarus. There were too many people held here to even contemplate using anything but a gun to kill the zombies when they arrived into the world. That had been the second one since Reece sat down. "Do you ever get used to it?" Jee asked.

"Depends what you're referring to."

"You deal with the risk of violence every day. I can't help but feel everyone we have to shoot is another example of how we've failed."

"You're doing the best you can," Reece noted. "I'm still amazed all this could be put up so quickly."

"So was I," Jee admitted. "It was all stockpiled in a FEMA warehouse on the edge of the city. Apparently the then Governor decided he wanted Texas to be ready for everything, especially the inevitable global pandemic we all knew was coming. The CDC and FEMA have similar operations going on in San Antonio,

Dallas and Austin. For once, someone actually did what they were supposed to do." A question suddenly formed in Recce's mind, but she kept it to herself. *Why would they need cages to fight a pandemic?*

"Is there any word on other parts of the country?"

"The rust belt states have so far been pretty much unaffected, some of them have even started cutting themselves off from the rest of the country where they can. But all the big cities are in trouble. We try not to talk about that here though, unofficial rule. Atlanta's doing alright, although for how long I don't know." At the start, Jee had been glued to the news, but now she barely watched it. It depressed her too much and she wanted to concentrate on the important job which was saving as many people as she could. Reece looked at her new acquaintance and for the first time noticed the bags under her eyes.

"When was the last time you slept?" Reece asked.

"Sleep? Oh yes, I remember that. I've probably had an hour in the last forty-eight."

"I won't tell you to look after yourself then. You're a doctor, you already know." Jee gave her a sarcastic look and then pulled something from a pouch on her suit's utility belt.

"Thanks Mom. Now give me your arm." Jee unzipped the pouch and withdrew the blood testing kit. Reece was already wearing a short sleeved top and she rotated her body so that the CDC doctor could get at the arm without the monitor on.

"I swear this place is actually run by a cult of vampires." Jee didn't need to stick a fresh needle in, all the patients here had Venflons inserted. Better to risk a needle stick once than multiple times. Once the blood was drawn, Jee put it into a clear plastic bag.

"Jee, can I ask you something?"

"Sure Clarice."

"What happens when you run out of room?"

"If needs be, we start doubling up on the cages." Jee knew she wasn't supposed to tell anyone that, nobody really wanted to be in a cage with someone that might turn into a zombie.

"Jesus," Reece suddenly had a flash to her future.

"That won't happen to you. I have assurances you will be confined to the room we have given you should it come to that. I told you, the soldiers running this place have got a lot of respect for what you did when you arrived."

"Don't you mean when?" Reece watched the doctor stand, a distant look now on Jee's face.

"You keep out of trouble now Clarice, okay?"

"I promise to be home before eleven thirty, mum." Reece could sense the tension in the doctor's voice. If they were already planning to double up on the cages, what happened when they had to triple up? The city had millions of people. As large as this facility was, could it even cope with what was coming? As if to answer Reece's question, another series of gunshots came from the maze below.

Jee walked away. She tried to supress the excitement that was threatening to grow inside her. The monitor Reece was wearing sent real time data to the computers they had set up. Whereas everyone else was showing a steady, and sometimes rapid decline towards the final stages of the Lazarus infection, Reece if anything seemed to be stabilising. It's not something she wanted to tell the Deputy just yet, because being given false hope only to have that dashed could be psychologically devastating.

Jee was eager to get this blood test checked, the CDC having set up an entire testing lab in the tent city now present on the Astrodome car park. If Reece was immune, then that changed everything.

23.08.19
Preston, UK

Whittaker lay in the dark, still struggling with the fate the Gods had decided for him.

The accommodation they had provided Whittaker was infinitely superior than his last residence. He had a room to himself for once, with a door that actually locked on the inside. The bed was more comfortable than any regulation army mattress, clearly designed for sick people who needed extra TLC. He even had his own bathroom. To the army corporal, it was almost luxury.

The guy called Nick had led him here and whilst they hadn't locked him up, it was clear to him that he still wasn't a free individual. If he really was immune, he would be invaluable to the war that was being fought on the streets and in the bloodstreams of every person in this country. Whittaker could live with that. He was a soldier, and he would be just playing a different part in the battle that was unfolding. As much as it was his job, he really didn't think he wanted to be on the front line fighting undead hordes. So let them do their blood tests. After the shit he'd seen, he would be happy to sleep and stay in this room for the rest of the month. Hell, the rest of the year.

Captain Beckington had been in to see him to let him know what would be done over the coming days. That was when Whittaker had learnt about the other immune individual in the room next door, the woman who was likely now asleep. At least he wasn't alone in this. If there were two of them there would be more, perhaps the start of something. The fight against the undead might be being lost, but maybe the virus could be defeated. That would mean people wouldn't have to be afraid of themselves and the soldiers would be freed from the NBC suits that had a finite life and came with gas masks that would eventually become useless as the filters all failed. Whittaker knew nothing about how vaccines were made, so his visions of his usefulness were perhaps somewhat exaggerated.

Despite how tired he was, sleep refused to come at first, the carnival in his head constantly going over everything that had happened. He had seen people die, had felt forced to desecrate their corpses to stop them returning from the dead. He thought that was something he could get his head around, but to witness an enemy as powerful and as relentless as the one they now faced left him feeling hopeless. The undead didn't seem to need sleep, and although it was said they craved the flesh of the living, they didn't need food to sustain themselves. They would just keep on going relentlessly. On the ride here,

Whittaker had shared a Land Rover with Beckington, and after an initial tense hour, the Captain had started opening up to him. Beckington had told him things the top brass had wanted kept from the lower ranks. Things were worse than the soldiers were being told.

Great swathes of the country were being abandoned, whole cities given over to the dead, the virus having spread faster than anyone could have imagined. London, Glasgow, Cardiff and Birmingham were the worst so far. There just wasn't the manpower to combat this menace, and much of the command and control structure that was in charge of running things was gone, the heads of the government either dead or dying.

The battle was also being hampered by the lack of air dominance, planes and helicopters being grounded in parts of the country due to the deadly threat of zombified birds. That was why they hadn't sent Whittaker north by helicopter, it was deemed too risky. Nearly a fifth of Britain's combat helicopters had been lost, the rest now waiting for the time when the undead birds could no longer fly.

Then there was the good news. The Colonel who was working on an antiserum. Not a full cure, but at least something to reverse the disease in those infected. Something at least to hold back the tide. And that was why Whittaker was here. It was hoped that his blood might hold the answers to the secrets of Lazarus. And yet he had seen the eyes of the condemned soldiers when he had been picked from amongst them due to his apparent immune status. There was a glimmer of hope there, but also envy. In one or two eyes, he had also seen hatred.

Whittaker was pretty certain he knew what happened to the men he had been locked up with. The army was not above sacrificing its own to eliminate an immediate threat. They had been kept alive because they were hoping for a miracle. When that miracle arrived, the fates of the rest of them were sealed. Perhaps that explained the hate. His presence in the room, even though not by his own volition, had sentenced the rest of them to an early death.

**

Jessica slept, although her body tossed and turned on the bed, the nightmare worse than usual. Every time she took a dream step, the desert seemed to be hotter, her skin more crusted, the fear of the horsemen more intense. Only later would she learn what the nightmares meant and why she shared the same dream with other immune individuals. It would warn of the battle still to come.

It would be Nick who would figure the enigma out, something in Jessica's conversation with Azrael that had sparked the neuron that sprouted the thought in Nick's head. Through Natasha he had asked Moros whether, given the information provided, the immune could somehow be linked. Moros had come back with its analyses.

Given the unknown neural affects Lazarus has on the brain, and the lack of reported nightmares pre infection by the limited patient base, I can only give a 57% probability that there is a causal link between immunity and the cognitive disturbance reported. More data is essential. My database does contain classified data on MI13 and CIA research into paranormal abilities, which were all deemed negative after countless trials. I cannot therefore speculate on the question as to whether the immune are somehow linked telepathically.

None of that mattered now. Infected by a disease Jessica had beaten, her mind had awakened to a network that spanned space and time. Across the globe, the immune were being exposed to a virus that was no more deadly to them than the common cold. As their bodies fought off the invader, it would give them a gift and a curse, unlocking something that had perhaps lain dormant for tens of thousands of years. The dreams would show each of them who they were, but only in a realm of utter torment. There they could suffer together and see the truth in each other's tortured eyes. It would also warn them of the threat yet to come.

The horsemen were not those beings depicted in religious fiction. If anything, they were much worse than that. The horsemen were the sons and daughters of Adam.

23.08.19
Manchester, UK

By the time Smith got close to the exit of the hospital building there was a full-fledged battle going on outside. Army reinforcements had arrived from their forward positions around Manchester and were engaging the undead as they stormed out of the hospital's front entrance. At least a hundred soldiers had turned up, enough to turn the tide in what would later be seen as a mere skirmish in the great battles that would erupt across the globe. To the men engaged in it though, this was utter carnage, the engagement further depleting ammunition stocks as well as sapping the courage of men who had always expected to be fighting other men.

At that moment in time, there were twenty-seven thousand infected individuals across Manchester who had yet to fall and rise. Even with the curfew, the numbers continued to grow as families, friends and loved ones continued to associate. Even with the threat of the undead, there were still people out there doing the essential jobs to keep the city viable.

Two further times, Smith had been able to send the undead on their way, the zombies seeming to act confused by what Smith represented. Renfield stuck to him like glue, not letting the Colonel out of his reach, never mind out of his sight.

"I'm not sure I want to keep him anymore," the Voice had whispered in Smith's head after the final encounter. *"What do you think he will do when we get outside?"* Smith at first didn't know what the Voice was referring to, still confused and somewhat dazed by what was happening to him. A moment later, the answer clicked. Would Renfield want to keep the witness to his crimes around? This left Smith in a difficult predicament, Renfield most likely just using him to escape the hospital. Smith's gun still rested on the hospital floor where he had been forced to leave it. He was defenceless in the presence of a maniac.

The question of his own broken sanity didn't come into it.

"*Let me take over,*" the Voice insisted. "*I can save you, I know just what to say. You just need to let me fully in, let me run the show. Just for a little while.*" As difficult as it was for Smith to get a full grip on his reality, he had been resisting the influence of the Voice as best he could. Sometimes he had felt his control slip like when Patel had been killed, but as the minutes ticked by, he had felt the influence of the Voice waning.

"But you're me," Smith had mumbled to himself, the words unheard by the Private who was becoming more and more agitated.

"*Then you won't have a problem with it. If he shoots you, he kills me, and I have no wish to see that happen. I'm enjoying the ride too much.*" Nearing the exit, he had seen the way Renfield had kept fidgeting with the gun. Smith felt he had no other real choice so he had relented and allowed the Voice to take over, although he had no idea what that even meant.

The world around him had gone dark, the sounds muffled as if spoken through a thick wall. Smith's skin had felt cold, and the words spoken were missed on the whole, only the odd syntax breaking through the barrier that had formed. At that moment a question had come to him that had filled the recesses of his supressed mind. *Was this what it was like to die?*

Although no longer in full command of his senses, Smith still saw the world. He was there to witness the Voice speaking to Renfield, saw them walking outside, witnessed Renfield kill a zombie that had come out of the pits of the darkness that engulfed Smith. He was getting used to the condition now, the sounds becoming clearer, his vision stronger as he rode on the back of the body now temporarily controlled by the Voice.

Things were reversing quickly though, the Voice unable to keep full control. Although Smith didn't understand the process, it was clear he was pushing the Voice back, regaining domination over himself, the wrongness of the situation too much for his mind to accept. It wasn't something he was actively trying to do, more likely the natural balance re-establishing equilibrium.

"*Not yet damn you,*" the Voice chastised, and Smith felt himself being squashed down again, only this time by force that he had not consented to. That did it, this wasn't what Smith had agreed to and he fought back hard against the Voice. It felt weaker, and Smith knew he could overpower it by exerting his overriding dominance.

"What did you tell him?" Smith demanded, not having heard the bargain made. Renfield didn't react to the words, so Smith guessed he had spoken them internally.

"*The Private is obsessed with death. I told him that he could be directly responsible for the murder of millions. Strangely enough he liked the idea.*"

"But how?" Smith felt his jurisdiction continuing to return despite the resistance of the Voice. What would happen if the Voice tried that again though, to usurp his mind perhaps when Smith was asleep? Did it need Smith's permission, and could he hold it off next time if the Voice tried to take control by force? What if it had the ability to adapt?

Inside Smith's brain, the virus had destroyed and created millions of new neural connections resulting in a second personality that was now trying to gain governance. XV1 had destroyed its lethality, but not Lazarus's ability to adapt and evolve, made worse by the fresh viral load that had been inflicted on Smith by the zombie that had bitten him. This was not the virus becoming sentient, the psychological anomaly just a by-product of the virus's attempt to survive. To put it in layman's terms, Smith was descending into the madness of two minds.

What was forming came from the darkest desires in Smith's subconscious. The wicked thoughts that creep up unawares in the dead of night, the strange notions that plague us, ideas that would make others recoil in horror even though their minds are just as rebellious. The distressing memory from the past that just pops into our head for no apparent reason. It's the thought that springs up about driving one's car into the barrier wall when you are doing seventy on the motorway. The salacious urge that grabs us when we meet someone we find attractive. Demons from the Id, the hidden part of us that demands immediate gratification of our most hedonistic needs. All this formed itself into another mind.

For some reason, deep down under all the hopes and dreams, the newly fractured part of him felt that only Smith should have charge over who was immune to the virus, the ego swelled with its own self-importance. With possession of the last of the XV1, Smith was the determinant on who would survive this plague until more was made. There was more psychosis there though, more to the bubbling insanity. This subconscious persona could no longer abide the thought of the naturally immune existing in the world.

With Patel dead, who was there with greater knowledge of the virus than Smith and the identity that shared his skull? As far as Smith knew, only he had used the power of science to beat this thing. The interloper, born of Smith's crassest emotions, could also not tolerate the existence of any other mind having that knowledge, jealousy churning it almost into a rage. This was why the Voice had killed Patel, taking Smith when he was at his most vulnerable.

Smith finally regained control, pushing the Voice deep down, its objections muted, its ambitions thwarted. A little bit of the Voice died at that point, but so did a bit of Smith. Perhaps they came that bit closer to being one again, but a great part of what made him human had been lost forever.

Renfield, for his part, resisted the temptation to shoot this new Colonel in the guts. The deal the Voice had offered up was too tempting, too sweet to turn down. With the bulk of the zombies now either still in the hospital or lying devastated out at the main entrance, Renfield and Smith made it back to their troops without too much trouble. A Lieutenant there who recognised Smith from a former meeting at the Fulwood Barracks was more than willing to arrange an escort for Smith.

"Private Renfield is coming with me," Smith had informed the lieutenant. "He saved my life in there, so I want him around for my safety and the safety of the data about the cure I am developing." The word cure rippled through the soldiers around them. Did the Colonel really have the key to all this? And when would they all be saved from the fate that had befallen so many?

The soldiers on the scene discovered something that they had forgotten over the last few days. Hope. It was a shame that such blissful expectations were to be shortly dashed on the rocks of the coming apocalyptic reality.

22.08.19
Washington DC, USA

When the black tendrils had begun to form around his nostrils, nobody had been able to deny that the man presently holding the office of President had no longer been fit for office. Ryan had volunteered to be locked in the room he had been sleeping in, a member of his Secret Service detail handing him a sidearm before the door was locked.

"I figure a marine would want to at least have the option."

The President's wife had been in hysterics and had needed to be sedated. Now the First Lady, she was unable to maintain the decorum that the position demanded, the pending loss of her husband too much for her to fathom. There was also the slightly worrying matter that she had shared the same bed with the man who was likely hours away from turning into a zombie. She had been given everything she had ever dreamed of, only for it to be snatched from her in the worst way possible.

Jessy was heartbroken, as well as scared for what this all now meant. She wasn't aware that she had brought the virus down here. If the President was infected, then that probably meant they all were, at least sixty per cent of the people down in the bunker now displaying symptoms that could be attributable to Lazarus.

Jessy's sore throat and runny nose had disappeared and in herself she now felt fine. It had been so easy for everyone to ignore what was now so blatantly obvious. The bunker doors were now being kept closed, not for the protection of those inside, but to stop the virus making the world above any worse, the state of the city above making the testing of the blood taken from everyone difficult to arrange. It would take time, something not everyone had, and the way people kept their distances from those around them indicated how trust was being rapidly eroded. So the bunker doors would stay locked, everyone down here with the authority to make such a decision in agreement that it was the best thing to do. If they started evacuating people, they would just be putting more aspects of the government at risk. President Ryan had already resigned himself to the fact that he would most likely have the shortest presidency in the history of the United States.

It didn't take long for Jessy to realise she was trapped down here.

As it happened, the President wasn't the first one to shoot himself. One of his Secret Service detail was the first individual to take their own life. Nobody had expected it, the man well liked and well respected by everyone who worked with him. But with the word that the President was now locked away, the agent had excused himself so as to apparently use the bathroom.

The agent's name was Nicholas Godfrey, father of two young girls, husband to a wife who tolerated his strange hours but honoured and adored the way he protected the country. Standing before the rest room mirror, Nicholas looked at his troubled face and decided enough was enough. His sinuses were feeling bunged up, and the skin on his back had started to itch with an annoying relentlessness that no amount of scratching could deal with. He was probably the last person anyone would have expected to commit suicide, but he did so anyway, the neurotransmitters in his brain so out of whack he was finding it hard to keep his emotions in check. Several times over the previous hours he had almost burst out crying.

All he could picture, towards the end, were the inevitable fates of the people he loved, each meeting a brutal and vicious end. It sent him down a spiral of despair that, with an immense force of will, he'd managed to hide under his professional façade. No more. Locking the door to the toilet, he took out his gun and stripped all the bullets out of it as if to make a ritual out of the whole suicide. Examining them carefully, he picked one and concentrated on the way it shone in the fluorescent lights. It seemed flawless to him, not marred by the slightest scratch or blemish which somehow mattered in the ritual he was about to perform. He loaded the gun with this single round and stared at himself in the mirror for several seconds. This really did seem like the only option open to him.

Was there any reason for him not to do this? He couldn't think of any, his thought processes disrupted by the virus that was manipulating his present actions. The thing that surprised him the most was how calm he felt as he placed the cold steel into his mouth, pointing the gun up into the roof of his mouth. It felt wrong against his teeth, a sudden concern striking him that he might chip something if he wasn't careful. The veneers on his incisors had cost him thousands of dollars and it was only proper that they survive him past death.

There wasn't much in the way of hesitation for him to pull the trigger, the bullet punching through the palate into the brain, taking the shock wave with it that decimated his humanity. The gun was flung across the room as his body slumped to the floor. Ten seconds later, there was a commotion on the other side of the bathroom door as people came to see what tragedy had occurred.

Bob Crane was the first man to break through the door, the forty-five-year-old head of the President's protection detail. The image that greeted him filled him with despair, Nicholas a personal friend, someone who Crane had mentored for several years. The loss of such a valued colleague sent Crane a little further down the path of overwhelming despair that experiencing the apocalypse was bound to create. There was no point in even checking the man's pulse, the brain matter that was dripping off the roof tiles showing the true fatality that had been inflicted.

The other thought that got into Crane's head was that at least the body wouldn't resurrect. Everyone now knew that zombies were killed by shots to the head, but it hadn't quite filtered through to the rank and file that it was a specific part of the brain that needed to be destroyed. The reptilian complex of Nicholas's corpse had escaped relatively unscathed, the virus working its magic as it turned the carcass into a tool for its own purpose. This one was to turn quickly.

The gathered faces at the shattered door were ushered away, and a thick sheet was produced to cover the dead body. With the shroud complete, Crane stood in the doorway and told one of the marine guards to help him move the body to somewhere that wasn't so frequently used. One of the storage cupboards would likely have to do for the time being because at least that way the body could be hidden from everyone. They couldn't just leave it in the open like this for everyone to see.

And who was going to clean this shit up?

Under the shroud, the eyes opened, black as the darkest of nights. The zombie sensed people nearby but was still acclimatising to its new form so it was already being carried by the time it got a full sense of itself. With what was left of its nervous system, it could feel hands holding it above the floor, its feet and armpits being used as leverage points to move it out of the restroom.

The craving for flesh was already strong, the sheet rising up as if a magic trick was being performed. The arms lifted it, dead hands clasping around Crane's surprised and vulnerable throat. The marine dropped the feet, the zombie's body pulling Crane to the floor with it as it was released, Crane's hands trying to pull at the vice that was crushing his neck.

As the soldier pulled out his sidearm, the zombie formerly known as Nicholas bit down into the neck of its former mentor, tearing a huge chunk out of the jugular vein as well as damaging the carotid artery enough to cause a fatal bleed. Due to the angle, the blood shot across the room, hitting the marine in the eyes, an impressive shot aided by randomness and perhaps fate. Momentarily blinded, the marine staggered back, giving Nicholas(Z) time to push its writhing victim off its body. The zombie itself rose off the floor with the chaotic grace that only a zombie could muster. Despite the hand that pressed against the pulsing wound, the blood loss was too severe for Crane to stem, and he rapidly began to lose consciousness.

Despite still being half blinded, the marine got off several shots before the zombie was upon it, the pistol swiped from the soldier's hand with a blow that broke the marine's wrist. The marine was a big man, and he tried to valiantly fight off the clawing hands that grabbed for him, his uniform ripping as the zombie propelled him fully out of the bathroom and into the well-lit corridor outside. The two impacted the wall opposite the bathroom doorway, teeth snapping in the marine's face, mere centimetres from inflicting injury. So close were those blood stained lips that tainted phlegm splattered across the human's face. An iron grip began to squeeze his larynx closed, the neck of a human so ridiculously vulnerable.

There were three bystanders to witness this, two armed and now aiming their weapons. So vigorous was the conflict that the marine was clearly losing, nobody felt confident they could line up a shot without hitting one of their own. It was only when the marine finally lost the battle and became overpowered by the stronger force that one of the watchers, a fellow marine, fired. Shooter one's bullets impacting into the back of the zombie with little apparent effect. The result was not what the shooter had planned for.

Nicholas(Z) by then had its teeth firmly embedded in the cheek of the marine it was attacking, and it spun its head around, pulling the flesh away with cataclysmic force. At the same time, it pushed itself away from its prey, the claw like grip having crushed the throat that was so pliant and weak. It seemed to glare at the man shooting it, even though it had lost the gift of sight upon its death. It let go of the man it was killing, the marine falling to the floor clutching his ruined neck.

The zombie was rocked back by multiple shots, one taking it in the left eye, the shooters moving towards the zombie as it was pushed away from them by the deadly impacts. None were enough to finish the creature off, but it fell to a knee, the damage inflicted momentarily becoming too much for it. Distracted by the immediate threat, nobody noticed Crane(Z) rising up from the bathroom floor, its conversion as quick as the zombie that had created it. Nobody would ever learn why the time to resurrection differed in different deceased.

Crane(Z) was on its feet and out the door despite the lack of coordination it had in its legs. It collided with the second shooter (part of the Secret Service detail) just as he spotted the new danger in his peripheral vision. Inhumanly strong fingers wrapping themselves up in his hair, pain firing through the agent's scalp. Propelled sideways by the zombie, he was forced into the first shooter, all three of them falling to the ground, teeth already finding their mark. Nicholas(Z), no longer under assault, lifted itself off its knee and hobbled off in the opposite direction, ignoring the marine it had attacked whose death throes would soon begin.

The third witness to all this had been Jessy, and she backed away, terror filling her soul as the true ferocity of what humanity's most pressing threat now was. Other people came running, more people hesitant to fire due to risk of shooting human rather than zombie flesh. A gun fired from within the downed group on the ground, the back of the zombie exploding as the bullets ripped through its lifeless body.

Jessy backed away further, pushing through the people around her, suddenly colliding her back into a slab of iron. Only it wasn't iron, it was a stern and sour faced looking General Roberts. He looked down at her gravely and then pushed her aside with an unexpected gentleness. Forcing himself to the front of the spectators, he ripped a pistol from the hands of a seemingly paralysed marine and surged over to Crane(Z) that was now attacking the second shooter.

General Roberts had no hesitation in grabbing Crane(Z) by the hair with a gloved hand, putting two shots in the base of its neck after pulling its head back. His arthritic fingers objected to the insult that was being forced upon them, but he held the creature still long enough to do what needed to be done. Jessy went from being thankful for the General's presence, to suddenly being shocked by what he did next. Barely had the General dispatched Crane(Z) than he had fired more shots into the downed secret service agent who was now clearly infected. There were others that needed to be dealt with.

"Sorry Marine," the General said, lining up to do what needed doing.

"Please wait, no..." the first shooter managed to beg before his life was ended by what some would consider an act of mercy. Others would look at the General as if he was a rampaging barbarian. Both the men Roberts shot had several bite marks on both hands as well as other wounds.

With shouted orders, men were dispatched after the zombie that had caused all this. Roberts stepped over to Nicholas(Z)'s first victim. The dying man lay there trying to breathe, a look of unexpected calm on his face, the last of his life slipping from him. He looked into the General's eyes, and seemed to give the faintest of nods, perhaps knowing what the General felt he had to do. Nobody saw it, but there was a single tear that fell from General Roberts's eye as he dispatched another brave and indispensable Marine. Roberts had sent men into battle knowing many of them would die. But this was different. To kill your own so directly, even when it was vital for the safety of everyone here, was the most difficult thing he had ever done.

Jessy was about to say something when the sound of further gunfire in the underground facility broke through the tension. Whatever had started was a long way from being over.

23.08.19
Preston, UK

It had been several hours since Smith had escaped from the hospital that had thankfully now been reclaimed from the undead. Safe for now, Smith lay on the bunk of the room he had originally been given at the army barracks. Most of his personal effects were gone, incinerated when he had discovered the terrifying truth that he was infected. No matter, there was nothing missing that couldn't easily be replaced. The vials of XV1 he told nobody about, choosing to make that revelation when he was fully rested. They sat in the fridge in his room, safe only because of the secrecy over their existence. He would decide what to do with the samples in the morning, the door to his room locked for good measure. Smith was still finding it difficult to determine if he was fully in command, or if his actions were being *guided* by the other part of him that refused to go away.

Sleep came easily, his body still weak from defeating Lazarus. Having two competing minds inside your head also took it out of you.

Renfield also slept. Now once again surrounded by regular army, he was forced to play the waiting game one more time, the murderous high finally leaving him. He felt drained and depressed, the after effects of his addiction hard to ignore and bone chilling. The craving was still there, gnawing at his mind and he knew that this time he wouldn't be able to deny it for long. Sooner or later his resolve would break.

It was hard for him to hide these feelings, appearing sullen and uncommunicative to fellow soldiers. Being stationed at this barracks, the rank and file had previously felt he was likeable enough, although on occasion he was considered to be a bit of a prat. Before sleep finally came, he had lain there, staring at the ceiling, listening to the sleeping sounds of the night and of his fellow soldiers. The urge to kill them was great, but the need to survive was presently even more powerful. Trying to slaughter the men around him would only result in his own death.

He was no longer amongst sheep, although he knew at some point his need for self-preservation would be overwhelmed for his painful need to kill.

As a lowly Private, he shared a room with three other people, his fellow soldiers just assuming he was traumatised by the things he had seen at the hospital. They saw him as a hero now, a man who had saved the life of the Colonel who had the cure in his grasp. Allowances were thus made when it became obvious that he wasn't ready for conversation just yet, the other squaddies leaving him to his own devices. Nobody saw the madness in his heart, Renfield's crimes hidden from them by the chaos that had engulfed the hospital as well as the silence and conspiracy he and Smith shared. If time had allowed, Renfield's actions would have likely been uncovered, but events were going to make such irrelevant.

When the new day came, Renfield knew he would need to try and hide below an exterior of banter and jokes, to show the face the normals expected to see. It would not be good to be seen as the outlier for too long, strangeness being rejected and fought against if it persisted. When he awoke, he intended to once again wear the mask and wait for the moment Smith had promised him. That was all assuming he didn't lose control before the blissful moment he could be given what the Voice had promised him.

In his sleep he saw the face of Lucy. Not the sweet visage that had so enthralled him, but a shattered image that berated him for his atrocities. Renfield was not disturbed by this and in his dream he merely laughed at her weakness. She was in him, and it was he who was the tormentor. His resting body lay still as if in total contentment.

***

Whittaker also finally slept and dreamt, the nightmare coming to him for the first time. Nobody would ever understand the mechanism surrounding why the virus triggered this lost part of the human mind in the immune. Across the globe, the few who shared this genetic abnormality began to join the damned in the desert. Also, scattered amongst the stalking, battered figures a statue of human ash would occasionally appear. There it would stand, seemingly invulnerable to the sometimes hurricane strength winds, never moving and yet forever in the sight of those who walked the desert of the damned.

Not all the immune survived, and everyone who died became represented by this permanent addition to the hellish landscape. Exposure to the virus triggered the dreams, which was why Azrael had been plagued with them for over a year. Even though the virus in the vaccine he had injected himself with was dead, it still brought him to the realm of sorrow. Ironic really that one of the few people given Gaia's cure turned out to be naturally immune.

As numerous as his fellow immune were in that kingdom of pain, it was clear they were a mere fraction of the seven billion people that risked becoming the army of the dead. Surely such low numbers could never defeat the power of the dead.

Occasionally Whittaker moaned, a sound that drifted to the corridor outside where Nick sat. Nick had always trusted his intuition, and that sixth sense had saved him more times than he could count. Whether it was purely due to his superior training or down to something more supernatural, Nick didn't even try and speculate. He listened to it though, the little voice that told him not to put his foot down on that particular piece of earth in that seemingly deserted Afghan village. The little voice that told him to go left instead of right at the top of the stairs when he was hunting for insurgents in Basra. Whatever it was, it resulted in him living where others might well have died.

His intuition now told him to watch over the immune. Sat in the corridor outside their rooms, he knew that Jessica would assume he was guarding her to prevent her escape. Nothing could be further from the truth. He trusted her at her word, so his vigil was purely for her protection. Nick also knew he had to watch over Azrael, as odious as the man's crimes were. As yet he couldn't explain why. He could have delegated this task, but he was never one to ask someone to do a job he was more than capable of doing himself.

Something different but just as devastating as the undead plague was coming, he was sure of it. Whilst not afflicted by their night terrors, he was still fascinated by them. When Whittaker woke up, Nick would be there with a single question about whether he dreamt the same as Jessica and Azrael. That was the other reason he was here. He wanted to ensure there was no chance Whittaker and Jessica could communicate until Nick got an answer to that riddle. He wanted no doubt in the theory he was formulating. As crazy as it sounded, he went where the evidence took him. If the immune did share some ethereal connection, there had to be a reason. And if there was a reason then perhaps that also meant they would have a weapon against the undead. He knew he should tell Smith of his discovery, but the same intuition held him back. There had always been something in Smith's eyes that had told him his superior officer couldn't be trusted. There it was, the intuition again, the thing that had kept him living where so many others had perished.

"Can I ask you something Nick?" Brodie asked. Nick wasn't alone, not trusting his own mind to stay awake throughout the night.

"Anything mate, although I can't guarantee I'll give you an answer."

"How much of a hardship was it for you to leave the army?"

"The army life was everything," Nick answered. "It was who I was, especially when I went into special forces. I'd reached as high in the ranks as I knew I was going to get though, and my body was starting to betray me."

"Do you think you could have survived the civilian life?" Brodie seemed pensive, nervous even.

"Nope," Nick answered. "If MI13 hadn't come along I would have eventually been squeezed out of the forces in one of the many spending revisions. Likely I would have ended my days doing mercenary work in some third world shit hole."

"So MI13 saved you?"

"Most definitely," said Nick. "Plus they made me a Lieutenant Colonel, which was nice of them." Nick turned in his chair to look at his team mate. "What's up Carl?"

"I'm struggling boss." There, he'd said it, the words falling out of his mouth even though he feared saying them. Never had he ever wanted to show weakness in front of another human being, but Nick needed to know. He would gratefully have told a psychiatrist, they were professionals and he knew that his exposure to them was a mandatory part of his training and his progression through MI13's ranks. Fixing the fracturing and troubled mind was their job.

"It must be hard," Nick said, "raised to protect a realm that might not be here a week from now." Nick understood. He'd had a similar revelation a year into his SAS induction. He'd woken up one morning with the realisation that the politicians in Whitehall weren't actually interested in the health of the nation or the welfare of the people who fought to defend it. In fact, sometimes, their very actions seemed to be counter to the nation's benefit.

"It's like my life has been slit open and gutted."

"You know your mission is far from over though, right?" Brodie looked at him, surprised.

"The country is failing," Brodie said, emotion welling up inside him. "What is there to protect when this virus has taken so much already?"

"Those two," Nick said pointing to the two doors behind which Jessica and Whittaker slept. "They, and others like them. They are now the realm, its hope and its future. That's your new mission Brodie. We have to protect those who can fight off the virus. We might lose the war, but we won't necessarily lose the country."

"Two people though?" It wasn't much to rest his hopes and dreams on.

"Where there are two there are more. I even think Azrael might have immunity, and not from Smith's experiments."

Nick shared his thoughts about the nightmares.

"That's a lot of speculation, boss."

"I know." There was another sleep induced cry from Whittaker's room, "although it sounds like someone's having night terrors." Brodie mulled over what Nick had told him. As much as he was sceptical, a lot of it made sense.

"You know, that helps. That helps a lot. Thanks boss." Brodie still had his doubts, but his mind felt lighter. Protecting people, he could do. If he concentrated his efforts on keeping the likes of Jessica safe, maybe he could get through this.

Perhaps there was a need for him in this world after all.

23.08.19
Lake Conroe, USA

Rodriguez was ripped from the loving embrace of sleep by the piercing sound of his wife's scream.

He had managed to get his family out of Houston a mere hour before the National Guard had shut the city off, the spreading infection there deemed a threat to the surrounding areas. He had learnt about this via the CB radio in his SUV, something he had installed several years back. Past the check points, he had started to pick up the radio chatter as people reported the quarantine zones that were spreading across the state of Texas. At that moment he had been so thankful that he had insisted his family leave. Relief had turned to exhaustion, and safely unpacked at his father in law's cabin and the children put to bed, he had easily fallen asleep with his wife in his arms.

The bed rocked, the cries from his wife terrifying. Without any night vision, all he could see was the dark shape, mere seconds since his sleep was ended by a barrage of confusion and violence. But he could feel what was happening. Someone was attacking his wife. She had been asleep on the side of the bed closest to the bedroom door so she could get up in the night to tend to her sick daughter. By the time they had reached the cabin, their youngest had been running a fever, and they had sent her to bed with Tylenol and love.

The fear of what the hospitals now represented was greater than the symptoms that had afflicted their daughter. Rodriguez didn't want her around those who carried the contagion they had just escaped from. And all the time, his little girl had been harbouring and growing the very thing he had feared the most. Perhaps in his heart he had known that from the very start of the trip out of Houston, the fateful words all but forgotten.

"Mummy, I don't feel very well."

How many parents would be devastated by those softly spoken words? His daughter had been taken quickly by the virus in her sleep.

Jumping from his bed, he almost knocked the bedside light over in his urge to switch it on. He needed light, needed to see what this was, even though deep down he already knew. His eyes flared as the brightness filled the room and the first thing that struck him was the blood. The once white pristine sheets were defiled by it, the two writhing figures engaged in a battle for life. Death was winning, death in the guise of his daughter who was tearing at his wife's face with her tiny fingers. Those fingers shouldn't have been capable of inflicting harm, but they did.

"Honey, stop," was all he could weakly say, shock and the futility of everything ripping any courage and hope out of him. His wife screamed again, this time begging for him to help. His daughter was seven, and yet she seemed to possess the strength of a demon. His despair finally broke into action and he moved to contain the child, his arms grabbing it around the waist from behind. The girl writhed like an eel, slippery with some kind of residue on the surface of its skin. He tried to pull, but all the child did was to wrap its fingers in his wife's hair. There was no way to wrench what had once been his daughter off, his wife's head even being lifted off the bed.

Rodriguez saw it then, the destruction in his beloved's face, the skin torn by teeth that were still growing, the cheek and eyebrow a ruin that would never be healed.

"Please," Rodriguez begged, only for the zombie to release its grasp allowing him to pull it off his wife. He felt the thing try and turn in his grasp, the head moving desperately so that it could bite. With more luck than anything, he managed to evade the small arms that flailed for his eyes. He knew the undead were supposed to be strong, but he had never imagined this.

What broke his heart more was how this thing made no sound. No cry, no hiss, just a silent assault by a beast whose power defied its size. Once its voice had been able to laugh and sing, not now. Despite his best efforts, the zombie managed to wriggle free, falling to the floor where it scuttled away almost crab like, disappearing out of the bedroom and into the hall.

Rushing to his wife, she grasped him, desperate for his strength. She wept hysterically, clutching at her face, trying to stem the blood. The wound itself, although disfiguring wasn't life threatening. But he had seen what the virus did to people, had seen it on the streets, the utter madness it caused. Were the dead insane? They were certainly driven by some desire he could not even hope to comprehend, forged on by their clear defiance of all the so called facts that medical science had discovered.

His wife clung to him like he was the last hope she had on Earth. There was no hope, even though she still breathed and wailed, there was no denying the fact that she was already dead.

"Why?" she asked. He couldn't answer and he gently pulled himself from her grasp. This wasn't over, not by a long shot. They still had a feral creature in the house and another daughter to protect. That was assuming he wasn't already too late, both his daughters having shared a room together. Emily, the oldest daughter, was still unaccounted for.

"I need to find Emily," he said almost wanting his wife to tell him now that he needed to stay with her. "Lock yourself in the bathroom. Can you do that?" The lawman was finally coming out now, the training starting to kick in. When he stood up, he pulled the pistol from his gun belt which he had slung over the post at the foot of the bed. He had wanted it to hand, a hand that was now slick with the gore that had covered the zombie. Almost as an afterthought, he wiped the hand on the bed, desecrating the sheets there even further.

"Save my baby," his wife begged as Rodriguez left the room. He didn't look back at her, for he knew that to do so would break the final strand in his heart. Incredibly, he found himself suddenly wishing his father in law was here. Not for the help he might have given, but for the very real fact that he might have been the one the zombie would have attacked first. If the man he had never really liked had been present, his wife might have been saved. But the father in law wasn't here, and Rodriguez was alone to face the most torturous experience in his life so far.

Off in the furthest bedroom of the expansive cabin, floorboards creaked. Rodriguez ignored the sound, instead stepping into his daughter's new bedroom, turning on the light with a heart stopping moment. There were two beds here, one empty, one occupied. The figure in the occupied bed stirred with the light, bleary eyes looking out from under covers that were pulled up to the chin.

"Dad?" Emily said. She sounded upset that she had been woken. There was no injury visible, no evidence of violence. Thank God, he thought. At least I have one.

"Dad, I feel sick." The words cut into him like the sharpest of knives.

"It's okay, honey," Rodriguez heard himself say, and he stepped into the room. The other bed was fetid, the covers thrown back to reveal its occupant had pissed themselves. There was a bloody stain across the virginity of the pillows. This is where his daughter had died, from a disease nobody understood and that only the rare few could fight.

He had been worried about being on the streets and bringing Lazarus back to his home, only for the children to be the vector of transmission. This would be the scourge of mankind in the early days, infection rates amongst children high because of the way they were congregated together in schools and nurseries so as to spread the virus amongst themselves.

He said the words again, but it wasn't okay. Emily coughed then, a bone chilling affair as her body shook with the force her lungs used to express whatever it was that was irritating them. Blood appeared on her lips, splattering across the pillow. No, it wouldn't be okay, and she started to cry. Rodriguez wanted to rush to her, to hold her in his arms, but what could he do? He couldn't cure her.

He went to her regardless, pulling her out from under the sheets, holding her, the heat from her body far in excess of what was normal. The gun he placed at the foot of the bed within his easy reach. She was burning up now, clearly on her way to the same fate as her sister. In another part of the house, something shattered causing Emily to flinch in her arms.

"It's going to be all right," he lied.

"Mummy," Emily begged, the word slightly slurred. There was no denying the truth that she was infected. Was that why she hadn't been attacked? Rodriguez didn't know that sometimes the undead left those who were about to join their ranks alone. Holding her like that, he never wanted to let go, her quiet sobs his penance for all the wrongs he had committed in this world. He wasn't a wicked man, but like any Catholic, he knew his sins could never even be counted. In that moment he wasn't even sure if he believed in God anymore. What kind of supreme being would allow such horrors to befall its creations?

He still had the gun and he knew what he had to do.

"We need to get you back in bed now so you can be well." She resisted, but he was firm, breaking her hold on him, easily manhandling her back onto the bed. He didn't bother with the sheets, but sat next to her as he smoothed her hair with a loving hand.

"It hurts," Emily said between whimpers. She was fading fast, he could see it in her body, the ink like lines starting to spread across her skin. He could actually see tendrils moving, as if someone was injecting a deep, dark blue into every one of her veins.

"I know honey, but the pain will go soon. I promise."

"Promise?"

"Pinky swear honey." He kissed her then on the temple, knowing that he too was likely being consumed internally by Lazarus. With ease, he turned her over so she was facing away from him, meeting very little protest from her now. Reaching for his gun, Rodriguez brought it up, keeping it out of her sight.

"It will all be over soon." She didn't even have time to react, the trigger pulled as soon as he placed the muzzle of his gun into the base of her neck, closing his eyes so he didn't have to witness the destruction he created. He couldn't see that, the sound alone too much for him. Rodriguez didn't open his eyes again until he was standing in the children's bedroom door which he closed behind him. He never looked at Emily again, never got to see her sweet smile or her stern face when she knew she was being teased.

Whatever was left of him broke. There was no room for life now, not in this world. The creature came rushing at him once again, all fury and chaos, five bullets needed to bring it to the ground where it thrashed wildly. Rodriguez ended it the way he ended Emily, and in the echo of the blast, he thought he heard his wife scream again.

Still half a magazine left. Still enough to do what needed to be done. Numb now, Rodriguez made his way to where his wife was. He had one act of love left to give before he removed himself from this world. He hoped there wasn't an afterlife, because he didn't want to live an eternity with the knowledge of what he had to do here at this hour.

23.08.19
Preston, UK

Whittaker woke up early, a thin sheen of sweat covering his skin, the taste of ash lingering in his mouth. He'd never experienced a nightmare that intense. It stayed with him, into the waking time, the bulb above his head no replacement to the brightness of the desert sun. It took him several moments to figure out that the small room he found himself in was actually his true reality. He had a faint recollection of someone talking to him in his dream, but it had been mostly drowned out by the terror.

One of the greatest threats to a soldier was the failure of their own mind. Was this the first signs of that?

Somehow he wasn't surprised to see Nick and Jeff outside his room when he emerged to use the showers, Brodie having been relieved half way through the night. Natasha had offered to take Nick's place, but he had declined.

Wearing a dressing gown and bare feet, Whittaker looked at the two MI13 men expectantly.

"Chris," Nick asked, "tell me about your dreams."

"What?" What the hell was this, thought Whittaker? It was hardly a question a relative stranger was supposed to ask you.

"It might sound strange, but that's only because you don't realise how important the question is. Please, tell me about your nightmare." Neither of the men guarding Whittaker wore their gas masks, there was no need here. The only other people in the building were immune, and the regular soldiers knew to stay out. It hadn't taken much for Nick to be given total authority of those deemed to be safe from the virus. They were his to protect, and the soldiers in the barracks had been warned that this area was off limits to them unless they were specifically called upon.

"Well okay. It was pretty horrific, the worst I've experienced."

"Go on." Nick looked at Whittaker who stood in the doorway of his room. The soldier looked nervous to be talking about this sort of thing.

"There was a desert with a hot sun and I was walking in it." Jeff and Nick shared a look, which told Whittaker that this was what they were expecting to hear. "My skin was all burnt, and I felt like I was being chased by something."

"Something?" Jeff asked.

"I have an image of people on horseback, only they weren't people. I don't know what they were, but they sent a shiver up my spine just thinking about them. I never got to see them and yet I feel I know exactly what they looked like." Nick nodded as he heard the words.

"Come with me soldier," Nick ordered. Whittaker followed, the three of them moving further into the building towards the room that held Azrael. They didn't go in, but they took Whittaker to the observation window. There was no need to bother Jessica with this just yet, for she had woken up before Whittaker and was presently taking a walk in the early morning air. She had felt compelled to seek out something beautiful, the pending sunrise hopefully enough of a distraction for her.

Azrael lay there awake, his eyes moving to the new arrivals. He was no longer restrained to the bed, his limbs shackled to allow him a degree of freedom. When Azrael saw Whittaker, his face lit up as if this was an old friend come to greet him. Nick activated the room's intercom, desperate to see how the conversation would pan out. Azrael walked over and put his face right up against the glass.

"Do you know this man?" Nick asked Azrael. Azrael nodded.

"Another one," he said. "Another traveller from the desert."

"How could he know?" Whittaker demanded, fear starting to well up inside. He couldn't see how this could have been a trick.

"I know because I was there," Azrael said. Whittaker looked suspiciously at the sunken eyes that stared back at him. There was something about Azrael that was definitely familiar to him.

"Why is he tied up like that?" Whittaker demanded.

"Because this man is a killer," Jeff answered. "Isn't that right Azrael?"

"Yes I have killed, but I don't know if I'm still the man you say I am." It was true, Azrael felt changed. The urge to commit death and slaughter didn't seem to be in him anymore. He didn't know if he should be relieved about that.

"You still are," Nick said. "You never lose that part of you. Trust me." Azrael nodded his acceptance although he wondered if he would ever get a chance to prove his captors wrong.

"I don't understand any of this," Whittaker begged.

"There's someone else I want you to meet," Nick advised, indicating that Whittaker take a seat. "Jeff, can you go and get me Jessica from outside." Whittaker stayed standing for a moment, staring at Azrael, the man who would soon unlock the secrets to everything.

23.08.19
Manchester, UK

Superintendent Craig Soul had barely slept the last few days. It had fallen to him to organise the police response to the zombie epidemic that had rapidly been building in the northern part of the city. The army helped, but they were limited in number and had their own shit to deal with. Soul's biggest problem was that he didn't have enough men to do what needed doing, especially as large numbers of them had chosen not to come into work. He understood that, his own wife begging him to stay with her. How could he though, he had responsibilities and had been placed into a position of trust.

Specifically, he didn't have enough armed officers, a problem faced by the police forces across the country. You couldn't politely ask a zombie to cooperate with your lawful command, so many of the officers under his watch were of little use in fighting any zombie outbreaks directly. That was one of the reasons he had lost control of the city. He knew that now, because as he stood looking out of the office on the top floor of the Albert Hall, he could see hundreds of the undead surging across Albert Square. It was clear to him that they were sweeping across the city virtually unchecked.

He had been here to liaise with city officials on the best way to contain the problem that had been bubbling under the surface for so many days. The early hour didn't matter because sleep wasn't something people seemed to partake in any more. So many cities had reverted to anarchy, but Manchester so far had held it off, most likely due to the initial presentation of Lazarus here which resulted in early intervention. By being the first city to see the zombie outbreak at Wythenshawe Hospital, Manchester had been better prepared than any other UK metropolis. As gunshots echoed around the city streets, Soul realised it had all been for nothing. The antiserum, the quarantines of the passengers from the flight shared by Peter Dunn. All that had done was bought them a day at most.

Soul was alone in the room when the realisation of how badly he had failed finally hit him.

Stuart(Z) ran amongst its brothers and sisters, the humans falling before them. The horde had formed in the night in Salford Quays, formed from the frightened and defenceless citizens of Manchester. Many of them sported injuries, but some were almost strangely whole, their bodies still to me smitten by the bullet or the blade. What humans they found they quickly felled, the centre of the city teeming with life ripe for the conversion. Stuart(Z) was now just one of thousands, a collective that poured through the streets, breaking into every door and window that would allow them access. If one listened very carefully, you could hear the screams of the damned as the people of Manchester begged for deliverance. All they had to look forward to was starvation at best. For most, the virus would take them.

Stuart(Z) sensed the size of the building it entered, dozens pouring in after it. It didn't matter that the Town Hall was the heart of the city, it was just another place where meat could be found. Stuart(Z) paused briefly, buffeted by its kind as they rushed past, soaking up the cries and the anguish that this building gave out. Then it was off, finding the stairs, running up, its feet making easy work of the stone steps. On the second floor it found a woman who tried to run, but Stuart(Z) easily brought her down, smashing her head into the floor several times. Dazed, the hapless woman could do nothing to prevent the zombie biting a chunk from her shoulder. Even as the flesh detached, Stuart(Z) was off, chewing frantically so as not to waste the morsel it could not now swallow.

Two more victims and more flights of stairs saw it on the top floor of the building where it finally met capable resistance. Bursting into an open plan office space, bullets ploughed into its upper body, Stuart(Z) rocked by the onslaught. But it was not alone, zombie after zombie streaming past it, charging the valiant defenders who simply didn't have enough bullets or guns. Nine bullets in total weren't enough to stop Stuart(Z) and it walked past its feeding kind, fluid leaking out of the many holes that now peppered its torso. By perhaps a miracle, not a single projectile had marked its once handsome face.

It sensed a human step out of a side room into the bedlam and ran at him. When Stuart(Z) had been an aspiring lawyer, the superintendent's uniform would have made the human self-conscious, an emotion impossible for the undead to feel. The only thing Soul's uniform now represented was a barrier to the delicious flesh underneath. Stuart(Z) speared the man, bringing him to the floor, the cries from the terrified lips sending Stuart(Z) frantic as it ripped the skin off Soul's face with fingers that now acted like claws.

The twenty third of August was the day Manchester city centre fell to the undead.

23.08.19
Preston, UK

Despite the horrors of life there was always balance. Standing alone on the edge of the shooting range, Jessica gazed off into the distance and watched the sun as it began to crawl its way into the sky. Even though she had seen countless sunrises, it felt like the most amazing thing she had ever seen. Enthralled by the spectacle, it took her several moments before Jessica realised she was being watched.

Sometimes you just know, as if you could actually feel the other person's eyes burning into the back of your skull. A shiver went down her body, unrelated to the cold morning air and concern caused her to abandon the sunrise to seek out the source of her worries. Darkness hid him at first, but movement drew her eyes to a tree that was washed in darkness.

Fifteen metres away stood a lone, partly hidden figure, dressed in army fatigues. There was something odd about the way the man stood, a weapon ominously clutched in his hands. It wasn't pointed at her, but still it made Jessica nervous even though she knew that the people here were for her protection. Was he guarding her or making sure she wasn't about to abscond? She was unsure of his purpose because there was malevolence here, she could almost taste it. Something about this watcher was very wrong. Deep inside there was a part of her that knew a predator when she saw it. She had no idea how long Renfield had been watching her.

"Jessica." It wasn't the watcher who shouted, but a reassuring voice she recognised. Jessica had to move her body to see where the shout had come from, Jeff running over from the medical facility, the gas mask raised up on his head because he knew she was safe to be around. When she looked again at where the watcher had been, she was surprised to see that he had disappeared.

She knew she hadn't imagined him, and it had most definitely been a him. With the surrounding darkness, Jessica had never seen the face and part of her was glad for that.

***

Renfield had been dragged from sleep by his own desires. The urge was building, and lying there in a room with three men totally vulnerable to his addiction, Renfield suddenly sensed he couldn't stay in the room a moment longer. Dressing as quietly as he could, he had slipped from the bedroom before he had ended up doing something incredibly stupid. It would have been so easy to just slice the knife into pliant and vulnerable flesh. Renfield could almost taste the delight that such an act would have brought him, but there was no way he could have ultimately gotten away with it. He would have to talk to Colonel Smith about getting a single room. Renfield knew he wouldn't be able to do what Smith wanted of him if he were to fall foul of his own desires.

Going outside was supposed to mean wearing full NBC gear, but he eschewed that. He needed freedom and he had Smith's promise that the cure would be his if only he fulfilled the task. Renfield wasn't aware that the deal he had made was with Smith's alter ego, that it was Smith's subconscious that wanted to see Jessica dead. Renfield also didn't know why he had been given this task, the mystery of it an irrelevance. If the woman called Jessica was immune though, then he was more than happy to oblige Smith with her death and would enjoy every second of it.

Wandering up to the medical facility, his plan was to clear his head and get some control over himself. At no time did he actually expect to find Jessica standing out in the open because that would have just been ridiculously coincidental. And yet there she had been, vulnerable and alone. With his L86A2 gripped in his hands, it would have been so easy to kill her and he almost had. The knuckles turned white as he clutched his weapon, the burn within him needing quenching. As the seconds ticked by as he stared at her, he had steeled himself for the slaughter knowing that this was the time. Then she had turned and looked at him and the spell had been almost broken. The finger slipped onto the trigger of his gun.

Renfield knew that he was becoming dangerously reckless. There was a strong chance that he wouldn't have escaped the inevitable justice that would have been unleashed upon him if he'd gone through with it. Shots like that would have brought people running even at this hour, and here he was out in the open. The shadows hid him but it likely wasn't enough cover to get away with murder in the middle of an army base. Still the urge to go ahead with it became unbearable.

He couldn't really see Jessica in detail, it was still too dark. He knew it was her though, there was no doubt about that. Why else would there be a woman in civilian clothes walking around the base like this? It wasn't how he would want to do it, to kill her would be better up close so he could see into the pain her eyes would telegraph.

He stalled though, and that initial hesitation saved both of them because another intervened. If not for Jeff, there was no denying that Jessica would have been sliced in half by machine gun fire.

"Jessica."

When the shout occurred, Renfield slid further into the darkness, natural foliage swallowing him up. Renfield had no idea who the man was, but he too was armed. The NBC suit suggested army, but Renfield's gut said not. This was one of the men Smith had warned him about, the watchers who kept Jessica safe. The odds of him successfully killing Jessica at that moment dropped significantly. He would have to kill her and the man, and nothing was certain when you shot at people. Renfield abandoned any idea of murder at that moment. He would have to wait for a more opportune time that Smith had promised to provide.

The problem was, murder needed to be done, because the pressure in him was building. If he didn't act of his own accord, he might just find his addiction acting for him. It was then that Renfield truly understood the mistake he had made. As pleasurable as it had been and as awesome as it was to now have Lucy inside him, breaking the dam that had let his murderous desires be unleashed would be his undoing. There was no way of putting this particular genie back in the bottle.

In the state he was now, he suddenly found himself wondering if he was any better than the fucking undead.

23.08.19
Jersey City, USA

The fever had hit Gabriel quickly and with an intensity he had never before experienced. In the end he decided not to venture up onto the surface even though he was in sight of the platform at Grove Street Station. Instead, he broke into a tunnel service room he found near the underground station platform, the dirt and the grease of no concern to him despite his personal preference for cleanliness. Closing the door behind him after staggering in, he had sat with his back against one of the room's corners so as to let the infection have its way with him.

The delirium had worried him and with his thoughts swimming in and out of the real world, he had strongly considered suicide a way out. Several times the Glock had rested under his chin, Gabriel thinking the moment had definitely come to end it all. If he lost himself, if his mind started to fail, Gabriel had decided that this would be the indication that it was time to leave this fetid world. Each time he wavered, not sure if this was in fact the end. Each time he had been right, the darkness that had been descending upon his mind ebbing away to return clarity to his thoughts.

Even with the pain and the near delirium he was in, he kept himself together enough through sheer pig headed determination. He never fired the killing round, the heat in his flesh slowly subsiding as the infection began to lose the battle for his flesh. Inside, Lazarus had fought valiantly, but his defences had been too strong even if it had been a close won battle. The vaccine he had been given nearly a year ago worked, but it was far from ideal. Whilst it was enough for Gabriel to live, there would be consequences that would manifest only with time. Unlike his fellow assassin, Gabriel carried no natural immunity and had to rely on the chemical concoction he had injected into himself a year before.

His whole body ached, but better that than death.

It soon became clear to him that he would live, but the virus had taken a toll on him, sapping his strength and leaving him barely able to move. He could just about manage to pull the water bottle from the rucksack he had dumped onto the service room floor, the water harsh on his throat. It caused his body to almost retch, a shaking cough forced to descend on his burning lungs. Even that simple action of drinking took almost everything from him. Still he forced it down, knowing that dehydration was now his enemy. His clothes were drenched from the sweat that had poured off him, his skin still slick with it.

Safe for now, he had drifted off into sleep, the exhaustion too much to resist. No dreams interrupted his slumber, his body taking its time to try and heal the damage that had been done to it. When Gabriel eventually came to, he would find the world a much different place than when he left it. And he himself would be a much different person.

23.08.19
Preston, UK

As soon as Jessica saw Whittaker she felt like she knew him. There was confusion on her face, because this wasn't a passing familiarity that she felt.

"I know you," Jessica said.

"Yes," Whittaker agreed. He had risen when she entered, all chivalrous like. His dad had taught him that when he was young, repeated instructions on how to act around what his dad had called the fairer sex.

"And yet I don't think we've ever met."

"It's unlikely, I'm from London. I've never been this far north before." They both sat down in chairs facing each other.

"I really don't understand what's going on here." Jessica was starting to sound overwhelmed. Just a week ago she had been a lawyer recovering from the discovery that she was pregnant. The last few days she hadn't even been able to think about that.

"Let me tell you what I think, and I apologise if this starts to get a bit whacky bollocks." Nick looked at them both, trying to figure how best to phrase this. "Okay, you are both immune, as I suspect is the man in that isolation room."

"The killer," Whittaker added. Jessica gave him a tense look as if to tell him not to use that word, the gesture strangely protective in nature. He missed it, his attention on Nick. Nick caught it though, and stored that knowledge away.

"I believe you are somehow connected due to your immunity, and that connection occurs in your dreams."

"I'm not sure I can believe that," Whittaker contested, shaking his head dismissively.

"Would you have believed the dead would be walking and killing everything in their path if I'd told you such last week?" Nick countered. Whittaker looked at him as if he wanted to argue, but nothing came. He threw his hands in the air in resignation.

"Point taken. So what does it mean?"

"What does it mean? I have absolutely no fucking idea. But what I do know is that, as you have just shown, you can possibly recognise each other. We need to find more immune individuals to be sure though."

"I know we've never met in real life," Jessica said interrupting, "but I feel like I've spent time with this man. I feel close to him."

"Jesus, this is some crazy Stephen King shit," said Jeff.

"There's something else," the voice came from the isolation room, those sitting standing so as to look at Azrael. "The horsemen."

"What about them?" Nick demanded.

"I feel I know who one of them is now." When Azrael said the name, things actually seemed to make more sense to Nick. He didn't know why, but it just seemed to fit. The name Azrael said was Smith. "I see him there, following us through the dessert. He's dangerous."

"I don't remember that," Jessica countered. "Surely he would be with us in the desert though," Jessica insisted. "You told me he cured himself."

"I'm not sure that's how this works," Nick pointed out. "We are only at the very beginning of understanding this and I think we have to put a considerable amount of trust in Azrael. I believe the immunity has to be natural, not acquired. But why would Smith be in your dreams?" Jessica was shaking her head.

"I'm not ready to believe that until I experience it myself," Jessica said. "I still can't trust the word of Azrael, not after what he did." Nick was going to counter this, but Jessica stopped him. "Yes, I appreciate all the mind control shit, but that actually increases my distrust."

"I would never lie to you Jessica, not now." Azrael was staring right at her with an intensity that was almost pain inducing to witness.

"You say that, but I don't even know what to call you. I knew you as a man called Kevin. And yet you sit before us with a different name and a different personality."

"I..." Azrael faltered. He didn't have an answer to that. No matter how he looked at things, he saw no reason why Jessica should hold any confidence in him. Finally, he said the only thing that made any sense. "I hope with time that trust will come."

"So you didn't see Smith in your nightmare, Jessica?" Nick didn't bother asking Whittaker because the Corporal wouldn't have any idea what the man from Porton Down looked like.

"I don't know," was all she could say.

"Okay, well for the time being it might be better if you didn't go wandering off, just in case."

"Why, you can just have your minions watch me like this morning. Why don't you trust me?" *Where the hell did that come from?* thought Nick.

"I don't understand what you mean," Nick said truthfully.

"Don't give me that. Why else are you having your goons follow me around outside?" Nick looked at Jeff who just shrugged.

"Nobody is following you around Jessica."

"Then who was the man watching me when I went outside? Was it Brodie?"

"Brodie is asleep," Jeff said. "I didn't see anyone when I collected you Jessica."

"I know nothing about anyone watching you. I've told you, I trust your word when you say you won't do anything foolish." Nick instantly regretted using the word foolish, but Jessica didn't seem to react to it.

"Well he was there and he gave me the creeps." She seemed to believe what she was being told, but to Jessica that was even more worrying.

"Maybe just a curious squaddie? Or one of Haggard's lads?" offered Jeff.

"No, Mad Dog would have told me. Jessica, why did this man make you feel nervous."

"You're telling the truth aren't you? Shit." Jessica was now feeling bad about accusing Nick. It had just seemed like the logical answer to why there were mysterious eyes on her. Nick nodded. "Well, it was just something I sensed about him, like he was up to no good. Even from the distance he was at, I could tell there was an intensity there. Plus, he wasn't wearing all that protective shit you guys always wear outside." *That I don't have to wear* she said to herself.

One of the things Nick excelled at was threat detection and threat avoidance. Once again, his little warning siren was going off in his head. If Jessica was telling the truth, and Nick had no evidence to the contrary, then there was an unknown man wandering around the base whilst breaking the cross infection protocols that were in place. Nick activated his radio headset which he now almost permanently wore.

"Natasha," Nick said. It took several goes for her to answer. Most likely she had been asleep. "Pack up your shit and meet me here with Brodie."

"Everything okay boss?" Natasha asked. There was a concerned edge to her voice.

"No," was all Nick would tell her. "Get Haggard and his men over to the infirmary as well. I might be wrong, but I have a feeling trouble's coming. I want everyone ready to bug out if we need to."

***

Moros was not self-aware despite its vast computing power. It was merely a tool for humans to use. Part of its job was to monitor all the data collected by the government listening station GCHQ, which was still fully functional and now heavily guarded.

With the shutdown to civilians of the internet and the cell network, the burden placed on Moros was released, allowing it to concentrate on the few communications that were still being sent. It was like the digital version of post 911, when, following the disaster, the skies had been clear of all civilian air traffic. In such an environment, communications stood out, which was why Moros was working to decrypt the messages that had been sent back and forth between Clay and Brian's encrypted phones. With its ability to slip into the quantum realm, the encryption wasn't that much of a chore. Moros could make billions of calculations every second so it wasn't difficult for it to connect the mysterious satellite phone messages with the disappearance of the three soldiers couriering XV1.

Moros calculated there was a 97.3% chance that the two were linked and it easily established the GPS coordinates of Clay's end of the communication. With only one person now to tell, it sent that information for human scrutiny. The three missing vials of XV1 now had a location. All that needed to happen was for Natasha's laptop to be powered up and for that message to be read.

23.08.19
Leeds, UK

He had almost fallen asleep several times during his night-time vigil, boredom creeping up on a mind lacking stimulation. Iain had not returned however, and now with the day's light wiping out the night, Andy knew it was time to end this once and for all. The thought that he was actually prepared to kill a man like this was somewhat of a shock to him.

He chose to leave the ground floor shutters down, only the front door to his property not protected in that manner. At some point he would cut up the ply board he had stored in his garage to cover the broken window, but that was a job for later, something perhaps to distract his mind from the after effects of what he was about to do. Andy had no idea how he was going to fare with this act psychologically, but Iain had proven to him that he was a threat that needed eliminating.

The cul-de-sac he lived on was quiet and deserted. He saw no twitching of blinds or curtains at any of the windows he saw. This did all represent a basic flaw in the position he found himself in. He was alone, and even with his barriers and his gun, he was vulnerable to the external threats that existed in the outside world. Andy should have thought more about that when he had considered the security measures he had originally taken. He had friends, some of them even in this city, but did he dare try and reach out to them? The phones didn't work which meant going out to their locations physically. A mere ten minutes by car could be the best or the worst decision he could possibly make.

What if he was ambushed on the way? The shotgun was not a weapon that could easily be deployed inside a car. What if the people he sought out were infected, or not even home, the trip pointless? There were so many maybe's that staying put and doing nothing seemed to be the only viable option at present. A car ride that had once been commonplace now held countless threats.

When he had turned the TV on this morning, there had only been three channels that contained anything other than snow. All the local radio channels were playing messages on a recorded loop, only Radio 4 still having any semblance of a live broadcast. The news it gave was grim, still repeating the mantra that people should stay indoors and wait for further instructions. Perhaps worst of all, he had been unable to access the internet which had been the source of much of the information that swirled around his head. Had this all been done deliberately, or was it a side effect of a failing infrastructure? Andy didn't believe things would fall apart that quickly which suggested to him this was what was left of the government, possibly even the army, trying to control the flow of information.

The world around him was falling in on itself. How long before the electricity went out? How long before the taps stopped running?

He wore the belt with the extra shotgun rounds over his chest, enough there to do the job that needed doing surely. The shotgun was loaded, and Andy made his way around the side of the house, unlocking the gate so as to get around the back of his property. Here he had relative privacy except from Iain's house, Andy examining the shattered border fence from a distance. Satisfied that Iain wasn't outside and that no missiles would be thrown at him from an open window, Andy moved closer to the felled barrier.

There was blood on the pale wood, as well as on the white stone patio that led to Iain's back door. Andy had definitely hit the wanker with his shot last night, the amount of blood indicating he had inflicted a not insignificant wound. He paused as he prepared to step onto enemy territory, for once he did this, there was no taking it back. If order was restored tomorrow could he justify this? Would the law of the land see that this was the only choice he could have taken? Or would they apply the rules that existed prior to the crisis and see him as someone who needed locking up for the safety of the whole? It had not been deemed proper for people to take the law into their own hands, vigilantes and mob justice crushed wherever it occurred. Were any of the politicians who made those laws still alive though?

The back door was closed, and the blinds to the patio door open, giving Andy unrestricted vision into the dining and living room areas. There were boxes everywhere, piled up against the walls, accumulated rubbish that filled much of the free space. Was Iain a hoarder? He tried the patio doors but found them locked. The back door however, that allowed access, which saved him having to shoot the patio glass out.

The door led through to the kitchen which was in a worse state than the living area. And it stank, the fetid aroma of decayed food and bleach making him almost retch. Suddenly, Andy didn't want to go in there, the kitchen surfaces hidden underneath piles of trash and unwashed dishes. There were flies as well, a lot of them, indicating that maggots could be found in their multitudes throughout the kitchen. It was also dark, rubbish piled up so as to obstruct much of the natural light that was trying to penetrate the gloom through the windows. How the fuck could anyone live like this? Jesus, his neighbour really was a nutcase.

"Iain?" Andy shouted. "Get your arse down here." At first there was no response, but then he heard movement upstairs as the floorboards above his head creaked. Better to let Iain come to him than go hunting through this defiled place, thought Andy, and he stepped back from the door, careful not to step in the blood.

Something upstairs fell over with a crash. More garbage? Andy found himself taking another step back. It was difficult to tell now if Iain was going to make an appearance, but Andy readied the gun anyway. Would he even come out if he saw that Andy was armed? For some reason, now the nerves started to hit and he was beginning to feel that perhaps this wasn't the wisest move he could make. Just when he was getting ready to shout again, Iain appeared at the far end of the kitchen. The man seemed to stand drunkenly, slightly unsteady on his feet. When Iain took a step forward, Andy noticed there was a limp there, as if the leg was damaged. Most likely the result of being shot.

It was, that had been where the blood had escaped from. The shotgun blast from the early hours had ripped through the flesh, rupturing the posterior tibial artery. The problem for Iain had been the vast amounts of alcohol he had consumed which had helped induce his arsonist rage. He had been drinking heavily since the outbreak had been confirmed, choosing the bliss of inebriation rather than facing up to what it all meant. Alcohol didn't go well with his pathological paranoia, thus just exacerbating his already diminished mental health condition.

Suitably drunk, Iain had initially been somewhat anaesthetised to the reality of the injury that had been dealt to him. After fleeing from further shotgun blasts, Iain had staggered upstairs in a daze, agony slowly starting to descend on the damaged limb. He had attempted to deal with the injury, but had ended up passed out from the alcohol and the pain which had allowed the artery to continue to bleed. With no hope of medical intervention, Iain had died of blood loss in the small hours of the morning.

Andy had come here with the intention of killing a man who was already dead. Lazarus took care of the rest. Right before Andy was the proof that the virus had also reached the city of Leeds.

If he was honest with himself, Andy saw the truth almost straight away, the darkened figure just not standing right. There was something about the way the head seemed to lol to one side, the body looking limp as it twitched.

When Iain(Z) surged forward, storming from the kitchen despite the damage to the muscles in its leg, Andy felt panic rise. He stepped back further, and that was when he lost his footing on a loose stone bordering grass that was well overdue mowing. Falling onto his back, Andy almost lost the gun as his arms tried to break his fall. The sound of garbage crashing to the ground could be heard, caused by Iain(Z)'s flailing arms as it ran for the door, heading towards the delicious meat that now lay outside. It could smell Andy, even through the stench of the kitchen, the flies in the kitchen whipped up into a frenzy by the zombie's rampage.

Winded, Andy tried to gather himself, managing to bring the shotgun up so it pointed up towards the heavens. With one hand he tried to push himself up, but then Iain(Z) was there above him, the end of the shotgun planted into its chest, propping the zombie up, its fingertips brushing across Andy's face as it tried to grab hold of him. With the stock almost buried into the soft earth beneath it, Andy had difficulty reaching the trigger, but he managed to snake a finger in there.

Stuff leaked out of the zombie's mouth onto Andy's face which alarmed Andy almost as much as the very present fact that Iain was now one of the undead. His shotgun was a double trigger design, and he pulled down on both of them at once, duel cartridges ripping through the zombie's upper abdomen, blood and matter exploding up into the air behind Iain(Z), the blast sending the enraged zombie backwards and to the side, much of its spine destroyed. Where it landed on Andy's legs, it began to thrash violently, fingers trying to grab whatever was near. Andy managed to pull himself from beneath it and for a second he thought he would lose the shotgun. Iain(Z) grabbed its barrel with one of its hands, almost yanking the thing out of Andy's grasp.

Fortunately for him, Andy was able to retain hold of the gun, and getting to his feet he pulled himself away from the ruined thing. It didn't seem able to use its legs properly anymore, perhaps the spine being too badly damaged. The legs still tried to move however, digging into the ground to try and propel it forward. Iain(Z) just wasn't able to stand up.

Frantically, Andy reloaded, two fresh cartridges slamming into place. With the gun closed, Andy lined up for what he hoped to be the ending of all this. Grabbing tufts of grass, Iain(Z) pulled itself forwards, obviously not willing to give up on the food that was right there in front of it. Andy used two more cartridges to finish the thing off, the first taking most of the left side of its face off, the second obliterating most of the head completely. The thing twitched slightly for several seconds before falling still.

There was moisture on his face. Was that enough for the virus to be passed on? The news had said it could be spread easily by exposure to bodily fluids. He needed to get inside and get himself cleaned up. Surely he wasn't infected? That wasn't part of the plan, Andy never even considering that Iain might have been a Lazarus carrier.

My God, what had he done?

23.08.19
Preston, UK

Smith woke up to news that the Fulwood base commander had decided the prospect of fighting zombies wasn't something he had any further interest in. Without having given any warning, the commander had selfishly hung himself, the men who discovered the body dangling from the rafters of his office distressed but also relieved that their commanding officer hadn't been infected with Lazarus. It would have been a bit shit for them to have had to cut down a wriggling zombie which was sired from the man who had routinely shouted orders at them.

That made Smith the ranking officer, even if only temporarily. He wasn't in command though, the station executive, an army major, taking charge. The night had also seen the death and resurrection of the country's Chief of the Defence Staff. Any form of leadership in the UK was rapidly disappearing up its own arse.

There was no real emotion within him regarding all this, except for an unusual feeling of dread. Smith just hoped his own brain wouldn't betray him like it had last night. Shaving in the mirror, he was relieved to find there was no hint of the Voice from the previous day. His mind felt strangely silent and at peace.

With Smith now being as good as cured, the new base commander consulted with him and other officers about how to deal with the morning's outbreak in Manchester. As with other cities, the army and the police had finally lost control. A new quarantine block had also needed to be opened to house the increasing number of men who were falling sick with Lazarus. Even with the cross infection procedures that were being taken, the soldiers were still somehow catching the virus, obviously when they were interacting with each other. You couldn't wear an NBC suit for days on end. Sooner or later the invisible was going to get through your defences. So far, three of the quarantined men had died and had needed to be dealt with in the middle of the night.

The Major's first unofficial act was to take up residence in the commander's office whilst he waited for confirmation of his new position. As the early morning progressed, the news of what was happening in the world began to build, most of it a continuation on the depressing theme already set for the morning. The couriers transporting the antiserum from the North Manchester General Hospital had gone missing. Soldiers hadn't been able to find any evidence of foul play on the expected route the couriers took, and there was a general feeling that the men might well have absconded with the vials of XV1. Three men, three vials, you do the math. It was believable because it was what many who heard the story wanted to do themselves.

In the Major's first hour in command it seemed like a barrage of information was hurled at him, his office filled with officers requesting orders about operations Smith knew little about. Not being party to the quarantine operations, Smith was only present to give advice relating specifically about the virus, his senior rank almost an afterthought. There was something in Smith's manner and in his eyes that several of his fellow officers became wary about. He was clearly much improved from the illness he had been suffering, but for those who had previously met him, the Colonel definitely seemed different. There was a greyness to him, as if only part of Smith's personality was in the room with them. At no time did Smith tell anyone about the vials of antiserum that were in his possession.

Things only got worse for the Major. If the imminent loss of Manchester to the undead wasn't bad enough, there was the fateful news that the Porton Down research facility was being abandoned. Satellite surveillance was watching a horde nearly three thousand strong heading in its general direction from Southampton. Whilst there was every real chance the mass of zombies would just give it a wide birth, there was also the problem that one of the research scientists there had come down with the virus. They were frantically trying to discover if anyone else was infected, no acceptable explanation being found as to how Lazarus had overcome all the containment protocols. To some, the only logical answer was an unthinkable act of sabotage.

Being in charge of much of the facility, Smith was definitely of the opinion that any failure in containment there couldn't be down to human error.

"I helped design the protocols myself," Smith had insisted. For some reason, many of the officers in the room weren't reassured by this.

Smith finally outlived his usefulness and left the emergency meeting to go and check on Jessica, his new lapdog, Renfield, waiting outside for him. As he walked, Renfield followed silently behind him, now resplendent in full NBC finery. There was hardly any memory of the way Smith had killed Doctor Patel, the images in his mind indistinct and shattered. There certainly wasn't any guilt and he didn't even consider himself responsible for the act. It had been the interloper in his brain, of that he was sure.

His other self had been quiet all morning, and Smith wondered if he had been able to get the parasite under control. Maybe it had vanished all together, a temporary insult to his psyche caused by the trauma he had endured. He wasn't to be so lucky.

"*Aren't you forgetting something?*" The Voice suddenly asked out of nowhere. Damn!

"I thought I was rid of you," Smith said to himself softly. It wouldn't be good for rumours to start that the Colonel who was set to cure the world was talking to himself. The desertions had spiked this morning, despite the murmurs of a cure. If word got around that Smith was a complete fruitcake who knew how many more men would flee. Renfield heard Smith mumbling, but he ignored it. Renfield's mind was going through its own turmoil.

"*No such luck,*" the Voice mocked. "*I'm not going anywhere.*"

"And what is it I've forgotten?"

"*We made a promise to Renfield.*"

"No, you made the promise."

"*Don't split hairs. We have a job that needs doing.*"

"What do you expect him to do, just walk in and kill Jessica?" That would be an almost impossible task. Carter had them under his team's protection. Renfield wouldn't stand a chance against them.

"*That's exactly what's going to happen,*" the Voice said. There was menace there, as if some plan was being formulated without Smith's knowledge. Right now, Renfield was walking guard behind him, both men intent on keeping a close eye on each other. There could be no illusion that Renfield was there for the Colonel's protection. "*Let me tell you how.*"

***

Something drew them, pulling their decaying forms towards a central spot. With no conscious mind, the zombies went where their feral instinct led them, creating more of their kind as they skulked through the streets and the back alleys. Most of the homes they came across were easy to penetrate, the terrified occupants offering no resistance to the army that fed off humanity's weakness.

Stephanie(Z) was one of them, its dead form hardly damaged except for the occasional cuts that failed to bleed due to them being delivered post mortem. The blood had already begun to coagulate in its veins, foul smelling fluid leaking out of every orifice. The feet, bare of shoes, were mangled by the sharp detritus they had encountered, but were still able to propel the creature forwards to whatever horrors it was wont to commit. There was no pain, so there was no hindrance to the speed it could produce, dozens of times Stephanie(Z) having to chase down the humans that so often fled from it rather than fight. Stephanie(Z) craved the flesh that it could never force down its gullet, but something else was the focus of its attention now. As with the Hounslow variant, the virus here had also begun to mutate.

If the wind had just blown in another direction. If Jessica had chosen not to go outside that morning. If Stephanie(Z) had become trapped in its fetid hotel room. None of those happened, and the scent from Jessica's immune flesh floated on the breeze, just waiting for the decaying nostril of some random zombie to suck it up. This was what drove Stephanie(Z) on, zombies gathering behind it as the crowd of undead grew larger, concentrating in one mass, going against their usual habit of spreading out. It didn't take long for the few to become dozens, for dozens to become hundreds. Still miles from the army barracks that Nick and his team were hiding out in, but getting closer with every passing minute.

With the army being overwhelmed in central Manchester where the bulk of the outbreaks were happening, they were spread too thin to initially detect this specific mass of undead developing. There just weren't enough men, enough drones. The CCTV network spotted the zombies gathering, but there were no human eyes to watch the screens, most people employed in that role staying at home. The one strength the British surveillance state had in detecting the zombie menace turned out to be all but useless.

The zombies were coming to destroy the immune, but they wouldn't have things all their own way. If they wanted the meat of their enemy, they would have to fight for it.

23.08.19
Manchester, UK

Susan woke to the dire haze of fear mixed with dehydration. She had finished her meal with Clay yesterday and had listened to his continuing proposition, more out of terror than any real interest in what he was offering. Her choices, it seemed were catastrophic. Be Clay's occasional fuck toy and live in the house with all the creature comforts someone could want. Or be what amounted to a maid with the knowledge that her existence here would likely be a life of drudgery and toil…as well as vulnerability. The threat hadn't been made overtly, but there had been a hint that without Clay's protection, the men working under him might consider her fair game. Several dozen men, all with the same urges and no other women around to fulfil what nature demanded of them except for a skeletal looking surgeon who was their one and only avenue to any kind of medical care.

She needed to talk to Brian, surely he could talk some sense into Clay? After all, Brian had brought her here, didn't that mean she was under his protection? She was sure he had some clout in the criminal underworld in which he resided.

Susan realised she shouldn't have drunk so much yesterday, but the shock of it all had exposed her weakness. And that, above everything, was perhaps the most terrifying thing that Clay had threatened, words said casually as if to just pass the time.

"*Only those of value get to enjoy luxuries here. Alcohol will shortly become a rare commodity that will need to be strictly rationed. The delightful wine you are drinking will become a reward, and there is no need for a maid to be rewarded.*"

Could she survive without drink in her life? It had been her whole world pretty much since her husband had killed himself, all-consuming as it swallowed her existence and much of her pain with its intoxication. It helped numb the impossible, it helped stop her thinking about what life could have been. Alcohol helped block out the images of her smiling and laughing daughter's face as she had once so freely run about the house. Even now, years after, such happiness plagued her with its absence. How was she supposed to cope with the way her joy had been so callously ripped away from her heart?

Her head ached from the amount of wine and vodka she had consumed, the urge to obliterate herself almost relentless. Clay had given her time to consider her options before having her escorted back to this room, and all she had done was drown herself in her emotional crutch. Could she even contemplate what Clay had asked of her? Could she get through having his fat sweaty body heaving on top of her without throwing up? What was wrong with men, why did so many of them think that their urges were so fucking important?

She had fallen asleep in the dress Viktor had chosen for her. It was clear that she stank and, standing, she stripped the crinkled garment off, no nearer to being aware of the cameras that spied on her presence in the room. Susan avoided looking at her reflection in the bathroom mirror, shame and self-accusation waiting there to claim her if only she would just cast a glance at herself.

The shower was warm and delightful, and it took the edge off the dilemma she found herself in. But it also highlighted another problem…was hot water classed as a luxury? If she turned Clay down, was this the last time she would experience any kind of comfort? He had shown her what the extravagance of his wealth offered…was she willing to experience the darker side of that?

Then the other memory from yesterday wandered into her consciousness. Clay had told her that whatever path she chose, she wouldn't be allowed to leave so long as the plague was running amok on the merciless streets. He couldn't have relative strangers out there telling people about the setup he had. She was trapped, stuck behind the mansion walls. Safe from the viral evils of the world, but at the mercy of men who clearly had no regard for her self-determination. It was clear that Susan didn't have a choice. She had to make a decision between the lesser of two very unpleasant evils. Susan found that once again life had dealt her a shitty hand.

Brian had slept little and lay on his back staring up at an ornate ceiling that defied his understanding. Why would anyone go to the effort of putting so much work into a bloody ceiling? What was the point of all that moulding? Who thought that it was an essential requirement for flowery shit to be put up where people weren't even looking?

His bedroom was not as plush as the one given Susan, but then Clay wasn't trying to persuade him to give it up. It was certainly smaller, and with a single bed that seemed too short for Brian's bulk. If anything, the room was more functional, with an en-suite and a closet with the clothes he was now expected to wear. It was mainly filled with military style combat fatigues, durable and tough. Nobody could deny that a sense of fashion was irrelevant during the apocalypse. Was Clay expecting everyone to dress like his own private army? Yes, that was exactly what Clay was expecting.

As high up in the criminal organisation as Brian was, he felt a doubt bloom in his thoughts. Had it been a mistake to acquiesce to Clay's call? It was clear the paranoia was blossoming in Clay, and instability forming there that would only get worse as the days progressed.

Brian's skin still itched from the second chemical shower Florence had forced him to take upon returning in the small hours. That was why he lay on top of the bed, the sheets too much of an irritation, his lower half covered by fresh trousers that had been supplied after his shower. Brian would have hated to see how much washing Clay's estate was getting through, although he suspected a great deal of the clothes worn outside the wall were just being burnt. No doubt military fatigues were something else Clay had in great abundance.

The need for the chemical shower confused him. Since his blood test he hadn't been outside the walls without protective clothing on so there was little in the way of opportunity for the virus to have infected him. But Florence had insisted, and apparently Florence's word was law. He supposed he could have said no, could have forced his way past her. But then word would have got back to Clay, and as much as he hated to admit it, Brian knew that the crime boss just wasn't worth upsetting. Brian had seen the world outside, had seen the fear and the resignation in the eyes of the soldiers he had been forced to interact with. Now was not the time to go it alone. The fact that Florence hadn't required him to undergo another blood test suggested to Brian that the shower had simply been to piss him off. He wouldn't put it past her.

As eager as Clay had been to get his hands on whatever the courier was carrying, Brian's instructions upon returning had been to leave the package with the doctor. There was some speculation as to what the three couriers were transporting, but to Brian's mind there could only really be one thing that Clay would want so desperately. Attacking the military like that was dangerous, despite the precautions taken. Clay and his men could hold off the undead and the goons that passed for gangsters in what would be left of Manchester... but the army could easily flatten Clay's house from a distance without risking the life of a single man.

It was clear to Brian that he had acquired Clay some kind of antidote to the disease that was now known to everyone as the Lazarus plague. The question then arose as to how much of the cure was there? Enough for everyone, or just one man? It made sense for Clay to keep that under his hat. As loyal as the men here were, if they learnt that he had some sort of antidote, there was no telling which of them might decide to take matters into their own hands. Loyalty rarely went so far as to gladly offer up your life for someone, although Clay did have people like that under his charge. Brian wasn't one of them. He had been willing to do time for Clay, but he wasn't willing to die for the man.

His racing thoughts were interrupted as the door to his room opened without the hint of a knock. Susan stood there in a white dressing gown that seemed to swallow her up. She looked distressed, her eyes definitely agitated, and she hovered on the threshold as if uncertain that she was in the right place. Brian sat up and swung his legs over the side of the bed.

"Susan?"

"Brian, I need to talk," she said, finally entering fully, closing the door behind her.

"Okay, talk." He was tired, worried and irritable. If he could get this over with, it would be better for him. Brian expected her to berate him again, but was surprised when instead she started to cry.

"I don't know what to do." Her back was against the door, her body starting to shake with the sobs that were starting to crash through her. What the hell was this?

"Hey now," Brian said standing. He grabbed a shirt from where it was hung on the chair beside his bed. He didn't need his bare chest to complicate matters here. Buttoning it, he stepped towards her, uncertain as to how to approach the situation. A pub brawl he could handle, but emotional women? That had always been a bit of an enigma to him.

"Why did you bring me here?" she suddenly exploded. Whatever was troubling her was being unloaded now, Brian even stepping back as if the words were physical blows. *What the fuck is going on here?*

"Because I wanted to keep you safe," was all he could say. Was that true though? Why had he brought her here instead of just leaving Susan to her own devices? The look she gave him was filled with venom. Susan had come to him for help, but she couldn't get past the fact that, in her eyes, her predicament was all his fault.

"Well I'm not safe, not even close."

"What do you mean? What's happened?"

"Clay happened." *Oh shit*, thought Brian. *Now what?* "He wants me to be…" The words stuck in her throat. "He wants me to sleep with him."

"Oh, is that all?" Brian said to Susan's amazement. She looked at him open mouthed, the words seeming to float in the air in front of her. "What do you want me to do about it?"

"What? I want you to speak to him, tell him how fucking outrageous such a suggestion is."

"I can see you are shocked," Brian said using all the negotiating skills he possessed. Now he saw why Clay was so eager to invite Susan along. Really he shouldn't have been surprised, there had been stories about Clay's sexual appetites for years, although the people who worked for him rarely talked about such things. Would Clay really want to be locked up here indefinitely without at least one willing woman around? "And I can see that you find the idea of doing what Clay asks to be unpleasant. But you have to look at it from Clay's point of view."

"No I bloody don't," she insisted. The tears were still there, but now there was also hostility.

"Look, let's face facts here Susan. Clay has finite resources and he isn't a charity. You said yourself, the man is a gangster."

"But you said I would be safe here," she almost screamed. She knew now that she had been right about Brian all along. Had his white knight act been merely to get her here for Clay?

"And you are. Safe from the infection, and safe from the violence on the streets. And if you pay your way, you will be safe with Clay."

"Pay my way?" Was she hearing this correctly?

"You are under Clay's protection. That comes with a price. He isn't known for his altruism."

"You bastard." Susan stepped up to him and tried to slap him as hard as she could, but he easily caught her wrist.

"You should know by now I'm not the kind of person to try that shit on Susan. I rarely hit women, and I'd prefer not to start the day with such an act. Especially with you." He glowered at her, and she stepped back, realising she had judged this all wrong. She had seen Brian as an annoyance, an unhappy reminder of days gone by. Now she saw a part of him that only her subconscious had so far uncovered. Was he really capable of hitting her?

Yes. Yes, he was.

"How could you?"

"What the hell did you think was going to happen here? At the end of the day, Clay is a businessman. He expects a return on any and all investments. The people here, behind these walls all have a use. The only useful thing you possess is between your legs." The words stung her. Brian felt no guilt at the words as they fell from his lips.

"I can't believe you're saying this." The tears were coming fresh now. *How convenient that women had this power to turn on the waterworks*, Brian suddenly found himself thinking.

"I've been there for you Susan ever since my brother killed himself. I've put up with your desire to self-destruct, and what thanks have I received in return? No, I'm sorry my being around reminded you too much of the man you loved, but that's more your problem than mine. If anything, a bit of gratitude would be nice." Brian was angry now, with himself and with Susan. He should have just let it go and not answered her plea for aid the other night. He should have just let her self-destruct and left her to her own devices. His life would have been so much easier without having to deal with all of this. In his heart he knew he owed her nothing. It hadn't been him that had wrecked her life, that had been a path she had chosen all on her own. Here she was again trying to put him in a difficult situation with the one man he couldn't afford to upset.

"You want me to be grateful for your pity?"

"I never pitied you," Brian stated. And it was true. If anything, Susan had just been an irritation. Looking at her at that moment, he suddenly felt tired of having her around him. "Look," he said to try and placate her because he saw exactly where this was going to end up. A shouting match that would end in blows. "Let me talk to Clay. I won't give you any promises, but I will do what I can." Those words seemed to calm her, but she found herself hoping he wasn't giving her false hope.

Of course he was. There was nothing he could say to Clay that would possibly change the gangster's mind.

***

As with the day before, Brian was asked to join Clay for breakfast. Viktor was there as usual, Brian seeing right through his butler act. Why Clay trusted the Ukrainian thug was beyond him. The same feast had been laid out before him in the same room, and Brian tucked in, taking his time to savour the food.

"Good work yesterday, Brian," Clay said. He seemed genuinely pleased and it was always a good thing for a man like Clay to be happy with the work you did for him.

"Thank you, Mr Clay," Brian said, accepting the praise.

"I hear you talked some soldiers down into allowing you to take the warehouse supplies."

"Yes, I thought it better to try it that way. Better to save the ammunition for the Dead Heads, Mr Clay." The term for the zombies had caught on across the country.

"I agree," Clay said with a smile. He picked up his mug and drained off the last of the tea, Viktor there to refill it from the teapot on the table. Clay barely looked at the butler come bodyguard. "There will be more teams going out today because this might be the last chance we have before the zombie menace really gets out of hand. It's getting bad out there, they've lost the city centre."

"Do you need me to take any of the teams out?" Brian asked. Clay shook his head to Brian's internal relief.

"Shame we had to kill those three lads last night though Brian. I felt it was the only way though."

"Yes sir. I feel bad about that, but as you say, to get what you wanted we didn't have any choice." He put faint emphasis on the WE, subtly reminding Clay that there were other men with him. Clay seemed to pause as if mulling over his next comment, a piece of bacon rapidly disappearing from his plate. Clay's next statement was clearly an attempt to catch Brian on the back foot, the thread of the topic completely changing.

"Viktor tells me Susan came to see you this morning." Brian looked at Viktor who stood there, stony-faced. Viktor rarely showed emotion, unless it was to express some kind of menace. Brian wasn't surprised by what Clay told him though. Viktor had always seemed to have eyes in the back of his head. With the limited times Brian had interacted with the Ukrainian, Viktor had seemed to possess knowledge above his alleged position in the criminal organisations structure. It made sense for him to be in charge of the mansion's surveillance. Considering Viktor never seemed to be involved in the actual running of Clay's operations, the Ukrainian did seem to wield influence greater than that of a mere butler come bodyguard. Brian was certain that there was some sort of surveillance in the room he had been given.

"I'm sure then that Viktor will have told you she isn't happy with your proposition. I'm sure she will come around in the end though."

"Women," Clay said dismissively. "Can't live with them, can't punch them in the face in Waitrose car park. Am I right Viktor?"

"Very droll sir," Viktor managed. Wow, thought Brian, it speaks.

"I hoped you aren't upset Brian. That wouldn't do, that wouldn't do at all." Clay was looking at him now, as was Viktor. As big as he was, Brian knew he would lose against these two men if they suddenly decided to go against him. This was exactly what he was worried about.

"Your house, your rules," Brian said. That brought a smile to Clay's lips. "If anything, I should have known what her protection here would have cost. I'm partly to blame for her..." for a moment he was lost for the word, his mind stumbling to try and find what he was trying to say.

"Misgivings?" Clay said answering for him. With the word said the crime boss shoved half a sausage into his ravenous mouth.

"Yes Mr Clay, misgivings."

"I gave Susan a clear choice. I will have no dead weight here. She either works or she keeps a smile on my face." Viktor gave a quiet chuckle at that.

"Yes, I explained that to her," Brian agreed. Clay seemed pleased with Brian's responses so far. "I think she is just looking for assurances."

"I won't lie to you Brian, I won't force myself upon her. But if she doesn't oblige me my indulgences, she won't enjoy her stay here. She won't have my protection, and as much as I would like to think the men I employ are all gentlemen, we both know that's not the case."

"No Mr Clay. She does seem very reluctant though. I'll try and talk some sense into her."

"Good man. I knew I could rely on you."

"May I offer a suggestion?"

"Please do," Clay said, giving Viktor a sideways glance.

"She's been through a lot and she isn't a strong woman. Give her a couple of days to settle in fully, get the lay of what it all means to her. Perhaps let Viktor here show her the servants' quarters."

"The servants' quarters are a tent in the garden next to the kennels," Viktor stated. Perhaps the words were meant to shock Brian, but he didn't react. Instead he doubled down on his support of what Clay wanted.

"Vodka is probably your best bet whilst you weaken her resolve." Clay looked like he was taken aback, only to burst into raucous laughter.

"You see Viktor," Clay shouted happily, "that's the kind of loyalty I'm talking about."

Viktor watched the exchange with growing amusement. Brian was suitably respectful to Clay, as he should be, but he really didn't understand the mind of the man he was speaking to. Viktor did, because he was privy to many of Clay's much darker secrets. He could also read Clay, and could sense the way he was probing Brian for any kind of rebellion or judgement when it came to Susan. Fortunately, Brian had behaved himself, and Viktor saw no deception in the big man's face. Which was good because Clay was not going to tolerate any kind of disorder in the ranks. Clay had already had two men killed. Another one would hardly matter.

That was another reason Clay kept Viktor around. Growing up on the streets of Kiev as he had, you acquired certain skills to be able to survive. One such skill was the almost primal instinct that told you when someone was lying or being deceptive. Whilst not one hundred per cent accurate, it was something that had allowed Viktor to escape trouble more than once. He saw none of that deception in Brian now. As far as he could tell, Clay's lieutenant was on board with Susan's fate.

Brian's aversion to sexual molestation was well known throughout Clay's operation though, and what Clay ultimately had in store for Susan would present problems. A wise man would not go down the road Clay was hurtling down, testing the loyalty of his top lieutenant so early in the game. Whilst he was not a man to let passion overcome him, Clay was also not a man to deny himself when he had an opportunity. The problem facing Clay was that there was now a scarcity of women for him to indulge in what had likely become an addiction. Viktor knew how big a craving Clay had for the sins of the flesh, for it was he who acquired Clay his women. Susan was presently the only available option, the crisis happening too quickly for Viktor to acquire "clean" girls from his normal supply. Florence was too old and too useful to be a potential candidate. Clay's choices were thus limited which was possibly making him desperate.

Viktor could see that this was going to cause trouble. Getting the women to agree to his "romantic" advances was all part of the game Clay liked to play. Usually it was the promise of money and material wealth, Viktor choosing the targets from the desperate and the vulnerable. With Susan it was the promise of survival that would perhaps buy her compliance. That was a promise that Viktor knew would eventually be broken. For the game always ended the same way as it gradually escalated in intensity, the nearby forest buried deep with the hacked up corpses that had been created by Clay's murderous hands.

This was the true secret that Viktor helped hide from the world. It was also the character trait that Viktor knew would be Clay's ultimate undoing. Every man had a weakness, and for those who sought power, it was often that weakness that was used to destroy them. When that time came, Viktor was sure he could easily step into his boss' shoes.

23.08.19
Washington DC, USA

With his failure, Campbell had considered his career with the Defence Intelligence Agency to be over. Now he wasn't so sure. Upon relocation back to the United States, he had been transported to a non-descript building where he had been kept under guard. In a sense he didn't mind because the fewer the number of people he came into contact with, the less chance he had of contracting Lazarus.

He was in a DIA safe house, designed to withstand armed assault as well as ensuring the people placed there stayed put. Situated well away from the centre of the nation's capital, it looked like just any other suburban house, but it was strategically located to offer quick extraction in case relocation of those inside was needed. This was where his employers had put him whilst they figured out what to do with him. It was actually encouraging to Campbell and strongly suggested that his sins were about to be forgiven. He was an accomplished field agent and one that wasn't about to turn into a zombie like half of DC. That was a major plus in his favour.

He was not surprised when the short convoy of three SUV's pulled up outside the house in what had been a quiet and deserted street. There were no flashing lights to announce the importance of the people inside, and looking out of the bedroom window, Campbell watched as men got out to form a protective detail. One opened the back door of the second SUV so the woman who had interrogated him in England could step out of the car unhindered.

There was a lot of firepower on display down there. Only the woman entered the safe house though. Ms Winters was here, most of her face hidden beneath a high tech surgical mask. The very air held the prospect of death now. When Campbell finally came downstairs, she was sat in the living room waiting for him. One of the house guards had made them both cups of coffee, those same guards now conspicuous by their absence.

"Ms Winters," he said joining her. She had placed herself in a leather backed chair that gave her a full view of the room and she watched him with a calculating eye. Winters blew on the coffee which had been delivered in a large mug that seemed too heavy for her deceptively delicate hands. She looked tired, like she had the weight of the world on her slender shoulders. Winters obviously felt it was safe to remove her mask here.

On the coffee table, there was an electronic tablet which had been placed next to the second steaming mug of coffee. Royal Mile Coffee, no cheap shit here. A fine example of the taxpayer's money being spent wisely. Campbell sat down, ignoring the mug for now so as to wait for it to cool down a tad.

"I assume this is for me?" he said picking up the tablet. She nodded.

"You are being reinstated to active duty," Winters said. "We have information we want following up." Campbell flipped through the files on the tablet, the file of the woman seemed to be the dominant feature.

"Who is this?" Campbell asked.

"Maria Braun, ex KGB. Your friends at MI13 managed to get a name, and the computers at Langley did the rest. Very good of them to share it with us, considering." The look on Campbell's face told her the name didn't mean anything to him. "You might know her better as Mother." When Mother had given Nick her first name, he had told Natasha to input it into Moros with the instructions to share it with the other intelligence agencies, including the Americans. The CIA had huge files on the illegals program, and they had been able to connect many of the dots. The CIA went hunting for a piece of hay in a great big stack of needles and had actually come up trumps, their facial recognition software able to age the images they had of Maria whose identity was relatively easy to determine with all the other information they held. There were only so many ex KGB female agents left in their database.

"So, you know who she is."

"Better, we know where she is." Winters let the words hang there for a moment. "She was captured on airport cameras at LAX eighteen months ago. From there we easily followed her trail, despite the fake passport and private jets." A desperate trip Mother had made to see the top cancer specialist in California. Following her back through the international flight passenger manifests, they got lucky. The false name she had travelled under had chartered a helicopter at Brasilia International Airport which had taken her to a private address which the CIA had easily acquired.

"What do you want from me?"

"We want her, David. I'm sending you with a Delta team to extract her and bring her back to the States. We need what she knows." Why though? thought Campbell, reading through more of the tablet. What use could she possibly be?

"Where is she?"

"Northern Brazil. It's a simple exfil. In, out. You will be going in via Columbia."

"Will we be telling the Brazilian government?"

"No, that would be foolish," said Winters.

"Any word on a cure?"

"The CDC are working on it. I'm told they think they can synthesise the antiserum the Brits concocted with the data they shared. The Japanese have said they also have made a breakthrough. No luck on a vaccine yet though." She didn't mention that Tokyo was in a worse state than London or New York. Winters also didn't mention the Japanese had killed dozens of people in their attempts to hamper Lazarus.

"Okay, I can do this. When do I leave?"

"You have time to finish your coffee," Winters said, standing. She set her mug down and walked to leave the room before turning to Campbell. "We need this woman alive Campbell." There it was, the formality again. "If you are unable to retrieve her for us, don't bother coming back to the US."

"Will there even be a country for me to come back to?" Campbell enquired. Winters didn't answer that, instead she gave him a look that could almost be described as pity.

***

On the streets of Washington, order was barely being maintained, troops presently sweeping in from the west in a street by street action backed up by heavy armour. Most key government buildings were still secured, even though the virus was crawling through the people inside with a relentless pace. The one building that wasn't secure was the very seat of government, the fences along Pennsylvania Avenue no hindrance to the zombies that had easily scaled the metal barriers and overwhelmed the depleted armed men and women there. Thousands of them had amassed, surging north along Fifteenth and Seventeenth Streets, overpowering anything in their path. Just as in the UK, the Americans found its superior air power grounded due to the relentless assaults from birds who had fed off the carcases that were lain strewn in the streets of the nation's capital.

The Whitehouse fell from without and within, the deaths of the people around Jessy accelerating. Some died bravely, others less so. Then the dead had become all there was leaving Jessy the last person standing.

Now Jessy was alone, wondering if there was anyone left alive down here with her. When those around her had started dying in significant numbers, the human's defenders quickly became overrun. It wasn't a matter of just killing the zombies and waiting for back up because those waiting ultimately turned into the very thing they were fighting. There was no sign of imminent external help, the chance of aid arriving being shattered by the sheer numbers of undead that were making their way across this part of Washington above ground. One by one the people who held the reins of power began to succumb to the dreadful effects of Lazarus.

The moment she knew it was all over was when she had heard the gunshot from inside the President's bedroom, the man she admired shooting himself rather than becoming one of those things. That had been the final straw for Jessy, part of her breaking inside. She did the only thing she could do, she ran and hid, barely escaping from a zombie that had grabbed her briefly before the last remaining marine had shot it.

272

She should have left when the President had subtly offered her the opportunity. It was too late for that now. All she could do was sit and listen to the fists that pounded on the other side of the steel door in the room she was in. A bunker within a bunker, the panic room designed in case foreign agents were able to storm the supposedly secure subterranean fortress below the White House. The designers had thought of everything.

She had food and water, as well as a direct satellite uplink that allowed her to communicate to the various installations of the military industrial complex. There was also fear in her heart, the bite wound on her hand painful physically, and also mentally devastating due to the ultimate death it surely represented. The wound hardly bled, the teeth marks red and angry with the disease that had been implanted beneath the surface of her pale and freckled skin.

How long did she have? Hours?

Weaker people would have collapsed into despair, but Jessy chose to do what she knew needed to be done. For her country, for the memory of her President, a man who had almost been a father to her. It was Jessy herself who told the world the President of the United States was dead along with the Head of the Joint Chiefs and the Secretary of Defence. She also told the world that she was bitten, the woman on the other end staying on the line with her to keep her company in the finality of her life.

Twenty-seven minutes later, Jacqueline Fairchild was given the news that filled the Attorney General's heart with joy.

Sat on the desk beside Jessy, the pistol that had been discarded there was in no way inviting to her. Committing suicide was a mortal sin and it was not something she could even contemplate. So she sat and she talked, a broken stream of conversation often punctuated by sobs and prolonged silence. Minutes would turn into hours and as she stayed alive, the thought began to dawn on Jessy.

Was she immune?

On the other end of the radio, that thought also occurred to those who listened in on the words spoken by President Ryan's Chief of Staff. There was a survivor, someone who had been bitten and was yet still alive. Was this the hope they were looking for?

23.09.19
Houston, USA

Dr Lee had done the blood test herself, and the results were unmistakeable. Deputy Reece was immune to Lazarus, a modicum of hope in the finality that the virus now meant. In the last hour, thirty-seven people had died and resurrected. It was only a matter of time before the sick started to die faster than the rate at which the infected were presently being delivered. Lee had feared the moment they would need to double up on the cages, but now she feared the speed of the deaths from the infection even more. What would it be like a week from now?

Clearly this was why the tens of thousands of plastic coffins piled up in the Astrodome car park were designed to take more than one corpse. The human body was so miraculous, but at the same time so devastatingly vulnerable.

Lazarus was definitely airborne now, spread by touch, by bodily fluids and the expired moisture from people's lungs. Animal studies had shown that it was also contagious to a host of non-human species. With the way it was spreading, the whole planet risked being overwhelmed by it. Earth risked becoming a world owned by the undead. Army engineers were presently busy within Houston segregating the city up so that future outbreaks could be more easily contained. A monumental task that would eventually mean abandoning most of the suburbs.

Lee had inputted her findings about Reece into the central CDC database and, sat at her computer with the echoes of gunshots ringing out across the Astrodome, the first email response came. To date Reece was only the second person to show immunity to Lazarus on the continental United States, a depressing statistic given the size of the US population. There would be more, but would they be enough to stem the tide of the virus? Sitting in front of her computer, she listened to the hum of the machines that were keeping her cool. Would there likely come a time when air conditioning became just the myth of stories?

Lee no longer looked at the computer predictions. Quite frankly they scared the shit out of her and she needed to focus on saving as many people as she could. She couldn't worry about the state of the world, just her little part in it. Connected to the secure CDC email server in Atlanta, it took Lee several seconds to notice a new message had been delivered.

Michael Perry <Michael.perry@secureCDC.org.gov
DrJee.Lee@secureCDC.org.gov

Re: Immune Individual CR28HT

Jee, I knew I could count on you. We've looked at the tests you sent, and it's been confirmed. Arrangements have already been made to have your patient transferred. I know you aren't happy with that, but it's out of my hands. The CDC isn't running the show any more.
The military want her, a containment team from USAMRIID will likely be with you within the next five hours.
Do me a favour and don't fight them on this. I no longer have any say in how things are being handled. Atlanta isn't faring well, there are just too many of us infected to be effective anymore.
You're one of our best Jee, so I've arranged for you to leave with this Reece woman. The army brass took one look at your resume and almost demanded you join the team they are putting together to fight this.
They want the best and the brightest in one place. I'll put Dereck in charge of Houston once you leave, he should be able to handle things in your absence.

Regards,

Michael Perry MD
Director
Centers for Disease Control and Prevention
Direct line: 800-232-4636

Lee read the email through several times, dragging the subtext out of it. She only knew Perry on a professional basis, so the formality in the email was to be expected, but she already knew that he too had been infected with Lazarus. How long was there left for him? If they could get the antiserum synthesised then maybe he had a chance.

For the CDC centre of operations in Atlanta to be abandoned was as bad as it got so she pleaded quietly that this wouldn't happen. And the army taking over worried her. She'd had experience with military scientists before and found that sometimes they pushed the ethical boundaries further than she would have liked. Perhaps that was what was needed here though. Maybe worrying about the rights of individuals was now less important than throwing everything available at the contagion. They were already under martial law, how much worse could things get? Jee would learn the answer to that question.

Perry was right, she was one of the best and she knew it. Lee had a PhD in Medical Virology as well as a PhD in Virology and Microbial Pathogenesis. It was crazy, but the doctorates hadn't meant anywhere near as much to her parents as the medical degree she also held. Her parents had always wanted her to be a doctor, and not just a doctor of letters. What she wasn't aware of was that Lazarus had actually saved her. If not for the outbreak, Gabriel would have soon received a courier package with her name in it with the instructions that she was to die by heroin overdose. Sometimes just killing someone wasn't enough. Sometimes you had to destroy their reputation as well.

Clarice Reece would be very thankful that one of Mother's assassins never got to practice his art on Doctor Jee Lee.

23.09.19
Preston, UK

Smith was stunned to see the barrack's medical building under full security lockdown. The four SAS soldiers guarding the entrance to the barrack's medical facility were unmistakeable in their unique protective gear.

"*What the fuck is this?*" the Voice screamed in Smith's inner mind. Smith didn't answer. He wanted to know himself.

"Can I help you Colonel?" one of the soldiers asked. The four men were clearly positioned so as to stop people entering the building. None of them bothered to salute.

"Out of my way soldier," Smith ordered. "I need access to my patient." Instead of letting Smith in, one of the SAS detached himself from the group and went inside himself.

"Sorry sir, but I have orders not to allow that."

"Orders? Orders from who?" Smith demanded. Behind him, Renfield fidgeted. The Private had the sense to keep his hands well away from his weapon. This wasn't what Renfield had been promised. Should he have taken his chance this morning after all?

"From Lieutenant Colonel Carter sir. I'm sure he will explain it all to you." With the gas mask on, Smith couldn't decipher the facial expression of the SAS soldier who was giving him the outrageous news. Smith felt though that there was a very strong possibility that the SAS man was mocking him, and Smith seethed inside.

"*I'm not having this*," the voice squealed. Smith felt it pushing at him again, but found he could easily push it back down. Now was definitely not the time to lose control.

"Are you alright sir?" the SAS man enquired. "You've suddenly gone all pale."

"I insist you let me in," Smith tried again, almost petulantly. Nobody answered him, so he took a step towards the door causing the three remaining guards to raise their weapons ever so slightly. The closest soldier even put a hand against Smith's chest to halt his progress. "You have to be kidding me. I'll have you on a charge for this."

"As I said, Lieutenant Colonel Carter will explain everything."

The standoff lasted a further two minutes, Smith's blood pressure slowly starting to boil. When Nick finally appeared, Smith was ready to strangle the man. Of course he didn't do anything of the sort. Nick could have laid him flat within seconds.

"Carter, why are you denying me entry?"

"Because I don't trust you," Nick answered. He wasn't wearing his gas mask.

"What does that have to do with anything?" Smith demanded. "I need to get to my patient. This is outrageous."

"And you will," Nick stated calmly, "but under my terms." If Nick had any real choice, he would have kept Smith well away from Jessica and Whittaker completely. But no matter how wary he was of Smith, the army doctor was still needed in the hunt for the cure. Looking at Smith now though, Nick saw the wrongness in him, as if something was broken.

"*Tell him to go fuck himself*," the Voice insisted. Despite himself, Smith almost did.

"What bloody terms, man?"

"What happened to your hand?" Nick asked, pointing at the now freshly bandaged appendage.

"I got attacked by one of the zombies in the hospital. It proves that the antiserum works. We lost all that had been produced at the hospital which is why I need to continue my work." None of the soldiers guarding the building seemed to react to the news of the antiserum's success.

"And Doctor Patel?" Nick asked.

"He...he didn't make it." Nick watched the doctor's face as he said the words. He didn't see any guilt or attempt at deception there.

"So the terms. You will not be allowed anywhere near Jessica for the time being. She has withdrawn her consent to be directly used in your experiments. Any blood taken will be by my team." Smith was about to protest, but Nick put his hand up to stop him. "Corporal Whittaker has also volunteered to give blood, and the same rules apply."

"Who the fuck is Whittaker?" Nobody had told Smith about the Corporal's arrival.

"Another immune individual that arrived last night. Captain Beckington will oversee everything as he is army medical corps. We will give you what you need, but I don't want you anywhere near them."

"Another immune individual?"

"And what authority makes you think you can make these demands?" That was his ace in the hole. Smith was a full Colonel, Nick only a Lieutenant Colonel, a lower rank.

"Under the authority granted to me by the now deceased Director General, the Security Service Act and the Intelligence Services Act. There's also a host of other legislation that was never made public that I won't bore you with. Needless to say, it's all official, but feel free to make any complaint with the acting Director General...if you can find out who he or she is. I also have the authorisation from the acting base commander, God and these fine gentlemen from the Special Air Service."

"He can't do this," the Voice screamed.

"This is outrageous," Smith persisted.

"Yes, you already said."

"I'm going to have your head on a fucking spike for this, Carter." Even with the words, Nick noticed there was no real anger in Smith's voice. If anything, he sounded resigned.

"Not really a recognised punishment under UK law, but I'll take it under advisement. Now if there's nothing else?" Smith was about to say something, but the sound of unnervingly close machine gun fire ripped the words from his mouth. It was amazing how quickly petty squabbles became irrelevant in a time of war.

The undead were here.

***

Stephanie(Z) led its battalion into battle. Thousands strong now, they came from all directions. Fulwood Barracks was a collection of buildings positioned around two main parking areas. To the north east were two shooting ranges, the medical complex to the north. The whole facility was surrounded by either walls or razor topped wire fences. But as a defendable position it was laughable. It wasn't designed as a fortress, and perhaps it should have been.

The guards that were on duty reacted too late to have any real impact, the undead washing over them with their speed and undeniable strength. The main bulk of the zombies came at the south gate, the machine gun fire laid down on them barely cutting into their numbers. Stephanie(Z) was near the front of the mob, its body partially shielded by the kin in front of it. Still, it did not come away unscathed. Three bullets entering its lower abdomen. Stephanie(Z) was barely put off its stride.

The front gate was not designed to keep people out. It had been fortified by sand bag emplacements and erected razor wire barriers. Unfortunately, zombies didn't care if their skin was sliced to smithereens. The hastily constructed wood and wire obstacle collapsed under the weight of the onslaught, soldiers abandoning their defensive posts as it became clear there was no stopping the ravenous legion.

As with armies across the world, the British were slow to adapt to the realities of what the undead truly represented. They were a primal force of nature that used brute force to overwhelm any kind of technological advantage mankind thought they held. There weren't enough bullets in the country to fight what was coming. Normally an aggressive force could be kept pinned down by sustained and devastating supressing fire, but not the undead. Fractured bones and ruptured organs meant nothing to them, crawling where they couldn't run when irreversible damage was done to their legs.

They seemed to come in never ending waves.

Around the base's perimeter, the undead easily scaled the walls. Some got themselves entangled in the razor sharp wire on top of the fences, but with the numbers they had, it was inevitable that the whole structure of the fences would fail in parts. Stone was formidable, but it was no real hindrance to the creatures with the strength to defeat the wall's inadequate height. Over the walls, they went straight for the buildings, doors and windows smashed in even as the soldiers there fired out in desperation. Within minutes half the defenders were out of ammunition.

With the base officially in the process of being decommissioned, some of it had even been turned into a museum and it was the archway of this structure that the zombies who had attacked the southern gate streamed through. Stephanie(Z) made it past the outer perimeter, and into the main car park which had no doubt once been a parade ground. If it had been human, the wounds inflicted would have been lethal. The already liquefying liver inside of it was virtually blown apart, the large intestines perforated in several places. What was left of the clothes it wore were ruined beyond salvation and a long scar ran down the side of its cheekbone where a bullet had almost performed instant plastic surgery to its warped and visceral features.

The undead were here and they wouldn't be denied.

***

Renfield couldn't resist it any more. He had been made a promise that hadn't been delivered on. Smith had brought him here to kill the woman called Jessica, only there were fucking SAS crawling all over the building like the damnable rodents they clearly were. Those men had not been in evidence earlier that morning when he had stalked Jessica. What was even worse was that those present were watching Renfield like a hawk watches its frightened prey. To merely twitch in the wrong way would likely mean one of them shooting him between the eyes. It was clear that they didn't trust Smith, and by association that meant they didn't trust him.

He had watched the exchange between Smith and Nick with growing despair, the urge within him almost at bursting point now. Renfield was well aware that his failure to shoot Jessica that morning had been a grievous error on his part. An opportunity had presented itself and he had likely fucked up his one and only chance. The madness inside him was clear where the blame lay. As Smith argued fruitlessly with Nick, Renfield began to berate himself in his own head, the anger at his own cowardice building. The need to feed his addiction was presently at breaking point. It was inevitable that he would snap.

Then came the proof that Smith had lied to him, the conversation about other immune individuals making Jessica almost irrelevant. Smith had told him Jessica was the only one, the only chance to save the human race. He had also told him that by killing her, he would ensure no more antiserum was available which left the samples Smith owned the last of it.

"*Kill her and you kill the world, and also save yourself.*" The promise the Voice had made to him was clear. If he did this one thing, then Smith would give him the antiserum and make him immune to the undead as well. Be one of the few to travel the land without fear.

All lies, it was clear now, the finger moving across his gun's trigger guard slowly, anger growing inside him to a peak. Then the gunfire started and everything changed. Renfield got the chance he thought he needed.

23.08.19
Pennsylvania, USA

Jaqueline Fairchild was no longer the American Attorney General. She was now the first ever female President of the United States of America. Having just been sworn in, it was now her job to try and gain some order in the country that had so long ago lost its way.

The zombies weren't the only problem, and the crisis she was faced with presented her with the opportunity only God himself could have dreamt up. America had been wayward of late, allowing heathens and those damned liberals with their loose morals to corrupt the good work done by the Founding Fathers. This was a Christian country and she was going to make sure people remembered that.

She was reassured that everyone in the facility was free of the virus. Whilst a prototype field test for Lazarus had already been developed, conventional blood tests had been used just to be sure. Jacqueline had needed to consent to such herself. The field test would be a game changer and would only require a drop of blood so as to give an answer within five minutes. Basically an antigen test strip, there were already factories setting up production lines to pump these things out. Once ready, everyone in Site R where she would be living for the foreseeable future could be tested as often as was deemed necessary.

Jacqueline was already formulating a scheme to have the field tests distributed country wide. Once ready, she had ordered that road side testing be done in every zombie free city, block by block if they had to. In the areas of the country where the undead were yet to make their presence felt, any incidence of Lazarus had to be stamped out before it got a foot hold. She had been impressed by how Texas had come out against the disease, and this would be the model for the rest of the country going forward.

Jacqueline had Martial Law on her side. She could pretty much do what she damned well pleased, including removing some of the undesirables from the streets of her beloved country. As she sat at her improvised desk, plans began to form in her mind. She was going to mould and shape this country to her image using the King James Bible as the blueprint for how a country should be.

The work would really start when the nuclear football was delivered to her from where it sat in the bowels of the Whitehouse. She had already asked General Roberts' replacement to put forth a feasibility study on the use of nukes to reduce the numbers of undead and infected in the worst hit cities. Specifically, those replicas of Sodom and Gomorrah that corrupted and festered on the west coast of this great land. The new head of the Joint Chiefs had been picked specifically because she knew he was a hawk and a fellow believer. He had the nickname 'Fire and Brimstone' for his somewhat unorthodox views on how to fight a conventional war.

As much as she would put on a suitably stoic act when she finally pressed the button, Jacqueline was rather looking forward to cleansing the sin from this country with the Lord's own atomic fire. And then she would turn the missiles to those other countries that were so in need of redemption. The ones that decried the teachings of the Lord Our God. She wasn't just going to change the country. Jaqueline Fairchild knew with every fibre of her being that she had been put in this place at this time to change the very essence of the world. The heathens and sinners had better make the most of the days they had left because God's holy fire was on its way.

Say his name and speak it loud.

23.08.19
Preston, UK

The old instincts kicked in as if he hadn't missed a single day without war.

"We have to go," Nick said in a way that expressed the urgency that was building within him. He was inside the medical facility now, the rest of the team present. They stood in the observation room, Whittaker and Jessica now well aware of the situation outside. Machine gun fire was pretty much unmistakeable.

"What about him?" Natasha asked, indicating Azrael. The assassin looked at them all through the reinforced glass almost blankly.

"We bring him with us," Nick decided.

"I don't like that boss," Jeff added. Nick nodded, accepting the nature of the advice but rejecting it.

"I don't like it either, but my gut is telling me that he is important. Keep him shackled, but bring him." Jeff didn't need to be told twice, and he slapped Brodie on the arm to indicate that the two of them were now in charge of the assassin.

"Where will we go?" Whittaker asked. Inside, the Corporal was panicking, but he wasn't going to let that show, not in front of his fellow soldiers. Nick didn't seem to have an answer for that.

"I know where," Jessica suddenly insisted. "It's safe and secure and out of the way." Where better than her brother's farm, the one place she could guarantee would be secure and virus free. She told Nick her idea, and watched as he clearly mulled it over.

"Let's get out of here first, decide when we are on the road." With the extent of the firefight happening outside, Nick knew they had one chance to make it out of this alive and that all depended on Haggard doing what should come as pure instinct. As if to emphasise that fact, the sound of battle outdoors intensified.

When they finally left the medical facility, the sound of carnage was deafening. Close to the entrance two APC's stood idling with their back doors open, another being driven the short distance from the car park where most of the base's military vehicles were parked. A lone zombie ran at the third APC, only for it to fall beneath the wheels of the several tonne beast. Even those already dead couldn't survive that kind of trauma.

It was clear to Nick that there was no saving the base, its perimeter too vast for the meagre defenders who, even now, were easily being overwhelmed. He should have guessed this would have happened, but could you really predict that the undead would hit so strategically and so surgically? Of all the places they could have attacked, they came here? They were supposed to be mindless, but to Nick's strategic mind, this felt coordinated. The military's ability to control the streets of Manchester had led everyone into a false sense of security. They had overreached themselves and had ultimately left their flanks vulnerable.

"Everyone into the first APC," Nick ordered. He was now stood by Jessica, almost protectively, Azrael and Brodie stood beside him. In his peripheral vision, two SAS soldiers could be seen backing towards him as they fired rounds at half a dozen zombies that were barrelling towards the group. They were alternating between head and leg shots, the torso of the zombie a complete waste of bullets for the guns they were using. The technique seemed to work. Any zombies they didn't kill became crippled, slowing them down considerably. Still the undead crawled for there was nothing else they knew. Nick looked around, but he couldn't see Smith anywhere.

With everything that was happening, Nick never expected for someone to suddenly push into him and throw him roughly to the ground.

"Down," somebody shouted.

Nick hit the concrete floor hard, the wind being kicked out of him, the multiple machine gun reports blending into the surroundings. Pain shot through his left arm, a burning sensation that he was all too familiar with. Someone was screaming, and despite the agony that was pouring through him, he scrambled to his knees pulling the sidearm from its holster. At his side, Azrael lay sprawled from where he had speared his captor. Nick instantly knew that Azrael hadn't been attacking him. If he had been, there would have been more follow through from the handcuffed man. Azrael's actions had been to protect Nick.

He saw that Jessica was safe, Brodie on top shielding her body. A hand appeared, Jeff helping him up, the awareness of what had just happened still forming in his mind. Someone had fired at them, and Azrael had pushed him aside. Lying there in his hospital scrubs, Azrael appeared uninjured.

"Fucker," Nick heard one of the SAS soldiers shout before shooting a body that lay sprawled several metres away. The picture began to clarify, Renfield's corpse evidence of a betrayal that had almost been perpetrated.

"Brodie, get Jessica into the APC," Nick said absently, only for Jessica's tear ridden pleas to drag his eyes away from the body of the dead Judas. Brodie had rolled off Jessica and now lay on his back. All around him was mayhem as soldiers retreated to this position, but the centre of Nick's world seemed to shrink down onto his fellow MI13 agent. With arms that reflected the weakness that was overtaking him, Brodie pulled off his gas mask, blood bubbling into the air as a rasping cough ripped open his shredded lung just that little bit more.

Two of Renfield's bullets had penetrated Brodie's right chest, one passing right through, another lodging where it had deflected off a rib.

"He saved my life," Nick heard Jessica say. The gratitude and the sorrow in those words seemed to clarify what Nick already knew.

"Med kit," Jeff screamed. "I need a fucking med kit here." Nick knelt by Brodie and grabbed his hand, trying to assess the damage that had been inflicted. In response, Brodie looked at him with an almost bewildered look. The pain in Nick's arm melted away.

"Guess…guess I found what I was here for after all," Brodie wheezed, his breath raspy and forced. Nick used his knife to cut away at the NBC suit concealing the damage done and instantly he knew it was hopeless. A pressure dressing was thrust into Nick's face and he forced it down onto the bubbling wound despite the obvious futility of it. If they had immediate access to a highly skilled trauma team and several pints of O negative blood, then maybe something could have been done. But the shrinking SAS cordon surrounding them was barely holding the undead off and there were more of the zombie fuckers coming than anybody could even count.

"We need to go, we need to go now," someone shouted. Nick thought it sounded like Haggard, but he couldn't be sure. He pulled off his own gas mask, the virus be damned now.

"Don't you fucking quit on me," Nick ordered his man as hands and arms appeared, Brodie being lifted off the unforgiving earth, the injured man moved into the back of one of the APC's where he was roughly deposited on the floor. Nick did what he could to keep pressure on the wound, the red already soaking through his feeble attempts to keep Brodie alive. People piled in after them, the gunfire more insistent, more desperate.

Something thudded against the side of the APC as if a body had been hurled against it. Over the endless turmoil Nick heard a man scream. At the rear of the APC a severed head appeared to fall out of the sky, one less SAS soldier left to protect the world.

Brodie coughed again, agony ripping across the Orphan's face. More blood was propelled into the air as his lungs finally began to fail him. He was drowning in his own blood and there was nothing anyone could do to help him. The engine of their vehicle revved and, kneeling by his fallen comrade, Nick was almost propelled to the floor as the APC lurched forward. Natasha, the last person into the vehicle, almost missed her ride. A zombie appeared at the back door scrambling to get in, but Natasha was there to obliterate its head with the auto shotgun she was wielding. Where bullets had little impact, the awesome power of her weapon decimated the skull of her attacker.

In Natasha's rucksack was the evidence of how lucky she had been in the initial altercation, the laptop that was hers to guard having returned the favour, its presence likely saving her life. One of the bullets Renfield had fired had been stopped by it, the screen completely shattered, the laptop now pretty much useless without repair. Some would say she was lucky, but they weren't going to be around to live in the world that was now quickly forming.

The back door closed with a formidable clang. Was everyone safely aboard? Nick hoped the faces he couldn't see were on one of the other APC's. Jessica, Jeff, Azrael and Natasha were all here. But where the fuck was Corporal Whittaker?

"You're going to make it through this," Nick insisted, knowing the words were a lie. Brodie didn't speak, instead he gripped Nick's wrist weakly to indicate that Brodie knew the attempts to stem the bleeding were pointless. The two men looked at each other, an internal torment punching through Nick's mind. Brodie smiled weakly, nodding to Nick that he understood there wasn't any point anymore.

Any words he could have said would have been drowned out by the bedlam. Brodie gave a final breath, and then the life seeped out of him. All Nick could do was kneel there and watch him die. Another man to list to the long list who had perished under the command of Nicholas Carter.

***

Smith had run. When the gunfire had started he had all but ceased to exist in the eyes of those around him, Nick turning from him without a word so as to retreat into the building where Jessica was. Why he ran, he wasn't quite sure. Was it even him that had instigated that flight, or had the Voice suddenly made that decision for him? It wasn't so much fear that was the controlling emotion, more a regard for his self-preservation. When the shooting had started, Smith had been smothered in the overwhelming sense that Renfield was going to kill him. Unarmed as he was, and with the SAS troops distracted, it would have been so easy for the private to have done what so easily could have happened in the hospital the night before.

The Voice had made Renfield a promise that hadn't been fulfilled. How could Renfield ever forgive such a deception with the clear insanity that dwelled within the lunatic's mind? By running, Smith had likely saved himself for now, a lone figure running through the centre of madness. Strangely nobody or no thing paid him any mind.

And all the time, the Voice inside him screamed its ultimate dissatisfaction. Jessica, Whittaker and Nick had all got away, the three APC's driving past him minutes earlier. They had ploughed through the zombie menace, several other army vehicles following behind as those who could escaped the base before it fell to the totality of the viral horde.

Even as the gunfire around him lessened in frequency, Smith realised he might very shortly be the only human being here. Now what the hell was he supposed to do? As to the answer to that pressing question, the Voice was strangely silent.

23.08.19
Everywhere

One by one the cities began to fall to the armies of the dead. London, New York, Beijing, Los Angeles, Berlin, Paris, Chicago, Mexico City, Tokyo…the undead did not discriminate in their purge of the living. All races and creeds were welcomed into the battalions of chaos.

Mankind had no choice but to retreat. By midnight of the twenty-third, the world was home to zombie hordes numbering into the millions. Even worse though was the way Lazarus continued to cut into the human population, nearly two hundred million infected, more being added to the tally as the zombies marched and the people fled, the huge exodus of humanity washing the virus across whole countries. As the centres of civilisation toppled, the rotting legions spread outwards, devouring everything in their path, swallowing up whole communities despite the resistance fielded against them.

Tanks, bombs, planes and guns…all ultimately useless against an organism that hid in the blood and the cells of those it fed on. And just as with the Hounslow strain, mutations began to appear, Lazarus adapting to the human host, corrupting the DNA and thus creating something even deadlier. More and more the immune found they became the hunted, the virus singling them out whenever the undead detected them, in some cases the zombies being able to smell them from miles away. The immune became the true enemy.

As the zombies rose, the governments began to fail along with human civilisation itself. With the fall of man, now all that was left was the struggle to survive.

The End

Coming Soon……

Book 3 in the Lazarus Chronicles

THE FALL

Did you enjoy this book? If so you can make a big difference

Reviewers are the most powerful tool in my arsenal when it comes to getting attention for my books. Much as I'd like to, I don't have the financial muscle of a big New York publisher. I can't take out full page ads in the newspaper or put posters on the subway.
(Not yet, anyway).
But I do have something much more powerful and effective than that, and it's something that those publishers would kill to get their hands on.

A committed and loyal bunch of readers.

Honest reviews of my books help bring them to the attention of other readers.
If you enjoyed this book I would be grateful if you could spend just five minutes leaving a review (it can be as short as you like) on the Amazon page.
Thank you very much.

ABOUT THE AUTHOR
Facebook - https://www.facebook.com/seandevillesnovels/
Twitter - https://twitter.com/seandeville666

Get free chapters to try before you buy, as well as a free book
Building a relationship with my readers is the best thing about writing. I occasionally write blogs and send newsletters with details on new releases, special offers, and occasional free gifts relating to my books.

And if you sign up to my mailing list, I'll send you all this free stuff:

• Free Chapters to my zombie horror "Cobra Z"
• Free Chapters to my apocalyptic book "The Defiled"
• A free copy of my horror book, "The Profane," Book 1 in the Sheol trilogy

You can get these, for free, by signing up at www.seandeville.com

ALSO BY SEAN DEVILLE

Have you read them all?

In the Necropolis Trilogy

Cobra Z

What if one day you find your world suddenly torn apart? Entranced by your daily routine, you hear the terrifying news that makes your blood run cold. A devastating man made virus has been unleashed on the world, a virus so lethal that it rapidly turns everyone it infects into rabid, blood crazed killers. Maniacs so devoid of humanity that their only goal in life is to rip the flesh from your very body, and kill or infect the people you love the most. Would you panic? Would you rush from your desk in a frantic attempt to save your children? Would you hunker down, and hope the infection somehow passes you by, praying to whatever God you think will help? And what if the very people you care for so deeply are the ones clawing at your door, their blood smeared faces screaming for the destruction of your soul? How would you survive in such a world? And would you want to?

Buy it here

UK: https://amzn.to/2xb8b3S

US: https://amzn.to/2NDCbip

The Contained

When the infection struck, 64 million people never stood a chance. It only took a day for the country to collapse, for the five largest cities to be overwhelmed by the onslaught of the viral hordes. Merciless, relentless, they ripped their way through humanity. They were unstoppable, almost biblical. With no way to protect itself against the deliberate act of bio terrorism, a once great nation began to feed upon itself. Violence and chaos reigned, and those who had vowed to protect a once proud nation did the only thing they could....they fled leaving millions to their fate. At the end of the first day, a tenth of the population had become infected....7 million blood crazed killers whose only purpose in life was the consumption of human flesh. Stranger, friends or loved one, the infected did not discriminate. They did not care, only the burning hunger within them filled their rabid, predatory thoughts. And as the infected surged out of the cities, their numbers grew, those they fed on swelling their ravenous, inhuman ranks. And with every hour that passed, the infection spread, and humanity bled.

Buy it here

UK: https://amzn.to/2CPYRaQ

US: https://amzn.to/2p5Ff90

Necropolis

As the virus spread across the globe, the world slept on, oblivious to the threat that was about to be unleashed upon it. And as the armies of the Horsemen threaten Europe, a new force joins them in the destruction of humanity.

In Britain, the survivors from the devastated MI6 building flee to the only safe haven left in the now quarantined country - the military stronghold in Cornwall. With their walls, and their tanks and their guns, will the last surviving remnants of the British Armed

Forces defeat the slaughter hurtling towards them through the roads and the streets and the fields, or will they be washed away by the devastating force of the Infected.

Who will live, and who will die when the Infected arrive? And what kind of world will be left when the smoke clears? Will humanity prevail or will they be cast aside by the force of Abrahams insane gift to the world?

So begins the final battle of the Necropolis

Buy it here:

UK: https://amzn.to/2MrAG2j

US: https://amzn.to/2COe0JQ

In the Lazarus Chronicles

Book 1: The Spread

Book 2: The Rise

Coming soon... Book 3: The Fall

SEVERED**PRESS**

f facebook.com/severedpress
◯ twitter.com/severedpress

CHECK OUT OTHER GREAT ZOMBIE NOVELS

RUN
by Rich Restucci

The dead have risen, and they are hungry.

Slow and plodding, they are Legion. The undead hunt the living. Stop and they will catch you. Hide and they will find you. If you have a heartbeat you do the only thing you can: You run.

Survivors escape to an island stronghold: A cop and his daughter, a computer nerd, a garbage man with a piece of rebar, and an escapee from a mental hospital with a life-saving secret. After reaching Alcatraz, the ever expanding group of survivors realize that the infected are not the only threat.

Caught between the viciousness of the undead, and the heartlessness of the living, what choice is there? Run.

THE DEAD WALK THE EARTH
by Luke Duffy

As the flames of war threaten to engulf the globe, a new threat emerges.

A 'deadly flu', the like of which no one has ever seen or imagined, relentlessly spreads, gripping the world by the throat and slowly squeezing the life from humanity.

Eight soldiers, accustomed to operating below the radar, carrying out the dirty work of a modern democracy, become trapped within the carnage of a new and terrifying world.

Deniable and completely expendable. That is how their government considers them, and as the dead begin to walk, Stan and his men must fight to survive.

 SEVERED**PRESS**

f facebook.com/severedpress
🐦 twitter.com/severedpress

CHECK OUT OTHER GREAT
ZOMBIE NOVELS

900 MILES
by S. Johnathan Davis

John is a killer, but that wasn't his day job before the Apocalypse.

In a harrowing 900 mile race against time to get to his wife just as the dead begin to rise, John, a business man trapped in New York, soon learns that the zombies are the least of his worries, as he sees first-hand the horror of what man is capable of with no rules, no consequences and death at every turn.

Teaming up with an ex-army pilot named Kyle, they escape New York only to stumble across a man who says that he has the key to a rumored underground stronghold called Avalon..... Will they find safety? Will they make it to Johns wife before it's too late?

Get ready to follow John and Kyle in this fast paced thriller that mixes zombie horror with gladiator style arena action!

WHITE FLAG OF THE DEAD
by Joseph Talluto

Millions died when the Enillo Virus swept the earth. Millions more were lost when the victims of the plague refused to stay dead, instead rising to slaughter and feed on those left alive. For survivors like John Talon and his son Jake, they are faced with a choice: Do they submit to the dead, raising the white flag of surrender? Or do they find the will to fight, to try and hang on to the last shreds or humanity?

www.ingramcontent.com/pod-product-compliance
Lightning Source LLC
Chambersburg PA
CBHW022025240626
47154CB00007B/2260